A Life Cycle Reborn
Carolynne Raymond

BY CAROLYNNE RAYMOND

NOVELS
The Crinkled Page
Titles available in The Earth & Airus Series

(in reading order):

A Life Cycle Reborn

A Life Again

NONFICTION

Newbie Author – This Chick's Journey to
Becoming a Self-Published Author

FOR CHILDREN

What Does Teddy Do While You Are Away All
Day?

A Life Cycle Reborn
Carolynne Raymond

A Life Cycle Reborn

By Carolynne Raymond

Copyright 2013 Carolynne Raymond

Cover Design by Carolynne Raymond

Published by Carolynne Raymond

For Mom & Dad

Chapter 1
Who is Robin?

2:55pm: Robin, you have worked enough for today time to go home. I am packing up because there are no other little odd jobs that need to be finished at the office. The only ones left to do will take way more time than the five minutes left in my workday. The sun is shining, and it is my little sister, Samantha's birthday today, she is eighteen years old. Last night I made her a necklace of glass beads, colored pearls, and lace. The thought I had was to either give her money or make something. What teenager doesn't like money? Then I thought about when I was her age; someone who is no longer here made me a beautiful pink freshwater pearl necklace; to this day I still cherish the gift, and maybe my sister will feel the same about the necklace that I will be giving her later tonight.

It is a long, lonely drive home. Normally my husband Kyle and I carpool together, but last Thursday was his last day of work. Now Kyle is off, and our guess is, he will be without work for the next month until a new contract comes up.

Geez! The traffic after work makes the drive so ridiculously long. I am not sure about anyone else, but I wonder, my mind is always on the go like a hamster on its exercise wheel, and it is not always the normal stuff; well sometimes, it is. The random thoughts are things like, what I need to pick up at the grocery store. I sometimes wonder why my boss is so incredibly retarded. Today on the drive home, my brain is pondering the thought; how does a psychic know that they are channeling their specific clients loved ones? Personally, I believe that psychics are frauds because they always seem to find the dead relative that is close to the inquirer, and the dead person is always sending their love to them. Why is it that we never hear the psychic say that they couldn't make a connection because the deceased is now reincarnated, or that the deceased is upset with them and haunting their house, or something? I'm not super religious, and I hope that I'm not coming off as one of those philosophical, religious, push their beliefs onto others kind of person, but I know that there are religions on earth that follow this belief, and that some do believe in reincarnation. These psychic readings reflect the beliefs of the psychic and not the client. Why am I thinking about this psychic stuff anyway? Well, it is because this morning, on the radio show they have psychic readings once a week. This morning the psychic was on the air. It was funny because a woman called in and said that she was cheating on her husband, and she wanted the psychic to confirm whether her lover had more feelings for her other than the physical relationship. The psychic said that it was just a physical relationship, and the woman seemed completely relieved by his answer. Wow, I had a good laugh. Normally, the callers who inquire are all sad, choked up crying, and asking for the psychic to make a connection with dead loved ones, and it is always the same answer, like a broken record... "Someone is being channeled, and they are sending their love to you..." Blah, blah, blah is what I think. Anyway, this nonsense daydreaming is getting to be too off the deep end for me, let me change subjects.

The roads are a parking lot; I am just sitting in traffic staring ahead. This is so annoying; not even moving really drives me nuts. I must tune out of this traffic frustration.

Let me switch the subject to books. I do love to read because it helps me to get my mind off things. Too bad, I cannot read and drive at the same time. I read every night to fall asleep. Currently, I am in this sensationally popular one that "Everyone," and when I say everyone, I am visually making air quotes with my hands as I drive and saying the word "Everyone." Anyway, "Everyone" is talking about it. It is a story about a girl who is swept off her feet by this incredible handsome young and extraordinarily rich man, the catch. He has kinky tastes in the sac…. Hey, I am not complaining, I do admit it is an enjoyable read. Would I say great; nope, it's not even close in comparison to my favorite books, none the less, it's good enough for me to keep my attention; get my mind off all the day dreaming that I do, and that helps me fall asleep at night.

Recently the idea of writing my own story came to me. Do I know anything about writing? No not really…Do I know anything about copyright, publishing, and stuff to make a story get to a bookshelf? NOPE. What is the drive? Well, I have a story to tell. I doubt anyone thinks like me, and if they do then, they keep their daydreams secret. I want recognition and hey, all these first-time writers seem to get rich. I laugh to myself. Boy, if I could just be rich, or at least win one million dollars I could do so much with it. There are so many places to see and things to buy and I would have that freedom to follow my dreams. Wow, so many dreams from the daydreamer. I should help in the creation of the commercials that the lottery companies put out. I do believe in lottery tickets. I buy one every time I stop for gas, but so is a billion others. I know my chances are slim to zip and really, it will only be a dream and nothing more, but I continue to buy because I enjoy that idea of knowing that there is a tiny chance of winning.

There we go, now we are getting somewhere! Finally, the traffic is starting to clear, and I am moving off this downtown street and onto the highway. Now that we are moving, I am starting to feel a little closer to home. YES, I internally jump for joy at the thought of getting home. I continue to wonder. Why do I even daydream, it's almost as though I'm playing some evil game by tormenting myself, and I know logically that I will never come close to winning the lottery? For starters, it is because I want more out of life. I think that I can do better in all aspects. Don't mistake these thoughts of me being ungrateful for what I have. I recognize that I have a fantastic life, and I am sure that without sounding too presumptuous that my peers would agree. I am a thirty-year-old woman. I would rate myself as a seven point five. I have a very handsome husband, Kyle, he is thirty-three years old, tall, blue eyes, and he keeps his hair short, shaved bald short. Kyle has his head on his shoulders and is a true provider, even with his little set back, currently being out of work, he still does so much for the both of us, and I do love him to bits. I have a wonderful career. I'm an office worker for a private company that sells and installs solar panels to corporate companies and the general public, I am proud of what I do for a living, and I do sleep well at night in knowing that the small roll I do is good for this world. I own a home, two cars and a four-wheeler. The only major debts I have is a mortgage, which is the norm these days. Lastly, the only child that I have is a little three-year-old black Havanese dog named Smarty.

So even though I know that life is good, why is it that I always want more? Well, I feel that I have gotten so used to my lifestyle and have fallen into a rut. In the past year, I have dropped thirty pounds. I was by no way fat, just a wee bit chunky, and I would like to lose another fifteen to twenty pounds just to get the little rolls off my body and have a more athletic and toned look. I feel like I am stuck in a rut and lack the motivation to reach goals. I need to do this to fulfill that need that I have of my body image. Kyle and I do have fights; just like any other couple, but I feel that I could be a better wife for him. I know he gets annoyed with all my daydreaming for starters, and yesterday he told me, "Robin please, I am not sure what world you think your living in, but everything you want, as it is right now isn't going to happen."… Can't a girl dream? I guess after six years he is getting tired of it. My career is good, but that is just it. I love my job, but it is not exciting. I could look to climb the corporate ladder, but nothing has come up. I am keeping my eyes open for opportunities, but I need to do more and really look. What person doesn't want to make enough and have no limits?

Finally! I am coming up to my off ramp. Five more minutes and I will be home. So that is it, my life as it is in this moment, normal. Only normal…. The realization is I know what I need to do, and I need to start doing more to make my life more than just the norm. Easy said okay lct's do this! My car is idling at the red light at the end of the off ramp. The light turns green, and I touch my foot to the gas.

When I set foot in my house, I am going downstairs to work out in my gym, do a bit of running on the treadmill, and work out like a rock star!

Chapter 2
Toast and Chocolate Spread

I step through the front door and see Kyle; just seeing him makes the drive home frustrations go away. I smile at the sight of him and say, "Hey babes! How was your day?"

He peeks over the back of the couch, he was watching television, "Oh, hey Robin. It was good. My Dad called earlier, I took Smarty for a run, and I watched a couple of movies that you wouldn't like. How was your day?"

I take my shoes off and put my purse away, "It was ok, nothing new to share and sadly no office gossip to tell you about, I got nothing interesting for you." I smile and shrug at him.

Kyle asks, "What time did your mom and dad want us there for?"

I snuggle up with him on the couch, "They said 5:30 PM. We won't eat until 6:30 PM, I am a little hungry now and was going to make myself a toast with chocolate spread did you want one?"

He flashes the cheesiest smile and flutters his eyelashes at me to exaggerate just how touched he is that I am even considering making him a snack and in the most exaggeratingly appreciative voice he says, "That would be great Robin, thank you." He smiles and gives a clearly fake bashful flirt with his eyes, and I go to the kitchen to prepare our snack.

Kyle is my husband and best friend. We balance each other out. After six years of marriage, we are still finding ways to make each other laugh, and we keep each other on our toes. He is the type of person who always tries to make you laugh. His personality ranges from carefree and playful to a more down-to-earth provider. I also have a playful personality and often I am the "instigator" with the nonsense that goes on in our house, and he will always roll with it, but if I am not careful, I will get my fun, games and nonsense handed back to be tenfold. Like, for example let's say I go to give him what looks to be a loving innocent hug, and it is, but I have an ulterior motive, for example that my hands are cold and need warming. I will hug him and touch my icy cold hands to his bare skin, wrapping my arms around him and resting my hands on his bare back. This will usually result in him screaming and jumping out of my grasp in sheer surprise and shock. Kyle will often return the prank by making his hands cold by putting them in the freezer and then chase me down. He will hug me just as I did to him, only he will leave his icy freezer hands on my bare skin for minutes on end as I scream while trying to squirm out of his grasp. The only difference is I can't break free from his hold. We are outgoing people, and when we want to achieve something, we do, and if we fail, we don't let the failure eat us up, we just push through it. For instance, Kyle being out of work now, we are embracing it because he does work hard, and we take the mentality that he will eventually land another job soon, and this period is just an "extended" vacation.

I smear the chocolate spread onto the toast for the two of us and find my way back to the couch to eat and watch the rest of the show with Kyle.

What now? Shower and then change into something a little more comfortable for my sister's Birthday dinner at mom and dad's house. Well, I guess working out like a rock star isn't going to happen tonight. Ah well, there is always tomorrow... I do hope my little sister Samantha loves the necklace.

Chapter 3
A Bead and Pearl Necklace

We pull up to my mom and dad's place; they live out in the country, surrounded by a golf course. There are a few acres of land between each home on their street. My younger sister and brother, Samantha, and Brandon both still live at home. Brandon is twenty-three, and Samantha, as you already know has just turned eighteen. As Kyle is parking the car, I see Brandon and Samantha's boyfriend, Phil on the back of Brandon's four-wheeler; they are tearing up the yard and having the time of their lives. Kyle parks and we both get out and watch.

My brother drives up and parks. In a teasing voice I say, "Brandon! What? No helmets? Geez you are bad!"

Brandon smiles and quickly makes a smart-ass comment, "Robin it's like this, I don't have a second helmet for Phil to use, so I figured if he doesn't have a helmet than I wouldn't wear mine, and if something happens, than I have done a noble thing and not put myself first."

I role my eyes, "Brad, that makes no sense" I giggle, he is ridiculous, "Anyway…So where is Samantha?"

Brandon shrugs his shoulders and says, "Not sure, in the house maybe?"

Suddenly, I hear the creak of the front door open and turn to see, "Hey there she is!" I holler.

Samantha must have heard the four-wheeler shut off, and now the boys are all talking about guy stuff around the machine. Samantha comes out onto the driveway to meet me.

I walk over and say, "Happy Birthday Sam." I give her a big hug; I must reach up; she is a little taller than I am.

She answers, "Hey Robin, thank you."

I hand Sam the heart shaped tin, "Here you go."

She opens the tin carefully and picks up the necklace, "Ah Robin it's so pretty and heavy!" She smiles as she examines the necklace.

I stop holding my breath and blurt out, "I am glad you like it because I made it." I beam and can't help feeling proud of my crafted creation.

"Ah thanks Robin, I love it!" Phew! She really likes it! I can tell by the expression on her face! Yes, my subconscious is jumping for joy, and I give myself an imaginary pat on the back. I feel that in general, I am not an incredibly good gift giver and often find myself giving others money, or gift cards. I know that money and gift cards are great gifts, but I feel that if you give the same thing repeatedly, I think that the receiver may think that you didn't put any thought into them. For me it feels good to think of something original and try to be as authentic as possible, and when the receiver genuinely loves the gift, it really feels good to know that you did well in thinking of something nice for them.

Samantha puts the necklace on and says, "Robin, let's go inside, Mom is just setting up the dinner table and Dad is on his way home with pizza." Sam and I go inside while Brandon, Phil and Kyle continue to chat around the dirty four-wheeler.

My parents have a beautiful home and property. It is a bungalow and there are many mature trees in the yard, and off to the north side of the lot is a creek that runs through and divides their property from the neighbors. The backyard backs onto a forest, which is perfect for Brandon's four-wheeling hobby. Across the street is one other home, and off to the left of it, you can catch a glimpse of the eighteenth fairway to the golf course. My parent's home is a little run down inside. The house shows the signs of raising a family with some wear and tear on the walls and carpets. Their furniture shows signs of being well used and it is a bit dated. I would say late 1980s early 1990s. With my brother and sister pretty much all grown up and almost out of the home, my parents have only recently started upgrading and replacing things. Recently, a few of the rooms were painted and they have just replaced all the kitchen appliances with stainless steel ones. Slowly it will all be replaced.

Samantha and I find Mom in the kitchen, and I walk in to greet her, "Hey Mom!"

Mom sets down some plates and says, "Oh hey Robin, I didn't see you come into the driveway! How are you?"

I smile, "I am good, you?"

She smiles, "I am doing well. Could you take these forks and knives, and place them? Oh, yah and Robin, I have some wine here, do you want a glass?"

The thought of wine at this time, makes me shudder because I am already a bit tired from having worked a full day at the office, a glass would put me to sleep for the night, "No thanks, not tonight, I will just have a diet soda."

Mom looks a bit disappointed. She enjoys sharing a glass of wine with others. "Okay Robin, help yourself there is a case in the basement fridge." She smiles but showing glimmer of disappointment in her eyes that I won't join her for a glass of red.

"Thanks Mom." I shrug at her and give her the, "I am too tired for wine right now" look.

My mom is a quiet type. My entire life, she has been dedicated to her kids, but not in the overbearing Mom way that some moms portray. She is not like that. Her style has been more of a "Plant a seed in your mind" and let you decide on what is best, she kind of makes her children think that they have made a decision to do the right thing on their own when really she gave small pushes along the way. She got mad when she needed to, but overall, she was more of a negotiating type of Mom. My Dad on the other hand was and still is a prankster. He is the exact opposite of my mom. He is an extremely outgoing and outspoken person. Now that I think about it, how does that go? Opposites attract, well that is my mom and dad, and that is likely why they have a successful marriage. I am the oldest of their three children. My little brother, Brandon, is a mix of my mom and dad in terms of personality. Like my mom, he is a listener and observer; he always strives to do what is best, but when he wants to have fun that is when my dad's personality comes out of him. I guess like any twenty three-year old, he loves to party and socialize. He is the one that will quickly become the life of a party. People are naturally drawn to him because he is so likeable. My little sister Samantha, I have always known her to be silly. She likes to kid and joke, especially with me, and now that she is older, we have conversations that are more meaningful. We talk to each other just like she is one of my old high school girlfriends. Sam is smart, an honor roll student, she graduates from High school this June and has already been accepted to University for Nursing.

The Boys have just come in which means Dad is back with the pizza. I am coming up the stairs from the basement with my diet soda. Dad opens the door holding two boxes of Pizza. It smells oh so delicious!

"Robin, take these to Mom, would you?" He hands over the pizza.

"Sure" I take the food to the dining room where Mom is.

Everyone sits down together for dinner at the dining room table, and we all feast on awesome, cheesy, pepperoni and bacon pizza and a vegetarian pizza. Oh yes and don't forget the healthy stuff, a Caesar salad as a side dish! We all laugh and kid, talking about the most recent happenings of our lives, overall, a great evening. Dad tells us about the silly stuff that happened this past week. Mom is quiet, listening and enjoying the conversations around the table. Brandon is telling us all about the possibility of him going to France in the next year to gain some life experience abroad and learn the French language. It feels like no time has passed and the table is soon cleared so that dessert can be served, Samantha's cherry chocolate cake served with vanilla and moose tracks ice cream. She blows out her candles, and we all have dessert. Before we know it, it is time to head home.

"Bye everyone," Kyle and I give my sister and Mom a hug and wave good-bye to Dad, Brandon, and Phil. In no time, Kyle and I are back in our car driving home.

"Did you have a good time tonight, Robin?" Kyle asks.

"Oh yes and I could tell Samantha really liked the necklace I made her."

Kyle says, "That's great. What did you think about that cake?"

"It was good. It was a little on the sweet side. I could only see myself having a sliver of a piece at a time, but that moose track ice cream; that was amazing." We are approaching the highway on ramp. Kyle puts the turn signal on, then turns onto the ramp. This highway has four lanes; two lanes that run east and the other two go west. Kyle turns onto the eastbound ramp and accelerates, the on-ramp lane is merging into the highway, and we are now at a cruising speed and are about ten minutes from home.

"KYLE!" I shout and point ahead, there are two cars about one hundred feet in front of us, they are beside each other, one is in the left lane passing the car on the right, but it isn't passing the car on the right at breakneck speed, but at a steady cruise, basically taking its time passing. The driver of the car in the right lane must have been distracted, or something, my guess, a cell phone because without any notice he has crossed over to the left lane and hit the slow passing car and this is it...

Kyle reacts as the two cars in front of us spin out of control. He breaks hard, steering right, off the road and onto the gravel shoulder, just missing the two cars in front of us. Our tires hit the gravel and send up a spray of stones that hit the car, it sounds like hailstorm. We are just inches from going into the ditch, but Kyle manages to bring the car to a stop before the decline. The front of the car is pointing in the direction of the ditch, and the trunk is facing the highway.

"Are you okay?" Kyle asks. His breathing is more of a panting from the sudden surge of adrenaline.

"Yes, I am fine, a little rattled, but I am good." My entire body is trembling from the adrenaline, but I don't feel any bumps, bruises, or pain whatsoever. I smile back at Kyle gazing into his concerned blue eyes, he kept us safe, and he returns the smile. His eyes dart beyond mine, the last thing that I remember is Kyle screaming "NO!" I look over my right shoulder, out the passenger side window, and I see is two headlights.

Chapter 4
Into the Blank

There is no going back, no rescue and no doctor resuscitating me. That was the end. It was fast, too fast, I feel like the joke is on me and this is just a dream, but it is not. I am no longer Robin. I am nothing, a spirit, energy, whatever you want to call it; all I know is that I am nothing now. It is funny in a dark sort of way because I always wanted to go out fast. I was never fond of pain, but the only thing about going out so quickly is that I can't help but feel that I never got to say goodbye. It is queer how wishes come true. At least I got to be with my family on my last day, seeing my mom and dad, Samantha, Brandon, and Samantha's boyfriend Phil and leaving this world with Kyle, my love and best friend at my side. I can take some comfort in knowing that I didn't die alone in some hospital bed. Am I disappointed? Yes, for sure, there was so much that I wanted to do with the life that I had. I wanted to grow old and be with my loved ones. Will I miss them? Of course, my core aches to be with them and be Robin again, but time will heal, and I hate to say this, but it's true, once I make a decision I will forget who I was, I will forget my life as Robin when I make a choice. I will explain the choice a little later and instead move forward and explain some more about the aftermath.

Kyle survived the crash. My side of the car took the brunt of the hit, and now Kyle is in a hospital, in a medically induced coma for his body to heal. He had no breaks or permanent damage, just some severe bruising that the medical professionals prefer he heals in sleep. He is expected to make a full recovery, and my parents already called his parents. They are driving to the hospital now. My parents are more reacting in a state of total numbness, and this is a good thing because they need to think about Kyle and everyone that they need to phone. The family will have their time to grieve, but right now people need to be told what happened.

As for the rest that were involved in the accident, the driver to blame was indeed texting someone which caused four cars to collide with multiple passengers. He caused injuries to others and one death for being careless. The police were able to retrieve the data off his phone as proof that he was distracted.

This absolutely sucks big time. You always hear about these things happening to people in the news. It is sad for everyone left behind. I guess, in a selfish sort of way I am grieving the loss of my own life and how I will miss all those souls that I have left behind in my life as Robin. I loved them all so much, but at the same time, I am happy that Kyle will be okay. It is hard enough to lose a member of your family, but the loss of two lives at once. That gives me some relief that the family only lost me.

So, I am dead now, and this state that I am in what is it? I had a Catholic upbringing in my life as Robin. I didn't go to church every week, or every year for that matter. I didn't say prayers before I went to bed or anything like that. Do I believe in a god? Yes, there is some greater unknown in the universe that we on earth have named as a God, or Father. I believe it to be much more than we have perceived it to be. I can't describe it, my soul just knows there is something more, and even in the state that I am in, I still don't know what this heaven is. I haven't run into anyone that has died before me, from my life as Robin nor have I met God, or any angelic figures; nothing has come to bring me to heaven. Go figure, I went to a catholic school growing up, and we were taught that when you die you go to heaven and meet God and reunite with all the loved ones that you have lost. In this state, I can think, and I feel like I have a body, but I don't. I am free and I remember the life I left behind, but it is nothing like what I was taught.

In this state, I remember everything that my soul has experienced. This is weird for me to describe but let me put it this way. Have you ever wondered how stories of fairies, dragons, centaurs, griffons, vampires, werewolves, and creatures came about? They don't exist on Earth. Even the concept of time travel, or the idea of traveling to other worlds with life in the universe? Hell, so many sci-fi shows and movies capture the attention of many. How do you think writers have been able to imagine such creative unique creatures and worlds?

Let me tone this down a bit and step back. Have you ever had a dream that you were flying, or falling? Do you remember how vivid those dreams were? That it truly felt like you were in the air. How do you suppose you know what those feelings are without experiencing that? You don't. In my life as Robin, I had the experience of going sky diving. I only did it once, but I never forgot the feeling. The feeling of falling from thousands of feet, it is something that you never forget. The feeling you get in your stomach, that heart-stopping feeling the wind going past you as you are accelerating to earth, and your adrenaline coursing in your veins as you scream at the top of your lungs, only the funny thing is you can't hear yourself scream because you are falling too fast. I remember thinking to myself how amazing that was, but I found it so weird that the dreams that I have had up to that point, the dream I used to get where I was falling off a cliff and waking up just before I hit the ground. I couldn't help but compare that, that dream, the feeling of falling, was the same feeling. How do you suppose that I knew that feeling of falling before actually experiencing it? It is because you have experienced it before, but the experience was in another life.

These writers and storytellers that imagine fictional characters, creatures, and worlds, they didn't imagine it out of thin air. What we see and experience influences us. All these storytellers have seen these things and places at some point, but it was in another life. It is the soul bringing that recollection to light for us. The writers and the readers know nothing more than calling it fiction, or a great imagination, but really, it is a truth, from a previous life, and we pawn it off as creative thinking.

In this state that I am in I have the comfort of knowing who I truly am, and I remember my lives before I was Robin.

Chapter 5
Travel and Rest

Going back to the people that were in Robin's life, the day after my sister Samantha's birthday. My parents are exhausted from all the running around and making telephone calls to the rest of the family. They have been up all night. Kyle is in the hospital and my body is in a fridge waiting to be prepared for the funeral. At least my corpse didn't go to waste. Last night the doctors were able to talk to my parents about my wishes of being an organ donor. They managed to harvest a few vital organs that were protected by my rib cage before that window of being able to harvest them closed. Kyle is going to remain in a coma for the week as his body heals. He won't be awake for my funeral. His parents are now by his side along with my brother Brandon. Samantha and my parents were with them, and my dad finally got the courage to go home with Samantha and Mom to rest.

Roger and Liz are Kyle's parents. They are clearly tired because they are about a five-hour drive from us, and they made the trip to Kyle's bedside last night as soon as they heard what had happened. They love their son dearly. He is the youngest of his family and has one older sister, Tammy. She will be making the drive to see Kyle this evening to be with the family.

Brandon sees the fatigue and grief on their faces and decides to speak up to encourage them to go home and rest. "How are you two doing?"

Roger pipes up, he breaks the silence, and he is clearly tired. "I am as okay as I can be for the moment." Liz is resting in a chair; her hand is holding Kyle's and is none responsive to Brandon's words.

Brandon continues, "Do you think it is time to head home? I mean to Kyle and Robin's home. Their dog is at home by himself, and he needs to be fed and let out. Do you think we should at least head over to care for Smarty?" Brandon asks carefully.

Roger responds, "Yah we should head out now and get that out of the way. Liz what do you think about that?"

Liz is trying to ignore the conversation, but because the discussion is now waiting for her response, she forces herself to murmur. "What about Kyle, can't I stay, and you two can go home and rest?" She isn't thinking straight, and the two men know that she is hurting for her son and his heartache to come. She doesn't want to face the reality that her son's life is going to be rough when he wakes up.

"Come on Honey lets go with Brandon." Roger says to her in a quiet, but soothing voice.

"I need to be here." Liz is a little flustered at the thought of leaving and is holding onto Kyle's hand and not wanting to let go.

Roger convinces her. "Liz dear, the doctors are keeping him asleep for the next six days at the least. If he were awake, he would urge you to go home and get some rest. Come on love, Brandon is going to take our car and drive us back to Kyle's." Liz reluctantly comes around and Roger lightly massages her shoulders while she is still sitting in the chair next to Kyle's bed and he gently reaches down and takes her hand from Kyle's into his own hand.

"Come on Liz," he murmurs. Liz slowly gets up and reaches over the bed, giving her son a kiss. Brandon leads the way out of the room with Roger and Liz following behind. Roger, guiding his wife, holding her with his arm around her shoulders, walking side by side, as Liz takes one last look at her son with a quick glance over her shoulder as they leave the room.

It is the early hours of the morning and Brandon, and my in-laws are on their way. My mom, dad and sister are already home, and they are finally drifting off into sleep. Samantha is asleep in her own room. For her, it is now sinking in and unfortunately feeling very real. She has curled up in her bed and has cried herself to sleep. For my mom and dad, it hasn't sunken in yet, it doesn't feel real to them, but none the less they are finally resting.

My dad, I hope that he doesn't bottle any of this stress up and I wish that he could get some peaceful rest before it sinks in. Like any other dad, he wants to be strong for his family, but sometimes acting in that role can take its toll. I hope that he can see when that happens and be strong enough to take a step back. My beautiful mom, I wonder what she is dreaming about. I hope her dream is taking her to a place that is less tragic than this reality.

I remember a few years back my mom once admitted to me that she had dreamed more than once that she was giving birth when she was pregnant with me but when I was born in her dream, I was a baby horse instead of a human baby. We had laughed about it, and we thought, how odd that I ended up being a child and then an adult who had such a huge passion for horses and equestrian riding. I was never influenced to love horses in this past life as Robin. I didn't have friends who introduced me to the sport. Neither my mom nor anyone in my family ever rode. I don't recall any artwork, or paintings in the home that had any relation to horses. I developed this passion on my own and without the influence or introduction to the sport by others. It is funny in the state that I am in, I can put the pieces together, and it is humorous that my mom had these dreams when she was carrying me in her belly. In a way, it was a premonition to my hobby, but really, she had an insight from my past. That was what my soul was before I became Robin; I had lived the life of a horse.

I was nothing special in my past lives, or the life before I was born as Robin. I was never an overly intelligent being, I didn't aide in advancing a civilization, like finding the cure for a disease, or anything special like that. I didn't come from riches, and I was never any sort of idol like, a movie star, or professional athlete. It never works quite the same, as you leave one life you don't necessarily jump into a new life right away. Don't get me wrong, you can if you wanted to, but for me, I have always re-collected myself and remembered what I have done and what I would like to do, to be, and to experience.

Going back to my last day as Robin, after work on the drive home, when I was thinking about the psychic on the radio, that I still think and know that they are full of shit, but what I didn't realize in the car that I realize now is the beliefs that people have. Souls do sometimes linger. It is not what you think though. When you are just a soul you can see everything you want to see, you can't go back in time, but you can see everything that you want to see and know stuff as it happens, kind of like being in two or more places at once, if you feel that you need to be.

My soul has taken many forms. When you leave a life behind you have the choice to decide on what form you want to take. If you want to be a human you can, but you can't decide where you will come into the world, or if you will be born into riches, or poverty. You can take the form of any living creature. If your soul wants a good rest, you can take the life of a plant and sleep as little as a season, like if you choose to become a flower, or a blade of grass, or you can sleep for thousands of years if you become a monstrous tree in a tropical forest. My soul has done that, I have slept; it has been a while since I have taken on the form of a plant, I am not ready for a rest yet, but I do need to think about what I will become next; maybe a bird?

The weird thing is I have never taken on the form of a male although it would be interesting. I do think the male body is fascinating, but it is just not me. I think that I have always been and have picked a female form because it is familiar and comfortable to me. There was one life that I had really enjoyed a long time ago and I will tell you about it   now.

Chapter 6
Tale of Taylan

I was a human, well sort of. The closest thing I can compare this to would be of a human form. I had the body, shape, and size of a human, but some of the characteristics that my body had were not human. My hair for instance, was different. I had a full head of beautiful silky long hair that never seemed to tangle, even in the most humid heat. The thing that was neat about my hair is that it took on the colors of what my eyes set their sights on. It did not change color instantaneously, it was more of a gradual change over the course of a few minutes, and when a color change was occurring, which was always, it was like seeing a dry cloth soaking up water. It was a wonderful trait to have. It was that of beauty and that of an item of protection and camouflage. It was interesting because even after sleeping for hours, even if you have dreamed of places and things, no matter what, your hair is black when you wake because that is what your eyes have seen while asleep, darkness. My skin was another beautiful part of this body. Unlike humans being prone to acne, getting rashes from illness, or irritants in our environments, or the bumps you obtain after a bug bite, or allergic reactions and the factor of living for many years and showing signs of age, this skin that I had didn't do that. The skin was similar in that there were the same shades of skin in this world as in the world that we know to be Earth, but the skin that this body had was more resilient. It simply didn't show signs of age or was not easily susceptible to elements in the air, or illness. It was a strong, smooth skin, from birth to death, even if you were at the end of your life, you never looked old, as people do on earth, because of their strong healthy skin they had and the fact that the color of their hair was what you set your eyes on. You needed strong and resilient skin in this world. It was a tropical warm climate, the skin protected the body from heat, water loss, the sun, it kept the temperature of the body, and organs cool during the day and warm at night. As well as it protected the body from parasites and the environment. There weren't any more bugs in this world than on earth, but the bugs on this planet were stronger and generally lived longer because there wasn't much of a climate change, and the skin protected the body from everything that a tropical climate had going for it. If I were injured, for example like getting a cut, or puncture to my skin, which rarely happened, but when it did, I would bleed like my human body. The difference is this body would let out as much blood as it needed to fill the wound and the blood would dry and scab quicker to seal the wound, which in turn would heal faster than a human body. You were not invincible. For injuries that are more serious, you would still need medical assistance just like the bodies on earth, but the healing process in this world was much quicker since the body's tissue was stronger.

Like humans, we can swim. This body, just like humans is slow moving in the water, but this body is a little better suited because in between the fingers and toes there was a small web of skin to aid in propelling yourself through the water. The webbed skin ended at the first knuckles. I was also able to hold my breath a little longer in this body so diving and swimming underwater was more of a breeze to do. I could hold my breath for a few minutes at a time.

This world was like earth, but the temperature and climate of this world was more balanced. Snow and ice didn't exist. There was only tropical humid climate as well as dry hot climate and variations in between. The world was beautiful, lush with forests and vegetation, the air was full of the sweet smells of beautiful flowers and life. The oceans, lakes, and streams were fresh and clean. Unlike Earth, its civilization took on more of a natural state of living. The elements of light, wind and water were used to power its cities. The use of coal, or gas to power machines simply didn't ever come into the minds of this civilization because coal and fossil fuels were never discovered. Civilization in this world is intelligent, and even though they had more advanced ways of powering cities, they held a remarkably similar relation to that of a medieval world that existed on Earth. More people held trades for jobs, selling food, clothing, tools you name it even though the option was there to work for companies. The majority specialized in a product, or a trade to make money, or to simply barter and trade with others. There was no reason for someone to be poor unless they chose to do nothing, and if someone were physically incapable to work, families and communities came together and cared for loved ones that could not manage on their own. People were closer and there was a better sense of community because society was more in line for people to go out into the world and create their own wealth, which meant really getting to know who was in your community. This world sounds perfect right. Well, an element exists on this world as it does with Earth and that is greed.

The populations, or cities as you will, always have a leader appointed, a king, queen, and royal family. They can be voted into, or out of power, as its people and the power of wealth see fit. At times, there could be corruption from who was leading. These leaders were committed to the success of their Kingdoms and their people. These leaders were level-headed, informed, and smart individuals who thrive on the success of their people and the success of themselves. Like I said it does sound like a strong and well-grounded society, and for the most part it was because they care for the general wellbeing of others but do keep in mind that their drive and motivation stems from other factors and they will do what it takes to make sure that they are successful.

In this previous life, I came from an area of the world that was tropical, humid, and next to a beautiful ocean that had a massive reef. I was born into a family that was successful. I had a mother, Nafeeza, and two older sisters, Ashlea and Saydira, however, I never knew my father. I never asked my mom about him or my sisters. My sisters and I all had different fathers. I suspect that it was always a short relationship, and they shared a moment with my mom and that was all. My mother didn't talk about them because to her, they were part of her past and that was it. She felt that we, my sisters, and I were gifts. We earned our living by gathering food and supplies as well as creating crafts. Our supplies came mostly from the ocean. Gathering was something that my sisters and I loved to do. We would visit the ocean, spending the day diving in the reef and harvesting food and other items for our family to use. We also traded and sold things that weren't so readily available to others. I loved this life and everything about that world, but it wasn't always so simple, I have a story to tell.

Chapter 7
Waking in old eyes

This was my life, long before I became Robin. It is an hour before dawn, and my two sisters are already up, getting ready for a day of work and play at the beach. My oldest sister Saydira is about twenty-one years old, Ashlea, whom I am a little closer to, is nineteen and I have just turned eighteen. Ashlea is whispering in my ear. "Come on Taylan we are heading out soon, get up."

"Yes Ash, where is Saydira?" I whisper.

"She is getting some breakfast and snacks ready for the day ahead of us." Ashlea climbs into my bed, deciding to rest on her stomach, supporting herself on her elbows, looking warmly at me as I become more awake and alert.

"What is she putting together?" I let a yawn escape when I ask as I rub my eyes open.

"I think I saw some dried sugar kelp, berries and some dried fish chips for the afternoon." Ashlea says with a twinkle in her eyes. She is looking forward to the day. I have no idea where she gets all her energy from this early in the morning and I can tell she has been awake for a bit, because her hair is a warm honey brown color. The color of our home.

"Oh wonderful" I reply. I love sugar kelp; in fact, I love anything that is sweet. Ashlea gets up off my bed, convinced that I am awake and rejoins Saydira downstairs.

Saydira is a great sister and a natural leader. She has grown into a matriarch of our family. My mother is still heavily involved too, but she and Saydira have more of a partnership that works very well. Saydira manages my sister and me with gathering, and my mom works exclusively with the sales and trade of what we gather.

I roll out of my comfortable satin sheet covered bed that is surrounded in netting to keep the bugs out in the night. I brush my teeth in the bathroom, tie my hair back, get into a t-shirt and shorts, and head down the staircase that spirals around a massive tree trunk to the kitchen area where Ashlea and Saydira are. Mom usually is not up for another couple of hours as her workday starts when the rest of the community opens their shops.

Saydira sees me as I am descending the stairs, "Hey sleepy head." She says in a teasing voice.

"Morning Saydira, which areas of the beach do you have in mind for us to visit today?" I ask as I sit down at the table.

"Ash and I were just discussing that; today we are going to visit the North Shore; it has been a while and who knows? I was just telling Ash that we could keep an eye open for oysters; my guess is there are some beautiful pearls to be captured. Hopefully today we will be in luck?" She turns her back to me as she grabs a dish from the cupboard.

I say, "Sounds like a plan." Ashlea and Saydira join me to eat.

After about ten minutes, the three of us have finished breakfast, packed and ready for the day ahead. Saydira locks up, and we are off to the beach. It is a short walk to our destination. My family lives in an area that is the equivalent to a suburb, well sort of. It has a very lush and dense forest that we live in, and the homes are different, instead of tearing down the vegetation the community has built around it. Our home is one of many massive tree homes. It is built from the ground up and around the trunk of the tree. The trunk is the main support of the structure. The tree is a great insulator to our home, and the canopy of leaves provides added shading and protection to the roof. The home is a two-story structure like many of the homes in the community.

It couldn't be a more perfect morning. We approach the clearing of the forest and step through the dew-covered grass. We are approaching the North Shore cliffs, and I can start to feel the light fresh morning breeze that is coming from the ocean. What a sight. After clearing the trees, and there it is nothing but sky and water. The sun is just coming up in the East, along the cliff line and the sky, is a bright orange. The water is sparkling with the sun hitting its ripples. This world Airus; has that in common with Earth, this planet orbits around its sun the same way Earth does with its own sun.

"I think I am going to catch me a couple of pearls girls." Ashlea says with such certainty and playfulness in her voice, while skipping along the path.

"How long did it take you to come up with that rhyme?" I reply. Ashlea just sticks her tongue out at me.

"I hope you do!" Saydira winks at her. We make our way down the cliff path stepping carefully on the worn-down rocks to the North Shore.

The sand here is beautiful. It is the whitest sand I have ever seen, and it is so fine that when you walk bare foot on it, it feels as though you are walking on soft cushions. The one thing about it that always makes me laugh; it's childish really, but when you run on this sand it makes a squeaky noise, it kind of sounds like a toot, or to put it more bluntly, a fart. We often kid with each other while making farting sounds with the sand and tease each other with fart jokes.

This morning there isn't anyone at the beach yet, except for the three of us, it is still early. We find a good spot next to the base of the cliff in the shade, away from the water to store our clothes and bags. We all strip down to our bare skin in the morning sun; our hair has turned to a whitish color because of the abundance of sand. We all strap on a couple of pouches.

Saydira says, "Okay so the plan is we are going to spend the entire morning treasure hunting, focusing on finding oysters. Fill your bags and by noon we will stop for lunch, head back to the beach, open them and have a snack."

One thing that I love is the taste of a fresh oyster, oh so delicious. We walk down to the water's edge, happily playing and teasing each other. The one thing that I do have a tough time with is getting used to the water. Don't get me wrong, the water is always warm, but it is the first shock of entering, it is always cooler than your body temperature.

"It's so cold!" I protest.

"Taylan you're just being a baby." Ashlea chirps back. She is already in up to her neck in the sandy water.

"I hate this part." I whine. Getting into chilly water is the worst.

"Taylan, do you want some help getting in?" Ash hollers, she is starting to get under my skin. Ashlea is making her way back to me. I am only ankle deep, and she is starting to threaten me with a few playful splashes.

"Come on Ash; let me ease my way into it." I beg.

"Taylan you're just dragging it out just get in and be over with the shock already. The water is so nice and warm, it feels like a bath." Ashlea encourages.

"Yah Ash, just leave me alone for a few minutes. Hey, did you hear that? I think Saydira is calling for you?" I lie to get her to go away. Ash looks over her shoulder, and spots Saydira in the distance, who has made her way up to a sand dune and is now waist deep and re-adjusting her bag. Ash then turns away from me and makes a splashy dive along with some playful kicks in my direction. Oh, she is so annoying. Ashlea drenches me, and I growl in reaction, I wanted to go in on my own terms. Ah well, I walk out and dive into the fresh open water, following Ashlea who is swimming over to Saydira. Ash and I swim up onto the sand dune and re-adjust our bags, just as Saydira and we are all ready for the descent.

"Ready girls," Saydira encourages. Even though Saydira is the oldest and is the one looking out for my sister and me, she does have a playful side to her, and I know that treasure diving is one of her favorite things to do. It is more of a passion than a chore. We all dive down together; down to the depths to the ocean floor, my guess is that it is about thirty feet. As I mentioned earlier, we don't have the ability to breathe underwater, but our bodies can hold our breath easily for a few minutes at a time before needing to re-surface.

Down we go into the depths; the reef is colorful and full of different corals and millions of fish. The odd small shark patrols the reef for food. Sharks don't care for us; they are more interested in the brilliant schools of fish. I see my first stack of oysters that are attached to the reef. I dive down to retrieve them. You only take a few oysters out at a time and never the entire cluster because if you ever do remove the entire cluster, other oysters in the future won't attach themselves to an empty spot. Oysters like the company of other oysters, so you only ever take a few at a time and hope that you get lucky and picked ones that have the pearls. I pick a few from the cluster and swim on to the next.

Back up to the surface for air and then back down to the world of exotic colors and the beauty that is the reef. I feel free down here. I do a couple of flips with ease, making use of my webbed fingers and toes as I make my way down to the next new bed of oysters. I can see that my sisters are doing the same. I imagine that swimming in a way must be like flying, the feeling of being almost weightless, and propelling yourself through the water must be a similar feeling to wings flapping in the air during flight. There are so many oyster beds along the North Shore, and I would imagine that we have a few undiscovered pearls in our bags right now.

From the ocean floor, I can tell the sun has risen because the ripples of the rays of sun are glistening on the ocean floor. It feels like heaven down here. I make my way back up to the ball of light that is now in the center of the sky. My sisters go to the surface too. We all pop up and make our way to the sand dune.

I quickly pipe up, "Hey Saydira my bag is full; how did you do?" I move a wet lock of blue hair from my eyes.

Saydira smiles, "I think I may have some lucky oysters, I picked up a few larger ones with some tinges of pink and blue on their shells, so hopefully those colors are lucky; we shall see."

Ash is up on the dune, standing waist deep; her naked body is glistening in the sun. She says to Saydira and me as we swim up to the dune, "A little wager, whoever has the most pearls gets to keep one for her own?"

"I think that is fair." Saydira pipes in giving her approval as she is walking up onto the dune. I am the last on the dune and hastily adjust my bag and jump off the other side and swim to the shore following my sisters. We walk up onto the beach. A few families that have gathered and they all are enjoying picnics at the beach. A few moms and dads are lying naked on their beach blankets as their young children frolic on the shore. We sit down and open our bags.

Between the three of us, we must have close to seventy oysters to go through. We sit by the rocks and one by one, open each of them with our shucking knives that were in Saydira's bag.

It's seeing the few families that are here, but I think aloud to Saydira, "Why do you suppose there are no other people here, our age?" I ask as I am reaching for an oyster to open.

Saydira looks at me and then off into the direction of the ocean. Her demeanor is as if she is somewhere far away, she focuses back to me and sighs, "I'm not sure, I suppose there are many reasons."

I look at her and respond, "Things don't add up, and why is there so many women and children and so few men around? Why do they always seem to come and go?"

Ashlea gathers up a few oysters to open and chimes in, "Taylan, there are men in our community, the older gentleman a few homes down and the two men resting over there with their families."

"Ash, I don't mean none whatsoever, I mean, shouldn't there be more of a dynamic with genders and different ages? Like a more even playing field?" I stop opening the oysters for a moment, "Shouldn't we be winning the affections of young men our age, or something? We are pretty well all grown up." My two sisters look at one another with some sort of unspoken acknowledgement.

"Saydira, Ashlea, what is it that you two know that I don't, and why am I always left out of these discussions?

There are only a few years between us, so what is it that I am missing?"

Saydira looks right into my eyes, with a seriousness to her, "Taylan, it's not a conversation that you are missing. You need to pay attention to what goes on around you. Figure it out. Look at the few men that are in this community, the old man a couple of homes away from ours, the man on the beach over there. What do you see?" I look over at the man with his wife, they look to be enjoying the afternoon in each other's company. Smiling at one another and enjoying their conversation.

"Saydira, I, I don't understand, what is it that I am looking for?"

In a hushed voice Saydira says, "Taylan, his leg..." I focus on the man's leg. I know that he can walk because I saw him playing with his two children earlier when I had been in the ocean.

"His leg has a massive scar from his knee to ankle." I answer and look to Saydira for approval. That was what she wanted me to see.

"Yes, Taylan and how do you suppose he got it?"

I glance over at the man and his wife and try to figure out what it is my sister is leading me to figure out. "Well, if he would have been injured here, we would have known all about it."

"Yes, so where and how do you think?" Saydira urges.

"A fight, or maybe an accident, it had to have happened somewhere else?" I look to Saydira and Ashlea for confirmation.

Saydira confirms, "Yes Taylan, nobody speaks of it, but there are reasons for that. It takes a toll on the people around us. Families sacrifice their young and strong for protection as well as payment for their safety. The young people who are mostly men leave their homes and families to become trained and taken in as members to a new family. They normally spend their lifetimes serving and protecting for the major cities. When they are old, or no longer have the strength that it takes to protect, they sometimes return home to where they came from, but most of them find new lives within the city. If they are injured like that man over there, they will come home and re-start their life."

"Well why haven't any of us gone?" I ask completely confused. Ash is also looking to Saydira for an answer, but then decides to tease me just before receiving Saydira's response.

"Taylan, don't be silly we are women, Saydira said that the majority are men that leave." Ash smiles and waiting for a smile in return. I glance at her and give her a quick smirk then look to Saydira.

"Mom has us gather the goods for more reasons other than because she needs to manage the store front. Our neighbors know about us because they see us in the mornings and evenings, but it is not they who do the calling. Our community has regular visitors who come to buy our merchandise, and they go home to their cities. They not only buy our goods, but they report on whom they see. That is when letters and requests come, calling for the young and strong. The young men are usually called and the women, especially the young, are sometimes taken as motivation for the men that serve. The women care for these men that help defend the cities; and they serve as companions. We have not been called on because these visitors have not seen us. Mom keeps us busy and away, to gather while the visitors come. So, they simply don't call on us." I don't know what to think about this; how could I be so oblivious to reality? I pick up an oyster and open it, my first pearl of the day, white and a perfect sphere. Saydira looks at me to see that I understand.

I know it sounds ridiculous that I didn't really notice or understand until now but in my defense with growing up on this island, I saw people come and go often. Our island was more of a holiday retreat, a place for people to visit. My sisters and I never really had any long-term friends because the kids that where our age would only stay a short while before heading back to where they lived. Most of the families that did stay on the island didn't have children at least that I knew of. I was too young to remember them. I knew something was up; it was just that I couldn't place it and at least now, I know.

I break the awkward silence and say, "I understand Saydira, but eventually we will be seen and then what? We are all grown up, we can't stay here forever?"

Ashlea speaks up, "How many of us would have to go if they found out about all of us? They can't take all the young and strong of a family, can they?"

Saydira opens an oyster, and it is her first discovered pearl, as she slips the pearl in a pocket for safe keeping, she answers Ashlea, "I really don't know how they decide on who to call on and how many a family can manage to lose. All I can speak of is what I see, and from what I have seen, Taylan is right and there are hardly any young people left here. There are some, a few other women our age, but very few men. I think that all the young men in this area have been called upon, and my assumption is the women have either been called on to help or followed their men to the cities."

I murmur, "Nothing would ever happen to Mom when the visitors figure out, we have all been here the entire time, right? I look to Saydira for her thoughts.

Saydira's hair has turned to a light blond as her vision sees the white sand around her as well as the afternoon sun in full effect, with the bright rays shining down in a clear and cloudless sky. "I think she would only see trouble if we were to run, or disappear when, or if we were ever called to serve."

"So, we just need to keep doing what we are doing, I suppose." I say to Saydira as she uncovers her second pearl.

"Yes, we just have to be honest with who we are and what we do, and if that time comes, we just need to do what is asked of us."

We are all sitting cross-legged in a semi-circle facing the ocean, each with our bags of un-opened oysters to one side and a second pile of empty shells to the other side and a few discovered pearls between the three of us. Even though we just had a serious conversation, I somehow feel a little better. We haven't done anything wrong up to this point, and my mother can't get into trouble by putting us to work. If that day ever comes, than we do what is needed so that there are no problems for our family.

The oysters are delicious, and we have more than enough to fill our bellies. There really was no need for Saydira to pack a lunch for us, but it is always best to be safe than hungry. We work our way through our oysters, there were so many of them that we needed to give some of the meat away to the few other strangers at the beach. We did well; from our three bags, we have uncovered six beautiful pearls, and from Ashlea's wager that would mean that I get to keep a pearl. I had uncovered three, Saydira two and poor Ashlea only uncovered one. I decide on a medium pearl that Saydira uncovered. It wasn't the largest pearl of the six, but it was unique because it was a light blue color.

We all take a walk to the ocean, rinse off and rest for an hour; lying in the sun, as our stomachs' settle from the feast. We then go back into the ocean for the second half of the day. Ashlea prepares three spears for each of us to use for fishing, and we strap on our bags and head back out. Getting into the water now is much easier. It is more of a relief than anything. The sun and the air make the atmosphere feel like a sauna, and the ocean's water feels warmer than it did this morning, but it is still cool enough to feel like a relief to your skin, but not so cool that it stings when you first touch it. We all walk up waist deep then jump in and swim to the sand dune and dive back down to the reef below.

I take my time. It is not the quantity of fish because I can catch as many fish as I would like. Let's face it; I don't want to spend my entire evening gutting fish after going through a ton of oysters earlier. I want to catch one large fish, something with a lot of meat on it and something I can get close enough to and spear successfully. I am looking for this fish, and so far, nothing meets my wishes, back up I go for air. I break through the surface and gauge how far out I am. I can see that one of the families that were sitting near to us as we were opening the oysters has decided on cooling off; the entire family is jumping and playing in the waves that are rolling up on the shore. I go back down to the vibrant reef. Many little brightly colored schools of fish swim by but where is my fish? Hmm, Okay back up for air then back down again, I swim to the bottom now touching the sandy ocean floor and look at the reef in front of me and then in the shadows, I see him. I slowly move a little closer, spreading my webbed fingers and close in. Quickly, I spear him. His blood clouds the water. He is mine, and I make sure the spear is all the way through so that there is no chance of escape, and I quickly rise to the surface and swim to the dune. I take one final glance before going to shore and peer down into the reef and see that Ashlea and Saydira are still at work: trying to catch their own fish. I decide to swim back to the beach and take care of my catch. I clean up after packing my fish and treasures, and I have some time to relax; that is when Saydira and Ashlea have come up with their own catches to take care of for the short walk home.

I say, "Oh Ashlea what beautiful fish, Mom will be able to sell that one tomorrow and Saydira you managed a fairly good size catch of your own, very nice!" Saydira and Ash smile and you can tell that they are happy. I have food for tonight and a pearl of my own for keeping; what a wonderful day this was.

The sun is setting as we reach home and Mom has finished her day at work managing the store. We reveal all the pearls to her, five in total to sell, and she is just beside herself. "Oh girls, today has paid off for us. These pearls are beautiful, and they will earn extra profits. I am going to display them in the glass box tomorrow. Taylan, that indigo pearl that you are keeping, have you thought about how you want to wear it?"

"Yes, I want it as a pendent on a medium size necklace." I smirk at Mom knowing that she is surprised that I have already decided.

"Very nice Taylan you will have to work on that, I can't wait to see that gorgeous piece of jewelry when you're done creating it and if you don't mind, can I borrow it?" Mom winks.

"Yes Mom" I say with a giggle.

Soon dinner is finished, and before long I am resting in my comfortable bed, lying under the netting, and thinking about this perfect day as I drift off. What is the next adventure?

Chapter 8
A Routine

I am the first to wake. I quietly roll out of bed, wash, and go down to start breakfast for my sisters. Before long, I hear the light footsteps of Saydira descending the spiral stairs followed by Ashlea.

Ashlea rubs her eyes. Her hair is as dark as the night; she hasn't been awake for long. "What are you making?"

I smile; for once, I am not the sleepy head, "Fresh fruit with cocoa."

"Oh, you have read my mind, cocoa." When Ashlea says cocoa, she drags out the word cocoa so that it sounds more like cooooccooooooaa! She smiles sleepily. I bring the food over to the table and sit down with my sisters; Ashlea asks, "So what is the plan for today?"

Saydira ponders aloud, "Well we can hit up the forest today and look for fruits and nuts, Mom is selling the two fish, that we didn't eat last night, and she is also displaying the five pearls later this morning."

Ashlea nods, "Sounds like a plan. Not sure about you guys, but a day of swimming really tires me out; this will be a bit of a break if we decide to go to the forest today."

I speak up, "I don't mind, the forest seems like a good plan, my body could use a bit of a break." We all agree on the forest. Fortunately, our lunch and tools from yesterday are still packed, and before long, we are off to the woods for gathering. An hour, or so later at the house, Mom wakes after we have been gone.

She is a beautiful woman and even though she is older than we are, here on Airus, the body ages differently and she doesn't look it. Her skin is just as ours, and her eyes capture the most vibrant of colors that reflect in her long gorgeous silky hair. The only thing that really sets her apart from my sisters and I is that she keeps her hair much longer than ours, down passed her waist, and it is simply because she can. She works almost every day at the storefront, but because her job doesn't require an extremely high activity level as my sisters and I, she can manage to keep her hair long.

Mom is just setting up her storefront, which is about a ten-minute walk from our home, and it is on an ocean front boardwalk, where other vendors also set their shops. She displays the five pearls. She writes on the display board that she has fish for sale. It is another beautiful day, and she suspects that all the pearls in her display will sell today. She just has that knowing feeling.

The morning soon turns into the afternoon. The fish are sold, and only the five pearls remain. It has been disappointing. She had some who were curious, but it ended in them continuing along the boardwalk. It is now the late afternoon and mom is contemplating on closing, but immediately puts that thought to rest as three women walk up to look at the pearls. They are dressed in brightly colored sundresses, blue, orange, and yellow with gold bangles and uniquely designed earrings. Each woman is wearing a unique design, but they all seem to be coordinated. They gaze down at the display to view the five pearls, all with yearning expressions, which tell her, that she has buyers.

One of the women whispers with a noticeable accent, "Oh these are beautiful." The way that she articulates her words sounds like song. Her voice is like velvet.

Another one says to the other two, "I don't think I have seen such pearls. These would be ideal for your collection."

My mom, Nafeeza waits behind the display. She isn't interrupting; instead, she is carefully letting them admire the pearls. Nafeeza quietly asks, "Would you like to touch them?"

The one in the blue dress smiles and says, "Yes please."

Nafeeza takes them out of the display and onto the counter.

The one in orange says, "Oh these are exquisite. Where did you acquire them?"

Nafeeza answers, "These were found in a reef just off the North Shore."

The one in yellow, surprised says, "Oh these were grown in the wild?"

Smiling, Nafeeza answers, "Yes"

The woman in blue says, "I really like these, what would be a fair price for them?"

Nafeeza is used to bargaining on goods, but a fair price for such rare finds; she isn't sure where to begin. She answers the woman in blue, "You have a good eye, these are rare finds, and we can do a couple of things, a trade, or cash. I suppose if it were money alone, I would feel that two hundred kiros would be fair per pearl, that price would include setting the pearl in a jewelry piece that I have on hand of your choice, but I am also interested in a trade."

The woman in blue is listening to Nafeeza as she proceeds with her proposal. Nafeeza continues, "Your clothing, the fabric is so vibrant in color and looks to be of a high quality, and I know that what you are wearing is not something that is readily available. Are you a dress maker; are you in the clothing trade?"

The one in blue smiles and replies, "You are kind and also have a good eye," she smiles, "this is Ashanthian silk. I am not a dressmaker, but I do employ tailors to clothe me as well as my servants. I can have my tailor see to you if you wish for clothing?" Nafeeza realizes whom she is speaking to, and her excitement of selling the pearls to these women quickly fades and becomes a nervous fear, however she manages to conceal her fear.

The young princess of Thresolon is the daughter of King Wolfrim who rules this area, which also includes the middle continent. She is right here, right now, and Nafeeza knows that this could be the end to life with her daughters.

"I am sorry Princess. I didn't realize who you were. You are so kind to offer a tailor to make me a dress, but what I am interested in is a trade for the fabric that you use." If a tailor is included in this negotiation and as a result brought into her home, it will raise the odds that her daughters will become known to these visitors and will be called upon to serve.

The princess is pondering her proposal and with some resolution to her demeanor she suggests, "I want all five pearls, divided into three necklaces. I want three pearls incorporated into one, and the two remaining pearls are to be set on individual necklaces for these women who you see with me. I will give you one hundred kiros per pearl and for three settings, and I will do a trade of Ashanthian silk, enough silk to make three dresses, and I insist that my tailor sees to you for a proper dressing."

Nafeeza smiles, she can't refuse the princess of her kind offer. It could be viewed as an insult. Nafeeza accepts. "My princess we have a trade. Thank you so much, you are so generous." Nafeeza touches Princess Rosaleen's hand and bows here head to her.

The women continue to chat and work out the details of their trade with the decisions of the settings for the pearls. The princess's tailor will see her tomorrow to take her measurements and to pay the five hundred kiros and accept the finished jewelry on the Princess's behalf. By the end of the day, the tailor will deliver the remainder of the payment being the three finished dresses.

Towards the late afternoon, my sisters and I are now on our way home from a day of gathering in the woods. We didn't meet any other gatherers, which is a little out of the norm, considering that we weren't too far from home. Ashlea and I are leading the way, side by side along the dirt path, and Saydira is trailing not far behind.

"Do you think Mom sold the pearls?" Ashlea asks me.

"Um, I am not sure. I am not even sure what she would ask for them; let alone how much interest they would receive since they are nothing more, but fancy trinkets."

"Taylan, fancy trinkets, you should talk? Hey how does that pearl feel around your neck?" Ashlea teases.

I laugh, "It feels quite nice. I never said that I didn't love trinkets." I wink at her.

We enter our home. Mom is already in the kitchen cooking dinner. The table is set, and she is putting the final dishes out so that we can all sit down and eat. There is a spring in her step. Her hair is shining in a warm brown shade and flowing like ribbon behind her as she moves about.

Ashlea concludes, "You sold the pearls, didn't you?"

Mom smiles, "Of course"

I ask, "All of them?" Mom nods and smiles.

We all sit down and eat. Saydira asks what we are all wondering, what the price was and who the buyers were. Mom shares all the details.

Ashlea is blown away, "How exciting, a Princess, and you get to have a few dresses made for you with the same fabric that a princess wears! Mom you are so lucky! I can't believe it."

Mom is beaming from ear to ear. The trade was good. The kiros will go a long way, not that we were starving for kiros, we have made a comfortable life for ourselves. It is simply great to have that extra breathing room and the dresses, what a treat for all her work.

Saydira asks and suggests, "So the tailor is to see you tomorrow. We should leave while the visitor is with you. I was thinking that we have gathered food for the last two days, the berries and nuts today and the fish the day before, we should head back to the forest and collect some wood. That will keep us busy for the morning, and we can take the afternoon off to relax. We will make sure to stay away from home until the evening."

"That would be best."

We know what could happen if the Princess's servants see us.

Chapter 9
A week later with Kyle

A week has passed, and my old body, Robin, was laid to rest. Family and friends have come to give their condolences and things have started to quiet down since all the ceremonies have finished. My parents are still taking time off, and my parent-in-laws, Liz and Roger are still in town looking after Kyle, our home and Smarty, the dog.

My soul is with Kyle for the moment. He is resting in his hospital bed, and I can honestly say that he looks much better than when he had first arrived a week ago. He is alone, only I am here watching over him. Touching his hand, I know that he is ready to wake. He slowly opens his handsome blue eyes to an empty hospital room. Daylight fills the room, and he can hear the soft rumbling sounds of the machines behind him and the activity in the hallways. He slowly looks around the room, a little confused and then slowly looks down at the hand that I am holding and sees the IV in his skin. It all comes back to him.

I can't talk to him now, for I am nothing, and I know that he can't see me, only I know what is going on in his head. He wants answers. Carefully he sits up in his bed, his eyes have adjusted to the light, and he looks around the room. This isn't a private room, and there is another bed separated by a curtain. For the moment, the bed is unoccupied, but Kyle can't tell because the curtain pulled out; he can only see the wheels at the bottom of the bed and the bottom of that bed's nightstand.

He whispers, "Robin, are you there?" He waits a moment. My soul hurts for him. "Robin, are you awake?" He says a little louder. I touch his cheek and kiss his face, but he doesn't feel, or see me. His curiosity is urging him up; Kyle was never one to sit still. He rolls back the sheets and moves the bed rail down swinging his legs over the edge of the bed. Just then, a nurse comes in to check on him.

She says, "Great to see that you are awake, I am just going to check your IV, and we will have the doctor here to check on you shortly."

Kyle asks her, "Where is my wife?" The nurse knows what has happened and she can't give him the courtesy to say it. She thinkers with his IV and fails to bring herself to look him in the eye.

"The doctor will be with you shortly." She repeats like a robot. Kyle knows something isn't right and begins to get cross with her.

Kyle demands, "Is she in this hospital?"

The nurse murmurs, "I am sorry I can't say." She makes with haste to the door and that is when Kyle's temper makes its appearance. He sits up and rips the tape from his arms, which is holding the IV line in place, unhooks it from his hand and arm, and then he unhooks the things monitoring his heart. Beeping noises start sounding, and the nurse turns, rushing back to him, "You can't do that sir." She pleads and tries to reconnect him, but Kyle isn't having any of it.

He snaps at the nurse, "If you aren't going to tell me I will find someone who will." He starts to get up, and she is gently trying to ease him back into bed. Even though he is still recovering, his strength is more than she can manage, and he is winning this match.

Before Kyle wins his battle with the nurse his mother, Liz, and father, Roger walks in. Liz gasps and runs over to him, "Kyle" she says, and it is enough to distract him for a moment and the poor nurse re-hooks him back up to the IV and heart monitor and gently lifts his feet back into the bed and makes her exit. Liz goes over to him, starts to sob, and hugs him as Roger stands behind her waiting for his turn. Liz looks up at him knowing that he is off, "Why are you angry? The nurses are only here to help you; you must let them do their job."

"Yes Mom, I know, but the least she can do is answer me, and tell me what is going on when I ask. I know that she knows, and I don't understand what the point in keeping it from me is. That is what pisses me off, I am a grown man." Kyle is still fuming despite the arrival of his parents.

Roger speaks up, knowing that no matter what the approach, it won't be easy, "Kyle, I am not going to beat around the bush, Robin didn't make it, I'm sorry." Kyle looks at him and then back to his mother whose eyes have turned red. There is a tear streaming down her cheek. Whatever Kyle was going to say has left his mind, he has no words and just stares at the two of them in disbelief. Liz shakes her head and gazes down; a couple of tears leave her cheek and absorb into Kyle's bed sheets. Roger puts the bed rail down, sits on his bed and says, "I wish I had better news."

"This can't be." Kyle says, but he knows deep down that this is the truth. The details of the crash come back to him. He knows. The three of them are quiet, and after a few moments have passed, Kyle gets the courage and asks, "When can I see her?"

Roger answers, "You have been in the hospital for a week; they have already laid her to rest." Kyle's anger turns to frustration, and he hangs his head down, trying to hide his tears.

Chapter 10
Nafeeza's fitting

It is another early start, and I'm still lying in my bed, looking up into the netting that surrounds it. Ashlea peaks through the netting, "Hey Taylan, time to get up. We got to be out of here early."

"Yes, I know." I pitifully roll out of bed. I am not as good at waking early as Ashlea and Saydira are. I go through my morning ritual, and before long, we are out on the path to the forest. Noon quickly arrives and Saydira suggests that we go back to the North Shore to relax for the afternoon.

The North Shore is an excellent choice because just the other day, there weren't many others on the beach, and it should be the same kind of turn out this afternoon. We come to the clearing of the forest and make our way down the grassy path. I spot a ship that looks anchored just off the deeper side of the reef and stop.

"Saydira," I whisper her name. I don't know why.

"Yes, I see it, they are far enough away. We will stick to the plan and head down." Today is no exception; we are the only ones here and set up on the sand for an afternoon of lazing in the sun.

"That has got to be the Princesses' ship." I say as I stare at it while lying in the sun. Saydira is off cooling herself in the ocean and it is just Ash and I lying together.

"Yes, I think so too." Ashlea answers.

"What do you think they are doing here; shouldn't they be anchored closer to the harbor near home? It's not the typical ship route." I think aloud.

Ash says, "Who knows with them? This princess is a bit of a free spirit. I thought royalty had their servants do the bidding, but I was wrong." We both watch Saydira come out of the water and approach us.

"Hey girls, I want to swim in the reef, would you like to come?" In no time, we are all out on the sand dune and ready to dive into the depths of the reef.

"Let's go girls" with a smile and a look of playfulness, Saydira dives with a splash down into the depths of the reef. Ashlea and I follow, and down we go, flipping, twirling, and following each other as we explore.

A short distance away, on board the ship the Princess and her two servants talk. "They look like mermaids, the way that they are swimming, they are dancing in the depths," says the taller servant as she looks on. They have tools to view from a distance, even thru the reflection of the sky on the ocean's surface, they can see through, into the reef.

"Yes, I want to do what they are doing. Nafeeza said our pearls were found here. I want to see it up close." The princess puts down her gazing tool. The princess requests, "Can you have a boat prepared for us to go to the shore?"

"Yes princess." Not long after the princess and her two servants are dropped off on the shore. They walk along the shore and want to come into the water, but they are unsure of just how. She knows how to dive and swim, but isn't sure on the currants and path that we took to go in. Saydira is the first to spot them, when she comes up for air.

"They are on shore. How did we miss that?" Saydira gasps with disbelief. The three of us have surfaced. It looks like two of the three people on the shore are now waving us over. We can't ignore them now; they see our stuff on the shore and can tell that we have seen them because they start waving more frantically with excitement.

I grow shy, but say, "Shall we?" It would appear odd and suspicious if we were to try to swim away. We all swim up to the dune and return to the shore. It is a funny encounter because we swim naked. As we approach, we know from the details Mom provided us yesterday that this is the princess and her two servants. I never imagined meeting royalty, let alone meeting them completely un-clothed. The taller servant walks up to greet us unfazed; she is the first to speak.

"We saw you from the ship and were wondering if you can take us down into the reef?"

Saydira answers politely, "It would be our pleasure." I know she is lying.

The princess says, "I am Rosaleen, and this is Izavelle and Soolena." They bow their heads.

Saydira says, "Princess, what an honor it is to meet you, I am Saydira, and this is Taylan," I bow my head, "And this is Ashlea." Ashlea bows.

Izavelle asks, "Do you always swim without clothes?"

The slender woman's accent is a little distracting, but I can understand her well enough and answer, "Yes, it is easiest for propelling yourself through the water, and your clothes don't go through the wear and tear or get soiled with the salt of the ocean." My sisters and I quickly smile nervously, it is infectious, and in half second, all of us are giggling. The first-time encounter nerves quickly dissolve. Rosaleen, Izavelle and Soolena remove their clothing and leave the garments with ours. Saydira leads the group out to the sand dune and back down to the reef. Just like the other day of pearl hunting, the ocean is warm, and the sun's rays pierce through the ocean water and ripple along the reef. My sisters and I flip and spin through the water. Rosaleen, Izavelle and Soolena are quickly mimicking our movements and genuinely enjoying themselves, as we swim over the vibrant corals, pinks, blues, yellows and so many schools of bright, shiny fish. After a long swim, we finally swim back to the shore and sit with our new companions on the white sandy beach.

Princess Rosaleen asks me, "That pearl around your neck looks familiar. Do you know if your pearl was found here on the North Shore?"

I answer, "Yes."

Rosaleen grins and says, "I purchased five pearls yesterday, just like the one you are wearing. They are being delivered to me this evening. The woman I purchased them from said that her pearls were from this shore. Did you purchase your pearl from her?"

"No," I swallow, and am a little nervous; her questions are growing more personal.

Princess Rosaleen asks, "Did you find the pearl that you are wearing?" I nod.

Rosaleen persists, "Were you the one that supplied the pearls to the woman that keeps a stand in town?"

Saydira speaks up, "We went diving for them a couple of days ago."

Princess Rosaleen doesn't back away with her questions, "What was your price for the trade with the woman?"

Saydira answers, "Food, clothing, shelter."

Rosaleen knows our connection and nods in understanding. She isn't surprised. Soolena has been quiet the entire time, but asks, "Do you have a father that has been called to serve?"

Ashlea answers, "I have never known him."

Princess Rosaleen asks, "None of you have been called upon by the visitors nor have followed a young man to the City?"

Saydira replies, "No Princess, we have been fortunate to remain here for so long and we have sort of been unfortunate in finding love, there hasn't been many options who have stayed long enough to notice and for us to be able to fall in love with and to follow them."

Princess Rosaleen looks intrigued and asks, "Please join us on the ship for dinner. I will send for your mother to join us." Her words come off more as a demand than as a question.

The small boat that brought Princess Rosaleen, Izavelle and Soolena to the shore earlier has returned. The driver turns the boat off in the shallows and allows it to drift up onto the sand. We are trapped without a way out. We can't run, or hide, and besides at this point I'm not even sure that this is a good princess or a bad one because we are so far removed from the Thresolon City and the happenings of the Palace.

Little is known about Princess Rosaleen. We know that she is young, but King Wolfrim hasn't really brought her into the spotlight. She has a confidence to her and isn't afraid to show it. My guess is that she isn't much older than Saydira and probably has a suitor lined up for her at home. Why is she here? Why do I get the impression that there is more to this than a dinner? Something isn't right, but all we can do for now is go.

The small boat comes to a slow along the side of the ship. We climb a ladder to the main level. The crew who greeted us is left to store the boat. This ship is jaw dropping. It is like a smaller version of a cruise ship or a massive yacht. It is so much wealth for one person. It is white and everything is clean and new. Leather bound seating, huge spacious decks for lounging and servants. The inside is a spacious home, white carpets and lightly stained wood flooring, white leather couches and loungers and windows from floor to ceiling on both sides in the living room area. We don't get a full tour of the ship, but from what I can see so far, our home fits into this ship at least ten times. We settle on the front deck at a more intimate table. A servant quietly approaches and asks, "Is there anything that I can assist you with?"

Rosaleen nods, her warm confidant eyes, and a smile to match, "Yes, sangrias for all please and a couple of trays of assorted fruit."

The servant nods with a rehearsed smile, "As you wish, my Princess." He quietly departs.

Rosaleen starts the conversation, "Today, in the reef was amazing." She turns, saying to my sisters and me, "I have never experienced anything quite as beautiful as what you have showed me today."

Saydira answers with a kind, but bashful expression, "Your welcome Princess."

"So, what do you think?" When we glance at Rosaleen she glances around her; showing she is referring to her ship.

Ashlea says breathlessly, "It is something that we have never experienced. You do have a magnificent ship, and your servants are so kind."

Rosaleen chuckles, "I guess that today is a day full of firsts for all of us." She lifts her glass, "Cheers to that." We all copy her, lifting our glasses and then sip our refreshing drinks.

Another servant, escorting my mother approaches the table and introduces her, "Princess, Nafeeza is here to visit."

Rosaleen addresses the servant then my mother, "Thank you; please sit down;" and she gives one more request to the servant, "and before you leave a glass for Nafeeza as well." The servant returns with the drink, and he disappears again.

My mother looks at my sisters and me with a bit of uneasiness. I can tell that she is wondering how much this princess knows of our family. Funny as it seems, my mother is the only one who is clothed at the table, wearing one of her new dresses made of a purple and rare Ashanthian silk that the princess offered in her trade. The dress drapes her body and ends at her knee. She looks regal. Mom makes a joke of it to break the silence. "Princess, I love the fabric and this dress. Your tailor did a wonderful job, but I can't help, but ask; should I undress?" Everyone looks to one another and laughs. We never dressed when the boat returned to take us to the ship.

Rosaleen says, "No, please wear your dress. Your daughters have taken us to visit the reef, and that detail escaped us. We never dressed afterwards."

Mother says to Saydira, Ashlea and me, "How kind of you to show the princess the reef." We all look at Mother and can see in her eyes, buried far down for only her daughters to sense, that she is now worried for us.

Princess Rosaleen replies, "They are truly kind and welcoming. They have the same characteristic as you. It amazes me that no one from your family has been called to serve or has followed a loved one to the city. Your family is very intriguing to me, and I want to know more. Tell me your story."

Mom and Saydira explain our life to the Princess, our home, our way of living, our likes, and dislikes. As the conversation continues, servants continue to bring out appetizers, the main dish, lamb, followed by desserts of sweets and chocolate. This has been the most delicious meal that I have ever had. We have eaten so much that we are all sluggish. There is still a hint of uncertainty that lies within Mother, my sisters and I, but the impression that I have is, that the princess is better than bad and unconsciously I let my guard down.

Rosaleen concludes, "Shall we dress now and move inside?" We all follow Rosaleen's lead.

Rosaleen instructs Izavelle and Soolena, "Soolena please see Nafeeza to the living room. Izavelle assist the girls and me, and we will meet back in the living room, when we are back, Soolena you can excuse yourself and dress and quietly return to us." Soolena nods and escorts Mom to the living room. My sisters and I follow Izavelle and the Princess.

We are quickly washed down with soap and a damp cloth by Izavelle and sprayed with a perfume, and like Mom's dress, we are clothed in what I assume to be Rosaleen's beautiful dresses. Izavelle works her fingers and quickly fastens our hair into simple tied up hairstyles, and we are shown to the living room where Mother is already sitting on a white leather couch and sipping her drink. We sit with Mom on the couch and Rosaleen, Izavelle and Soolena sit across from us. The sun has just set and the sight of the sky through the large living room window is revealing a canvas of pinks and oranges.

Rosaleen starts the conversation, but this time her tone is more serious, she sips her drink, sets it down and speaks, "Even though I have known you all for a very short time, I find myself liking all of you in such a way that it feels that I have known you all forever. I think of myself as a good judge of character and find myself intrigued by the life that you lead. I am not stupid and know that neither are you. I know that you are worried, especially your mother." My sisters and I glance to Mom who is looking at the princess with worry. The princess continues, "You are worried that one day your family will be called upon to serve. It isn't your daughters to blame for your family being discovered, it was fate of me coming to see your pearls and fate in my curiosity to see where the pearls came from. I have a proposal that you should not take lightly," Rosaleen takes another sip and sets her drink down. "I am a kind master, and you can clearly see from the way that I treat and provide for my servants. Give me two daughters Nafeeza; I will leave you one, so you are not alone. I promise that you will never receive a letter to serve." Rosaleen pauses, staring down her nose for a second to let Mother process and continues, "They will remain and serve me, just as Izavelle and Soolena. They will be cared for and treated kindly and I will never trade them." Rosaleen smiles with confidence then takes another sip from her glass and sets it down. "These daughters of yours are young and beautiful; they will never see or be subject to the violence that the ones who are called to serve normally see."

Nafeeza knew that this was coming. She felt in in every muscle of her body even before she boarded. Should she have lingered, or even worse, deny the Princess's request, the letters would soon be received, and her girls could be hurt, or even worse, lost in a battle. Women normally aren't called to fight, but they are called into dangerous situations to help soldiers, feed, clothe, care for, and be companions to them. I am holding my breath and the tears that are pooling in my eyes. I know this is the last time I will see Saydira and Mom.

Nafeeza speaks with a tremble in her voice, "I accept; Ashlea and Taylan are yours." Her voice cracks a bit as she tries to hold herself together. The princess is clearly overjoyed that mom has agreed.

Rosaleen commands, "Girls, hug your mom." Ashlea and I wrap our arms around her. She is shaking.

Mom whispers to us, "You know that this is better than receiving a letter; don't you?"

I whisper back to her while failing to hold back my tears, "Yes I know Mom, I will never blame you."

"I love you both so much." She kisses us on our foreheads and holds us tightly for another moment. Saydira comes from behind and hugs my sister and me as Mom continues to hold us.

Saydira whispers to us both, "Stay safe, obey your Princess. I love you, and I will take care of Mom. Keep us in your hearts."

I whisper back to Saydira, "I will forever keep Mom and you in mine."

This is our parting, and I never thought it would happen as suddenly as it has. Mom and Saydira are escorted to a small boat that drops them off on the shore. Ashlea and I are ordered to remain in the living room. We watch in the light of dusk, as Saydira and Mom are being dropped off on the shore. I can see that Saydira has her arm around Mom, guiding her up the path that leaves the shore into the forest. They are gone. I feel alone even though I have Ashlea. We are with people who seem nice, but the truth is, we are no longer free, and we haven't a clue what is expected of us.

The princess returns alone, she dismisses Izavelle and Soolena for the night. The princess quietly walks in and sits in the white leather couch she was sitting in earlier.

"Don't be scared; be excited, this is the start to your new life." Rosaleen calls to a servant, "Three more drinks, white wine please." The servant quickly pours the drinks and hands them to us.

"Drink to your new life, cheers." The princess raises her glass, and we reluctantly do the same and drink.

"Girls I have much to teach and show you before we return to the city. The good thing about both of you is you really haven't a clue of what is going on in this world, and you will need to be taught and trained before our return. Don't be sad in my presence. Come let's go to sleep."

Rosaleen leads us down a long straight hallway leading to double doors with crystal knobs. She opens them. We step down three steps into a spacious room. Her bed is at the end of the room, opposite to the doors, and its three steps up to her bed. Off to the right are two doors. One leading to a massive walk-in closet and the second door is a luxurious bathroom with a giant shower with multiple showerheads and a tub that can hold more than a few people at a time to bathe. The wall to the left is floor to ceiling windows; the windows are facing out towards the open water. It is dark now, and the sky is sparkling with the moon and stars.

"Come here my girls," Rosaleen retrieves a couple of nightdresses. "Put these on." Ashlea and I remove the dresses that were lent to us and put on the nightdresses. "You are sleeping with me tonight."

Ashlea is hesitant and looks at me, and I shrug not understanding and say, "Princess, are we to share your bed?" I don't bother to mask my confusion.

"Yes, into bed with me now." Rosaleen orders us over. She steps up to her bed, draws back the silver-colored sheets and climbs in. I climb in first followed by my sister. Rosaleen reaches over to her bedside table and touches a remote that turns off the lights. The bed is huge, and there is more than enough space for all of us. I settle down on my left side in the middle and it is the princess to my back, and she is snuggling up to me from behind and I am holding Ashlea in my arms.

"We have a busy day ahead of us, sleep" and just as Rosaleen has ordered, I close my eyes and dose off. I have too many questions, but one is why is this princess keeping us   this   close?

Chapter 11
Ship Life

It is the early hours of the morning and just outside of the windows, the sky is not completely tenebrous as it was in the night. The sun will rise in the next hour. I lay there, holding Ashlea, though she is awake, she is lying ever so still not to disturb anyone. There are other rooms on this ship. Why would the princess want us to lay with her? I have a few ideas already forming. She made this arrangement so that we could not talk to each other about the events that happened over the past twenty-four hours. I think that she did not want to give us a chance to be alone together, and I think that she didn't want us to think of escaping this arrangement. Not that we would try because we are known, and if we were not tracked down my mom and Saydira would be, and who knows what would happen to them? Neither Ash nor I would ever put my mom or Saydira in that sort of situation. One question remains, the Princess; what does she want with my sister and me? She could have taken anyone to be her personal assistants. I lay there holding onto that thought. I close my eyes, ponder for a bit, and drift off into a short rest that only feels like I have blinked my eyes. The rustling behind me awakens me again. The princess is waking.

Rosaleen gently starts to play with my hair. She whispers to me, "You have been awake for a bit." She says this because my hair is not black, but deep, deep brown since my eyes were open earlier looking around the room and out the window at the dawn that was soon to come.

"Yes Princess, I was awake, but I stayed in bed not to disturb you, or Ashlea, and I drifted back into sleep."

"Is this bed not comfortable?"

I murmur, "It is very adequate Princess, it's just that so much has happened in such a short time, and it is hard to take it all in."

"Do you like all that I have shown you so far?" The princess nuzzles up to me and rests her chin on my shoulder.

"Yes, my Princess, you are so kind. It is just... that I am starting to miss my mom and Saydira." I let go of Ash and roll over on my back, staring up at the ceiling. The princess has no netting that surrounds her bed like the one my bed has back at home. It is another reminder of this nightmare. The princess leans over and gives me a gentle kiss on my right cheek.

"I am your family now, and you have Ashlea to accompany you into this new life." She sits up and looks down at me.

"Come, let's get up." She playfully gets out of bed, walks to the window, and stretches while gazing out at the ocean. She turns slightly to face me and Ashlea, slips out of her nightdress, tosses it to a hamper, and walks away with a grin, into the bathroom. I nudge Ashlea awake.

"Come let's get ready." We cautiously walk to the bathroom where we find Rosaleen preparing a bath for all of us. I am surprised that she is doing this and not a servant.

"Come, ladies, get in." We reluctantly undress and step into the oversized tub. Rosaleen steps in after we each find a spot to sit.

"You two have a long day ahead of you. Do you have any idea what we will be doing?" She smiles warmly at us. Ashlea and I look at each other for a hint of knowing in the other's face; with have not finding anything we look back to Rosaleen for an answer.

She leans back against the tub and says, "Come on girls humour me, you two showed me such a wonderful time in the reef yesterday surely you can take a guess?" She looks on intently.

I murmur, "Are we traveling to the city today?"

Rosaleen laughs, "Oh no not today, you aren't ready for the Palace...good guess though, Try again."

Ashlea concludes, "Are we receiving lessons today?" It would make sense in assuming that we are officially the Princesses' new servants or better yet, pets.

"You are both smart, you are going to be shown by us today how to properly present yourselves and how to represent me. You are going to receive the goods and background to palace life." Rosaleen smiles, "You two women are going to do so well, I just know it. If you stay true to me, I will treat you as well as I treat myself."

We all wash one another, massaging each other's shoulders and backs and braiding each other's hair. Oddly enough, this helps me to relax a bit and forget for a moment the truth, that I am no longer free. We all finish bathing and step out of the tub. Izavelle and Soolena appear out of nowhere with soft fluffy white towels, and they wrap us up in the warmth.

The princess still wrapped in her towel gives instruction. "Izavelle please take care of Taylan for the morning, and start her lessons, and Soolena please do the same with Ashlea. I have things that need my attention, and I will meet you all on the main deck for lunch."

She leaves the room with purpose in her step, and I think either Izavelle, or Soolena had laid some clothes out for her before entering the bathroom because when Ashlea and I enter into the bedroom there is no sign of Rosaleen, but there are two dresses laid out for us. We dress, Soolena escorts Ashlea to another area of the ship, and Izavelle gestures me, and I follow the slender, petite woman. We walk out onto the back deck of the ship where we sit at a table. The ship is on a slow and steady pace, there is no sign of land, and we are at a cruise.

Izavelle starts the conversation with her warm exotic voice, "So how do you feel about all of this?" Her eyes speak to me, and her voice echoes her princesses' words, and I wonder if she even cares or if this is part of an act. I know that she is referring to this entirely new life of service to the princess.

I lie, "It is really nice, and you are great hosts." I can't help it, but there is a bit of sadness in my voice, and really what can I say? The truth is I want to hit rewind.

She leans towards me, "Let's cut to the chase, do you know why you are here?" Izavelle asks.

I answer, "Because the princess needs more servants?"

She shakes her head no but says, "Yes, but do you know why she wanted you and your sister?" She can't help but smirk at my obvious observation of the fact.

I pause for a second, look up then back into her persistent eyes, "Izavelle I have no clue?" I look to her for answers.

"You and your sister are free spirits; from the little time she has known you; she has seen your love and dedication to one another and your interest in exploring. Rosaleen has said so herself, she is captivated by you and your sister's absolute trust in each other and in strangers." Izavelle picks up my hand and holds it on the table. "She was keen on taking you because she knows that your family was intact, and it was only a matter of time before others would find out, and the city would come, seeking out your family to serve. Rosaleen felt compelled to take you for her own because serving royalty is much easier than doing the dirty groundwork of serving the city." She looks into my eyes, and I cannot look away, "She did your family a favour by taking you two before the city did. We are going to mold you into a strong creature. Don't get me wrong, but you will see things that are not right, but at least the good outweighs the bad with the life the princess will create for you, and trust that this is for a greater good."

"What things?" I ask.

Izavelle looks at me, "You will find out soon, just remember what we have talked about." I do not feel like we have really talked about anything. Nothing has really been explained to us and I only have more questions. She smiles and takes a strand of my hair that fell from my braid and tucks it behind my ear. "We have to teach you some etiquette this morning, let's start with the basics, please and thank you." I sigh.

Izavelle gives me the rundown on when to use and apply different manners that they use in Thresolon and the Palace. Not that my sister and I are rude people it is just as Izavelle explains it, manners are a bit different in Thresolon and the Palace. She spends the morning teaching me and having me mimic her movements, her walk, her bow, her smile, her eye contact, and the way that she annunciates. I find myself liking these mannerisms even though this feels silly.

We take a break and lean out on the banister, both looking out at the ocean, "Izavelle, can I ask, how did you come to serve Princess Rosaleen?"

Izavelle smiles, "How do you know that I serve her?"

I pause and look at her, "Umm...well, I assumed by the way she instructs Soolena and you?"

She laughs, "Just because you see that I take instruction from her does not mean that I serve her or am loyal to her. This is your first real lesson, and you need to remember that. Everything in the palace community and the city is not always what it seems to the onlooker. Never assume. I might be your mentor today, but later I may become your enemy."

I ponder that thought. How am I supposed to serve this woman who has taken me from my home? I am being taught by her servants' things about her life, how to act and told not to trust her servants, and to only trust her? I just don't understand. I am confused. This is some sort of disarranged social game.

"I am sorry Izavelle." I look down to my toes as I curl them, do I trust myself, my intuition? Can I trust my judgment? I know that I am in a situation that is bigger than what has been revealed to me so far. I feel in my heart that this princess will be good to me, but what I don't know is, is she good?

Izavelle sits down beside me and whispers, "I didn't mean to upset you. You need to be shown that this world is vastly different from the world you have known. You need to serve your master, and you need to protect yourself by remaining reserved, by watching and by paying attention to your surroundings. Let us end on this note. You have done so well this morning. Come Taylan; let's meet the others for lunch." Izavelle and I walk hand in hand to the front deck to meet with Rosaleen, Soolena, and Ashlea. Rosaleen stands to greet us as we walk up.

"Ladies come and join us." She joyfully motions us over to sit with her at the table.

"How did she do, Izavelle?"

"Marvelous, she is a quick and eager learner." Izavelle beams.

"Good and Ashlea did just as well I hear." Ashlea smiles and I return her smile and look to her for signs that she is okay, and her glance back brings comfort because her silent gesture says that she is good despite all of this.

"Let's eat." Rosaleen is the first to fill her plate with fresh bread and fruit and fill her glass with white wine, and we all follow her lead.

"I think you two will really enjoy what we are doing after lunch. You showed me how to flip and spin and play in the depths of the reef, now I will show you something that you have never experienced." She smiles and pops a grape in her mouth; swallows and splashes a sip of wine to wash it down. Ashlea glances at me, excitement in her expression, and I feel my uneasiness settle with my sister's glances. Her excitement is infectious, and I feel myself sharing the same emotion. I feel a little guilty for feeling this way after having lost everything. This arrangement isn't bad.

Chapter 12
Light as a Feather

While Rosaleen, Soolena and Izavelle talk, I quietly ask, "Ashlea, do you know what Rosaleen is talking about?" Ashlea shrugs and in a whisper says, "Not a clue." Rosaleen, Izavelle and Soolena each laugh obnoxiously and their eyes hint of something fond and they sit back in their chairs and seem to relish in our anticipation.

Rosaleen stands from the table and still laughing, "You two are a dream, so trusting, come let's get you out of those dresses and into something more suitable for the afternoon's lesson. Izavelle, Soolena, take the afternoon off, you are both dismissed until the evening, thank you for your work, ladies." Soolena and Izavelle are still sitting at the table. They gently nod as a thank you to the Princess. Ashlea and I tuck our chairs in, Rosaleen hooks her right arm into my left, and her left arm into my sister's right and leads us down the hall to a door on the left. We enter and go up a couple of flights of stairs and enter one large open concept room, full of skylights and equipment. The floors and walls are a pale grey. The room is full of suits, I see some diving suits that have compressed oxygen compartments within and breathing tubes to allow for the person to not have to come up for air. I see flippers, some look to be for the feet and others seem to be for the hands. What catches my eye is that Rosaleen is leading us to this row of suits that reflect. She picks out two, handing us each one. I study the strange fabric, rubbing my fingers on the smooth surface. It is a stretchy material so that it is skin-tight, and the material has a soft feeling to it. The entire suit looks like it is made of mirrors. From the arms to the ankles of the suit, there is a piece of material that looks to be like a sail that extends past the length of the arms, like wings on a bird. Rosaleen smiles and asks, "Do you have any idea what we are doing now?"

I smile, "Is this for flying?"

"Precisely" She answers, glancing at me through her grey bangs.

"How, Princess?" Ashlea asks confused.

"The shiny material on the suit captures the sun's rays to help you become weightless. There are no engines, or built in propellers, it is more like, when you try to push together two magnets with the same ends facing each other, they repel. The suit kind of acts like that, but its repelling itself from the ground, helping you become weightless."

I ask, "Well how come these suits aren't floating around this room?"

Her head tilts back and her bangs fall away from her eyes as she giggles, "So many questions! The suits are inside out and are in a state of charging. Remember that. If you take the suit off, flip it inside out, or else you risk it floating away."

Ashlea and I start to giggle, and it is the first real giggle since last night. Go figure, what a silly concept. Rosaleen gives us instruction. "Okay girls please follow my lead and watch what I am doing." She first slips out of her dress so that she is in nothing but underwear; she turns her suit so that it is no longer inside out and lays it on the floor in front of her, she spreads the wings out and opens the bodice up. She climbs into it on the floor as you would a jumper and carefully, puts her legs and arms through the pants and sleeves of the suit and fastens it. Rosaleen is still on the floor to my amazement.

I ask, "Rosaleen why are you not floating?"

She can't help but laugh and give me a wink, like she is silently saying to me with her eyes, watch this and just like that she gets on to her feet, knees bent, so that her bum is just inches from the floor and then does a sort of bunny hop into the air. She is floating three feet off the ground and opens her wings and just like swimming, she glides around the room as if she is under water only, she is in the air. Ashlea and I are frozen in amazement. We have never seen anything like this. We didn't realize that these suits even existed.

Rosaleen puts on an act to pretend as though she is bored; somehow crossing her legs in mid-air, as if she is resting on an invisible couch. "Ladies we haven't got all day, hurry up!"

Ash and I both take our suits and copy what Rosaleen had done to get into them and we are ready for flight, or floating. I don't know what to call it.

"Taylan, a gentle push into the air is all you need, remember you are in an enclosed room, if you push off to hard you will hit the ceiling." I follow Rosaleen's instructions and just as her, I find myself floating a few feet off the ground.

"That is very good Taylan!" Rosaleen complements, "Okay, Ashlea your turn." Ash, just like me, has managed to float around the room. "Girls, this is the hardest part, judging the force of launching yourself, you're weightless now, just like swimming in the reef you steer and propel yourself in the air. The only difference between the water and air is the air has less resistance, so that means that the stronger and more forceful movements will take you farther and faster."

I realize that this is the first time that I forgot of the loss with having to leave Mom, Saydira and our home. I spread my arms out and flap the sail and I move forward. I flap up to the ceiling then make the motion of diving, and flap back down, moving around the room, smiling from ear to ear.

"Oh my, this is amazing." I twirl about the room and gently bump into Ashlea.

"Hey, watch where you're going!" Ashlea laughs at me and pushes me away from her; only I float into the wall.

"Ouch, Ash I am trying to fly, you don't need to be so mean about it."

Rosaleen is patient and allows us to get comfortable with this new feeling of being weightless. "Okay girls, now that you have experienced being pushed by each other, I need you to practice taking control of yourselves after something has happened to you that is out of your control. That push could be a gust of wind. Start with pushing each other gently and work the force up as you get comfortable with being able to quickly adjust to the change." Ash playful goes at me first, but I push back, and we both back into opposite walls, giggling.

I say, "Okay, okay, Ash come here, push me again, I think I know what to do."

Ash gives me a push, and I swim into her push, which is the easiest way to describe it.

Rosaleen applauds. "Good!"

I push Ashlea, and she swims into my push and keeps herself from backing into the wall behind her. We continue, back and forth, at different strengths and different angles and trying to throw the other off. We switch gears and race each other around the room and practice diving and soaring in the room. I can easily say that flying is now the most enjoyable thing that I have ever done. It is easy and feels natural, like we were built to have wings and fly. Rosaleen has a look of satisfaction and asks, "Are you two ready to put your skills to the test?"

"Yes," we answer in unison.

"Okay out to the front deck we go." We fumble out onto the main deck and both grab hold of the railing as we can feel the light breeze on deck.

"How do you two feel?" Rosaleen asks.

Ashlea answers, "I feel like I could quite seriously blow away."

"You will feel that don't panic, it is the same as practice, remember push into the wind. Okay let go of the railing."

We let go, and instantly I feel myself drifting, my feet are dragging lightly on the deck as though the ship is moving without me.

Rosaleen says, "Taylan, you feel that right. Okay lightly push forward like you are treading water in the ocean." I do as I'm told, and my feet are no longer drifting, but I am instead feeling a sense of control of my footing and have control on where I'm moving.

Rosaleen encourages, "Taylan you got this. Ash let go of the railing and remember your treading water." Ashlea lets go; she is a natural. Ashlea seems unsure of herself, but really, in my eyes I know that she has this.

"You are going to follow me, keep up, this will seem hard at first, but it doesn't take long to get used to, and once we are done you will be so good that it will feel like you have been flying your entire lives."

We have an audience; Izavelle and Soolena are sitting in loungers on the deck and being loud about it; cheering us on and clapping. Rosaleen runs and leaps into the air, spreads her arms so that the suit's wings extend, and she flaps into the air to gain speed and height. My heart is in my throat; I can hear my own heart beating; it is pumping so hard with adrenaline. It is a good excitement, and I copy my master and run, spreading my arms to extend my wings and flap them up and into the air. Ashlea follows.

"WHOA" I scream, laugh, and look back at Ashlea; she has the exact same reaction.

"This is so amazing!" I call out at the top of my lungs; we follow Rosaleen into the sky. The height we get is nothing I have ever imagined. The ship looks like a toy now that we have gotten so high. We follow Rosaleen and continue to climb up into the sky. Soaring and learning how to dive, and then slowing ourselves down before hitting the water. We learn to steer, circling, gaining speed and slowing ourselves. We are flying for what feels like such a fleeting time, but really, we have been up in the sky for a couple of hours. Flying does feel like second nature. Rosaleen calls us to follow her, and we go back to the ship. As I am coming in for a landing, I slow my speed by tilting my wings and doing shallow dives to get down to the level of the ship. In a steady motion, just few feet above the deck, I swing my legs down, so that I am in a standing motion, and I do a treading water motion to bring my feet to touch the deck. Izavelle and Soolena come over with a skip in their steps to meet us, clapping eagerly.

"Very good ladies," they both say as they come to help us out of the suits. We get out and carry our suits back up with Rosaleen, to the room that housed them.

Rosaleen asks, even though she already knows the answer, "So I take it that you both enjoyed that?" We both smile and nod.

"Very good, flying will help you get out of any weird situations that may come into play, especially where we are going." She hangs her suit up and there is a bit of seriousness in her voice. She turns to us, "Can I trust you?" Rosaleen looks at us, studying our expressions and eyes for any hint to say otherwise. I thought that was part of her reason for taking us.

Ashlea replies, "Yes, you can trust both my sister and me. We are sad to have left our home and family behind, but having you as our master, we couldn't have asked for a better alternative. You have been so kind to us, and we would never do anything that would go against your wishes." There is certainty in her words and Rosaleen seems satisfied with Ashlea's sentiments.

"That makes me happy to hear this from you." Rosaleen replies, "Let's wash up and get dressed for dinner."

Rosaleen escorts us back down to her bedroom, and we quickly wash up with a damp cloth and then we each slip into light summer dresses and meet Izavelle and Soolena for dinner, but this time the location is in a dining room that is just off the living room area of the ship. The table is large for our group of five; caters to twelve guests, but with the room closed off to the living room area, it gives the space a more intimate and a private feeling. We all sit at the far end, opposite to the door. Rosaleen takes a seat at the head of the table, Ashlea, and I to her right and Izavelle and Soolena to her left. Dinner is served. It is some sort of white fish, served with sugar kelp and a red wine to accompany the meal.

Rosaleen sips her glass of wine, turning her attention to severing the fish on her plate into more manageable bite size portions and says to us, "Your first day has gone very well, and I feel more confident with having picked you." She takes a bite of her fish and slowly chews, savoring the taste of the meat. "This evening you two will share your own room, and I trust that you won't do anything that would jeopardize the trust that I have gained in you." She eyes us both and takes another bite of the fish. "I want you to feel at ease here. This is your home now and even though you are here to serve, you need to think of us like family. We are all here in this room to protect one another."

Rosaleen raises her glass, "To family!"

Everyone follows her lead and raises their glasses, "To family, cheers."

We all sip our wine, Soolena says, "Enough of all this serious discussion lets enjoy ourselves."

For the rest of the dinner, it is all lighthearted conversation of the day's events, and I can't help but wonder why me, why us? What does Rosaleen want with us? I can sense that she is holding back. My gut is telling me that she has a specific plan for us and has yet to reveal it. What I don't understand is why they haven't asked more of our backgrounds. They feel that they know enough but then again, trust seems important. I have lived a safe and sheltered life before Rosaleen walked into it and plucked Ashlea and me out. When you hear the word servant the first thing that comes to mind is someone that serves another in the form of work, so far Ashlea and I have been given lessons about their lives and we are being groomed and treated as equals to the Princess. I know that, once Ashlea and I are alone, we can talk, like really talk without the pressure of Rosaleen, Izavelle and Soolena around to listen in.

Ashlea and I continue to engage in the dinner conversations. We smile and are polite, showing off our newly learned manners from this morning's lesson and showing our appreciation for how well we are being treated, which is like honored guests.

Rosaleen finally dismisses us for the night, "Soolena please show them to their room." We rise from our seats, thank Rosaleen for the lovely meal, and follow Soolena to our chamber.

"Ladies, sleep well, you have another busy day tomorrow." Soolena exits the room, closing our door behind her. I don't hear the lock being turned on our door to keep us contained. It is kind of weird because the princess seems to emphasize trust with us, and to me it seems that her trust in us hasn't been fully developed, which I understand because she has only known us for a couple of days. Still odd considering her actions lead me to believe that she is still a little guarded when it comes to Ashlea and me. The room is lavish and like Rosaleen's room, there is a step down into the room and the bed is on the opposite wall, it is a step up to the bed. We also have floor to ceiling windows to our left and a bathroom and closet on the right. It has the exact same layout, but on a smaller scale. The door to our room is a single door and the closet is smaller. The washroom has only a stand-up shower, toilet, and sink. I go to the bed and sit, watching Ashlea's reaction to our newly given privacy. She circles the room and drinks it all in with her eyes looking up and down and walking slowly, completing a full circle.

Ashlea motions to the door and whispers, "She didn't lock it."

"I know, but don't even think about it. This is a test, to affirm her trust in us." I sit back on the bed, leaning on my hands and take in all the details, the white trim and light grey walls, the closet door is open part way and from the little bit I can see it seems to be full of dresses, cloaks and light tops made of flowing fabrics. Ashlea decides to come and sit cross-legged on the bed next to me, she is clearly in deep thought, as am I.

I murmur, "Now is the time to talk." I look over to her sitting beside me and ask, "What do you think about all of this?" I catch myself asking the same question as Izavelle had just asked me this morning.

She inhales and exhales, "I have no idea and was hoping you had some thought about all of this."

"Well for being servants the last day hasn't really shown us just how exactly we will be serving our Master. I think she may be carefully grooming us for something that we can't even begin to imagine. Flying, why, is all I have to say; I have never seen anyone fly before, it's almost like we need to learn the skill to get away from something, or someone, or the opposite, move in, get something, and get out. We will be groomed to steal, or spy?"

Ashlea doesn't reveal what is on her mind right away and is carefully absorbing my words with an agreeing look in her eyes, "Yes, but for what exactly?" She asks.

"Well so far we have had a lesson in etiquette and a flying lesson." I shrug, my head hurts with this entire pent-up curiosity and no answers, just ideas, or a better word would be suspicions.

Ashlea looks at me as if waiting for me to say more and then realizes that that is all that I have and then she jumps in to encourage me to continue along this train of thought, "How do these two lessons connect?"

I sigh, "Back to square one, no clue. What do you want to do?"

Ashlea states the obvious, thinking aloud, sharing her thoughts with me, she whispers, "Well the door is unlocked, do we make a run for it? Grab the flying suits and go?"

"Well, it's a clever idea if we knew all the pieces that are in play here. Neither of us knows if those suits work at night." I pause, "Let's stay put and wait this out. I don't feel like she is going to bring harm to us if she is taking the time to teach us, and besides, we must think about Mom and Saydira and if we leave then what happens to them?"

Ashlea looks to me quizzically, "Why do you suppose she just didn't take all of us, Mom and Saydira too?"

I shrug, "It's just another unanswered question only Rosaleen can tell us."

"Yah, I guess, anyway this whole room to our self-bit, we know that the door isn't locked from the outside should we at least lock the door from the inside?"

I roll the idea around in my head and conclude, "trust is a two-way street. They are giving us this much, lets show her by leaving it unlocked. She is treating us like guests, let's act like trusting guests."

Ashlea nods, "For sleeping arrangements I am not sure about you, but I still feel like there is something else in play here. I just have a feeling that I can't ignore. Do you think we should rest in different parts of the room?"

Tilting my head sideways I whisper, "What did you have in mind?"

Before she replies, she opens a dresser drawer that is in a corner, pulling out two nightshirts and tosses one over to me. It lands on the bed. "Well, I think we should have one of us sleep in the bed and the other can take some of the extra cushions and lay them out in the closet for the other to rest on. Should something happen then the chances to defend ourselves are better because we are spread out.

"I think you are on to something" I stretch my arms out and yawn. "I have a feeling that I can't ignore; a feeling of being watched." I remove my dress over my head, toss it, missing the hamper and slip on the nightshirt.

"Yah me to Taylan, we should get ready for bed, you are yawning, and you are making me yawn." Ashlea yawns, stretches, and smiles back at me.

We take the cushions off the bed and lay them out on the floor of the closet. A spare blanket is folded up part way to be pulled up if one is cold in the night. We use it as the blanket for our makeshift closet bed.

Ashlea quietly whispers, "I will take the closet, and you take the bed. If we have problems, what do I use as a defense?"

I look around the room, "That small stone sculpture over there, looks like it could do some damage." Motioning in the direction of the bedside table where a small stone sculpture of dolphins is placed.

"Yes, good idea Taylan." She walks over, picks it up, and weighs it in her hand. "Yes, this is a good size." Smiling wearily, but she does look a bit more relaxed with knowing that we have put together a bit of a defense in case something should happen.

Ashlea whispers to me again and looking a bit amused, "You understand I really feel better about sleeping, but you know with all this strategizing we have done, nothing will likely happen."

I return her smile and murmur, "Well that would be good, right?"

She chuckles and holds her hand to her mouth to quiet herself, she finally breathes and lets her hand down, "Yes that would be good, but Taylan, when they see that I have been sleeping in the closet what do I say?" She raises her eyebrows and wrinkles her forehead, her eyes wide making a silly expression on her face.

"Just tell them that you got tired of me kicking you in my sleep."

We both laugh quietly, "Okay will do. Let's get some sleep." Ashlea gives me a hug and a kiss on my cheek. We crawl into our beds. I must have fallen asleep immediately. A day of training and flying and with all my nerves and excitement at their peak, allow me to drift off into sleep quickly.

I have been asleep for some time when suddenly, I wake. Why am I awake? The room is dark. I haven't had any unsettling dreams, come to think about it I haven't dreamt at all. I lie there in bed and listen. Ashlea was making noise. I listen in the silence. If I concentrate hard enough, I can hear the soft rhythmic breathing of my sister sleeping, but there is something or someone else in here. I lay still and listen trying to figure out if this is my mind running wild or if there is someone else here. There it is I see someone standing at the foot of the bed, a dark silhouette.

Chapter 13
A Dark Shadow

The figure is large. Do they know I'm awake? They sense it because my breathing has changed from the slow, steady rhythm of sleep. What do I do? How long have they been watching me? Oh shit, what should I do? I'm frozen with fear. Do I say something, do I run, what? I lie still and glance at the foot of the bed to see the silhouette, but my heart stops—the silhouette isn't there. My eyes dart around. Shit, where are they? I sit up and look to the closet to see if Ashlea is okay.

I feel the blade across my throat and then hear a deep, familiar voice, authoritative and quiet. "Lie back down, you little wench.

I lie back. I can't even muster the voice to speak, to cry out for Ashlea. He straddles me with the blade still at my throat. I can feel the point lightly piercing my skin and the warmth of a small stream of blood running down to the back of my neck, pooling on the sheet beneath. He murmurs, "Servants... I will show you what it's really like. Don't you dare think of moving if you want to live."

Aggressively, he pulls the sheets down to my knees. Where is my sister? I lie back silent and still, obeying him. I refuse to cry or close my eyes. My ears start to ring, and the smell of metal fills my nostrils. Stay awake, I urge myself.

"What's wrong, little pet? Is this not what you had in mind?" He laughs, amused by my fear. His weight is too much for me to struggle against. Even if I tried, it might anger him more. His blade is at my throat. Then there's a sound, like a rock hitting a thick board of wood; he falls over me. The blade is still in his hand, and the point lifts out of my skin slightly as it falls, lightly severing the surface of my throat. I am frozen until I see my sister.

"Hang in there!" Ashlea demands, rolling him off me. The intruder is out cold.

"Get up," Ashlea urges. She sits me up on the bed, then holds my hands as she leads me off the bed. I can barely hear her through the ringing in my ears.

"Come," Ashlea says, wrapping my arm around her shoulder, allowing me to lean on her for support as we leave the room to go to Rosaleen's. Ashlea bangs hard on the door, then twists the doorknob; it's open, and she walks us both in. Rosaleen is startled by our entrance and turns on the lights to see who has disturbed her. She looks ready to scold us but stops suddenly at the sight of us. Blood is trickling down my neck, and droplets are hitting the floor. Rosaleen draws her conclusions. She runs to her bathroom and gets some cloth to press on my throat.

"Sit her down," Rosaleen says with anger in her voice. She approaches with the towels, covering my wound and applying pressure. I can feel the warmth on my neck as the towel soaks up my blood. "Keep it pressed on her throat, Ashlea. Keep her attention; I'll be right back." Rosaleen runs down the hall to wake Soolena and Izavelle. Izavelle instantly comes to my aid. Without hesitation, she takes a second towel, quickly removes Ashlea's hand from my neck, and replaces the first towel with the second, pressing firmly.

"It's not that deep, Taylan. We'll get this closed, and you'll be good as new, but you must stay awake for us," Izavelle instructs me.

"Can you see me?" Izavelle asks.

"Yes," I answer.

"Are you dizzy?"

"Yes, the room is spinning, and my ears, I can barely hear you—the ringing."

Izavelle instructs Ashlea, "Grab her legs, and turn her so we can lie her down." Ashlea gently lifts and pivots me so I'm lying across the foot of Rosaleen's bed.

"Keep her legs up," Izavelle orders, and Ashlea does so without hesitation. Izavelle turns her attention back to me. "How do you feel?"

"Thirsty. Can I have some water?"

"Not yet, dear. We're going to keep your legs elevated until the color returns to your face." Izavelle peeks at the wound. The bleeding has slowed, but it's still oozing.

"She needs stitches. Can you reach for those cushions without dropping her legs?" Izavelle asks.

"Yes," Ashlea responds, grabbing them.

"Okay, put them under her legs. There's a first aid kit in the bathroom. Run and get it quickly. Go!" Ashlea is back in a fraction of a second.

"Open the kit. There's a small hook-shaped needle; find it and a spool of thread."

"Got it," Ashlea says, anxiously waiting for more instructions.

"Okay, Ashlea, I'm going to have you switch with me. Put pressure on her wound."

Izavelle works effortlessly, threading the needle and knotting the string. "Taylan, I don't have any painkillers. You'll have to bear this. I'll be quick; four stitches, okay love?"

I nod, and Izavelle says, "Okay, here's number one." She gently lifts the towel, carefully lifts a piece of my skin, loops the needle through, and then pierces back through the other side. With no effort, she knots and cuts the first stitch, then moves on to the second, warning me as she goes. It hurts, but I can manage this. "Taylan, this is number two." She repeats the process, knotting the thread and cutting the ends. She pauses to dab the blood away, then warns me again and does the third and fourth stitches.

"I'm thirsty," I whine, my head pounding, wanting to close my eyes.

Izavelle instructs Ashlea, "Go fetch some water." Ashlea is back in a flash.

"Taylan, you've lost some blood, and you're still pale. I'm going to slowly lift your head up. Don't help; let me take your full weight. Just relax. I'm going to give you a sip, nothing more." Izavelle puts her hand under my head, raising me slowly and holding the glass to my lips, tilting it slightly so I can take a small sip.

"Swallow," Izavelle encourages, and I do as I'm told. She gently lowers my head back down. Izavelle continues to treat my wound, dabbing at it. The bleeding has stopped, and she applies antibiotics before dressing my wound with white bandages from her first aid kit.

"Ashlea, she's still pale and clammy. Run to the kitchen and fetch an ice pack from the fridge."

"Where's the kitchen?" Ashlea asks quickly.

"It's the door across the hall from the dining room, the door before the living room area."

"I'll be right back," Ashlea says, and she's gone.

"How do you feel?" Izavelle asks, feeling my forehead.

"A little better, but I'm still thirsty." Izavelle repeats the process, lifting my head and giving me another sip.

"How is that?" she asks.

"Better," I reply.

Ashlea returns with an ice pack and hands it to Izavelle, who places it on my head.

"I think we're doing well. Taylan, you need to stay lying down for a bit. I don't want to deal with your fainting. This will take some time, and we'll treat your thirst and feed you in moderation. No sudden movements, especially if you start feeling better. We'll help you until you no longer show signs of fainting."

The ice feels wonderful on my forehead, and I start to feel my strength return. I can't feel the pain of my wound at this point; it feels numb. However, I still feel tired and weak. I lie there and let Izavelle and Ashlea care for me. Every few minutes, Izavelle allows me another sip. I'm on to my second and third glass, but my thirst is never quenched.

"How do you feel now?" Izavelle asks.

"Better. I'm starting to feel hungry."

"Okay, we're going to change the pillows and remove them from your legs, then put them under your head and back. Keep the ice pack on her head. I'll be back with some food." In the blink of an eye, Izavelle is gone, and it's just Ashlea and me.

"How are you feeling?" Ashlea asks. I relax at the sight of my sister, relieved that the attacker didn't hurt her.

"I feel better now that I'm all patched up," I say calmly.

"I mean, how are your nerves?" I chuckle, realizing I misunderstood.

"I've been more distracted by my thirst than anything. You really did a number on them." I pause and then look up at her. "Thank you for saving me." I smile with a tear in my eye, and she returns a warm smile, wiping the tear from my cheek.

"You're welcome," Ashlea says, pausing to gather herself and tucking a strand of her red hair from her face. "I think your attacker was one of the food servers. I didn't get a good look at him. I didn't even hear him enter the room." She looks down at her hands, sadness evident, but she's clearly trying to bury it. Now isn't the time. "I woke when he spoke. His voice was so

familiar. I listened and knew you were in trouble. I slowly opened the door and crawled across the floor. When I saw his back was to me, I leapt up and struck him in the back of the head with all the force I had using the dolphin sculpture. I never got a good look at him to know for sure who he was; my attention was on you. I know I knocked him out. He never moved or flinched when I rolled him off you. His voice was so familiar." Ashlea takes my hand and holds it to her face, kissing it.

"Oh, Taylan, we need to know why this happened. Do you think we're being used as bait?" Before I can respond, Rosaleen, Soolena, and Izavelle enter the room. Izavelle has a tray of sliced food and fruit juice.

Rosaleen comes to my side. "I'm so sorry this happened to you," she says with sympathy in her eyes and a quivering voice. "Soolena has tied him up and locked him in your room as an extra precaution. However, I'm not sure it's necessary; he's still out cold and barely breathing. His skull is cracked. Soolena has tended to his wounds, but he will die today. If not by us, it will be by his wounds. Tell me what happened?" She looks concerned, and Ashlea tells her everything.

After Ashlea finishes, Rosaleen confides, "You two are very brave." She looks at me. "How do you want to dispose of your attacker?"

Chapter 14
Kyle My Love

Kyle is leaving the hospital for the first time today with his parents Roger and Liz. It has been another week since he woke from his extended bed rest and Kyle is still weak and stiff but can manage on his own. He is numb from life and is just moves through the motions. The three of them walk out to the car and get in. The plan is to take him back to his home and take it easy for the rest of the day.

From the driver's seat, Roger asks Liz and Kyle, "How about we stop for a coffee and donut?" Roger looks in his rear-view mirror for a reaction from Kyle, but he just looks out the window.

Liz answers, "I could go for a coffee and donut, and we can just go through the drive thru, make it quick."

Rogers says, "Yah I think that's what we are going to do." They find a coffee shop and place their orders and even though Kyle has said nothing, Roger goes ahead and orders him a chocolate milk iced cappuccino and an apple fritter donut, Kyle's favorites, and hands them back to him; Kyle quietly accepts, still saying nothing. Roger and Liz talk amongst themselves as they continue along the drive home about light topics, like the songs they are listening to, the weather and things they need to remember to do.

Kyle stares out the window as he begins to eat his donut. He is appreciative that his father ordered it for him even though he didn't ask for it. He is still working everything out in his head; he knows that the accident was real, he knows that I, Robin am gone; he believes what he has been told, but for some reason the thought of disbelief still lingers. In the back of his mind, he can't ignore the feeling he gets that when he gets home, Robin will be there on the couch watching television.

They are about halfway home when Kyle clears his throat. Liz and Roger stop their conversation at the sound and Roger glances in his rear-view mirror back at Kyle. Kyle looks back at the rear-view mirror into Roger's eyes and says, "I want to see Robin."

Roger answers, "Sure Kyle, let's get you home first, and we can make plans to go see her."

Kyle snaps back at him, "No, I want to see her now."

Liz looks over her shoulder back at Kyle and carefully she suggests, "Dear, you have been through a lot, maybe it would be best to take you home so that you can rest, and we can make plans to go tomorrow."

Kyle's voice erupts; "Don't tell me what is best; I want to see my wife, now, today. Dad, turn the car around." Roger without fighting back at his own son turns the car around.

Rogers says as calmly as possible, fearing that he may hit a note with Kyle sending him into more of a temper, "Kyle I will take you to see Robin, but please don't be upset with us, or your mom, we are just trying to do what is best."

Kyle is rattled by his own temper; he can go from zero to one hundred in a heartbeat, abruptly he answers, "I'm sorry, sorry Mom, I didn't mean it." He glances at Liz and then down to his hands.

"It's okay dear." Liz quietly says.

It is not long before they arrive at the graveyard, park the car, and walk down the path towards Robin's grave. Liz tries to hold Kyle's hand as they walk down the path, but

Kyle is too distracted to realize, and Liz takes his sudden motion of his hand breaking away from hers as a rejection to her gesture.

Roger sees, stepping in and holds Liz's hand as he leads them down the path and Kyle follows a step behind. They turn down a grassy row of small head stones arriving at one with the dirt still freshly turned. Robin's grave is a small metal rectangle that is flat to the ground and has an urn built in, which is full of silk flowers. Kyle falls to his knees, still not wanting to believe, or let go of that lingering feeling that Robin is still alive. He reads her name and the dates marking her life. Kyle studies the urn, the flowers; he knows that he is really without his soul mate.

Roger and Liz give him some space and take a few steps back, Liz with tears in her eyes. It is still fresh for everyone. Roger silently gives her a gentle embrace as they look on at their son.

Kyle has known since he woke up in the hospital that Robin is no longer, but in this moment, he knows it in his heart. He blinks trying to keep the tears from coming, but they manage to escape, running down his cheeks and dropping into the dirt. He speaks aloud as though he were alone with Robin, "I just wanted to see you one last time."

Chapter 15
Rosaleen's Ship

I look at Rosaleen with disbelief, "You said he was likely going to die today from his wounds?" I reply breathlessly.

"There is no point in dragging his suffering out, it is an unnecessary strain to our resources and besides after an attack like this, to my guests, my inner circle; this is a betrayal to me, and I want no such person on my ship." Rosaleen asserts herself and asks me again. "How do you want him disposed of?" She demands. I can't bring myself to speak, let alone to answer and I just stay quiet. I can't help myself and feel shaken by the idea of being responsible for another's death. Rosaleen removes the ice pack from my forehead and gently touches where it has been, "I know that you are troubled with the thought of what I am asking you. Understand that his death isn't your fault, but his own. If he were loyal and had any respect for me, or the people aboard this ship, this would not have happened."

I nod, but my hands are shaking with fear as to what I am about to say. "Okay, he will be disposed of quickly to reduce the suffering." I pause, to gather my nerves, my voice, quivering, "His throat will be slit as he had threatened to do to me, and he will be thrown overboard as soon as we know that he is dead, so that he doesn't wake when he is eaten by the creatures of the ocean." I close my eyes to contain the horror of my own words. I sense that any more signs of weakness-like tears in this moment will not look good, so I hold them in. Slowly, I open my eyes to the sight of Rosaleen looking relieved by my answer.

Rosaleen says, "I know this is hard for you, you are very strong and very fair to give a quick death." She places the ice pack back on my head. "You need to eat." She glances to Izavelle who is standing behind her with my tray of food in her hands, "See to it that she eats a full three servings, she needs to gain her strength quickly, we need her strong for the day to come. I won't allow this mishap to delay our plans." Izavelle nods and the two of them switch places. Izavelle lays the tray on the bed and begins to feed me. Rosaleen continues, "Soolena keep watch over the betrayer tonight, and Ashlea will rest with me for the remainder of the night. In the morning Taylan will carry out her sentence before breakfast." After she gives the orders she turns and leads Ashlea out of the room, and I assume that they must be taking Izavelle's room for the rest of the night because Izavelle and I are still in Rosaleen's. Soolena follows them out, and I am left with Izavelle. She feeds me and encourages me to drink. I slowly finish all the meals.

"I feel sick." I quietly moan to Izavelle.

"Yes, I know, but trust me you will feel your strength come back to you." She removes the tray from the bed. "You need your rest; close your eyes and I will stay with you for the rest of the night." Izavelle lifts the sheets on the opposite side of the bed and gently crawls in beside me. She leans over to the nightstand and turns off the light. I feel secure and protected as I close my eyes.

After a few hours of rest, Izavelle and I wake to the morning sun. Izavelle checks my temperature and gently opens the bandage to see that the stitches are good.

"Come let's get you dressed." Izavelle says.

I ask, "Are we not bathing this morning?"

Izavelle explains, "Taylan you have forgotten. Your attacker needs to be dealt with before anything else. You sentenced him last night and you need to be the one to carry out the sentence."

The color that I worked so hard at getting back has gone from my face.

"Is this your first kill?" Izavelle asks.

"Well yes, I mean no, I have killed animals for food, but never people, isn't this against all morals? We don't kill people where I am from."

Izavelle sits beside me on the bed. "You are no longer just any commoner; you belong to Rosaleen, and you need to trust her and respect her words and wisdom. She is a princess, and her conclusions rule out any jury. Your sentence was fair and just." She pauses, gazing deep into the souls of my eyes, "This isn't a punishment for him, you have sentenced him to a quick death; if you don't act, it would be an injustice to let him suffer even though he has harmed you." She reaches for my hand and holds it in hers, "You need to carry this out and show your princess that you can stand behind your words and her command." Izavelle speaks with certainty. She genuinely believes that what is being done is fair and I suppose it is, considering the attacker won't recover. This still doesn't add up though. The attacker has been a member of her crew longer than Ashlea and me. Without any questions, they accepted Ashlea's and my account as truth. Yes, I sustained an injury, but it is just, I don't know. I thought they would take more time in deciding guilt and the fate of a life. Okay I can do this.

I answer Izavelle's words of encouragement. "Yes, I can and will carry out the sentence." I hold my gaze back at Izavelle to show that I am not taking any of this lightly.

There is no wavering in my voice, fear yes, concern yes and sorrow yes.

Izavelle smiles encouragingly, "You can do this, and it will be quick. Come let's meet everyone outside." She helps me dress in loose fitted white linen pants and a shirt. She dresses the same, and we go to the deck.

Ashlea and Rosaleen are already standing before a crowd, all the servants on the ship have gathered and are all greeting Izavelle and I as we come out into the fresh salty air. The crowd parts as we walk over to Ashlea and Rosaleen. As we approach the front of the crowd, I can see that Soolena has my attacker bound and sitting in a chair, he is unresponsive and still unconscious; tying him up wasn't necessary. Rosaleen looks at me and gives me a nod and pat of encouragement, and she begins to speak to the crowd.

She deepens and projects her voice for the crowd, "You have all been pulled away from your duties this morning because you need to be advised that a terrible act has been committed last night." Rosaleen pauses and looks out at all the faces in the crowed, her crew. She speaks with such authority and presence. "One of our crew on this ship, my crew and our family has committed a foul and vial act to one of our newest members to our family. This girl:" Rosaleen places her hand gently onto my shoulder as she says it, still looking out on the crowd, "This girl, has been attacked by this poor excuse for a person." She motions and looks over to my attacker with such anger in her expression and in her most powerful voice continues, "In the middle of the night he crept into Taylan's room and attacked her while she was asleep. He held a knife to her throat and put her life in danger. Taylan has been under my close supervision since she has arrived on this ship, and there was no reason for the attack. She did nothing to him." She pauses, looking over to Ashlea, "If it wasn't for Ashlea," Rosaleen gazes at Ashlea with gratitude, "Taylan would not likely be standing here this morning. Ashlea ambushed him and injured him with a single blow to the back of the head to stop the attack and rescue her sister." Rosaleen pauses for a breath while everyone applauds for the heroism that Ashlea displayed in coming to my rescue. "My dear Izavelle mended Taylan's wounds and kept her safe by her side for the rest of the night, and now we are before you all to put an end to this man's life. As voiced by Taylan and approved by me, I sentence this man to death." She looks out to the crowd to see if there are any objections, there is none. The crowd has a look of shock, anger, and somberness to them. "Taylan has sentenced her attacker a very fair and quick death, and she will carry out the sentence." Rosaleen motions me with her eyes to accept the blade that she is holding out. I take the sharp shiny knife in my hands and lightly touch the point; instantly it draws blood.

Soolena whispers to me, "Hold the knife firm, I will hold his head up for you. Put the point in as deep as you can push, just under the side of his jaw, you are going to, with a firm grasp of the handle, carve the knife down and forward to sever his major vein lengthwise. This is going to get messy, but remember deep, firm, and quick, but not too fast and steady will give him a quick death." She holds up his head and tilts it so that I can see his vein, his pulse. My hands are shacking. This feels wrong to do this to a man who is already near death. Rosaleen is clever to have me do it because if there is any retaliation for what is about to be done, it will be on me. Soolena looks back at me and nods to tell me in unspoken words to do it now. I step forward towards him and take a deep shivering breath; I refuse to look at the faces of the crowd in fear that my already shaken nerves will overtake and prevent me from carrying out the sentence. I push the blade's point a couple of inches in, and a light spray of blood ejects between the cut skin and the blade. I know I must do this quick so that there is no suffering. Despite what he has done to me, he doesn't need to suffer. I close my eyes and quickly glide the blade, opening his neck and his vein. The blood sprays onto my linen clothes and pours out in a pulsing flow onto the deck of the ship. Izavelle is still holding him steady, even if she lets him go, he won't run he was as good as dead before I drove the blade into him. I don't take my eyes off him, I don't shed a tear, and I just watch, his face relaxes, his mouth opens slightly, and I can see the tip of his limp tongue. His eyelids are slightly open; there is no movement, or life in them. I watch as the flow of blood slows to a throbbing stream. Respectful of his body, I put my hand to his chest to feel a heartbeat, nothing. I take his wrist to feel for a pulse, nothing. I wait for a twitch, any sign of life, nothing. He is gone. Izavelle gently lets his body droop to the floor. She is also covered in his blood. I face the crowd. I can't believe I had the capacity to do this. To kill, I am not a killer. I look at the crowd and can see what I think is sympathy on their faces, but not for the dead man, for me. It was his fault, and it had to be done. I stand there still and silent facing them holding the knife down at my side. Rosaleen steps towards me, and without looking up at her, I hand the bloody blade back.

Rosaleen addresses the crowd, "We can't afford to turn on each other and attack one another. We are family. We need to respect each other and protect one another." She pauses, capturing the eyes of many, "We need to feel safe on this ship. I hope that this is the last act of violence amongst our family, and if any other who wishes to attack another one of my crew, I promise that they will suffer a more agonizing death than the one you witnessed here." She gazes into the many eyes of the crowd, reading them and making sure that they are with her.

Rosaleen directs her attention on me, "Taylan you will clean this deck and rid it of this mess." She says it like a punishment. Rosaleen's eyes still peering into mine, she addresses Soolena and my sister; "Soolena and Ashlea will help you dispose of the remains overboard. Make sure to weight it down, we are not a far distance from the shore." She turns quickly, angered by all of this, and walks through the crowd hastily. If I were to guess, she went to her room to wash up in privacy and reflect. Izavelle is left without orders and without any instruction. She decides to converse with the crew of the ship and explain in more detail with smaller groups of them the details of the actions that had taken place last night. I watch Izavelle converse. They seem confused and surprised at first but after a few minutes, Izavelle seems to accomplish an understanding. I start to wonder about what Izavelle said to me, that things are not always what they seem and hinted at the fact that she may not be loyal to the Princess, but now she is on Rosaleen's side in easing the stress of the crew.

I approach the slumped over body and touch his side. He is already cooling off. My hands are still shaking. He looks like he could glance up at any moment. I slowly fall to my knees before him. His short hair is a dull black and his narrow face almost looks rat like now that he is gone. He doesn't even look like he is at peace. I do not know him, other than the fact that he would bring out trays of food to us. I never spoke to him, other than a quick nod of my chin to thank him for the food. Do I hate him? No, it seems like the attack happened a long time ago and is something of the past especially after having all of this happen. His body is blood soaked. My clothes are covered in his blood. Puddles of blood are pooling all around me as the wounds from his corpse continues to ooze.

A woman comes up from behind me, I know she is older just from the feeling I get in her presence, "Dear let's get you up on your feet." She gently places her hands under my arms, and I rise to my feet at the gentle feeling of her touch. I can sense that she is a much older and much wiser, I would guess much older than even my mother. The rasp to her voice and the maternal instinct in her demeanor, which comes with time. My guess is she has raised many children, or she was a guardian.

She encourages with a smile, "You don't have to explain yourself, and I know and can see what you have been through. You have never done anything like this before, have you?" Her eyes are a beautiful blue a bright topaz. They peer right into my soul and make me feel vulnerable. I shake my head no and a tear trickles down my face. She takes her finger, touching my skin and stops the tear from running down to my chin, "Hun I know, but you must understand that this is a part of life, and there are things that you must do that are for the greater good. Keep that in your heart." She rubs my back and helps me out. She motions to the doors leading into the ship, "There are some cleaning supplies just over there; I will help you take care of all of this."

I answer, "You don't have to do this; I already have help." She doesn't hear me decline her offer; she is gone to get the mops and buckets. Soolena and Ashlea have already started getting supplies together to clean the mess and without me paying any attention to them, they have gone to retrieve a small anchor from one of the lifeboats. The anchor will be used as a weight for the corpse, and Ashlea has already retrieved some rope to secure the anchor to the body. Ashlea and Soolena dispose of the body. Soolena gently sits the corpse up by taking her arms and clasping them around the torso of the body under the man's armpits, and she quietly instructs Ashlea how to secure the anchor to him.

The woman returns with a couple of mops, rope, sponges, and an empty bucket and sets everything down. I instinctively take the bucket and the rope; tying the rope to the bucket handle and then tie the other end of the rope to the railing of the ship. I lower the bucket down over the side to get water and then pull the bucket back up. The woman is behind me by helping me, carry the weight of the water as I tug it back up the side of the ship. We both take a mop and dip it into the water. Then we start directing the pool of blood off the deck and over the ledge of the ship.

I glance through my red strands of hair, "Why are you helping me?" I ask in a defeated. I am so tired from all of this, both physically and emotionally.

She glances up at me as she continues to mop away the blood, "I can see that you needed the help and the company."

"I never got your name, I am Taylan." Despite my fatigue and sadness, I try to welcome her company as best as I can. I know deep down that I need her company, a stranger's company that is outside of the social circle of Rosaleen, Soolena, Izavelle and even Ashlea. Just for now, until I can wrap my head around everything.

She smiles, "I know who you are Taylan. Rosaleen introduced you to everyone."

"Right, I am sorry" and I shake my head at my own stupidity; of course, she knows who I am, especially after all of this.

"Don't be sorry, your right I never said my name, I am Zethel."

"Zethel, where are you from?"

"I come from a small remote area that is near to here. I believe that Rosaleen has plans to visit my homeland today." She says as she continues to mop.

"How did you come to work here on this ship, I mean you seem to be much older and to my understanding only the young are kept serving?" She smiles politely but drops her eyes to the floor and doesn't answer my question right away. I feel like I have overstepped an unspoken boundary, "I am sorry, I didn't mean to offend."

"No, it's alright," she assures, "I am not here because of a calling to serve, I came because I love Rosaleen."

I ponder her words for a moment, "Are you Rosaleen's Mother?"

Chapter 16
A Mop and Bucket

Zethel seems a bit amused, and I think flattered by my suspicion that she could be a direct member to Princess Rosaleen's family, "No love, but I am a dear friend to her family and helped watch over Rosaleen when she was a baby." I'm intrigued and want to understand. While Zethel explains, her mind is somewhere else, like she is re-living a moment in the past. She continues to mop away the blood, dipping it into the bucket and carefully soaking up the mess as though this is some sort of regular routine. "Taylan, I think it is time for a refill." Her blue eyes glance from me to the bucket.

Oh right, I'm distracted by my new companion. There is only a quarter of the water left in the bucket, but what is left is a deep dark red. I dispose of the soiled water over the side. The metallic smell as the dirty water leaves the bucket makes me queasy. I lower the bucket down the side of the ship by the rope and pull up more water. Zethel comes behind me and helps pull the bucket back up. I dip my mop into the water and continue with the cleanup. Glancing over my shoulder, I see Soolena and Ashlea. They are preparing the corpse for disposal. There is still a small crowd on deck, and the conversations seem to have died down when they notice that Soolena and Ashlea are ready to throw the body overboard.

Without acknowledging, the crowd Soolena instructs Ashlea, "Take his legs at the knee, hold him firmly, and on the count of three we are going to lift and rest him on the ledge, okay?"

Breathy, Ashlea responds, "Okay."

"One, two, three" with some grunts and force the two manage; the corpse is now balancing on the ledge of the railing with the two women supporting it.

Soolena and Ashlea are both lightly panting; Soolena instructs, "Okay Ash, carefully move your hands from under his knee, you are going to rest your hands on top of him, I am going to do the same so that our hands are free from him when we are ready to drop him." Ashlea does what she is told, and Soolena follows the same motion. The crowd has quieted, and everyone is watching.

Soolena and Ashlea are now balancing the remains of my attacker. Soolena continues giving Ashlea guidance, "We are going to push on the count of three so that we force him as far away from the ship as we can so that he doesn't hit the side on his descent. Put as much of your strength into it. Are you ready?" Ashlea nods.

"Okay, one; two; three…" Just Like That, my attacker is gone. I stop moping for a second and look over the side of the ship. I know that he is dead, but I just want to see, and make sure that he is not trying to swim or get out of the ropes. His body sinks and bubbles surround the point of entry into the water. The bubbles slowly fade away. Oddly, a light warm shower starts as if it were on queue. The remaining crowd disperses and Soolena and Ashlea seem relieved that their work is done.

Soolena and Ashlea walk over to me. Soolena wipes a bead of sweat from her head with the cuff of her sleeve and asks, "Do you want us to help you finish?"

"No thank you, go ahead, this shouldn't take much longer." If Soolena where a more emotional person I think that a warm embrace would have occurred just now. Instead, Soolena gives me a good long, meaningful look as if she is telling me with the souls of her eyes to be strong; she grasps my shoulder as she decides that it is best to take my suggestion and leave me to finish. Ashlea's hair is the first to change color, a reflection of the grey sky above, she is dripping wet as we all are, as the warm shower helps take away the blood from our skin. She retreats with Soolena into the ship. It is now only Zethel, and I left on deck.

"You don't have to stay with me, I got this." I say to convince Zethel politely that I can manage on my own.

"I want to help." She assures me.

We start using sponges and gently scrub the floor where the blood had started to get tacky. The two of us continue cleaning up in silence. The rain has done a thorough job rinsing away the last remains of the blood.

Zethel calmly rises from her knees to her feet and squeezes out her sponge over the side of the ship. I don't have to look, but I do anyways, that metallic smell of the blood is stronger when an effort is made to rinse and wring out the mops and sponges. Zethel in a calm casual tone says, "I see what Rosaleen sees in you and your sister." She smiles, puts her sponge down. We are finished. She walks into the ship without giving me a chance to question her. What is that supposed to mean, is Zethel hinting at something specific, or is she just trying to be polite?

I spot a bit of mess that is left on the railing, wipe it clean, and do one last check for missed spots. All I see is a clean ship floor and clean railing. If someone were to set eyes on this deck, they would have never thought of the possibility of the brutality that took place just a brief time before. I squeeze my sponge out, place it next to Zethel's and dump the remaining water from the bucket. I untie the rope from the bucket and the railing and neatly twist it back up and place the sponges in the bucket along with the rope and put it all away. Just when I have put everything away the rain stops, and the sunshine pierces the clouds. It already feels like I have lived through an entire day. However, it is still morning; this day is going to be long. Instead of taking a moment to enjoy the warmth of the sun peeking through the clouds, I go inside to wash up for breakfast.

It is not long after I have washed and dressed that I meet Rosaleen, Izavelle, Soolena and my sister in the dining room. Everyone is washed up and wearing light flowing dresses, their hair all done up as is mine. I have tied my hair back into a simple bun. My bandage in clear sight, but I don't care, it is not like it is a secret.

Rosaleen looks to be in better spirits from when I last saw her. "Taylan, you are looking much better, come and sit." Rosaleen no longer seems angered or phased by everything that had happened. She is sitting at the end of the table, and to her right is an empty chair, which I take. My plate is full. It is double the amount I would take. There is fresh fruit, meats, and bread.

Izavelle is sitting to my right, "Taylan, I put some medication in your juice, it is going to taste a little off, but I need you to finish it." I nod, understanding. I know the serving on my plate is large; they are trying to help me regain my strength.

Rosaleen starts, "Soolena tells me that you have met an old friend of mine?"

I look up at her, "Yes, Zethel."

"What do you think of her?" Rosaleen asks.

I fidget with the food on my plate while saying, "She is a really kind person and tells me that she wasn't called upon to serve, but instead came on her own account?"

Rosaleen nods, "Yes I met her recently, after being separated from her for many years; we reunited about a few months ago just on the mainland that we are going to be visiting after breakfast."

"She said that she cared for you when you were very young." I volunteer the information in hopes that Rosaleen will elaborate.

Rosaleen smiles: taking the bait, "Yes, she was my mother's personal maid. As I understand she would keep my mother company and care for me in my mother's absence."

"She says that she loves you." I murmur and then quickly take a sip of my weird tasting, medicine-filled juice.

"She is a sweet woman." Rosaleen confides and changes the subject.

"After breakfast we are going to have a bit of an adventurous day." She pauses as she glances at the reactions of all of us. "I will make sure that we will keep everyone's levels of strength in mind as we go about the day." Everyone at the table seems to be satisfied with the thought of getting off this ship even though the evident sign of fatigue is on everyone's faces.

Izavelle concerns herself with me, "How does your throat feel?"

I chew the food that is in my mouth and reflect for a second on all the points of my body before I answer, "It doesn't hurt, it feels a little hot, and it also feels like the skin is a little tight, but there isn't any pain."

Izavelle nods, "Okay that is good, the heat and the tightness mean that it is swelling a bit, the medication in your juice will help bring the swelling down."

I go to touch my bandage but notice that my pearl pendent is missing. I glance around and then across the table to Ashlea and calm my nerves; Ashlea is holding onto it for me, it is placed around her neck. Over the past two days, I have watched Ash turn into someone who is still fun and loving, but showing a new side of her, that of bravery, and someone who I know will always be there for me. She saved my life last night, and she took on the strength this morning of helping rid of my attacker. I am starting to see why Rosaleen has placed her with Soolena for instruction. This is only the second day on this ship with my mother and Saydira gone, and in the last couple of days, I have observed so much. I gather that Soolena is that of a solder, a protector, and my sister is opening her eyes to that world and really shining through as being someone who is brave, and then there is me being placed with Izavelle. I am not sure what the intention is quite yet. Izavelle is obviously a healer, but her comments that she advised me of the day before, with telling me that not everything is as you see, leads me to wonder. Is this what Rosaleen wants me to become? Another Izavelle?

Ashlea who is clearly starting to become more confident and surer of herself. I don't mean to say she was ever timid or a shy person because she never was. This place is transforming her into a more serious person and giving her direction.

Ash has always had spunk and whether we see the silly or serious side to her, both those sides, she doesn't hold back and thankfully she goes for it and asks the obvious question that has been on my mind all morning, "Why was Taylan attacked?"

Chapter 17
A Trip to the Island

Izavelle answers before Rosaleen opens her mouth, "Ashlea, just as I told Taylan yesterday morning, you must know that in our world, this ship, these towns that we visit, the Palace; nothing is always what it seems. We will talk later, but here is not the time." Izavelle, daring her not to urge for an answer stares at Ashlea.

Ashlea clearly understanding murmurs, "Okay Izavelle, later." Her voice, a pitch higher than usual and her posture, slumped down like she has shrunk. She has the passion and desire to know why, and it is more important than anything else to her in this moment. Izavelle nods as a confirmation that she will follow through and tell her later.

Soolena goes back to today's planned trip to the mainland she turns to Rosaleen, "I was thinking that I could take Ashlea for a flight to the mainland, Izavelle you can also come along with us, I wanted to show Ashlea the landscape and teach her some tricks." Soolena looks to me, "The plan I had was to also bring you on the flight, but with your injury I don't want to risk you re-opening your wound. Instead, I was thinking that Rosaleen can bring you by boat this morning to the mainland, and you can see the sights on foot."

I answer, "Yes that is fine with me." I rather curl up in a bed by myself for the rest of the day, but I know that I have no say in the matter, and these people don't seem to let an attack, or an execution get in the way of their plans. I look at Rosaleen who seems satisfied with the suggestion.

Izavelle says, "I think I will stay on board the ship today."

"Are you sure Izavelle?" Rosaleen says, "It is okay, I know that you love this area."

Izavelle shakes her head and refuses, "No, no it's fine, I will stay back and keep an eye on things and help where I can."

"Okay" Rosaleen doesn't push it, and I sense that she is a little relieved that Izavelle decided to remain.

"Well, I am full," Rosaleen says satisfied as she rubs her belly. I was able to manage three quarters of my overloaded plate; I really was starved.

Ashlea shows a glimpse of her light heartedness to this conversation and smiles, "Looks like you were hungry after all Taylan!" She blows her cheeks up with air, gesturing to me.

I smile a little embarrassed, "Yes I guess I was."

Izavelle touches my shoulder, "It is normal to feel hungrier; you are regaining your strength from the attack. Just remember if you are hungry you eat, and if you are tired then say so, so that Rosaleen knows to let you rest, okay?"

"Yes" I confirm. I wonder if I can get away with saying that I am tired right now. I had better not push it.

Rosaleen encourages, "Let's go now." We all leave the table, Soolena and Ashlea go upstairs to equip themselves with the flying suits, and Rosaleen and I go out to the side deck where the smaller boats are stored. Izavelle stays back, gathers our dishes, and disappears into the kitchen, since the servant who normally did this was the one, I killed earlier.

A man whom I have only seen a handful of times in passing since I have been on the ship greets us in a friendly deep voice. "Good morning princess and good morning, Taylan." He welcomes us with a smile and seeming unbothered by the events that happened earlier. I am guessing that he knows my name from the gruesome events that took place earlier.

"Good morning" Rosaleen answers confidently, but still politely.

I smile and say, "Good morning, Sir."

"I am guessing that you two are ready to make your trip to the mainland now?" He directs his question to Rosaleen.

"Yes" Rosaleen answers with a smile.

"Okay great the boat is already equipped, and I am just going to lower it now." He advises.

Rosaleen and I stand back and watch as the boat is lowered into the water. Rosaleen glances at me and suddenly seems startled by something. The immediate thought that comes to mind is if I have a bug on me, or something.

Rosaleen says, "Oh that is not good, I can't have you looking like this." She leaves and goes back into the ship. What, do I have blood on me? I look at my clothing and my skin, from what I see I am clean. I feel clean. The man has taken no notice to Rosaleen quickly leaving because he is still concentrating on lowering the boat. Rosaleen quickly comes back with a long dark red scarf. The material is light and thin. The ends float behind her as she quickly walks down the deck towards me.

"Face me." She barks.

"Chin up." She orders. I do what she asks, and she gently ties the scarf around my throat.

Rosaleen quietly confides to me, "I don't want strangers knowing that you were hurt. If people see, they will usually ask, and we have no time to wrap our heads around making

117

up some fabrication to cover up your attack. An injury stands out and I prefer we conceal it." She gently secures the scarf in place with a fancy knot. "There that is much better." Rosaleen seems happy with her own handy work.

Naturally, my fingers touch the scarf, and I reply, "I don't mind the scarf, but what is wrong with being truthful?"

"I don't want to startle anyone with what happened, and once things become known then it tends to branch out into exaggerations and then choosing sides and more problems. Keeping it hidden is better and easier for everyone."

The man calls up from the boat; having already gone down the ladder to do a quick check of the boat and is now climbing back up, "It is ready now." The boat's solar panels shine, and the propellers idle in the water. He takes a step back up onto the deck. As he steps off the ladder and in a synchronized motion Rosaleen steps onto the ladder like the maneuver between the two of them was choreographed and descends first; I follow slowly and awkwardly stepping onto the ladder and descend to meet her on the small boat.

Rosaleen un-hooks the ropes that lowered the boat and hollers back up to the man, "You can bring up the ropes." She takes the boat out of idle, and we are now on course to the shore. The sun is out with a few fluffy white clouds in the sky. The rays of light warm my skin. It feels so nice and soothing, mentally, and physically as we travel through the water. I sit back on the cushioned seat and relax. Rosaleen sets a good speed not too fast and not to slow just a steady movement. It is late in the morning and the water is no longer still. The wind creates a few small waves that cause the boat to bounce and splash the odd time as we make our way to the shallow waters. The warm breeze feels nice, and

I start to smell the aroma of spices in the air as we make our way to the shore.

Rosaleen slows the speed of the boat to a putter as we approach and then turns it off. We glide forward and ride the waves, as they are a little stronger now that we are in the shallows. Rosaleen takes a rope and hops out. The water is up to her knees as she walks up onto the shore and securely ties the rope around a tree. She runs back to help me out.

"Come Taylan." Rosaleen is back in the water knee deep, extending her arms up to me, and I grab onto her to correct my balance, stepping to the ledge and then step down into the water. It is a sandy bottom with the odd tree leaf under the water.

"There we go." Rosaleen says encouragingly, "What do you think of this place?" She asks clearly wanting me to be impressed by the surroundings. She has a special place in her heart for this place. Seeing this side of Rosaleen reminds me of being in the company of my own sisters.

"It is beautiful and the smell in the air is so wonderful." I look around; it is a narrow beech. You can tell that this part of the beech is not frequented because there are no signs of buildings, or walkways and the trees have grown close to the water.

Rosaleen catches me looking at the forest that has grown so close to the shore, "They are cinnamon trees, and they grow all around here. I am sure you will get to taste it. The locals use cinnamon in a lot of their cooking." I glance at the trees that surround the shore to make a mental note.

"Rosaleen, can we talk before we do anything else? I would just feel better in knowing what your thoughts are on everything that has happened." I feel a bit dizzy and need a few minutes to recuperate; she senses it too.

Rosaleen says, "Come let's sit over there." I fight the fatigue, and we walk not too far from the boat and sit on the warm light brown sand, facing the ocean.

She asks still looking out on the water, "Where would you like to start?" Her question is not needed, she knows what I intend to know. I ignore the stupidity of her question and just cut to the chase.

"Well let's start with the man who attacked me. Why do you think it happened?" I pause to watch her reaction, which is blank, emotionless, I cannot read her, and then I follow her gaze out on the water.

I can hear her swallow, "I didn't think you would be attacked."

"Well why do you think then?" I raise my voice; flustered by her vagueness and urge her. She has not revealed anything to me.

"There is more in play. Izavelle has advised you of this right?" She glances at me as she asks.

"Yes, Izavelle warned me to trust my instinct and understand that nothing is always what it seems." Izavelle never really explained what exactly was in play.

"Okay well, that man, his name was Shrago. He has been a member of my crew for the past year when I set course at King Wolfrim's approval. I took this ship to see my Kingdom and explore the world. I wanted to do this before my obligations of my palace role and the desire that everyone seems to have for me to marry would commence. Shrago was one of the men that Wolfrim personally approved to go with me, to serve and protect me. Until recently, I realized what the true reason was. He intended for Shrago to keep watch over me and to report anything that Shrago thought the king should be made aware of." Rosaleen squints like she is visualizing them before her, but the only thing that is really in front of her is the rolling waves of the ocean.

Rosaleen continues, "About few months ago we were here at this exact island. It was my first time visiting this area. Shaylo, who was his wife, Izavelle, Soolena and I came to the shore. We continued to the nearby town, exploring the shops, and taking in the sites. To my surprise, the people in the town recognized me as someone else, a person by the name of Newlyn. Newlyn is a familiar name to me. It connects to my past. I didn't correct these strangers and instead listened to their light conversations that they were having with me. Izavelle and Soolena were engaged in these conversations of this so-called Newlyn and genuinely curious while Shaylo kept silent. In retrospect, I understand why, but at the time, I just assumed that she wanted to return to the ship. Izavelle and Soolena were able to piece together where we could find this Newlyn. I was curious to see the person that I resembled. We ended up traveling to a secluded estate that wasn't far from the town. We entered the open ten-foot double iron gates of Newlyn's property and reluctantly Shaylo followed. Shaylo's argument at first was that we should stick to our day's plan and not disturb this stranger; however, I ignored Shaylo's suggestion. My curiosity was immense, and to my luck, Newlyn was there. We met and it was like peering into a mirror.

When I was young, I was told that my mom, Newlyn had left the Palace and years later, she had died. I never attended a funeral, but as a young child, I accepted what I had been told as truth. It turns out, that this woman was my mother. When we came face to face, she immediately recognized me and pulled me into her arms, holding me and hugging me as she cried. She thought that I had been killed because I have been kept away from the public, and she was surprised and in shock that I was standing before her. Izavelle, Soolena, Shaylo and I spent the entire afternoon at her home. Newlyn explained what had happened to her and my father, the real King Wolfrim and making a point to watch Shaylo. Newlyn's eyes burning with anger at Shaylo as if daring her to argue the truth or make a move.

Shaylo is a proud person and in hindsight, I can see why she didn't try to avoid Newlyn's home to avoid detection. Sometimes the smartest people make the most stupid decisions. Shaylo could have made up any excuse to leave and go back to the ship, but she didn't. I think it was part curiosity because, from what I understand even Shaylo didn't truly know the exact location of my mother's whereabouts, and the second is I think that she truly thought that justice would not come to her, and that she could somehow talk, or fight her way out of any confrontation.

Before my mother explained her story, this is how I understood my past. The King Wolfrim that is currently in power, the Imposter. I didn't always know him to be the Imposter that my mother calls him, but I did always know that he wasn't my real father. To the outside world, people didn't know any different, and I always acted like he was my family. In my reality, he was a dear friend to my family, and it was explained to me that when I was young my real father asked the Imposter to take over and rule for him. My father didn't want any part in me or my mother and abandoned his obligations and his family. As a young child, I felt lost but never questioned it. The Imposter King Wolfrim took advantage of my vulnerability, and in a way used it to draw me in. Needing someone to love me, I quickly learned to love him as my new father. The Imposter also explained that my mother was heartbroken by my real father's departure and never returned to the Kingdom, leaving me in the care of the imposter, King Wolfrim. The Imposter had explained to me that my mother wanted me to continue to live the life of a Princess, I believed this; that my father and mother left me, years later I was told that my mother had died, and my father was never heard from. Newlyn, in a single afternoon turned everything upside down and explained everything about my Family's past."

Rosaleen explained to me that her real father always had a couple of people around. They were his protection and his help that assisted in his duties. These people were his look-a-likes whose responsibilities were to represent the real King Wolfrim at public functions because her real father enjoyed and preferred that his time be spent outside of the public eye. His time was high in demand, and these substitutes were used to stand in for him. After years of representing the real King Wolfrim, the substitutes wanted to retire after their initial agreement had ended with the King. When the substitutes voiced this to Rosaleen's father, he refused their request and refused to pay them more to coax them into staying. He ordered them to continue to serve. These substitutes did not like the idea of being kept and instead, plotted and managed a short-lived success in escaping the Kingdom. They were captured soon after and imprisoned for treason. One of the substitutes was clever enough to bribe and make a promise to a palace guard to set in motion his escape on a night when Rosaleen's Mother, Newlyn, was not with Rosaleen's real Father and a simple switch was made. The real king was imprisoned in the clever substitute's place and soon after put to death by his own treason ruling. The imposture that Rosaleen had always thought of as a second father and a friend ordered his allies to take her mother away. Newlyn was given a small group of servants to live in a secluded area of the world. She was stripped of all her titles. The Imposter King Wolfrim, who is now in power, ordered her to never think of returning, or revealing the truth, or else her daughter Rosaleen would be murdered. Newlyn had feared, despite the threat on her daughter's life that the imposter King Wolfrim had murdered Rosaleen regardless of his warning because in her heart she could not see why or how such a killer and traitor would stand to raise a child whose father he had grown to despise.

I took a moment to absorb her story and could not help, but say, "That is insane, so you are the only true heir to the throne and this imposter killed your father and banished your mom, and you just happened to find your mother after all of this time, and by accident?" Rosaleen nods to confirm.

Scratching my head, I say, "I don't mean to come off as insensitive, but I am starting to understand what Izavelle means." I sigh in disbelief to this twisted tale. Rosaleen simply draws in the sand. She knows that I am still taking it all in and gives me the time to let this all-sink in.

Rosaleen murmurs, "Taylan the only people who know that I know the truth were the people that were there that day with me." I don't know why but I focus on Rosaleen's pearl pendant necklace that my mother made for her, and she is rolling one of the three pearls on her chain in between her index finger and thumb. It distracts me, all this talk about her family and those pearls they are reminding me of my own family. She says, "You are so innocent and removed from everything. My heart is telling me to trust you, and you do need to know this to understand the big picture. Never speak of this to anyone." She pauses as if reading my thoughts and continues, "Ashlea will be informed as well, and I instructed Soolena to tell her."

"I understand." I look at her while touching her hand to acknowledge. "Rosaleen, so where does Shaylo and Shrago fit into all of this?"

"Shaylo and Shrago were not my true servants they were eyes for the Imposter, King Wolfrim. Shaylo was with us and knew that Newlyn was my mother, but I didn't know this until my mother pulled me aside and spoke to me alone. I think that Shaylo didn't try to make a run for it because she also may have been hoping for some sort of truce with being a part of the reuniting of a mother and daughter. I am not sure what goes on in Shaylo's twisted head. She didn't run, or really, fight, she did fight with words. It was because she knew she was outnumbered. Who knows? Anyways, Newlyn explained that Shaylo was at the Imposter, King Wolfrim's side along with her husband Shrago the night that my mother was banished from the Imposter King Wolfrim Palace. Shaylo showed no loyalty to my mother, or for the people that were banished with her. Shaylo and Shrago were a part of the imposter's inner circle; Newlyn realized this the night she was sent away. She asked Shaylo to allow for her servant, Zethel, to continue to stay and look after me, just to have someone she trusted to care for me. Shaylo laughed in her face saying that she would never suggest it or give her any hope that her daughter would be cared for or could even survive through the Imposter King Wolfrim's reign. Shaylo made the final order to send my mother away and just like that, it was done." Rosaleen takes a breath, draws more lines in the sand with her toe, and continues.

"My mother suggested leaving Shaylo with her because if it ever got back to her husband Shrago that I discovered my mother, it would certainly get back to the imposter, which would change everything for me. I agreed to it. Zethel offered herself to take Shaylo's place as part of my crew."

"Rosaleen, what about Shrago he must have known something was up when you all returned without his wife and with Zethel instead?"

Rosaleen admits, "Shrago knew that something had happened. He asked me, and I simply advised that I believed there may be hostility in the area towards my father's Kingdom and ordered Shaylo to stay back and observe. I told him that we would move along our course so that our ship wouldn't attract the attention of the locals and then loop around back over the next few months and retrieve her."

"Did Shrago accept this?" I ask.

"Yes, he had no choice; I am the one in charge. He asked if he could join her to help on the Island, and I reminded him that King Wolfrim ordered him to remain by my side. Shrago was conflicted and knowing that if he were to leave me, his life would become more difficult by disobeying the king than letting his love slip away from him. He accepted and I assured him that it would only be for a brief time, and we would eventually go back for her."

"What about Zethel, he must have recognized her when she came onto the ship?" I ask.

"He wasn't there to meet us when we returned that evening. Zethel has never appeared to be a part of the group that included me, Izavelle and Soolena. Izavelle immediately took Zethel to her new living quarters and discreetly trained her as a house cleaner to clean the living quarters of the ship. No one really pays attention to the cleaners.

Izavelle trained her and handed her off to the younger staff that had no idea who she was other than the fact that she was a new face having been recently recruited from the Island. The pleasant thing about the younger generations on board my ship is they have no knowledge to any of what I have shared with you. They are as clueless as the public."

I ruminate all the information in silence and draw a conclusion, "So Shrago attacked me because he despised what you put him through, with leaving Shaylo behind and alone?"

She cannot bring her eyes to mine, but instead wraps here arms around her knees and sets her gaze somewhere in the sand, her hair is slowly changing to a shiny tan color. She replies, "Yes, I think that he saw how I have warmed to you and Ashlea, perhaps he worried that the bond that I once had with his wife was fading away and maybe that made him question whether I would really go back for Shaylo? I think that the arrival of you and Ashlea made him worry, and I think that seeing the two new assistants made him that much more paranoid or stressed for his wife not returning to her role by my side. I guess that he wanted to get back at me for sending his wife off, so he attacked you."

The waves are rolling up onto the sand, the light rhythmic swishing sound, such a beautiful relaxing place and oddly enough, I am trying to figure out why the worst experience of my life happened.

Rosaleen finally speaks, and with a shrug of her shoulders as though she is playing down everything that has happened to me in the last twenty-four hours, "You know Taylan, Shrago is better off dead. I couldn't just kill him even after knowing what my mother shared. It would have not reflected well for the rest who live and work on my ship. Your attack in a way, it was a good thing because it gave the ideal reason to get rid of him; he was a danger, not only for attacking you, but he was also aligned with the Imposter."

I shake my head in disbelief to her, "Do you expect me to buy that?" I accuse, "You knew deep down that this would probably happen, and you did nothing to prevent it?" I get up in a rush and walk down the beach away from Rosaleen. Just what I thought... Rosaleen was hoping that Shrago would screw up with the arrival of Ashlea and me. We were bait. Rosaleen catches up to me and jumps in front, drawing me to a halt. She extends both of her arms to catch my shoulders and holds me firmly within her grasp.

"STOP" she roars, "I am your Princess, your Master."

Chapter 18
In One Swift Motion

"Fine, I'm listening." Staring at her with rage, when she looks back into my eyes, I can't help but roll my eyes. In one swift motion, she slaps me hard across the face. It stings. I quickly realize that this woman is not like my sisters who I argue with sometimes. She is my Princess.

Rosaleen continues, "I admit, I knew that Shrago was mad at me for the orders that I gave them, but I swear to you I never thought that he would get back at me by attacking others in my command."

My cheek is warm from where her hand connected. Despite her reaction, I say what is on my mind and murmur to her, "Well it happened...I could have died if Ashlea wasn't there to protect me."

Rosaleen's expression relaxes and she regards me while still holding me in her grasp. I do not dare try to break free, but stay still and she admits as though defeated, "Yes Taylan you don't know how sorry I am and how angry at myself for not even thinking that this could have been a possibility." She pauses, collecting her thoughts, "Tell me if there is anything that I can do to make this right?"

Without hesitation I demand, "No secrets, I have no reason to turn on you, besides, you gave me my vengeance, we are even in respect to the harm that was inflicted on me under your watch." I have my doubts that Rosaleen has been truthful but all I can do is ask and hope that she gives me that much.

"Okay no secrets." I sense relief in her words, with sorry eyes she lets go of my shoulders. "Shall we continue down the beach? At the other end there is the town we can stop for lunch." Rosaleen suggests; I nod.

We come up the beach to a path that opens onto a cobblestone road. There are small colorful shops on both sides of the street; they all seem to specialize in certain things, jewelry, clothing, breads, meats, fruits and vegetables, and electronics. Shopkeepers and shoppers are active and engaged in their own activities, which seem to either be walking, riding bicycles or solar powered scooters. I spot a couple of travelers going about their business on horseback. This town reminds me of my home with the exception being that there is more of a variety of shops and the landscape has fewer trees. I can see off in the distance there are rolling fields of pale green and golden grass surrounded by mountains covered with trees in the distance. Back at home the setting is a little more closed off because where I am from, the town is surrounded by mature forest. The feeling that I get here is that this town is self-sufficient with its citizens equally contributing to its own success while at the same time it is also a relaxing place. I sense that the people who run their shops are happy in doing the professions of their choosing. I say this because each shop looks pristine. The people that are browsing from shop to shop seem happy. We walk down the street, and I notice people smiling and waving to others. Small groups of people conversing along the side of the road, and I hear snippets of conversations of things like, "How is your day going?" and, "How have you been?" Rosaleen even gets a few waves. She is being recognized as being her mother, Newlyn.

Rosaleen motions over with a nod to a sandwich shop that we are approaching, "Let's stop here and eat." There are a few round wooden tables and small chairs set out in front of the shop.

A woman with a petit build and dark tanned skin comes out to serve us; in a spirited voice she says, "Newlyn! It is so nice to see you today what brings you into town?"

Rosaleen does not correct her, smiling back she answers, "I am here to entertain a friend of mine." She glances at me.

I politely look up and smile at the woman, "I'm Taylan nice to meet you." I extend my hand, and we shake.

The woman smiles and says, "I am Kace." She sets down a couple of small menus for Rosaleen and me.

"I will give you two a few moments to decide; anything to drink?"

Rosaleen answers, "Yes could we have some Cinnamon Iced Tea?"

Kace nods, "Of course I will be right back." She disappears back into the shop.

Rosaleen says, "The cinnamon in the tea is so fresh, I would say that out of all the places I have been I have never tasted a fresher spice."

I smile politely, "Sounds wonderful, I can't wait. I don't think I have tried any of the sandwiches they have on this menu. What are you going to have?"

"I am having the cinnamon pork with sweet gravy and the braided brown buns."

"Okay I will have what you're having." I set the menu down.

Our server, Kace, returns with our beverages. "I see that you two have decided?"

Rosaleen takes the initiative and answers for both of us, "Yes two of these please." She points to the sandwiches on her menu.

"Good choice!" Kace politely takes the menus from Rosaleen and me, and she walks back into the shop.

Rosaleen begins the conversation, leaning back in her chair, "Don't you just love this town." She slowly leans forward resting her elbows on the table and in a lower voice so that only I can hear she whispers, "I don't think King Wolfrim ever envisioned this area that he banished my mother to would be such a beautiful haven." She winks and I sense that she is relieved in knowing that her mom was safe the entire time.

I ask, "Are we going to see her today?"

"Yes" Rosaleen smiles, "I have to introduce you and Ashlea to Newlyn, and I need to also get down to the more serious business by informing her on what has happened since we last met and seek her advice on how to proceed."

I sip my drink and gently set the sweaty glass down before answering, "That sounds like a good idea." I take a bite of the sandwich that Kace has quietly placed before me, oh; it is so good and has a nice kick to it with a light cinnamon taste. The spice is not overwhelming, but I understand what Rosaleen was saying earlier, and I can agree that this is the freshest spice I have ever tasted.

"Rosaleen I can't help, but ask please be honest, why did you take my sister and I from our home?"

I gaze on her as I wait for her response. I can tell that she was expecting my question, "You understand Taylan it's not wise to question your master in the way that you are. I have been honest with you and explained what I knew about the actions that lead to the attack and my thoughts on why it happened. For your own protection, some things need to be left unsaid for the time being."

"Princess I am sorry if I offended you, it's just that I don't understand you just promised me no secrets what is this?"

She takes a sip of her drink then sets her glass down and lowers her voice, "Taylan all these secrets will eventually be revealed as you gain strength and progress in your training. When you are ready, and I require you to do something for me, you will be told then what you are doing and why." She pauses as if calculating her words and then says, "You know Taylan I am truly sorry for what has happened to you under my watch, but you have to realize that when I ask of something, you know that my request will stand in the end."

"Princess can I at least have a say in the matter?"

Rosaleen says, "Of course, but understand my say will always be final."

There is more to Princess Rosaleen than I could ever imagine in any person. She clearly has a plan; she makes decisions based on her gut instinct, like being able to trust people and bring them into her inner circle. My feeling is that she trusts Ashlea and me, and bit by bit, she is slowly revealing herself to us. Rosaleen is passionate to those she loves and punishes those who betray her, and she carries the punishments out swiftly. She allows others to be a part of her world, but also knows her place in the world and commands respect.

I could never comment, or question Rosaleen on this, but her father, the real King Wolfrim who was murdered when Rosaleen was too young to remember; according to her explanation of the truth, her real father was a tyrant. He refused to let his substitutes go at the end of their contracts and then refused to agree to any negotiations that were proposed. The real King Wolfrim forced them to stay against their wishes. In the end, his lack of fairness led to his own death, followed by the separation of his wife and daughter.

Given the choice, I would like to go home because from the insight that I have gained into Rosaleen's world and the people in it, it is a dangerous mess. Everything that I thought of the Palace and its people that rule is wrong. To the outside world, the citizens and the armies that protect have clouded perceptions of what really goes on in the Palace. I had always thought that they were profoundly good, honorable people who strive to care and serve their people, but really, it is all a web of lies. Sure, you can give the leaders the fact that they ensure that their cities are run, and its people protected, but behind palace doors in the innermost circles it is a nightmare of power-hungry people playing dangerous games.

Rosaleen does not make me feel like a servant because she treats me as an equal. I find myself forgetting that I am obligated to stay and to serve. Seriously, what does that mean? She isn't going to tell me her plans of me, or my sister and I have no idea how long I need to stay? It makes me shudder to think that Ashlea and I could have the same fate as her late father's servants with being forced to work against their wishes and then being sentenced to death because of "treason" for trying to escape. I finish my drink and try not to let it worry me, I cannot leave Rosaleen, but I want to. She is so nice to Ashlea and me, but really, this revenge, which she feels obligated to see through, makes her a wolf in sheep's clothing. I do feel in the pit of my stomach that she does like us, but at the same time if

Ashlea or I ever faltered, I fear that we would pay a big price.

Instinctively, as if she is sensing my thoughts, Rosaleen asks, "What are you thinking?"

Startled by her question, I choke, "Nothing."

"That's funny; clearly you are deep in thought. I will need to talk to Izavelle and have her teach you skills on how to hide your emotions." I sit there like an idiot having nothing to say. Rosaleen demands, "Don't keep things from me. Share your thoughts."

I take a deep breath and only tell a half-truth, "I was just going over everything you told me. The story of your mother and father, I was thinking about how long you might keep Ashlea and me, and I was also thinking about how much I miss home, my mother and Saydira." I take a nervous breath to try to settle my startled nerves. She reads me like a book, I do need lessons from Izavelle. I continue, "I know that I am obligated to serve, I wouldn't think about deceiving you. It's truly the last thing I would ever think of doing it's just that I can't help, but think about these things, my heart longs for them." Looking up through my eyelashes, I nervously wait for Rosaleen's reaction.

There is a silence between us, and I cannot read her. She is finishing the last bite of her sandwich; licking the cinnamon flavoring that dripped onto her fingers. "Interesting, it is good that you are being open with me, and we will make everything right." She dabs her mouth carefully with a napkin and leaves some kiros on the table as payment for our meal. "I don't know how long I will need you, or if you will ever see your mother, or Saydira again. It's not something that I can foresee." Rosaleen rises from the chair, and I follow her. Glancing over I see that our server Kace spots us leaving; Kace waves to us, hollering out a "thank you" We return the gesture and continue down the cobblestone road. My heart is numb, but I am not going to challenge Rosaleen any further, not now because nothing is forever and surely, I should see them again. Why would she give me no hope? She is in control of Ashlea and me, but as for my mother and Saydira, I am not sure how closely they are being watched, or if anyone is watching out for them at all. Rosaleen has no control of whether something should happen to them.

Rosaleen says as we are walking down the road, "Keep your eye open we need to borrow some transportation to get to my mother's home."

Rosaleen gives no hint at her thoughts, and I have no idea what she means. I wish Ashlea were here with me so that we could talk and compare our interpretations of this discussion.

I spot some transportation, "What about those solar bikes over there?" I point just off to the right; a man in dirty clothing is tending to his bike shop. It is a small sand colored stucco building. Attached at the front is a bright ocean blue canopy that extends overhead to provide shade. The canopy looks new because the sun's rays have not yet bleach it. There are about ten solar bikes. They resemble a scooter, and the sun powers them. He strikes me as someone who is passionate about his products because when we walk up, he does not notice us. He is concentrating on polishing one of his bikes.

Rosaleen is the first to speak, "Hello, we are looking for some transportation for a couple of days."

The man startles at her voice, having been distracted by his work; and without hesitation welcomes our company. "Well, hello there!" he says while wiping the dirt from his hands with a towel, placing it over the seat of the closest bike and walks over to us to shake hands. He is tall and lean. His hair is a little un-kept and long, it is just touching the top of his shoulders. He has deep brown eyes and I notice that his hair is changing from the sand color that matches his stucco building to a reddish tone. He is picking up the color of my scarf. Just looking at the shape of his body, I would say he is a younger man, in his early twenties. He is lean and his muscles don't seem to be filled in, he is lanky, it is almost as though he is still growing into his body. He says to Rosaleen, "I can for sure lend you something for a couple of days what did you have in mind?"

Chapter 19
The Shop Keeper

Rosaleen says, "My friend is recovering from a little mishap so we will need something that can carry the two of us. We would prefer that it is a smoother and more comfortable ride."

His eyes automatically scan me looking for my injury, but he does not see anything. He is then conscious of the fact that he is staring at me, and I know. Our eyes meet, and I automatically look down. I can feel a slight blush in my cheeks, I quickly look back up, meeting his eyes again and he gently says to me, "I am sorry to hear you had a mishap, I hope that you feel better soon."

I find comfort in his warm gaze, "Thank you" I reply in a murmur.

He smiles then returns to the conversation with Rosaleen, "I have just the thing for the two of you." He hops back moving closer to his store building. Tucked in next to the front wall of the store is a clean white two-seater bike. He rolls the bike out, walking it over to us. The passenger seat of the bike looks comfortable. The seat is higher so that I would be able to see over Rosaleen. There are armrests and a backrest for me. I also spot generous footrests for the passenger.

He gestures and says, "Please come take a seat and try it out."

He extends his hand out to me, and I take it, accepting his lead while stepping closer to the bike. He explains, "So you will get on the bike first, take a seat, and your friend will take a seat in front of you."

I step up to the bike, straddle my leg over and then rest my body into the back seat. This is comfortable! Rosaleen quickly follows and sits in front. Even though I can't see her face, I can somehow sense that she is satisfied with the bike.

The man then gives Rosaleen a quick rundown on how to operate the bike. "Have you ever driven a solar bike before?" He asks.

"Yes," Rosaleen replies.

"Okay great, this one is the same as most of them. Your key is here, turn it to start it and stop it. Your break is here; your power over here and the kickstand is down here. The pleasant thing about this machine is, even though it is a little larger than your typical solar bike it is still light. If you happen to be unfortunate and fall the bike will sense the movement and shut off. There isn't much more to it. Do you want to take a quick test run to make sure that you like it?"

Rosaleen grins and answers, "Yes please."

"Okay" He smiles, hands the key to her. Rosaleen starts it up, leans back turning her head halfway to glance back at me with her right eye, "How are you feeling, are you ready to give this a try?"

"Yes" I reply, I am a little nervous, but at the same time excited. I have never ridden on the back of a solar bike. It is a welcome distraction to what happened in the last little while.

We head down the street, Rosaleen assesses the speed, and breaks, we then turn around, drive back to the store, and turn it off. She leans over to me, "Well it is perfect. How do you feel about getting this one?"

"I'm comfortable, it's a smooth ride." I return a polite smile, and the man seems satisfied that we are both clearly happy with his first pick for us.

She says to the man, "We will take this one."

He smiles and nods, "Okay great I will be right back with the form for you to sign and your fee." He hops back and quickly enters his store, returning to us seconds later. Rosaleen signs and hands him some currency. We are ready to go.

He casually asks, "Where are you two planning to go?"

Rosaleen replies, "I am going to visit Newlyn's home."

"Ah yes, I should have known. You know, I thought that you were Newlyn, but immediately thought otherwise; you carry yourself differently. You are related, right?"

Rosaleen answers, "Yes, we are related." Rosaleen leaves it at that, revealing nothing more. Even though the people from this area seem friendly, Rosaleen keeps her guard up at this friendly stranger.

The man says, "I am not sure how familiar you are with this area, but at this time of year the current from the ocean washes up tons of large fish and sea life on the flat rocks that are not too far from the road that leads to Newlyn's home just outside of town. The fish attract a lot of wildlife. There is a pride of large cats in the area. There have also been a few dire wolves spotted in the area." I gasp.

He continues, "The cats and the wolves will leave travelers alone. They care for the fish, but some have said that they are bold and have been seen attacking curious elephants that roam to close to them. My guess is if they feel threatened, they wouldn't hesitate and attack. If you see them near the road just keep your distance and wait for them to move along. They are protective of their families and defensive when it comes to their food supply so just remember that, and you shouldn't have any problems." Curiosity overcomes my shyness, I ask, "Have they ever attacked, or killed a person?" He gives an assuring smile, "No, not in these parts. The animals that are here are interested in the fish. It's a treat for them; the fish only wash up like this, on the rocks every six months. The fish are constantly migrating, and they only reach these parts for a brief period. The fish that wash up are the ones that happen to be too close to the rocks at high tide. Once the schools of fish move on the cats and the dire wolves retreat up to the mountains, beyond the horizon." Rosaleen does not look concerned, but kindly thanks him for the information and the solar bike.

"My pleasure ladies, see you in a couple of days, have a safe trip." He waves goodbye.

The cobblestone road narrows, turning into a dirt road as we leave the town. Rosaleen is driving at a conservative, but steady pace. It is open fields of tall golden grass and there are small herds of sheep, goats, buffalo, and elephants. I have never seen so many animals all together like this, enjoying the grassy vegetation. I have seen goats and sheep near my home, but the Buffalo and the elephants they are new to me. I knew they were large animals, but I never realized that they were giants. The heat out in the field in comparison to the ocean is much different. It is more of a dry kind of heat, there is a breeze, but it is not as cool, or as refreshing as the breeze that comes off the ocean. My eyes fix on the dirt road as we move along, and I spot tracks as well as the odd animal excrement on the road. The smell is hard to get used to in comparison to the sweet smells from the shore when we first set foot on the island earlier today.

Rosaleen slows the bike coming to a steady stop. She leans over and whispers to me, "They are beautiful, aren't they?"

I whisper back, "Yes" that is all I can say as I stare at the elephants that are grazing not too far off from the road. Rosaleen points in the direction of the ocean, "The flat rocks that the bike shop keeper had mentioned are just over there."

I follow Rosaleen's gaze and set my eyes on the shore. I see a pride of large cats moving along the rocks. The tide is down, and they are picking up what is left by carrying their finds back to the more comfortable grass to devour. I also see a couple of dire wolves patrolling the rocks; they seem to be a little timid and skittish around the cats. The wolves are quickly maneuvering to get some juicy fish without the cats noticing. There is a light breeze in the air now; coming from the direction of the ocean, carrying all the sweet scents of the area, the most noticeable scent of all is the cinnamon, even out here in the field away from the trees. You not only feel the breeze, but also you can see it approach as it ripples through the grass like gentle waves. A refreshing change to the smell of the animals. I cherish the sight of the ocean.

"Shall we continue?" Rosaleen whispers.

I nod, Rosaleen discreetly starts up the solar bike, and we are slowly gliding down the dirt road. We never came across any other people. There were not any homes, cottages, or tree huts, nothing. The road deviates, as it follows the ocean in the distance. The ocean is always to our right. Eventually, the open fields start to incline, and we emerge into a forested area. It is not a lush tropical forest like the forest near my home. My mother's house was built around a large tree. The trees in this forest are young; their trunks are at most just big enough that I could wrap my arms around them and still touch the tips of my fingers. The trees are spaced out nicely; you can really peer deep into the surroundings without getting lost in lush vegetation. Unlike the golden yellow color of the fields, the forest is a vibrant green, and lines of light pierce the canopy, touching the grassy green forest floor. Smaller animals live here. You can hear over the noise of the bike carrying us along our voyage the songs of many birds up in the treetops. I also spot the odd rabbit and chipmunk running across the road in front of us as we move along the trail.

It is not long before we are in the forest. The road begins to descend, opening into a new field. That is when I see it and know that it is Newlyn's home in the distance. It is like a mini castle, surrounded by large stone walls, as we approach the entrance there is a large, barred gate. Everything seems to keep to the same color scheme. These stone walls and the buildings within them are the same light beige except for their roofs are an orange-red color. For Newlyn being exiled from the Palace, this looks like some kind of holiday retreat. As we emerge from the forest, we descend into grassy light green hills and still to our right is the ocean. The gates to the home face the shore. The beach shores' sand is the same light beige as the home. On the far side of the home with looking passed, the walls there are more grassy fields, a couple of ponds and forest that turns into mountain. We descend into the field. I start to notice animals, mostly farm animals, sheep, goats, a few cows, and horses poke their heads up from grazing as we pass. When we approach, the gates are already open, we putter in, and Rosaleen parks the bike.

"Ah finally, how was that Taylan?"

"It was awesome; what a nice area." I look around at this retreat, I mean home. Wow, the yard has so many fruit trees that are evenly spread out, flowers that accent the yard and the buildings. There are a few small water fountains and neatly trimmed flowering shrubs that provide color to the yard. The main building is a two-story structure with a raised porch that surrounds the front and side of the home. I see a couple of tables and chairs as well as comfortable looking swings for lazing around in and wicker furnishings with generous fluffy cushions. There are smaller buildings that look to be homes that match, complementing the main structure. The only difference is that they are on a smaller scale, and the path that we are on that led us through the gate splits in two. One way leads to the main home. The split is at the entrance where the road turns right, from what I can see it hugs the wall of this retreat, going around the area of the inside walls. To the right, it looks like there is another building that is used for horses, livestock, equipment, and another structure that appears to be for storage. It is hard to tell what all these structures might be because most are tucked away within the confines of the wall, and they are behind the beautiful buildings of the main area where Rosaleen and I are.

Rosaleen gets off the bike first and then helps me off by giving me her hand. A young boy runs to us. He is about chest high to me.

"Hey Rosaleen!" he plants a big hug on her. "We missed you." He looks up at her while still squeezing her in embrace.

Rosaleen smiles and playfully says, "No you didn't, go on, run along." She winks at him and pats his head.

Before he takes her advice, he asks, "Rosaleen who is this lady?" He is not shy at all.

"This is Taylan my new friend and helper." Rosaleen looks to me and says, "Taylan, this little squirt is Sid."

I smile, saying, "Hey Sid."

He returns the smile, "Hey Taylan." Sid quickly sets his eyes on the bike then to Rosaleen, "Rosaleen can I play on your bike?" He begs.

"Sid it isn't mine. It is the merchant's from town. I only rented it for a couple of days. Tell you what, could you walk the bike around the back and store it for me, later I can take you for a ride?"

Sid kicks the dirt frustrated; he is old enough to understand that the bike is not hers to lend. He says, "Oh okay Rosaleen, maybe later then." Sid walks the bike around back to store it.

Rosaleen and I walk up to the main building where we see someone sitting out on the porch. I can tell it is Rosaleen's Mother Newlyn. It is as though they are identical twins.

She sits up, rises from her chair and steps down to meet us on the grass. She hugs her daughter in a long, warm embrace. "Rosaleen, I don't think I can ever get used to seeing you. I missed you."

"Oh, Mom I think about you every day." After their embrace, they hold each other at arm's length, gazing at one another and in unison, they laugh.

Newlyn peeks over at me, "Rosaleen, tell me who this beautiful creature is?" There is warmth to Newlyn's face. I blush when she compliments me.

"This is Taylan." Newlyn extends her hand to me, and she politely says, "It is nice to meet you and welcome to my home."

"Thank you, it is nice to meet you, your property is breathtaking." I smile.

"Thank you, that is so kind of you to say." Newlyn answers.

Rosaleen asks her mother, "I trust that Soolena and Ashlea have already arrived?"

Newlyn confirms, "Yes they arrived just before lunch."

Rosaleen explains, "Ashlea and Taylan are sisters that I met not far from a place called the North Shore, it's a couple of days journey by ship from here."

Newlyn answers, "Ah yes, I know that place and Taylan; you and your sister are lovely. Come let's go to the porch and sit." Rosaleen and I follow Newlyn; she leads the way up the steps. "Would you like anything to eat, or drink?"

Rosaleen says, "Could I have some juice please."

I answer, "A juice would be lovely, thank you."

Newlyn glances at a man relaxing in the hammock, "Could you be a dear?"

He nods, "Of course I will be right back."

"Thank you!" Newlyn turns her attention back to Rosaleen and me. "So, let's cut to the chase and figure this out together. Soolena tells me that there was trouble with Shrago last night." She leans forward with her arms crossed on the table as she speaks to us.

Rosaleen answers, "Shrago attacked Taylan in the night. We killed him this morning and disposed of his body overboard."

Newlyn glances at my scarf, "Taylan dear, come here, I want to see." I get up quietly and take a couple of steps towards Newlyn leaning over slightly to meet her at eye level. She carefully removes my scarf and sees my white bandage; looking up at me Newlyn asks, "May I?"

"Yes of course," I answer. Delicately Newlyn removes the bandage. It is late afternoon; it needs to be aired out and checked anyway. I don't mind her looking and from the moment I set eyes on her, I sensed that she was genuine. I trust Newlyn, even though she and Rosaleen are almost identical in appearance, Newlyn does not remind me of Rosaleen. She reminds me of my own Mother.

"This happened last night?" Newlyn questions but is not directing it to anyone specific.

I answer, "Yes," in a whisper.

"Who did your stitches?" Newlyn gently touches a couple of them.

"Izavelle" I answer.

"She did an excellent job; your wound is already healing well. The cut is clean, and the scab is nice, these stitches will be easy to remove."

Rosaleen peeks over, "Taylan it looks like your swelling has gone down already?"

Newlyn answers, "Whatever you gave her seems to be working there is only a touch of pink along the edge of the scab." Newlyn takes my hand, motioning me to sit down. I place my chair at an equal distance between Newlyn and Rosaleen. Newlyn continues, "You look to be doing well for someone that has been attacked and injured."

"The women have been taking diligent care of me, making sure that I eat. Today has been easier than I had expected." I have convinced myself that I feel one hundred times better than I did this morning.

"Good to hear." Just as Newlyn answers, the man returns with a jug of orange juice, and three glasses are set before us. The man smiles and retreats to his hammock. In a more hushed tone, Newlyn confirms leaning in closer to me, "I understand that you carried out the sentence?"

I nod, Newlyn looks a little relieved, "It is better that Taylan did the deed and not you Rosaleen. This certainly gives us something to think about?" I am not completely sure that her comment makes sense. I pretend to understand and try my best not to interfere with the discussion. I conclude to let them figure out whatever this is. This mess involves me however, these two women in my company are leaders with the strength to back them and I am nothing in comparison to them. If anything were to go against my favor, I am not sure what I would do, and I believe that I would be trapped. Right now, these women, I believe are acting with their best interests which also I think happens to be in my best interests. I decide to keep quiet and listen.

Newlyn is mulling something over, "What to do with Shaylo is the next decision that we have to make before your departure."

Rosaleen looks flustered, "How come you didn't do away with her while I was away?"

"Hun that wasn't a part of our agreement all I said was that we would trade. I would keep her here and you would take Zethel. Besides, had you returned to an anxious Shrago, and if he were to find out that his wife was disposed of then what?" She raises her eyebrow to Rosaleen and continues. "Out of pure luck these unfortunate events happened, and you walk away with clean hands." Newlyn sips her juice after making her point. I get the feeling that she is referring to me killing Shrago as the "unfortunate events."

I blurt out, "What about me; if she finds out what I did to her husband she will surely seek revenge on me. Am I wrong?"

Newlyn chuckles at my worry, "We won't let that happen. She will never find out."

Newlyn clasps her hands together "So now the question remains, do we keep Shaylo, or do away with her?" She asks Rosaleen.

Rosaleen asks, "Do you think that she is a threat?"

Newlyn without hesitation says, "Well of course. If word were to get back to the imposture King Wolfrim that you and I were reunited your life would be over, you know that Shaylo would be the one sharing the news as retaliation for us keeping her here."

Rosaleen satisfied with the answer, "Well then we must do away with her."

"Not so fast my child. It is safer no doubt if she is dead, but Shaylo could be an asset in figuring out details on the people who serve the imposture in the castle. If you want to avenge your father and me, I sense that you do because you wouldn't have left Shaylo with me if that was not your intent. You didn't want Shaylo telling anyone that the truth was uncovered in finding me. It may be in your best interest to keep Shaylo alive to gain information on relationships that you never knew existed."

I glance over at Rosaleen who is deep in thought and frankly looking to be having some kind of internal battle. "It's better to keep Shaylo alive; it obviously won't be easier to do it, but surely possible. Shaylo may prove to be an asset for us. I see the value if we keep her."

Newlyn says, "It is agreed we keep her; we will work out the arrangements later." Newlyn glances at the entrance gate, and automatically I look over my shoulder to follow her gaze.

Soolena and Ashlea are riding upon two large bay-colored horses. I admire Ashlea, this is her first time on horseback, and she seems to be a natural at it. They both dismount just inside the gate and Sid runs up, each handing over their reins to him. Sid's quick movements do not startle the horses. They like him because it appears from way over here that the horses are bringing their heads down to touch him with their muzzles as though they are saying hi to their little friend. Sid leads them to the barn that is situated behind the smaller homes on the property.

Rosaleen, Newlyn, and I get up, and I hurry over to hug my sister. I have last seen her this morning, but it feels like it has been a month.

"Ash, you learned how to ride." I have my arm around the mid side of her back. She matches my gesture. We follow the three women back to the table.

Ashlea giggles, "Yes, I think that I would say that riding is one of my most favorite things to do along with flying. I had so much fun this afternoon. Soolena taught me how to ride after we flew in from the ship. Before we arrived at Newlyn's, she also showed me the bird's eye view of the land. We went as far as the tips of those mountains up there and then down over the forests and the valleys." Ashlea points in the general directions to the different landmarks. Ashlea asks, "So, how did you and Rosaleen make out?"

I shrug, "Nothing compared to you. I am so jealous, but anyways, Rosaleen and I took that small boat to the shore and then walked along the beach and strolled through a town close to here. We stopped for a bite to eat, then after lunch, we rented a solar bike and drove here."

She smiles, "Sounds like just as much fun, I'm jealous."

"No, you're not!" I stick my tongue out at her. Just before we sit down with the women, I whisper into her ear, "We have to catch up later." She nods and we sit.

The women are re-acquainting, and the man in the hammock has retreated into the house, comes back out with more juice and now some beverages, and snacks for all of us. He sets them out on the table, like a ghost without interrupting the discussions and retreating to his hammock unnoticed.

Newlyn asks, "Ashlea how did you like horseback riding?" Newlyn pours some more juice as she awaits a response.

"Loved it and by the way, you have beautiful horses."

"Thank you; the one that you were riding, he is one of my favorites." Newlyn lights up as she tells Ashlea.

Soolena asks Newlyn and Rosaleen, "Will I be teaching Taylan how to ride tomorrow?"

Rosaleen begins to speak but is immediately cut off by Newlyn, "we have other plans for Taylan. She isn't quite ready physically to ride, but I have a better idea for her that I would like to propose to all of you to see what you think." My eyes must have gone wide because whatever this is its news to me.

We all give Newlyn the attention that she commands. "I hate to end the lighthearted conversation so soon, but we should hash this out sooner rather than later." Rosaleen nods in understanding and by no means seems bothered by her mother's interruption. Soolena tilts her head in confusion as if she isn't quite following where this is going. Ashlea and I have the same reaction, frozen and lost with no clue as to what to expect.

"We have a problem on our hands, and she has been here with me for a few months. Rosaleen's initial thought was to do away with her since we know where her true legions lie however my thought and Rosaleen has agreed that we keep her alive." Rosaleen nods. Newlyn grins, clearly pleased by Rosaleen's acceptance thus far, "We all know that Shaylo won't openly divulge anything that would be of value to us, if anything, Shaylo would try to mislead us." Soolena and Rosaleen nod while Newlyn continues, "Shaylo hasn't set eyes on either of these girls." Newlyn gestures to Ashlea and me.

Rosaleen leans over the table "Go on Mother."

"Yes, sweetheart." Newlyn says to Rosaleen in a teasing way and continues, "What better opportunity to introduce either Taylan, or Ashlea to her as a fellow prisoner? I would choose Taylan over Ashlea because we can work in the injury to the story of making it look like she tried to escape her obligations to her new master and make something up along the lines that Taylan is just too young and stupid to realize that she would get caught." I immediately look to Newlyn for more explanation. Do they think that it is a clever idea to coupe me up with a traitor let alone the wife of the person that I killed? Are they insane?

Newlyn continues, "Taylan wouldn't be a real prisoner, but instead she would be our spy, the link, in order to get information that we need out of Shaylo."

I wave my hand to get the groups attention, "I am not sure that I know how to be a spy, what if Shaylo figures me out, then what?"

Rosaleen answers, "We will guide you and won't let you fail. You must trust us and trust yourself." She is frustrated in my self-doubt. It is true. I am not a spy. I am not sure how to be one. I am sure that given the fact that Shaylo is older, I am sure she can sense a lie when it is staring her straight in the face.

I answer, looking into Rosaleen's eyes, "I will learn."

"Good." Rosaleen looks at ease with my response, she takes some snacks in her hand and pops them in her mouth with a satisfied look and washes it down with her drink.

Newlyn, just as she began, guides us along, "Okay, now that this is settled let's catch up on more lighthearted matters."

Everyone converses about their day and things that took place over the past few months and when they had last saw each other. The man in the hammock seems to know some unspoken queue, and over the course of a couple of hours, he serves us dinner, followed by dessert and tea. He disappears for the night. My sister and I catch up in running through our day in more detail.

Soolena is the first to retire for the evening. "The sun is going to set in the next hour. I am going to return to the ship and advise Izavelle what we discussed here."

Rosaleen says, "Yes that's a good idea, thank you."

Soolena excuses herself and as she leaves the table, she gives Ashlea a gentle pat on the shoulder. Ash gives a quick glance, and a smile is shared between the two. I can see that Ash and Soolena's bond is growing stronger. As a welcome change, Rosaleen decides to take a walk around the property with Ashlea. It is just me and Newlyn left.

"Okay dear let's get you cleaned up, and we will take care of that wound." She rises from her seat at the table and motions me through the entrance.

When you first set foot into Newlyn's home, you immediately feel tiny. The entrance is massive and impressive, all at once. The spacious entrance has a staircase that starts as one and then splits off in opposite directions. It is composed of stained wood, the same color as the sand on the nearby beach. The effect of it is a light, but also a warm tone. Everything is polished and has a clean shine to it. The floors are also of wood. They match the railing. Off to both sides of the entrance are rooms that are closed off by rows of smoky glass panel doors with gold color handles that are shaped like hooks. The ceiling above the stairway extends passed the second floor to the roof. It is in the shape of a small cathedral, and it is made entirely of glass to let the natural light in. Newlyn does not stop to give me a tour but instead leads me up the stairs, then off to the left and down the hall.

We enter a room with a massive four-poster bed; the posts almost touch the ceiling. They are as thick as mature tree trunks and carved into a beautiful spiral design. There is a fireplace to the left of the door and to the right a luxurious bathtub. Behind the tub, a smaller bathroom has a shower and a sink. On the far wall is a walk-in closet filled with clothes.

Seeing how taken aback I am, Newlyn chuckles. This room is more luxurious than the rooms on the ship. She says, "Don't get used to it. Remember you will be a prisoner tomorrow." She winks and I shudder at the thought. I don't remember it being decided that this was all going to be finalized tomorrow. I thought I was going to be trained a bit before having to face Shaylo?

Newlyn says, "Come on, it won't be that bad, you will never be alone, and you will get regular breaks with us to discuss what you have learned from Shaylo."

I ask, "How do you suppose there will be so many opportunities to talk?"

She smiles, "We have our ways." She walks over to the tub and lets the water run.

I undress before her without a second thought that this is weird that a stranger is tending to me. I am getting used to the peculiar lifestyle that they have. I step into the tub as it continues to fill. Newlyn sits on the top step of the tub, and she ties my hair up.

"Dear, can I ask you a personal question?"

"Yes," I am not sure where this is going.

"How old are you?"

"Eighteen," I answer a little confused because my age isn't something that I feel is personal.

She gushes, "You are so young, and this is good you will learn fast." Newlyn silently decides something. "How do you like Izavelle? I assume that she is the one who is teaching you, I can see that Ashlea's teacher is Soolena."

I nod, "Izavelle is kind, and I sense that she is wise. She is an expert in observation and appears to be well-liked by others. People seem drawn to her."

"Yes, she is well received." Newlyn turns the tap off; the tub is full, and I soak in it.

"You know I have someone here who is like Izavelle who can teach you how to listen and show you how to become someone that is easily trusted by others. He can teach you how to act to get what you need from different situations like for instance portraying compassion or appearing to be sincere."

Looking at Newlyn I reply, "I have Izavelle, and besides I think I know how to express myself." She is mentioning the same things as Rosaleen.

Newlyn sits up, "Taylan, explain to me, who are the loves in your whole entire life please name all of them."

I look up at her, hugging my knees under the water; I know where she is going now, "My mother, Nafeeza and my sisters, Saydira and Ashlea, and I really like my new family, Rosaleen, Izavelle and Soolena." I added them because I feel obligated.

Newlyn inhales and exhales, "You only ever known and expressed your emotions to people that you know, and they have only been real emotions. There are so many situations that you have yet to face like for instance, you have never loved a man, or have been subject to feel, or show compassion for strangers, or even act the part even if, you don't feel that way in your heart. Your entire life you have been surrounded by women and those you have known, your family and you haven't had to face, or express yourself in an un-sincere way to strangers, or potential foes."

"You're right, about it all, there were only a few that lived near to us, and the extent of my relationships with others was being a good neighbor. I never have faced a situation where I have had to act a certain way even though I didn't feel it." I confide, I am not sure why, but I feel embarrassed by this realization and divert my eyes to the water rippling around my body.

Newlyn asks, "Have you been with a man?"

"Yes, last night Shrago entered my room and me before my sister came to my rescue." That thought hurt. Newlyn knew this, why is she asking?

"I didn't mean to upset you I'm just trying to understand what your relationships have been up to this point in your life. You must realize that you are still green to many interactions that are crucial for you to become used to, and this needs to be learned if you want to properly serve my daughter and protect yourself. You need to learn to adapt so that you can better relate to and understand others. You need to develop some acting skills to get by until you become so good that you believe your own act. These are all skills that we need to teach you and need you to learn quickly."

"Why?" I feel like this is being forced on me suddenly out of nowhere, isn't it enough that they are ordering me to befriend their prisoner.

She touches her head for a second and explains, "Look Taylan please, you can't push this away. It is going to happen. Just think of it this way, one of Shaylo's strongest relationships was with her husband." Her eyebrows rise, putting little wrinkles across her forehead.

Rosaleen stands up, stepping down the steps of the tub, walks to the cabinet, then returns with soap, shampoo, and a container of first aid supplies. She sets everything along the ledge of the tub and starts with carefully cleaning my wound. "You know Taylan I have someone here that isn't much older than you. He is handsome, smart; he can teach you these skills quickly and step in for Izavelle since she is back at the ship. We need you to learn soon to perfect the task we are setting before you. Izavelle is a good teacher for you, but now Rosaleen needs Izavelle more than you do." Newlyn dips her hands into the water, cups them and slowly glides her hand back up my back, letting the water drain out through her fingers back down my back. She calmly takes her hands out of the water and pats them dry with a towel. "I will let you be for a bit." Newlyn gets up and quietly leaves my room, closing the door behind her.

I sit there in the tub considering the idea of this new teacher, not that I have a choice in the matter. Should I welcome the opportunity? Am I open to building a new relationship? Is this man also being forced into a situation just like me? Does he even want this? This is weird. I close my eyes and soak, trying to forget all of it. I go back to the day in my head, when it was just my sisters and I pearl hunting off the coast of the North Shore, carefree and oblivious of what was to follow. I recall the conversation where I asked Saydira about why there were so few people our age and on top of that even fewer men. I am ready for this. I was longing back then for building this sort of relationship without realizing that my heart was looking for it back when I was at the North Shore. Okay, I don't have the choice in this matter, so I am going to make the best of this and do what they ask. Hopefully, Shaylo won't figure out that I am just a spy, but here goes, I have this.

Satisfied with my reasoning and decision on how I am going to handle myself I carefully wash my hair; lather my body, mindful of my stitches, and rinse off. Wow, this is going to be the last bath like this for a while. Satisfied that my hair and body are rinsed I stand up to step out of the tub when I hear the door creak open. My first thought is, it is Newlyn, Rosaleen, or Ashlea, but it is neither of them. A taller figure enters the room. I immediately sink back into the water and wrap my arms around my body, feeling vulnerable. This has never bothered me before when at the beach with my sisters, but this is different, I am in a private place, and this is a stranger. He quietly closes the door behind him and looks in my direction.

His voice is warm, "Please don't let my presence make you feel uncomfortable."

I quickly muster up some authority in me. What does Newlyn know? I know how to act a part even if I don't feel it in my heart. I answer with a slightly raised voice, "What are you doing in my room?"

"I am here because Rosaleen and Newlyn ordered me here." He keeps his distance, sensing my discomfort; he decides to take a seat on the large bed. "Are you okay if I just sit here?" He asks.

"Not really, but I'm guessing that I don't have much of a choice, do I?" I answer a bit annoyed. I never catch a break, but I do have to admit that he is beautiful. Newlyn knows how to pick them. I know who he is; he was the man who was sitting in the hammock, the person who was serving us throughout the evening. He was like a ghost moving unnoticed, performing his duties. I really didn't notice what he looked like until now.

He says to me, "Look I understand that this is weird for you, trust me it is weird for me, and this literally just got sprung on me." He clasps his hands together and looks down.

"I know," I sigh, "So what were your instructions from Rosaleen and Newlyn?"

With calming eyes, he replies, "I was asked to be your mentor while you stay here; teach you how to blend and be accepted into unusual situations and teach you how to fend for yourself." He pauses as though collecting his thoughts, then elaborates, "I am basically teaching you to become a good liar and teach you some skills on the art of deception." He has a handsome smile and winks; I blush a little and I roll my eyes at him. Wow, I can't stay mad at Rosaleen and Newlyn for springing this on me; he is just too handsome to stay upset although, I find myself very self-conscious right now.

I am getting curious about him, "So you never told me your name?"

He smiles "No I haven't, Taylan." There is an awkward pause where neither of us says anything.

"Well, what is your name, stranger?" I ask as I lean over the tub with my arms crossed on the ledge of it.

He smiles "It's not my name that matters."

"Okay then what do I call you?"

"Call me Sir."

"Is that your name?" I ask; I am confused.

"You don't need to know my name right now, but if you need to call me something Sir will do." He is quite serious in his expression, and I decide not to push it any further.

Deciding on a new topic, I change the direction of the conversation. "So, you said your name doesn't matter, please tell me what does matter?"

He smiles again, "Good question, for starters we need to get used to each other, understand what our relationship is to one another and what we want others to perceive our relationship to be." He eagerly waits for my response.

"Well for starters we don't have a relationship." I say.

"Sure, we do, you know me as your mentor."

I pause for a moment to think about it and respond with a shrug, "Well sure I guess."

He elaborates, "You're going to be put in the presence of Shaylo for starters, my relationship with her is she is Newlyn's prisoner, and I am the one that cares for her. I make sure that she is cared for and that her living quarters is kept clean. I also see to it that she carries out her chores. When she miss-behaves she is punished, and when she does what is asked, she is left alone."

I ask, "Is your relationship with her good?"

He tilts his head; "If you're looking at it as a prisoner and guard relationship than yes, I am fulfilling all of my duties that Newlyn has asked of me," he pauses, "but if you're asking me specifically about the human relationship than I would say that it's pretty bad. Shaylo is nothing more to me, only a prisoner, she doesn't trust me, which makes sense, and because of that, I can't push her to divulge any intelligence. Apart from Shaylo holding back information the only good thing is for everything else that we have asked of her, like completing all the daily chores she does without hesitation."

I chime in, "So from what I gather from Newlyn, this is where I come in right?"

He clasps his hands together, "Precisely" he says and gets up off the bed, making his way over to the tub, "I think it's time you come out of the bath." I look up at him reluctantly and blush, not moving. He is now standing by the tub with a towel in hand for me. He says, "Newlyn told me of the place you came from, I understand that being nude is normal. People swim in the nude and sunbathe nude most of the time where you are from; am I wrong?"

"No, you're not wrong." I sigh "It's just that this is weird you are a stranger to me and it's not like we are out swimming in the ocean. You are here in the privacy of my bedroom watching me bathing. To tell you the truth this feels uncomfortable, and to be quite honest it's well, creepy."

He shrugs, "You have to put your feelings about this aside because this is going to be a fast-forming relationship for the sake of Newlyn and Rosaleen's plans." He glances down at the floor and says, "Come out of the tub." I blush and cross my arms in the soapy water. He peeks up at the splashing sound of me moving in the water and asks, "Would it help if I was nude?" He smirks, raises his eyebrows. He is still waiting for me to answer or to do something. Now he is holding a towel meant for me in hand.

I snort, "Keep your clothes on." I give in, this is weird, but I know that all of this is just the nature of the work that he and I must do. I step out of the tub slowly, mindful of my step and allow him to wrap the towel around me. I walk away to the closet to search out some panties and a nightshirt and disappear into the washroom out of this man's sight to dress my wound and clothe myself to get ready for bed. I emerge a few minutes later. He is back on the bed, but this time he is under the covers. I stop in my tracks and stare at him, what is he doing? He sees my reaction and somehow knows that I would react this way.

"Come to bed." He motions with his hand as if this is no big deal; I stand at a still. He urges, "Come, trust me I'm the least of your worries. Soon you will be put in the company of Shaylo." I reluctantly approach the bed and crawl in. This must be Rosaleen's bright idea of me getting comfortable with men especially only after a day of being attacked. He takes a strand of my hair and tucks it behind my ear, "This is your first lesson of many. I know that you are uncomfortable with this sleeping situation. I know, I am an intruder to your space, do you know how I can tell?"

"I hope you can tell because I am making it clear to you." I answer.

"You are." He says, "This is your first lesson on hiding your emotions and trust me you are going to need this skill when facing Shaylo. You are stiff and ridged right now. I need you to start with concentrating on your breathing, slow it down, in through your nose and out through your mouth." I breathe in deeply, he continues, "You are going to fool me into believing that you are relaxed in my presence even though I know right now that you aren't. Okay, so keep your breathing slow and rhythmic. Now you are going to think about every muscle in your body and you are going to relax them, let them all relax while continuing with your steady slow breathing." I can feel myself start to relax. "Good." He says, "The last thing with this lesson is I always think of something that makes me happy, it helps calm me, I want you to do the same. This will keep the act going, and I would even go as far as saying that you will start to actually believe your own act." My thoughts immediately take me back to the day on the North Shore, pearl hunting with my sisters, and I start to forget that I am in bed with another stranger who is preparing me to take residence with a prisoner. "Tomorrow, we will train you and get a solid story put together for you, for Shaylo, go to sleep."

I decide to turn over on my side; my back is towards him, I ask, "Where is Ashlea?"

He yawns, "She is safe you will see her briefly in the morning, rest now." I decide that he is right, and I drift off into sleep in the presence of this stranger. This has been such a long day and tomorrow promises more work. I drift off thinking about my family and all the landscapes that I have seen today on the back of the solar bike.

Chapter 20
Without a Name

I wake suddenly; sunlight is beaming through the window, lighting up the surface of the hardwood floor. I look around, where is he? Hopeful of finding some clues, I sit up and listen. It is too quiet. Slowly I slip out of bed, my feet touch the surface of the warm floor, and I lightly step around the bed and head towards the door.

"Taylan" He leaps out from a crouching position towards me. My reactions kick in; I dodge his attempted bear hug and give him an angry glare.

"Ah come on. Let me ask you this, did that get rid of the awkwardness of me being a stranger and all?" I try to hide my smile, trying to continue to glare at him, but I do have to admit it was funny and he got me good, mind you, that just shaved a couple of years from my life.

I answer, pretending to be still annoyed with him startling me, "You really scared me, that wasn't funny."

He stands in front of me holding me at arm's length, "Really Taylan, you are going to tell me that wasn't funny even though I saw a smile on your face." I look up at him and shrug my shoulders playfully, "That's what I thought." He winks and let's go, walking back to the bed to pull the covers up to make it. I follow his lead, going to the opposite side to pull up and tuck in the sheets. "So, the agenda for today is, I must tend to Shaylo, see to it that she is bathed, clothed, and fed. She is going to remain in her cell today until I have you up to speed on everything."

I fluff a pillow and ask, "So does that mean my morning will be spent with Ashlea?"

He shrugs, "Maybe I am not sure, but what I do know is that Rosaleen and Newlyn requested me to tell you to join them for breakfast."

"Oh, what time?" I ask.

"Now" He smiles, "I will come seek you after breakfast; the plans for the day will likely be decided by Rosaleen and Newlyn by then." He pauses and then says, "Make sure you get your fill, this is going to be a long day."

I nod then get dressed into some simple shorts and a shirt. He is still in the room as I clothe, but I keep my back turned. This is still very weird, but it seems to be a little less so since he is dressing too. We are ready at the same time and exit the room together, descending the stairs. He approaches the front door. I am surprised that he isn't coming to breakfast, he gestures for me to go ahead. I obey and find myself in a large sunlit kitchen. The walls are pale grey, almost white, and the ceiling is one large, slanted skylight. There are large windows along the exterior wall. There is a large whitewashed wooden table to the left and to the right, an island with stools, further past the island are more cupboards, counter space a large fridge, stove, and sink. The women sit at the table. I join them. Newlyn first notices me, "Ah Taylan, we were just talking about you, please come sit down and eat." I sit next to Ashlea; give her a quick touch on her hand under the table as I take a seat next to her.

Rosaleen says, "You are probably wondering what is going on?" She pauses and glances in my direction, trying to confirm her speculation, "You are going to stay here with Newlyn and Sit." That's his name, I grin to myself. Rosaleen continues, "Ashlea, Soolena, Izavelle and I are going to continue to the Palace. You are going to be-friend Shaylo to find out who the guard was, that did the switch long ago of the king and imposter as well as find out who else engaged in my father's murder."

"What is the time frame that we are looking at?" I ask anxiously, they are taking the last of my family away from me. I thought Rosaleen had promised my mother that Ashlea and I would only serve her.

Rosaleen seems pleased, probably because I am not questioning her on the plan, or showing doubt in myself, she says, "As long as it takes, we are going to set the ship at a cruise and wait for your feedback. Once we are satisfied with what we know then I will confront the imposter to avenge my family and take the Kingdom that is mine by rights."

I ask, "So, all of the training that you had planned for me..."

She answers simply; "Sit will." I don't bother asking any more questions.

Newlyn says, "So this is our last breakfast together for a while let me say cheers to the companions, servants, and friends we have all become!" Newlyn holds up her glass and everyone follows suit, "Cheers!" I am not completely sure if what she said is meant for Ashlea and me, as we have only known each other for a brief time.

I whisper to Ashlea, "So, what will you be doing while we are apart?"

She finishes chewing and swallows, "They will be teaching me different flying skills, offensive and defensive skills, and Izavelle will begin to teach me the skills she was teaching you."

I sigh, "I am going to miss you so much Ashlea."

She glances up with a tear in her eye, "Me too." She leans over and hugs me. Rosaleen, Newlyn, and Soolena let Ashlea, and I continue in our own conversation as they continue their own separate one. We finish breakfast and it feels like my heart has stopped. The last tie to my family is leaving, and we will each be alone to fend for ourselves in the company of these people. I am not even convinced that I am working on the good side. From what Rosaleen has told me about her family, I've concluded that there were no Angels in the matter and Rosaleen's family rather brought their problems on themselves. I'm not saying that it is okay to kill or side with the people who are righteous, but both sides had ill intentions. I feel like an infant about to go into battle with monsters.

The morning goes by in a haze, and before I know it, I am saying goodbye to Ashlea. The sick feeling in my gut is, not knowing when I will see her again.

"I love you, Ash." I hug her, failing to hold back the tears any longer, they are streaming down my face, and I am holding her in a tight embrace.

"I love you too, stay safe Taylan." Ashlea returns my embrace. We have a tough time letting go. Sit has a hand on my shoulder; I am not sure how long he has been here. Newlyn Sit and I watch as Soolena takes flight, and Ashlea takes my spot on the solar bike with Rosaleen; they putter out, exiting the gates and disappearing out of sight.

I feel lost in the absence of Ashlea and relief at the same time in the departure of my captures, Rosaleen, and Soolena. I know that I am still their servant and can't help but feel as though some weight has lifted by their departure. There is still no rest or freedom for me, and now Sit and Newlyn are my masters. I'm supposed to convince this Shaylo, whom I have never seen, that I am also a prisoner and am on her side. I hope that I can leech some information out of her. Newlyn retreats into her home leaving Sit and I on our own.

Sit whispers to me, "Let's get started on your training?" I turn and follow him back into one of the smaller homes off to the side from the main home. The one thing that ends up working out to my benefit is after Sit has spent some more time with me, he realizes that I am not ready. The departure of my mom and two sisters is weighing heavily on my mind, and even though I am starting to get used to him and this new life, Shrago's attack and his punishment are still fresh. Sit understands that I need more time to let that mental wound scab. I am not sure how he manages, but he somehow convinces Newlyn that we need more time or else they would risk me derailing their entire plan. Sit can grant me a few more nights of "freedom."

Chapter 21
The Heart Wants

I am starting to lose track of time; I have been here at Newlyn's home for some days and nights. This morning, I wake in a plain, but comfortable room with my mentor. Sit is in the doorway peeking in. "Help me with the breakfast?" He asks and I roll out of bed, dress, and head down to the workers kitchen. Sit is already there putting meals together for Shaylo, Newlyn, Sid, myself him and the handful of other servants that stay here. The meals range from some being extravagant breakfasts of freshly chopped fruit, meat, and bread to as simple as a couple of pieces of toast meat and milk, my guess is, that is Shaylo's meal. Sit instructs me, "Run these over to the main house this is Newlyn's and some plates for her assistants, and I will run this dish over to Shaylo. Meet me back here when you are done, okay?"

I nod, "I understand." I take a walk over to the main house. It is easy for me to find Newlyn, she is out on her front sitting area at one of the tables, and I quietly deliver her meal and set the other meals down for her servants that are there with her. She takes little notice to me, clearly engaged in a discussion and to my relief; I quietly retreat to the workers kitchen of the smaller home on the property. I don't wait long for Sit to return.

Sit and I finish our meals and Sit says, "Let's head down to the shore. You will like it. I think it will remind you of the North Shore." The shore is within walking distance from Newlyn's gaits. Sit and I take the path that leads to it.

He casually says as we walk, "I have put some thought into how we are going to do this."

"Yes" I answer, the word escapes slowly.

"There is no doubt in my mind that we have to come off as being as authentic as possible." That's a given, Sit continues, "The weakness with you is your inexperience." He sighs, "We can't throw you in the pen with her and have you pretending to be someone that you're not. Do you understand?" I look at him and nod, agreeing. "I think the good thing with you is, your real story can be used and built upon to get what we want from Shaylo." The path that we are walking down opens to a sandy shore, we find a spot to rest and talk more.

Sit volunteers his idea, "We will use your real-life story as a basis and simply add a little more to it so that even someone like you can act out. Who knows, you will even convince yourself that this story is true. Do you understand?"

"Yes," I answer.

Sit's voice has a hint of relief to it, "Well good." He winks at me. "Shall we?"

"What?" I ask,

"Swim silly; that's why we are here right?" He stands from sitting in the sand and strips down completely. I stare at his smooth, cinnamon tanned brown muscular body. His hair seems not to change as quickly as the women I know, but today his hair is the color of the sand, a dirty blonde and his eyes are a clear, vibrant blue. He catches me staring at him, instead of ignoring my gaze he acknowledges it right away while coming off as being over confidant. He changes direction from going to the water, comes to me and grabs hold of me at an arm's length after I have already removed my clothes.

"Do you like what you see?" Sit is gazing into my eyes. I turn my head to look away, feeling embarrassed that he caught me. He shakes me, to get my attention.

"No, go on, look at me." He urges. I look into his eyes, "Look at my entire body Taylan, don't be shy." I slowly look down and peek at his rippled chest, then down to his masculine parts. He makes it twitch and I immediately force myself free from his grasp.

"Oh, dear Taylan, we can't have any fun, can we?" He chuckles at my uneasiness. Instead of letting me walk away, he charges at me full force and tackles me to the sand.

I scream, "What are you doing?" He pins me on my back and looks into my eyes saying, "I asked you a question."

"What?" I say completely flustered.

"Answer my question." He demands while still pinning me down.

"I don't know?" I roll my eyes and try to squirm from his grasp.

"Now that's a lie." He laughs at me and still holding me firm says, "Tell me the truth."

I reluctantly divulge, looking into his eyes with all the little confidence I can muster, "I was admiring you, you're handsome and you are strong." I look away embarrassed for having been caught.

He smiles, "Well thank you, you are pretty good looking yourself." He gives me a wink and I muster up the strength to roll my body over. I have the feeling that he let me go. I free myself from his grasp. We are both on our feet again. He puts his arm around my shoulder and leads me into the ocean.

"That wasn't so bad, was it?" He asks.

"Which part?"

"The part where you admitted that you think I am attractive."

I shrug my shoulders, "No, I guess not." We dip our toes into the water to get used to it.

"You know Taylan; you're not a good liar. We will need to stick to the truth as much as possible to convince Shaylo of anything."

"Yes, I know." I skim my toes along the water's surface; the air is very warm making the water feel cooler than it is. We walk in about waste deep and wade in the water. There are no weeds, just a fine sandy bottom, the waves are nothing but a gentle ripple today, which makes it easy just to sit and bathe in the water and talk about all this stuff that we must do.

"What are your thoughts for a story?" Sit asks, shifting gears from being playful into being more serious and inquisitive.

"Well, I do admit that I have little experience in fabricating lies and to be honest, I could easily see myself getting lost within a lie. The last thing that I want is to disappoint Rosaleen and Newlyn." He understands my worry.

"Well let's start from the top. Tell me your real story on how you came to be here?"

"Don't you already know it?" I ask.

"Newlyn informed me, which means the information came from Rosaleen, but I want to hear it from you." There is silence between us. I look into those crystal blue eyes that are encouraging me to speak.

"Rosaleen met me and my two sisters on the North Shore one morning. She invited us all to her ship along with my mother. She broke up our family that day.

Rosaleen took Ashlea and me as her servants and left my older sister with my mom. Rosaleen hinted that she was being generous despite her tricking all of us with her false generosity, and in the end, she divided our family. Rosaleen started showing Ashlea and me what goes on in her life, teaching us different things that she felt was important. We didn't really work for her but were more her companions and extra eyes for her to keep watch. On the second night, a man attacked me. That is how I received the gash on my neck. The morning that followed, Rosaleen sentenced the man to death. He was well already dead from receiving a blow to the head by Ashlea who had come to my rescue. I was ordered to kill him. I cut his throat. I was told to clean up the mess of blood and to dispose of the body. Later that morning, the ship arrived just off the shore to this island. I accompanied Rosaleen from the main town to her mother's home, now I'm here with you and soon to be acting as a prisoner." I wade in the water, waiting for his reaction to my summary. I have a tough time believing it myself. My life has never been fast-paced, and I don't feel like I have completely learned anything new or mastered any real skills. It feels like they just plucked me out of obscurity just because they could, doing what they wanted, and now it feels like they don't know what to do with us. What's even worse is knowing that they won't just let us off the hook so that we can go home. It is funny because during these thoughts, Sit follows up and asks me how I feel about everything, as though he was reading my mind, and I repeat these thoughts aloud.

He answers, "Trust me, I know how it feels, but understand that what you are about to do has meaning. If Rosaleen and Newlyn didn't need you, you would be the first to know." Sit is thinking everything through. I don't bother to ask because it is obvious, and I allow him to mull it over on his own. I lay back in the water allowing myself to float along the surface. It is so relaxing, and the cut on my neck feels like nothing more than a scratch. It is healing nicely. I flip back so that I am wading, my knees resting on the sandy bottom. The water stops just below my shoulder, and I continue to watch him think.

He seems to have reached some resolve, "I am going to think aloud, stop me at any point." Sit takes in a breath and begins, "The events that first took place with Rosaleen, taking you and your sister from your home, we can use your real-life experience." He pauses, gathering his thoughts as he mulls this over while allowing himself to float in the warm clear water. He replies, "It's obvious you will need to leave out Shrago's attack from our fabrication for your new identity. We should tell it like this; prior to the ship leaving your home area you had tried to make an escape with your sister, however, you were caught and injured during the capture. If she asks about it in more detail, you can reveal that the injury was from a grappling hook that had grazed your throat, not because they were trying to hurt you with it, but because they were trying to grab a hold of the boat that you were using to escape. They succeeded in latching onto the boat and unfortunately you couldn't make the attempt of swimming because you were too far from shore and besides, the entire point of your escape was to go unnoticed and not have it turn into a chase." He looks up at me and asks, "What do you think so far? Do you think that you can manage sticking to that?"

I can work with this, "Yes, I think you are on to something, it sounds believable, but I have a question?"

"What?" Sit asks.

"Does Rosaleen's ship even have grappling hooks?" He starts laughing at me, I don't understand. It is an intelligent question. "What?" I ask clearly confused and now I am a bit annoyed.

He muffles his laughter, "Taylan did you not open your eyes when you were on board? They are on every ship of that size. They are used to secure ropes and anchor the lifeboats as sinkers and are used to catch and secure other boats. Rosaleen has a handful of them on her ship." Sit smiles at me meaning no offense to his laughing. I know this, but still, I can't help it and continue to feel annoyed. Deep down I am more annoyed with myself for asking a foolish question. Rather than admit that it was silly I just splash him and avoid his retribution by diving into the ocean to get some distance. I am attracted to him and his eyes. I can't get those crystal blue orbs out of my mind. I don't want to feel this with him, of all people, but my heart is decided, and I accept it. I'm totally smiting for him. I can't believe that I have fallen so fast for this stranger. I have known him for about a heartbeat, and when I first came into his company, he was nothing more than an invisible servant for Newlyn. I had not really noticed him until he was ordered into my bedroom that night. I have only had conversations with him that were focused on Rosaleen's and Newlyn's orders and not the kind of things that involve flirting or getting to know someone because you want to. We really haven't talked on a personal level so I really can't explain this attraction. Right now, it is only based on his good looks. There may be something more, but it is too early to know. I find myself asking this question repeatedly as I wade in the water. I am intrigued by him; not only is his toned body desirable, but I am drawn to his personality. He is playful, arrogant, but protective and a little guarded on how he is perceived. Right now, I don't know where we stand on this relationship dynamic. I know with Rosaleen and Newlyn, they are my masters, and Sit is on the same level with me when it comes to having to serve more elite people. However, the weird dynamic that we are creating is new. I will be posing as his prisoner. What is stranger is I believe what I am feeling with him is mutual. So how is this going to work? I can't even picture this man being a prison guard or coming off as being harsh to me. Then again, my first impression of him was nothing more than a shadow. He has taken on the role of a friend and mentor and something more. He chases me into the depths, and I let him catch up. He gives me a playful bear hug and the motion causes us to circle, as though we are doing loops in the air only, we are underwater. Feeling a bit dizzy and needing a breath of air, we both resurface.

"Where do you think you're going?" He asks playfully as he grabs hold of me in the water.

I giggle, which catches me by surprise, for the last little while my life has been more serious, "I was just trying to get away from you." The way that he is holding me in the water with one arm supporting me under my knees and the other arm supporting my back, I wrap my arms around his neck. The feeling must be mutual. He carries me to the shore and sets me down on my feet; we walk back up to where we left our clothes and rest in the sun.

"Sit?" I ask.

"Yes Taylan." He turns his head, giving his full attention.

"Is what you are doing, I mean how you are around me, is this all just an act?" He searches my face for hints to what I mean, or he is looking at me to see what I want all of it to really be so that his answer pleases me.

"What do you mean?" He asks.

"Us, this," I gesture my hands to refer to the both of us.

He looks at me, "Of course it's an act, you will be acting and so will I as per Rosaleen and Newlyn's orders."

"No, I'm not talking about that." I sigh and roll my eyes. I feel a little annoyed that he isn't grasping what seems so obvious to me. "I mean us; it feels like there is something more than just a partnership here." I pause to think about how I am going to convey myself, "Is what you are doing and how you are acting here with me just an act because of Rosaleen and Newlyn's orders, or do you have any real feelings for me?" I look up at him with nervous eyes. I've never done this, been so forward and never had a relationship as strange as this, let alone have any sort of friendships with the male population because back home, men go on to the cities and Kingdoms to serve and protect. They seldom return because they often end up re-establishing themselves there.

Sit hesitates and I glimpse a slight blush on his face although he is doing a fantastic job at not coming off as awkward like I am, "I think there is something between us and to answer the other part to your question, the answer is no, this side of me is not an act." There is a certain sense of understanding in those comforting eyes, and he gently rubs my back. "Don't worry yourself about what Rosaleen and Newlyn have instructed me to do. You know what they want and what we have made of this short relationship. The feelings are real. Everything that is discussed between us is real. We have a partnership and must be honest with one another." He shrugs, "What would the point of this partnership be if this were just an act? How would we succeed at this facade if we weren't transparent with one another?"

Again, looking to me for a response and I believe that Sit is being honest. I shrug and respond, "Yes you're right." I say with a twinge of relief, "It's just, I know everyone has a task to do and we are all under the rule of either Rosaleen, or Newlyn. I wasn't sure if they had asked you to act this way with me for some ulterior motive." Sit doesn't seem surprised about my reasoning.

"I can see how you may think that. It was good for us to get that all out of the way, but you do have something wrong." He raises an eyebrow.

"And what's that?"

"You're a servant to Rosaleen, but Newlyn isn't my master. I choose to serve her and can choose to leave when I wish."

"Why don't you?" I ask.

He smiles, "Why would I?"

I carefully choose my words, "Well for starters it seems like there is way too much drama here, wouldn't you rather be on your own and away from all of this?"

He allows himself a chuckle, "All of this drama is interesting, it adds spice to the everyday norm, and you will see that all the theatrics is only a small price to pay for the overall good you get from being a part of it all. Trust me it will get better." I can sense the passion for his work in his words. We dress and continue to rest and dry off on the beach.

I change subject, going back to building my story for Shaylo, "So what now after the grappling hook?" I ask.

"Shouldn't I be the one steering this discussion?" He glares at me.

I blush, "Maybe…"

He exaggerates his sigh so that it is long. He replies, "Oh Taylan, at least I have your interest in this." He recomposes himself, and I know that he is back into the thought process. "What to do after the grappling hook?" He thinks aloud, scratches his head, "Well I think that I have something, but it really isn't elaborate."

I respond, "Well simple is good. What's your idea?"

He regards me and continues, "Well how about, after you are caught from trying to escape, Rosaleen was furious with you and instead of keeping you on her ship, your guess, is that Rosaleen decided that she didn't want to keep you. Figuring that you would be too much of a liability on a ship with a limited amount of resources, so instead, she handed you off to her mother Newlyn to serve her. The last thing that she wanted was to let you have your wish by letting you go; Rosaleen couldn't have that."

I nod, "Yes that feels right to me, if Shaylo tries to ask anything more about the ship and Rosaleen I can just say that I don't know because it was all in a short time span, and that I was locked up after my failed attempt at leaving." I trail off; not meaning to say it aloud, "So now that leaves us, how do we mask our comradeship?"

"You know what I am, which is a fantastic actor." He winks, "and I can change my demeanor easily, but that leaves you, do you think you can hide your fondness of me?" He grins and I shove him. There is no force behind it, so it doesn't do anything, but lets him know how I feel. He doesn't fight back. Instead Sit laughs and replies, "I know how that came across, seriously, you are going to have to hide whatever feelings that you have for me."

"And how am I supposed to do that? I am not an actress, and I have never played this sort of game of deception."

I can tell that he has a solution to this predicament, "You aren't going to like what I am about to say, but for you to come off as a prisoner, I have to treat you like one, and I mean really treat you like you are beneath me. I'll be harsh and maybe even cruel so that should make you come to loath me; you won't need to act. I just need you to remember, I don't truly hate you. Taylan you must understand that this is all to help with the act."

I regard him, "I understand."

He follows up, "No really, you got to understand, I mean it."

I sigh, "Yes, I get it."

He stands up and shakes the sand out of his hair quickly, "Come let's go back to the house and get a bite to eat." We walk up the path to Newlyn's home and enter through the main door. In the kitchen, he helps me navigate where things are, and we help one another put together sandwiches and chips. During our lunch, he repeats the plan aloud so that we each have it memorized. He has me change upstairs into a simple light grey linen jumpsuit. I take care to tuck my necklace under the collar. Ashlea returned it to me prior to her departure and feeling that if Sit, or Newlyn see it they may object to me having it. He explains after I have dressed, that these are my prisoner clothes. We head out again, outside the walls, but this time to an open field where we review the minute details.

Sit explains, "So we have our story down and now to the details. If Shaylo asks you something that is outside of what we have discussed, you simply say that you don't know. To make anything that you say sound true maintain normal eye contact and don't emphasize like for example, I really don't know, just say that you don't know. Give eye contact to show confidence without staring her down, got it?"

"Got it" I confirm and to make sure that I really know how to do this he pretends to be Shaylo asking me questions, and I practice my deception on him; satisfied with how convincing I'm coming across he decides to move on to the next task.

Sit continues, "I don't think that Shaylo is the physical fighting type, to me, she seems to be more of a mental bully, but if she uses her strength, we should go over some basic defense skills, just to be on the safe side. I need you to stand in front of me with your hands at your side." I do what he asks, and he shows me different moves like how to break free from hold positions. He provides me with some offensive moves so that I can stand my ground. My guess, if there was an onlooker watching us it would look like we were doing an intimate dance, lunging, and turning back and forth. I appreciate his lesson, and have the feeling that it will pay off, if not with Shaylo, at some other point in my life. I feel disappointed that our relationship, this feeling I have in this moment will soon change to prisoner and master. It sounds negative, but at least right now, it feels more as though we are teacher and apprentice.

After an afternoon in the field, we retire back to Newlyn's home. I am tired, but I have confidence in what I am about to do. We enter the walls of Newlyn's property and stop at the same spot where Rosaleen and I were the day we had arrived on the solar bike. I look to him for the reason we have stopped.

"You are ready." He says encouragingly.

"Okay, but now?" The sudden change in tempo catches me off guard.

"Yes, let's do this."

I'm puzzled and feeling a little hurt that he is just throwing the last evening that I was looking forward to away. I ask, "What are we going to do. How are we going to do this?" I run my hand through my hair. I thought I was at least going to have one last night of a normal evening before I jump into this new identity.

Sit is either ignoring my reaction, or he is just oblivious to it, I am going to guess the first thought. He replies, "We are just going to jump into it, besides there is no more preparing that is needed, you're ready." With pleading eyes, I say nothing, and he holds me at arm's length resting his hands on my arms. He says, "Wait here, I need to get the chains to make this look believable. I will be right back." With a rushed walk, he disappears around the buildings.

The thought comes to mind, should I try to make a break for it? Are his feelings for me strong enough to let me go and claim that he lost me? This is my chance, I am alone, and no one seems to be watching, no Rosaleen, or Newlyn in sight. Will they really go after my mother and two sisters if I escape? They have bigger fish to fry. I must act now. I am going for it. I turn at a walk and exit the yard, passing through the gate at a casual pace. As soon as I am out of the yard I step right to get out of the site and run. It is an open field that has a gradual incline to the forest that is normally about a twenty-minute walk. I make a straight line to the cover of the forest. I hear nothing from Newlyn's home to indicate alarm, only the sound of the wind swooshing through the grass and the soft thump of my feet landing with each stride. I may succeed! Knowing how I have come across to my captors, as laid back and loyal, I think Sit will first assume that I may have gone back into Newlyn's home for something, if he thinks that, it will buy me time. I look back over my shoulder while keeping pace, there seems to be no signs of activity, or a chase, I will succeed, I run faster and without fatigue. My adrenaline is in full force; I am not winded from the sprint. Normally my leg muscles would be screaming at me by now. I glance over my shoulder and still nothing. I have been running for a while now and the forest is coming up fast. Wow, this is exhilarating; I am pulling this off. I reach the tree line and run straight in, not letting a second go to waste, and feeling safe, I slow to a walk. My heart rate slows and still curious about if I am being pursued, I peek through the branches to look back; weird still no action surely, they must know that I am gone it has been about ten minutes? Well, this is strange. I turn and sit down on the soft black mossy earth to regain my breath. My back is facing Newlyn's place, I can't put my finger on it. I had almost hoped that I would see signs of pursuit. The feeling of not seeing them is worse, at least if you see them, you know where they are and what you need to do. I lie back for a moment. The earth is cool, and my breathing slows. I let a sigh of relief escape me. Why didn't I had the confidence to do this sooner? The snort of a horse startles me; I turn to see a horse peering down at me and my heart stops.

Chapter 22
Just Kyle and Smarty

Imitating his mother, Kyle says to her, "Now I want you to call me as soon as you get home. I don't want to worry all night about you; you call me, you understand?"

Liz chuckles and gives Kyle a long heart felt hug, "Yes dear we will call as soon as we get in, I promise."

Roger says to Kyle, "Take care of yourself and call if you need anything."

"Yes Dad." Kyle's yes is dragged out and in a joking tone. Deep down Kyle is appreciative of his parents support through all of this. They say their goodbyes. Liz and Roger leave for home. It has been an extended stay for them with helping Kyle through his accident, the grieving process and the work that needed to be sorted after someone has passed. Kyle closes the door with Smarty in hand, as he peers out the side window looking at an empty driveway. He is at a loss with what to do with himself.

Smarty, realizing that something is off in Kyle starts to lick his hand, Kyle startles, putting the little dog down and goes to the kitchen looking for chores. Liz had already cleaned up after this morning's breakfast. The kitchen is spotless. Kyle goes to the bedroom where Liz and Roger have been staying. The bed has been made, and their room is clean. He looks outside, Roger cut the grass yesterday afternoon. His parents are wonderful guests, but they left Kyle nothing to keep himself busy.

Kyle decides that he hasn't taken his four-wheeler out in a while; maybe he can ride into town and grab an iced cream. He changes into some different clothes for the ride and goes to grab his helmet, opening the closet only to see that Robin's helmet is still placed on the top shelf. He grabs hers, holding it. All the rides and adventures they had shared; her screaming at the top of her lungs and holding him so tight as he sped up and down countless trails. The helmet smells of Robin, a combination of her sweat and the dirt from the trails. He can't do it, not today. He puts the helmet back and slams the closet door. One moment he is okay and the next he is brought right back into the realization that Robin is gone. Smarty scratches at this leg and whimpers.

"No Smarty." Kyle snaps at the little black dog and paces trying to pull it together. This is such a simple thing why can't I do it?

Kyle finally resorts to sitting on the couch to take a breather. He was fine when his parents were with him, helping him get through it all. He thought he was ready to do this on his own, but he knows in this moment that he can't.

After a long sit in silence, he turns off the television. Kyle decides and picks up the phone to make a call. He knows that a new contract should be ready and waiting for him with work.

"Hello, this is Charlene Mackhey speaking." It is Kyle's boss.

"Hi Charlene" Kyle says, clearing his throat.

"Oh, Kyle, how are you?" She asks, doing a poor job at hiding her surprise. She was not expecting his call for at least a couple more weeks.

"I'm okay," he lies. There is a pause. Kyle thinks about the words then says them aloud. "Charlene; I want to come back to work."

Silence again. Charlene says, "Oh, um well Kyle, that's great to hear, but are you sure you're…"

Kyle interrupts, "I want to come back now, my body is healed, I feel better I want to come back." Kyle still has some faint bruising.

"Well, um okay that's good to hear."

"Can I come back tomorrow? He asks.

Charlene takes a deep breath before answering, "Kyle, we weren't expecting you to be ready to return this soon, to be honest. Let me re-phrase that, we do have a contract that needs to be filled, and we had set it aside for you, anticipating that you would only be ready near the end of the month. If this is what you want to do, I will need to contact Human Resources and see what needs to be done first before you can return."

Kyle persists, "So how soon do you think?"

She answers carefully, "Let me place a call to Human Resources, I will do that today and find out what they need. We will not have it sorted out by tomorrow, but I am guessing it may take, two, or three days." Kyle sighs, but Charlene continues, "I will get this done for you, can I reach you at the number on my call display?"

This is better than staying by himself at home for another two or three weeks so he doesn't push it. Two, or three days is reasonable, Kyle confirms, "Yes, thank you Charlene."

Chapter 23
No Escape

"You could have told me that you wanted to go for a run, I would have accompanied you!" Sit shouts, exasperated. I look at the ground in defeat.

"How did you find me?" I ask; I don't have to say anymore. He knows what I am really implying which is; how did you find me without me seeing you coming?

Seeing the defeat and confusion on my face seems to amuse him, he chuckles mockingly, "Wouldn't you like to know? Someday I will tell you my secret, but not today." His horse is snorting and prancing on the spot. The beast seems excited to be out running and on the chase. Sit steadies his horse and dismounts. He grabs some handcuffs and small chains from a pack behind the saddle and approaches me.

"You know that I like you Taylan, and you already figured that I won't tell on you. If Newlyn, Rosaleen, or anyone on their side asks, I will simply tell them that I instructed you to run to build on to your story for Shaylo." He carefully approaches me; I am still sitting, defeated.

"You aren't going to try to run again?" Sit asks and I shake my head no; I am still catching my breath.

"Good" He says satisfied, "Now you are probably wondering what these handcuffs and chains are for?"

Shame and embarrassment must paint my face, deep down, I already know what the handcuffs are for, but I deny it to him. "No actually" Can he blame me for trying to get away? It wasn't a secret that, if I had stayed in the yard, I would have been locked up with Shaylo.

He regards me, "Don't play stupid, you know and besides, now I have a really good reason to use them, it's no longer just for the act." He grin's a fake smile; I can tell that he is slightly annoyed in the whole matter of me making a run for it and is acting as though I have made his work so much more difficult today. On the other hand, he is also annoyed that I didn't succeed in eluding him.

"Stand up, turn around." He orders, taking both my arms and putting the cuffs on, my hands are tied from behind. I can feel him securing a chain to the cuffs. He takes the other end of the chain, secures it to the saddle then mounts his horse, and barks at me, "We are heading back, keep on your feet, or else you will be dragged. The horse could startle, and I may not be quick enough to halt him."

"Is that a threat?" I ask. I get that half of this is the act and half of it is the truth. I ran. Would he really harm me?

"No honestly I am just stating the obvious." Sit answers coolly. He urges the horse forward to a nice walking pace. I follow along side. The first few minutes are in silence, walking out of the forest and into the field. Just the odd snort from the horse and the noise of his hooves hitting the ground, I break the silence, "Why do I feel like you are mad at me?"

"Because I am, you ran."

"What if I thought you were being a good friend and giving me my chance at freedom?" He did leave me alone.

Sit laughs, "If I was giving you a shot at freedom you would know." His eyes fall a few paces ahead of where his horse is headed.

"I'm sorry Sit, you've been good to me; I took off in the heat of the moment. I have only been within these circumstances for a brief time. All I wanted was to just go home and have everything go back to the way it was."

I catch him role his eyes as he asserts himself, "Heat of the moment, that's a load of crap, do you know what I'm really doing for you? I am trying to make this easier for you and am lying to Newlyn and whoever else, to convince them that your heat of the moment decision was all just part of the act. Do you realize that if they ever uncovered the truth, you would be punished?"

Angered, I raise my voice, "How much more harm could they inflict on me and my family? They separated us, forced some of us to work for them, forced me to kill another, and now I am being thrown into danger by being held captive, bound in chains?" He stops the horse. Sit jerks my chains hard forcing me closer to him and the beast. He asks, "Do you cherish your life? How about your sisters, do you cherish them? And your mother, do you cherish her well-being?"

I say nothing; he jerks the chain again, forcing a response from me. I murmur, "Yes."

"Rosaleen and Newlyn are probably the nicest masters you will ever encounter, they treat their servants fair and for the most part as equals, but never and I mean it, never cross them, it could be the last thing that you do." He pauses, gauging my reaction and continues, "Always remember that the people that are in power are there for a reason, and it wasn't because they were just nice." He looks into my eyes, "Don't let me down again, I trusted you today and you just threw it all to waste."

It is hard to look at him now, but I do, "Sit I am really sorry."

Even though he says nothing aloud after receiving my apology, I sense that he accepted it because the tension leaves him, and his body relaxes in the saddle. He nudges the horse on, and we continue in silence through the field. As I walk alongside, I step carefully in fear of tripping, it feels odd to walk with your hands behind your back, I don't think Sit would actually let me get dragged however the fear is more based on the fact that I don't have my hands as a buffer if I was to stumble. Neither of us are in a talking mood, we have both said what was needed. I am not really thinking of anything now and just focusing on one foot in front of the other and lose track of time and my inner voice during the silence. We make our way down to the entrance of the gates; Newlyn is out, sitting on the front porch and pretends not to notice us as we walk in. She has someone in her company, but it is no one I recognize. I hang my head in shame and embarrassment even though I don't have an audience watching me. I feel like an animal bound in chain. This is an entirely different level of treatment that I am experiencing right now, and even though this is supposed to be a cover, it eerily feels real. He continues to lead me, as soon as we are within the gates and around the back of the buildings, where the barn is, he dismounts. This home was built as a retreat but was used as Newlyn's exile. There are no dungeons, or jail cells per say, instead, they have used a couple of square box stalls that housed horses and converted them to jail cells. I see Shaylo immediately in a stall on the right, which is second to the end. She is up on her feet looking at us as we enter the barn. I notice our similarities. She is dressed in the same linen outfit as me, and she is about the same height and weight. Her hair is tied back into a simple ponytail. She watches us as we enter the space. She acknowledges Sit, "Master Sitrus" Weird; I thought his name was just Sit; Sitrus, what a strange name. Sit answers in his deep voice, "Good afternoon Shaylo." He leads his horse into a stall on the left with me following; I am still bound in chain to the saddle. He removes the saddle from the horse's back and then unbinds my chain from it. Showing no emotion, but instead just going through the motion of getting me placed in my new living quarters. He instructs me to enter the stall next to Shaylo's, closest to the exit. There are few words between us other than the orders he gives me. He removes my cuffs and exits the stall, locking it behind him. I take a seat on the cot that along the outer wall and listen. Later, I decide to get up and pay attention to everything that is going on around me. What if I have been fooled and this is real and not a cover? How am I going to get out of here? I did nothing wrong, why me? Sit goes to Shaylo's stall and opens it; he cuffs her hands and feet; it is done without any objection. It's routine for them. He orders her, "See to his stall." Referring to the horse's stall, Shaylo goes to work, without any hesitation and picks up a wheelbarrow and shovel that are kept off to the side down the aisle. Sit is at work polishing the horse's saddle and tack, then shortly brings the horse back out into the aisle and gives the beast a grooming. Shaylo finishes with the stall. They seem so coordinated, finishing each task at about the same time. Sit puts the horse in his freshly cleaned stall that is filled with grain, hay, and water. At this point, I am silent saying nothing, only watching. Sit says without any warmth in his voice to Shaylo, "I will take you to your bath now."

Shaylo answers, "Is my new cell mate joining us?" For a prisoner, her spirit seems unbroken, which comes as a surprise because the impression I got from the others was that she was terribly upset with her currant living arrangement.

Sit answers her, "No not today, come Shaylo."

They both leave and I am alone, well not completely, the horse is across from me, enjoying his meal, all I can see is the top part of his face, his muzzle is in his food dish, I can hear him chewing on his meal and smell the sweetness of the grain. I gauge my new living quarters. The stall is a perfect square shape, and there are thick wood panels that make the frame. The wood planks stop at about my chest and from my chest to the ceiling, the stall is composed of vertical bars. The difference between the horse's stall across from me and my prison cell, is that my cell, the ceiling of the box stall is fitted with chain fencing and the horse stall has an open ceiling. I run my hand along the wood walls as I walk the parameter. It is the early evening, just before supper, and I decide that I need to put the strategizing aside and rest. I just don't care. I go to the cot and climb under the sheets. It is small, but comfortable; I close my eyes and fall asleep for the night.

Chapter 24
An Unlikely Friend

"Hey" I hear in a whisper; I open my eyes. For a split second, I forget where I am, but it all comes back to me. "Hey are you awake?" I recognize the voice. It is Shaylo. I roll over, close my eyes, and pretend to be asleep.

"Hey, I know you are awake and besides it's rude; what you are doing isn't a very good first impression." Shaylo sounds annoyed. I sigh and roll over on my back and open my eyes. Let's face it; I won't be able to fall back asleep especially when you know someone else's eyes are on you. I look over and there she is looking back at me with both of her hands clasping the bars. At first sight, she is just a shadow figure; my eyes are adjusting to the light. I look over at her and things slowly come into focus; she is in the same linen jumper that I saw her in earlier only it is now clean. Her eyes are a deep brown, and she has a narrow, but beautiful face.

I look at her and say, "I'm awake" however, not being able to hold back a yawn.

She looks disappointed that I am still in a groggy state "You slept all night. Why are you so tired?"

"I have had a bit of a rough time lately." I sit up on the cot and rub my eyes. To be honest this wasn't how I was expecting this first encounter with her to be, I was expecting an evil villain with a negative personality to go with it, and right now, I have a very curious companion who seems interested in being aquatinted with me. This could be an act, but whatever it is, it does seem genuine, and I am compelled to get to know her also, but not just for Rosaleen and Newlyn's reasons. I have a feeling there is more than one side to everything.

I look up at her from my cot, "You are Shaylo." I confirm with her.

"Yes, and you are Taylan." She replies and I nod.

"Master Sitrus told me a bit about you. You tried to escape a couple of times." She half says it to confirm the truth, but also says it in a questioning tone. I simply nod yes, and she erupts into laughter.

"What's so funny?" I ask.

"Nothing" She answers.

"No, tell me." I insist.

Shaylo catches her breath and pulls herself together, "If you are ever going to try to escape again make sure that you're not going to get caught." She says holding back a chuckle her eyes are twinkling from her laughing fit.

"I thought I was going to succeed." I answer meekly; I feel a little stupid.

"You obviously acted on an impulse, especially the run attempt that you tried on Master Sitrus yesterday. You need to think about it, it can't be an impulsive thing. The people who have you caged up are expert planners, and one needs to anticipate their moves before you go making yours. Think about all the repercussions that will follow should you want to carry out another escape." Shaylo explains with certainty.

"How would you know all of this?" I ask, trying to keep my criticism in check.

"When you observe, you come to know things." She removes her hands off the bars and paces her enclosure, continuing, "I know about you from the nuggets of information Master Sitrus has given me yesterday evening.

I know enough to realize that he has an agenda to follow, and you have your own." I must admit that this woman is coming off as highly intelligent, and I get the impression that she knows how to play a good social game to get what she wants. Shaylo continues, seeming almost overconfident with herself, "Now Taylan, you're locked up here with me which means that we share a common enemy tell me, what you want in this very moment?"

I hesitate and then decide that it is probably best to answer, "Shaylo, I mean no offense, but after what you just shared with me how do I know you aren't just one of Newlyn's servants who were put in here to keep an eye on me and report anything of importance to your Master Sitrus?"

She grins and claps her hands in reaction to my point, "Well thought, maybe you are a good observer; you just act stupidly, that's all." She winks.

I change topics. I don't want to get into the gritty stuff with her at this point. I have been instructed to fool her and they instructed her to do the same with me? "What's your typical day like here?" I gesture at the fact that we are both locked up.

She explains, "In about an hour Master Sitrus will feed us, and we are then to feed and care for all of the animals, after that it is mostly various forms of housekeeping chores." It is a busy workday, and I think the true definition of what it means to be a servant. Shaylo goes into more detail, explaining where she goes during the day and where they take her.

I interrupt, "Did Sit, I mean Master Sitrus tell you that I would be helping you today?"

Shaylo looks at me quizzically, "Sit? You refer to him with a nickname?"

She searches me for a reaction. For what, I don't know but I quickly respond, "I thought that Sit was his name because that's what I heard others refer to him as."

Shaylo scratches her head and looks at me for a long moment, but was a couple of seconds, "I can see how you would think that, yes Master Sitrus mentioned that I would have your help today with all the chores. Please don't think about trying to escape because I could use the help." Shaylo answers with a hint of threat in her voice, but I don't care. I am relieved that she disregarded that little slip up. I wouldn't imagine running at this point. I have already tried it once, and if I do have people who are on my side, I wouldn't want to jeopardize those relationships. I think Sit is on my side, and I think Rosaleen and Newlyn want me on their side, and from what I gather from Shaylo, she wants me as some sort of comrade. I am going to have to take a step back to observe and then make a choice on what is best for me. The lines are a little blurred right now. We quietly talk for what feels like an hour and cover topics like where we are from, our families, hobbies, and even trivial things like our favorite foods. Shaylo comes from a small community that is like where I grew up. Despite what I had assumed, I thought she was a socialite that enjoyed the many lavishes of palace life. She is an accomplished hunter and tracker; hunting is her hobby of choice, but she has not done it since living within the palace walls although while there she has practiced on dummy targets. Shaylo said that she had both her parents growing up, but they have passed on, and she had one brother who had passed away while in combat. I noticed that she didn't bring up her husband, but it doesn't matter since I think I understand how she came to be in the company of Rosaleen. Shaylo obviously married into the socialite role with her husband being a close ally to the imposture King Wolfrim and made her way into being an advisor for a Princess.

The barn door opens, letting the sunlight in as well as Sitrus. He hands some bread and an apple through the bars to each of us, letting us eat before we begin to work. Sitrus opens Shaylo's stall first and then mine. He whispers in my ear "Don't plan on doing anything silly?" He warns.

I glance up and murmur, "No Sitrus."

He corrects me, "Master Sitrus."

I glance up at him through my eyelashes "Sorry Sir, Master Sitrus." With my apology, he pats my back, and I feel compelled to walk towards Shaylo and wait for Sitrus's instructions.

"Okay ladies, first things first, feed and let the horses out to pasture. Come back and clean out the barn. That should bring you to lunch. Join me in the servants' kitchen, and for the afternoon, you are going to the berry fields to pick four baskets worth. Newlyn has asked for jellies to be made and pastries." We nod and with that, Sitrus leaves.

I look at Shaylo and ask, "He doesn't stay and watch over us?"

She looks at me "No, he doesn't stay with us, he has other obligations, but that doesn't mean that no one is watching."

I ask, "What do you mean, I don't see anyone else here."

Shaylo brings her voice down and says, "Just outside this barn we have a watcher, you will see him."

She glances outside the door. I whisper, "I understand, I didn't know."

She replies in a hush "That's because you don't pay attention." With that, she walks to the feed room in the barn and starts to fill several buckets with a scoop of grain for each of the horses. I reflect, Saydira once told me that. I guess that is a fault of mine. I was watched yesterday and that is how Sit found me so quickly? I need to focus today and be observant of my surroundings of everything if I am going to play this game.

I help Shaylo carry the water and feed buckets to each of the stalls and then as a horse finishes feeding, we put a halter on them and lead them out to the field. I have never done this before and Shaylo teaches me as we go. I try to stay as observant as I can by glancing around the area to see who the watcher is, so far, I don't see anyone. I don't have the feeling that we are being watched even though Shaylo has said otherwise. It just feels like it is only Shaylo the horses and me. We let the horse go into the pale green grassy field and return to the barn for the next one only this time we will be walking two horses now that she has shown me how to do it. Shaylo starts up on a new conversation. "So, what is the deal with you and Master Sitrus?"

I answer, "What do you mean?" pretending that I don't know what she is hinting at.

She chuckles, "I'm not stupid, and I know there is something that is going on between the two of you. I'm older than you and have seen this before." My heart stops. I don't say anything, I can't; I don't know what to say. She asks me, "Have you ever loved a man before?" Is she going to tell me that she knows what happened to Shrago if I open up?

I swallow, "Um no, I have never loved a man."

She asks, "You're what eighteen years old and you never had a relationship?" I shake my head no and she says, "No suitors from where you lived?"

I answer, "No, it was a small community and a lot of the people who would have become suitors, when they became of age were already called upon to serve."

She nods "I see, well I suppose that will soon change. I can see that Master Sitrus has eyes for you, and it is clear to me that you have feelings for him." She laughs and shakes her head. "You youngsters are so foolish. You have feelings for your captor, oh what it's like to be young and full of hormones."

I say, "Well what does it matter? It doesn't change the fact that I am a prisoner." I take a breath and try to change subject, "So how come he didn't put chains on us this morning, but last night he chained you while you were out of the stall?"

Shaylo raises an eyebrow at me and starts with answering my first comment, "You are such a stupid girl; of course, him having feelings for you changes things. Sooner than later, he is going to demand more of you other than the chores he is asking you to do now." She pauses and smirks, "Take advantage and you will get what you want. As for the chains, I am only bound when I am taken to the baths or taken within proximity of Newlyn."

I comment, "You're lying about the idea of getting what you want. If that is so, why have you not tried to fulfill any?"

Shaylo quickly becomes cross, grabs me by the collar, pulling me close and through clenched teeth while on the grassy pathway she explains, "Before I became a prisoner I lived a lavish life within the Palace, I held one of the most desirable positions within the Kingdom. Now how is it that you think that someone like me, who came from the same upbringing as you, came into that position?" She shakes me, "Answer me." She demands.

I murmur, "You gave someone what he wanted?"

Shaylo whispers back "Precisely!"

I regain my footing as she lets go, "I don't think Master Sitrus is like that."

She snaps back, "and why would you think that?"

"Because, I just don't get that feeling about him," I answer.

She laughs, "You are such a credulous girl. Tell me, do you want to be locked up forever?"

I sigh, "No"

"That makes two of us. Master Sitrus clearly has something for you, and I think we can use that to our advantage to get out of here." She pauses, "Let me think something up."

We head back to the barn for two more horses. I figure now is the time to ask her about the people within the Palace to gather information for Rosaleen and Newlyn. "Shaylo will someone be coming to your rescue?" I dive right into it. She has been trapped long enough for people to take notice, friend's, anyone who is on her side and besides Shrago; Shaylo doesn't know what I know.

She glares at me, "You can't expect others to come to your aide immediately, sometimes your captures are one step ahead of you, and for me, they are I have to admit; besides that's the only reason why I am still here." I know that Shaylo is referring to Princess Rosaleen's ship. Everyone from the Palace and ship believes what the princess feeds them. That Shaylo is gone for an extended period. There is absolutely no alarm, and no one is aware from the Palace that Shaylo has been imprisoned and in Newlyn's hands, or for the people at the Palace they don't know that Shrago has been killed. The way that Shaylo answered leads me to believe that she only had Shrago. If she had an ally on the ship, it should have gotten back to the Palace. We walk back from the fields to the barn to clean out the stalls. This is good news for Newlyn and Rosaleen. I am convinced that all Shaylo had was Shrago. I feel like I made some headway this morning with gaining a bit of insight and then there is the whole Sitrus situation. I don't even know if he was sincere with all he has shared with me, or if he is playing me, lines are becoming blurred. I guess if Shaylo is certain that this man has feelings for me than I guess he was being true and now what do I do about it? I do like him even though I am supposed to be acting as his prisoner, but I think that I am in the clear on allowing some feelings for him to show besides, Shaylo can tell that there is something there. I believe that Shaylo believes I am a prisoner, and she is hinting at me to expect and use affections from Sit for some gain that she is working out in her mind right now. I am in the perfect position; both sides believe me to be on their side. We finish the stalls and meet Sitrus for lunch. The conversation during lunch is light, and we are given our afternoon chores.

Shaylo and I retire from lunch and head out to the berry fields to fill our baskets. Shaylo asks me, "So Taylan have you figured out who is watching us?" She asks.

I forgot to keep a look out and look all around me for a sign as to who it is, "I have no idea."

She chuckles, "Even after this morning's discussion you still don't pay attention."

I snap, "I do pay attention!"

She comes back, "No you don't, if you did you would know who."

I look around the open field. I look to the tree line for signs of movement, nothing. I see nothing when looking back towards Newlyn's. I decide to glance up in the sky, which is when I see someone soaring high above us. They are a little hard to spot because of the reflective solar suit that they are wearing; the thing that gives them away is the random flicker of the sun's rays reflecting from it. It is hard to make out who it is, but from the outline of the body, my guess is that it is a child. Sid, the boy who greeted Rosaleen and me the day we had pulled up on the solar bike. I had not really seen him since. I reply, "I see now."

She answers, "He is the eyes and ears for Newlyn, and he is tasked with keeping watch. He has been tracking me ever since I have become a prisoner here."

I ask, "Have you ever spoke to him?"

"A bit, but he hasn't slipped up and given away any information that would help me. He is a child, and his masters don't tell him everything, they only provide him with what he needs to know. I would love to get my hands on one of those flying suits, but he knows well enough to keep a safe distance from me."

I ask, "Has he ever reported to you on other things that he observes?"

She smiles, "Yes, he talked of when you showed up and mentioned when he saw a wild animal in the area. Come to think of it I have been meaning to ask; why do you think that Rosaleen and Newlyn didn't imprison you upon arrival?"

Shaylo is seeking truth; I remember my lesson with Sitrus, keep steady eye contact and deny any knowing, I pause, pretending to give it some thought and reply, "I have no idea, I didn't know that they actually had horse stalls being used as prison cells here. I thought that the extent of my capture was just that I was being closely watched. Someone was always by my side, and I was locked in a bedroom at night. The only time I was left alone was when I made a run for it." I must be pretty dam convincing because it's kind of is the truth. The thing that kind of messes' things up is Sid mentioned me to her, and Sitrus believed that Shaylo had no knowledge of me, prior to us meeting. Now I know that it was not the case. Shaylo is always watching me, reading my body language; the expression on her face does make me feel a little nervous.

She says, "Why do I feel like you are holding something back?" She is upfront, her brown eyes peer into mine for answers.

I am beginning to feel intimidated, but stand my ground, "I'm not sure. Why do I always feel like I am being stared down whenever you ask me a question?"

Shaylo gives me a long look, and I am not sure how, but she decides that I was just being funny, letting out a hearty laugh. I cannot tell if she is being sarcastic, or true in her reaction, she says, "you have a point Taylan. I will try not to stare you down. It's my nature to look out for myself and to me, everyone is sort of my enemy until I am convinced otherwise."

I don't share in the laughter, but instead change focus from me to her, "How do I know that you are on my side?"

She shrugs, "That is easy we both have a common enemy, we will need to work together to get what we want." I nod, agreeing with her. We finish in the field and head back to the house to meet Sitrus and hand in the harvest.

We help with washing and cleaning our berries in the servant's kitchen. Sitrus escorts us back to the stable for the night. Shaylo and I enter our stalls and Sitrus locks the doors. It has been a full day, I am still in the same linen clothes that I first put on before meeting Shaylo, and to top it off, Sitrus has yet to question me on the information that I have gathered. I feel so filthy from cleaning up horse crap and working out in the field. I was really expecting a bath;

as Shaylo had received the night, I met her. I was hoping for a break from all of this, to talk to Sitrus. I quietly and slowly pace the stall. Is he going to call on me to bathe? Do I retire to my cot and sleep in this state of filthiness? I look around the barn. Sitrus is already gone. I feel so grubby and decide to strip out of my linen outfit, I am completely naked and using the water bucket in my stall, I wipe myself down, washing away all the dirt and sweat with the cool water. It turns out to be soothing and I feel a bit cleaner. I dunk my head into the water bucket to soak my hair to rid it of sweat and dust. The shock of the cool water wakes me up and carefully, I run my fingers through my submerged hair and lift my head from the bucket to ring the excess water back into the bucket. I dunk my linen outfit into the water, scrub the fabric together, remove the garments once soaked, and drape them through the bars. Who needs a hot bath when you have a water pail full of freezing water? The water in the bucket is now a brown opaque and I just let it sit there. I don't want to soak the floor to my pen tonight. I drip dry, still pacing the stall calmly while running my fingers through my hair like a brush; it gives me something to do to pass the time. I look towards Shaylo's stall. She has been so quiet. She is just being courteous, giving me some privacy.

I walk over and peek through the bars to find that she is resting on her cot. Her eyes are closed. I can tell she isn't quite asleep, more just relaxing. I break the silence, "Hey Shaylo how often does Sitrus bathe you?"

She is lying on her back and just tilts her head in my direction, opening her eyes slowly, the way that you would if you were lying on the beach in the sun. "I would say that he lets me bathe once every three to four days."

"Three to four days?" I say in surprise, "Really?"

She chuckles, "Yes really, why are you surprised?" Her eyes are now looking upon me intently.

I look away, I am not sure why, but I am a little embarrassed, I can feel the skin on my chest and face flush; "Well it's just that, you seem so clean. I mean I know that you had a proper bath the night before, but even when I saw you briefly before you were called upon to wash, you didn't seem, well, dirty."

She rolls over onto her stomach and looks up at me, clearly amused. It is the fact that she senses my chagrin, "You know that I don't rely on Master Sitrus in order to bathe." She pauses clearly amused by something that I don't know, "If you wanted to wash you should have said something."

"What do you mean?" I am completely confused.

"Just ask next time." She lifts the edge of her mattress, motioning to a bar of soap.

Annoyed I ask, "Why didn't you say anything, you knew that I was trying to wash myself?"

She smiles and shrugs as if it is no big deal, "You never asked." She has the nerve to make a silly face at me.

I am cold, wet and don't want to play, or making jabs at her, "Whatever, next time I'll ask for yours if I don't snatch my own bar in the time being." Sit isn't too observant, or he is and dismisses it because it benefits him with having to spend less time with his prisoners.

I am almost dry. My hair is damp, so I decide to wrap myself in the sheet from my cot since my outfit is hanging to dry. I lay down for the night. I'm not quite sure when I drifted off, I have a feeling that I fell asleep quickly because I don't recall tossing and turning much. It must be the middle of the night. I feel a nudge to my side that wakes me.

Chapter 25
Awake in the Darkness

My eyes are wide open; adjusting to the darkness, there crouched beside me is a silhouette of someone gesturing for me to keep quiet with their finger held to their lip. They gesture me to follow them. I do so without even thinking twice about it, despite Shaylo's mention of planning the proper escape. Very quietly, we exit the barn and creep outside of Newlyn's gates, my night visitor turns to face me, and without a word, or hesitation they pull me into a passionate kiss. Sit holds me close in his warm embrace; it feels so soothing like the feeling you get when you are home. This is my first kiss. To be honest, I never really paid much attention to anyone before having met Sitrus. The warmth of him feels so sweet and inviting; I realize that I am still completely naked; I left my sheet on the cot. Sit takes my hand and leads me down the path to the ocean, periodically glancing back at me, making sure that I don't miss a step.

He smirks at me, "Where are your clothes?"

I decide to play it casual and shrug, "I knew you would break me out of my pen for a night swim."

Knowing that I am being sarcastic he replies, "I see, what else do you care to tell me?"

I hesitate and look up to the dark sky for inspiration, but nothing creative comes to me. "I don't know. I didn't think you felt so strongly about me?"

He looks at me, memorizing every feature of my face, "These things just sort of happen."

I can't get that weird discussion with Newlyn out of my head when she was hinting that I should start expanding on my relationship skills, which then followed with Sit, conveniently showing up in my bedroom shortly after, "Did Newlyn put you up to this, to break me in so to speak?"

He chuckles, "She asked me to help you get aquatinted with me and with Shaylo."

"And?" my eyebrows furrow.

"Newlyn bid it, but this side you see is me, it's not an act; come with me."

He leads me into the ocean after he has completely stripped down. I did not see it initially, but he has a bar of soap. We go in together about waist deep and wade in the water, just as we did the other day. He is so gentle, it is quite soothing, starting with my shoulders and hair and working his way over my entire body. He massages and I feel relaxed and safe in his arms. He turns me to face him.

"How is that?" He asks.

"Relaxing" I smile shyly; this is all new to me.

"Good" He smiles; he is down on one knee in the water and has me leaning on his bent knee as he holds me steady. He keeps his gaze while handing over the bar of soap. "I want you to do the same thing." What? He wants me to wash him. He gestures saying, "It is okay." He encourages in a whisper.

I change positions and slowly glide in the water so that I am now behind him. I start by washing his shoulders, then slowly lathering up his hair and running my fingers all over his body, massaging him thoroughly. I take my time and make sure that I am gentle. I am uncertain of the web that I am in so I do what I can to make sure that this moment in time is special so that he knows I care for him. I don't think I will ever get used to this. I have feelings for him, but he is my master. I am posing as his prisoner, the catch; Shaylo knows that I like him. She can tell that he likes me, but her spin on things is that I should take advantage of his feelings and use it to escape with Shaylo. The truth is that I don't know which option to decide on so instead, I am going to continue to play both sides. This intimate moment together ends in the dark of night in the warm ocean water and after we just wade in the shallows.

"Now down to business" Sitrus says, "What did Shaylo share?" Sitrus waits, confident that I am dedicated to this cause.

"Well, your plan has worked so far. I believe that Shaylo is convinced that I am in the exact same predicament as her. I feel that she believes that I am also a prisoner."

He nods, clearly satisfied with the news, "Well that's good to hear. So, you have gotten over that obstacle, please continue."

"It sounds as though she only had Shrago as an ally on Rosaleen's ship."

"Why do you think that?" He asks.

I answer, "Because; Shaylo explained the reason why she feels that no one has come to her rescue."

Sit seeming happy with this information asks, "What did she say?"

"Shaylo feels that if her acquaintances in the Palace knew the truth of her situation that she is certain she would have already been rescued. If she did have other allies on the ship other than Shrago, regardless that the ship is no longer here and still far away from the Palace, there would have been plenty of opportunity for allies to leave the ship to aide in her rescue and seek revenge for Shrago." This is logic to me, and I stand by my opinion, and continue with my reasoning, "If Shaylo was lying, then why hasn't Shaylo been rescued, or at the least have anyone ask about her whereabouts."

Sit seems to agree with my hunch, "That's a good point; Newlyn suspected that this was the case. The truth is that there has been absolutely no one that has come looking for her, or any suspicious sightings of strangers in the area." Sitrus pauses then asks, "Did Shaylo say anything else?" I continue explaining her background, where she grew up and how she came to be a part of the Palace. I try to talk to him as much as possible to make it seem that I am not leaving out any details; I left out the part of an escape plan. I don't want him to suspect and possibly share with Newlyn; I can't risk having more eyes on us, or risk being trapped forever. We already have that boy Sid watching us from a far, that is hard enough as it is, and from what I can tell once we are locked up in the stable there are no watchers. I want to ask Sit if we are being watched throughout the night but decide otherwise. I don't want to draw suspicion in the relationship that we are developing.

"You have far exceeded my expectations Taylan." He lifts me into his arms, carries me to the shore, setting me down near to the pile of his clothes and then realizing that something is amiss. "Oh yah, you have no clothes." I nod.

"Remind me, why where you naked?" Sit asks with a smirk.

"I tried to bathe myself." He makes a face, and I shove him.

He laughs while saying, "I'm just kidding with you. Well, do you feel better now that you have had a real bath with actual soap?" I smile and nod. "Well good, we should get you back to your pen; I can't have this raise any suspicions." I say nothing, feeling a bit of disappointment. I miss feeling normal, clean, and not being treated like an animal.

Quietly, we head back through the gates of Newlyn's and down the path around the servants' house to the barn. Sit quietly opens the barn door and we both slip in. He opens the stall door and motions me in after reaching into his pant pocket and uncovering a key, the lock on my door seems to have been clicked shut he opens the lock with his key and then clicks the lock shut once I am in. I just look at him, watching as he takes no notice of me, my guess is, he is avoiding eye contact on purpose, just in case Shaylo is watching, it is still the middle of the night. I would imagine that there are a few hours before sunrise. My eyes have long ago adjusted to the darkness, and I can make out his figure moving as quietly as a cat. He says nothing and just quietly exits the barn.

Unfortunately, I am wide-awake and a mess of emotions. This is not a game. This is my life. I am stuck in the middle of someone else's battle but, so, is he? I touch my clothes that are still where I left them hanging to dry. All I feel is just a few damp spots, so I re-adjust them by flipping the fabric over to dry and retire to my cot.

My eyes close, I should take back the wide-awake feeling that I had just mentioned because my fatigue quickly takes over and I slip away.

I am not sure how long I had drifted off for, but I hear a sound, and it is not coming from Shaylo's stall, its closer. Someone is in my stall.

Chapter 26
A Whisper and Warm Hand

My eyes are darting around my stall; I hold my breath, trying to figure out where the sound came from. A gentle touch of a warm slender hand rests on my forearm.

A whisper, "Sorry Taylan, I didn't mean to startle you."

I sit up, "Shaylo, how did you get in here?"

"I've been working on the screws with a modified twig and managed to loosen the ones in the corner. I slid a couple of the boards out to crawl in, see?" She points to a corner of the wall that we share.

I gasp, feeling partly excited at the idea of leaving and partly because I will need to pick sides, "Oh Shaylo that is great, do you think you could do that to one of the stall doors?"

She hesitates, looking at the door in my space, studying it, "Well, yes I can, but the only problem is that it takes time to unscrew using a twig, by the time I manage, it could mean wasted hours."

"Good point." I pause for a second and ask, "Well you managed the soap, what about getting real tools?"

She shrugs, "I already thought about that, we have access, but not that much. I thought about trying to hold onto a knife or something from the kitchen, but unfortunately, I have yet to have the opportunity and the strength of going head-to-head with Sitrus. It is not an option; he is too strong for me especially with him being rested while I am constantly worn down with work. If I were to succeed it would be a run, and there is only so much running you can do which is pointless if you don't have a good head start." I sigh, feeling like the idea of freedom just deflated right before me.

She sits on the cot beside me and nudges me with her elbow, "So I guess I was right, did you please him?"

I roll my eyes though she doesn't notice because of the darkness, "Yes I think he was happy."

Sounding satisfied she answers, "Stay on his good side and continue to make him want you. Did you notice anything useful that we can use?"

I ponder aloud, "I saw the grounds with him, but saw nothing new that I needed to make a mental note of, wait a second, yes actually, when we returned, I noticed that he keeps the key to my stall in his pant pocket."

Shaylo keeps her voice to a whisper, but I can feel her excitement with this news, "Excellent, that's our freedom right there. We have access to each other and now we have access to your key. It won't be hard for you to slip into his pocket and take it, right?"

I answer, "Yes, I think I can manage that, but when we came back the lock was shut. He needed the key to open it."

She shrugs, "We just must break him of the habit of locking it when you are not in the stall, and we can trick him into thinking it's locked. In the morning when he lets us out, we will just set the locks to make them appear that they are locked that way he won't need to reach for his keys."

"I think that's a stretch." I say.

"Well, it doesn't hurt to try." Shaylo suggests.

"Sure, I'll give it a go." I answer.

"Good, well the only part that is left is putting distance between us and them; I still need to plan something out.

Until I say so, if he calls on you don't go after the key until I say, got it?"

I respond, "Yes I understand."

"Tomorrow morning, we will see if our attention to the locks work, anyway, it's late and we both should rest, good night."

"Night Shaylo" She gets up, crawls through the opening, back to her stall, and puts the boards back in place leaving the screws loose. I roll over onto my side and curl up under my sheet, closing my eyes. Sleep comes immediately, but so does the dawn.

It feels as though I have only been asleep for a few minutes, but it has been a couple of hours. It is the same routine as the day before, caring for the horses and cleaning their stalls. When Sitrus was not looking Shaylo and I succeed in flipping the locks to make them appear as though they were shut, and to my surprise, it worked. He glanced at them just before leaving the barn but did not proceed in checking.

Shaylo asks while sweeping, "You have been really quiet all morning, or is it shyness I suspect, how was he?"

I follow her with my own broom and blush, "I'm not being shy, it's just that this is all messed up, and to answer your question he was kind and caring."

"Oh, come on Taylan out with the details." She urges.

I shrug, "He took me to the beach, everything happened in the water, in the moonlight."

She gushes, "I had a feeling he was a romantic."

I smile, "It really was nice. When I was with him, I forgot about this reality for a bit, I felt like myself again and not a prisoner."

Shaylo stops for a second and looks over to me, "Just keep him happy, don't you worry about how you feel, and we may possibly succeed, and Taylan don't kid yourself. You are his prisoner."

"Yes Shaylo." I roll my eyes and then go back to work.

The morning is slow, there is nothing different except for our conversations, we are learning more about one another, "Shaylo what do you think will eventually happen to us if we end up never escaping?"

"I think that they will just continue to use us for labor and whatever else they can think of."

"If we try to escape and they end up catching us then what do you think will happen?" I ask.

She sighs, "I'm not sure that they would treat us the same. I think they would give you a chance, Sitrus has feelings for you and Newlyn favors Sitrus but for me well, I think that they would kill me."

I ask, "How sure do you feel about that?"

"Well for starters I have separated Mother and Daughter for many years, Newlyn and Rosaleen hate me for that and the second reason is I am a liability to their plans."

I hesitate, "What do you mean by plans?" Secretly, I know, and I just want to hear it from Shaylo.

"They are keeping me because they don't want me to go back to King Wolfrim and inform him that Rosaleen knows everything."

I consider what I am about to say, "Are they correct with their suspicions, would you actually go back and tell Wolfrim?"

She looks around and then back at me and in a deep voice and reveals, "Yes without a doubt."

"Why wouldn't you just run somewhere far away from these families, this mess and start a new life without all of the drama?"

The emotions start flowing in her and I am not sure why, but she is upset about this. She looks at me in a way that her eyes pierce into my own. Her cheeks flush. She walks over to me at a steady purposeful pace and stops. We are face-to-face and eye-to-eye. I return her gaze only mine must be of confusion and with a single, swift motion; she slaps me hard across the face. It stings; I try to sooth it by putting my own hand to my cheek.

"You are such a stupid girl!" Shaylo is trembling with anger and has nowhere to go so she just retreats to her stall. I decide not to even try to sooth her, there is no point right now, I need to give her space, and continue with the chores alone for the rest of the day.

The only thing that makes sense for the reason she is upset is I think she believes that Shrago is still alive. Shaylo must think that if she gets to the king first, that it could be an opportunity to get her husband back before something happens to him. The only thing wrong with that is it is too late for Shrago. There is no mistake that her husband was a monster. My neck is pretty well healed after Shrago attacked me, but even with me knowing firsthand who Shrago was, I still feel sorry for seeing Shaylo so upset. Everyone is loved by someone. Even the monsters are loved.

I am going to keep Shrago's death a secret from her, for now anyway. I think that even if I told her the truth that she would not back down, she would still try to escape and run back, so really what is the point? I rather remain on her good side.

I work on all the chores for the rest of the morning and then meet Sit for lunch in the servants' kitchen.

I receive a cold greeting from Sit, "You're late."

I hate the tone he is giving me; it drives me bonkers, this entire act, "Yes" I reply, "and I am sure that you already know why besides, you don't need to act this way it's only me and you here."

He nods, "I don't, but it is still no excuse to be late." He has lunch already put together for both of us. I join him at the table.

"So, you are going to be on your own for the afternoon?" He is chewing a mouthful of food and reaches for his glass to sip his cool beverage.

"Yes, I guess? Isn't she your prisoner? Why are you letting her get away with not doing anything?"

He looks at me with an intimidating stare, "That is none of your business."

I decide not to add to this discussion. I don't see the point for the act that Sit is putting on. Instead, I remain silent, I am not going to pick fights and give him a piece of my mind for the way that he is talking to me, and he knows that I have checked out. If he wants to be like this for no reason, go ahead, I won't forget this.

He changes topic, "Have you ever ridden a horse?"

"No," Wow just like that, he is changing the subject, or more ignoring the tension.

"You are going to learn after lunch. I will teach you."

"Why?" I ask.

"Because you live with them, may as well learn to use them." We finish and head out to the fields where the animals had been let out to graze. Sitrus quickly runs ahead to a side door of the barn, grabs some leather straps, and runs back over to meet me. He makes sure to keep me far away from the stables, my guess that the reason is to keep out of sight of Shaylo.

"So how do you know Shaylo is actually locked up in her stall?" For all we know she could have decided to do her own thing instead of sulk.

"I know this because Newlyn actually paid her a visit today."

"Oh wow, it must have been a big deal?"

"Yes, it becomes a big deal when you stop taking orders."

Sit picks the tall black horse, the same one he used to chase me, leading him. "Despite his size this one is very gentle and cares for his riders, you are going to learn with him today." I gently touch the animal's velvet muzzle.

"So, first things first, your equipment, you put this into his mouth and slip the leather straps over his head like this." He equips the horse's bridle and then places the reins so that they are resting on the top of the animal's neck. "You check to make sure that it's not too tight, or too loose with your fingers, like this." He shows me different points of the bridle and sticks a finger between the straps that are on the horse's head to show me how much space there should be. "Now I'll give you a leg up." Immediately he picks me up and sits me on the horse's back.

I look down at him, "No saddle?"

"There is no need, this is just a lesson and you're not going anywhere with him." He has a point. A conversation I had with Shaylo immediately comes to mind; despite Shaylo being upset, right now I still consider her opinions. She warned me not to make a run for it unless I was sure that I would get away and right now, I don't think I could get far. I still don't know how to ride. If I take off after learning, who is to say that Sit wouldn't just jump onto another horse in the field and follow? He clips a long rope to the horse's bridle and then asks, "How do you feel?"

"I feel a little nervous about slipping off."

"We will take it one step at a time. I need you to relax all the muscles in your body, let your legs relax so that they extend on either side. You're not going to touch the reins just yet; instead, I want you to just let your arms rest to either side." I follow his instruction. He asks "ready?" I nod and he chirps at the horse. We start moving in a circle. Sit is standing in the center, holding the rope that is attached to the bridle of the dark horse. My immediate reaction without realizing is I clench my calf muscles and hold my breath.

"Breathe!" He shouts at me, "Relax your body, you are tensing up." I do what I am told even though my natural reaction is to hold onto this horse with every muscle. "I know that you want to hold onto him, but when this horse changes to a trot, or gallop you will fall right off. Relax, keep repeating that to yourself and breathe!" Sitrus has the horse walk for a bit and then he guides the horse to change direction. We walk, stop, and walk for a bit longer until Sit is satisfied that I look comfortable. He then warns me of the change in pace and brings the horse to a trot. This is hard, I feel like I am bouncing all over the place, he shouts at me some more. "Relax, your legs are tightening up, breathe!" I quickly react and instantly feel a bit more balanced. My butt is still thumping on the horse's back, but it's not as harsh as it was when I was tensing up. Sit quietly works with keeping the horse at a steady pace for me to get used to the movement, before long he has the horse moving at a cantor. Cantor is much easier than trot because the horse takes the movement of a rocking motion. Eventually he brings the horse to a stop. "Very good, you're a fast learner." I smile.

"Okay so next is steering the beast. You use these reins to help steer. Gently pull right to go right and left to go left.

You pull gently with both sides to bring him to a stop or slow him. Your legs are used for steering also. As you are pulling for the direction, you wish to go in, apply pressure in your leg to direct him in that direction. So, if you want to go right you pull on the right rein and keep you right leg snug and straight to support him in the turn and you take your left and move it slightly behind to encourage him to bend his body in the turn. You are going to do that to go left also. To urge him into a walk give him a gentle nudge with your legs. Do the same with trot. When you go into a canter sink your body into your seat keep contact with your reins, then one leg steady and straight and the other leg behind pick a direction, and you are going to go and apply the same rules of steering to urge him to a canter. Do you understand?"

"I think so." I reply.

"Okay let's start with walk." I go through the motions. Sit is walking alongside the horse, providing me tips and instruction, then to trot and canter. I appreciate the fact that Sitrus lets me get used to the horse before learning how to steer him. I feel in control, and it feels natural. I can sense the horse's muscles as he anticipates my instruction, it is like I know what he is thinking, and he knows what I am thinking. When Sit is satisfied that I have mastered the basics, he puts a bridle on a second horse in the field and joins me on horseback.

"Let's take a walk." Sitrus insists; we head up the grassy field to the tree line, not too far off from where I tried to escape. We enter a trail into the forest and walk side by side along the path for a bit.

"What happened today?" He asks me.

"I, well, I sort of hinted to her to remove herself from the situation that surrounds this family."

He looks at me confused, "You're encouraging her to run away?"

"No Sitrus, she already wants to run away, I didn't need to plant that seed. It was the direction that she was running in." I gather myself; my hands are shaking, and I am hoping that he doesn't see how much this topic bothers me because I am still undecided on whose side I will take. "If she manages to escape her plan is to run back to the Palace to warn King Wolfrim that Rosaleen knows the truth. She thinks that if she warns him, he will put a stop to Rosaleen and that he will help get Shrago back."

He looks at me surprised even though we had planned my cover before I was introduced to her, "She doesn't know that Shrago is dead?"

"No, I had thought about telling her, then thought it was best to keep it secret, it would only complicate matters and besides, I should try to maintain my cover." I take a breath and continue, "So really what is the point, and right now my relationship with her is more good than bad."

He nods, "Good point." In a muffled voice he asks, "Do you know how she plans to escape?"

I look at him and I can tell that he knows something is up and I am cautious with my answer, "Sit if I knew her plan, I think she would already be gone. I don't think she even knows how to escape?"

"Have you two talked about it?"

"Yes" I reply, wishing that I lied to him.

"Well then you surely know pieces of her plan." He wants me to spill the details, and I am not about to reveal my hand.

"We don't talk about it like that. It's more of a what if this, what if that conversation like what if you were free where would you go sort of thing. Shaylo wants to escape and all she said was she was still in the process of thinking." I look at him for his acceptance to the information that I have shared. His eyes are dark as night and his emotions seem to be running strong.

"I don't believe you."

"You don't have to." I am not going to try to convince him because I don't want to get caught in a lie and besides Newlyn is with Shaylo right now so who knows what sort of information is being shared.

He is clearly annoyed and rides his horse ahead of mine so that we all come to a stop "Get off!" He growls, I obey. He dismounts and ties both the horses to a couple of young trees. Their trunks are as thick as fence posts. He walks over to me. I don't know why I feel this because he has never hurt me, but I have the feeling that he will. I brace myself for the pain. I close my eyes and cringe, but instead he grabs me firmly and kisses me passionately. I slowly open my eyes in shock, not really looking at anything. I like this.

He pulls back and whispers to me, "You drive me nuts."

I say nothing and instead let him do as he wishes. It is no lie that I like him, but on the other hand, strategically, I need to keep him happy and remember to put myself first. I know where he keeps the key to my stall. I also need him to feel that he is in control and at the same time keep Shaylo happy with appearing to be on her side. I go through the motions without a word, just off the trail on the forest floor we share this time together, and I forget the web that I am caught up in again.

Sitrus says with a sigh, "We need to go back." I just wrap my arms around him and say nothing wishing that this moment does not end. I don't think he wants to head back either.

"Let's get out of here now and leave this life behind." I suggest as I feel his muscles starting to stir.

"Taylan you need to think, if you leave then what happens to Ashlea, or your entire family for that matter? Besides this is my home, my life, I can't leave. I hope that you won't think about escaping, or helping Shaylo?"

"No, I won't."

"I still don't believe you." He asserts himself. "I hope that you would stay here for me and for the sake of your family."

I don't argue and change the direction of this conversation, "Will you tell Newlyn everything that I shared with you?"

He laughs, "That my dear is none of your concern. Come on we should head back."

We walk our horses all the way back to the stable. It is the end of the day and Sitrus is first into the barn, followed by me. I peek into Shaylo's stall, but she is not there. My desire to know kicks in. Sit senses it. He says, "Don't ask." Surprised, I keep quiet. He is starting to know me well. I guess Shaylo must still be with Newlyn. We go back and retrieve the rest of the horses in the field. Sit keeps me company in helping with all the evening chores.

I can't put it to rest and blurt out, "I know that Shaylo is with Newlyn, I just want to know is she coming back? Will I need to continue this charade?"

Just as I ask Sitrus, Newlyn enters the stable accompanied by Shaylo. She is bound and looks ruffed up; she shoves Shaylo into her stall and gives me an angered look, "You caused this!" I don't understand I didn't do anything. I didn't force anyone to inflict harm on Shaylo, and I didn't mean for Shaylo to become upset. I certainly didn't tell Shaylo not do chores yet somehow this is my fault? Izavelle was right when she warned me that things are not always what they seem. I don't think that Newlyn is acting, she seems genuinely angry with me.

Without me having to answer her wrath, Newlyn storms out of the barn. I look back to Sit for some sort of answer. He just points for me to go into my stall, and he locks the door and exits. It is just Shaylo and me now. I approach the wall that divides us, "What happened?"

She looks at me "This happened," gesturing at the bruises all over her body.

I don't understand, "Newlyn did that?" She nods to confirm my suspicions.

"She found out that I wasn't doing chores." Shaylo does not go into detail. I decide not to ask. This is the first time that I sense her feeling of defeat, and I am sure that the details will eventually come out in time.

We are well into the evening. I am hungry and fortunately, took the lesson of the soap stash from Shaylo and applied her thievery lesson by looting some food from the lunch table earlier today, removing a small bread bun from my pocket, I eat to stop my hunger pains. Despite the situation that she is in, I go against my instinct to offer any of it to Shaylo. I know that it is not fair, but I am hungry, and besides, she never offered me her soap when it was clear to her that I was trying to clean myself.

I finish off the bun while keeping out of Shaylo's sight, its hard crust and soft center does the trick with putting my hunger at ease. I retire back to my cot and close my eyes. I am not asleep when the barn door opens; I sit up on the bed, expecting to see Sitrus bringing some food, but this time its Newlyn.

Chapter 27
A Visit from Newlyn

I don't believe Shaylo was asleep, but I also don't think that she bothered to pay any attention. Newlyn does not say a word and just unlocks my stall, motioning me to follow. We go around to the main house where I had stayed that first night and enter through the front door. She proceeds upstairs to the same bedroom from my first night here and she starts a bath, I say nothing.

"I'm not mad at you Taylan." I hear her words, but don't believe her and it really doesn't put me at ease because my heart is thumping out of my chest. "Get out of your clothes and into the tub." I don't hesitate and do just as I am told. I sink into the warm, soothing water. She sits on the step of the tub.

"Your injury is completely healed; I don't see the mark." Instinctively I touch my neck and relax a bit by her distraction.

"Yes, it doesn't hurt anymore." I answer softly.

"You know that you have been doing well with this project. Sit has provided me very insightful information that you were able to get out of Shaylo."

"Thank you," I answer shyly.

"What happened today with Shaylo won't ever happen again." Newlyn asserts herself.

"What do you mean?" I ask.

"She has been warned that if she ever acts in the way that she did it would be her last." I swallow slowly and know exactly what that means. Newlyn is the wolf in sheep's clothing just as her daughter.

"Taylan don't be frightened, people who do terrible things have terrible things happen to them, and I know that you are not like Shaylo." I am at a loss of words, and she continues, "With her outburst today we know that her weakness is Shrago. I need you to stay clear of mentioning him."

I find my voice, "Newlyn, can I ask you something?"

"Yes"

"I don't think there is anything else that we need to get from her that would be useful for Rosaleen. I am sure that both Shrago and Shaylo were the only ones who were resolute informants to King Wolfrim, and the only ones on the ship that participated in the things that happened to you and your family."

"Is this a hunch you are working off of, or are you defending her?" Newlyn looks down at me.

"I have nothing to gain in defending her. Look at what happened when I hinted at abandoning everything she knows." I am not sure if Sitrus or Shaylo admitted to Newlyn what I had just divulged to her just now, it is a calculated risk that I take in this discussion. "Shrago's safety is the main thing that is important to her. She worries about him constantly." This is a half-truth, and I almost believe my own lie.

"You know Taylan, I find myself constantly underestimating you and Ashlea."

My ears perk up, "You've seen Ashlea?"

She pours some warm water into my hair, "No, but I have heard news from the ship. They are halfway to the Thresolon. Soolena has been putting a lot of work into

Ashlea's training. I hear Ashlea is a quick learner, just like you and a natural in the work that they have given her."

I hold onto every word. This is the first news I hear of Ash since she has left. "What do they have her doing?" Newlyn enjoys my company; it is hard to tell if she is acting. Newlyn could have easily had a servant bathe me, but she chooses to do this work herself. She considers me a replacement to the missed time that she would have had with Rosaleen. It feels odd considering that I am a young adult, and I am being held here against my wishes, but what makes me get through this is the fact that I do welcome the company even though it's under queer circumstances. In some sort of twisted way, I accept Newlyn as a fill in for me missing my own mother.

Newlyn fills me in on Ashlea's work. She has taken on the role of being a protector for Rosaleen, and I find out that she has become an excellent flyer. She is good in the skill of stealth, she has become a skilled shooter, and she is mastering the discipline of knives and swords. Newlyn gushes over my sister explaining that Ashlea is the perfect apprentice. Newlyn points out that Ashlea is not someone that would normally come to mind as being a protector and admits that her daughter, Rosaleen has a good eye. Ashlea is small just like me, and people overlook her, which is such a huge advantage.

I reflect aloud, "I never thought Ashlea would ever take on a serious roll because she is such a fun-loving spirit, but I can see how she would be good with learning because it all sounds exciting, and it is her nature to care for the ones that she loves. She would want to do all that she could."

Newlyn asks, "Did you ever see yourself becoming an informant?"

I chuckle and can't help rolling my eyes, "I don't think that I'm any good, but to answer your question, I never thought that I would be picked to do this sort of work."

Newlyn lathers up some soap in her hand and washes my back, "My dear I don't think Rosaleen picked two better people."

"Thank you." I feel myself flush, "Newlyn, what are you having me do after tonight?"

She rinses the soap from my body and hair, "You are going back to the stall next to Shaylo to continue with the act. I understand your logic that there is not much more to gain, but I can't let her go just yet. I can't risk any warning of alarm to King Wolfrim. I don't want to do away with Shaylo because I want revenge; she helped in breaking my family apart. I want to keep her here and make her pay. Let's face it she owes me."

"How much longer do you think I will need to keep up this act?" I ask.

Newlyn ponders a moment, "I don't think it will be for much longer. It depends on how fast Rosaleen carries out her mission."

I instantly deflate; everything that is required of me is constantly changing. I had no choice, or say in the matter, but I had the impression that this act would only be a matter of weeks, but with Newlyn elaborating on it, this could take months. This also means that I won't see Ashlea for longer than I had anticipated.

Newlyn gets up from sitting on the step and holds a towel out for me. I step out of the tub and into it. The feeling of being clean is wonderful, but I am having a tough time enjoying it because I feel like Ashlea has been pulled even further out of my grasp.

"Cheer up Taylan, this isn't forever. You are going to keep close watch on Shaylo and see to it that she stays put." Newlyn approaches the dresser to retrieve some clothing. Instead of pulling out a fancy gown, she retrieves another simple grey outfit for me. The only good thing about it is its clean and dry. I dress myself, and Newlyn approaches me and brushes my silky hair that is reflecting a dirty blond color. It must be the mix of the warm wood tone in the room and the grey outfit.

"Such beautiful hair," Newlyn says admiringly to me, "Stay put for a moment. I'll be right back with some food for you." Newlyn closes the door behind her, and I hear the lock click shut. I wonder if Sit said anything to her about my own escape attempt. Adrenaline starts pumping in my veins, still remembering what Shaylo had said about the soap. I race around the room looking for things that would improve my living situation in the barn. There is some soap at the tub, candles, clothes, and towels. I open the dresser, there is a variety of clothing, undecided as to what to take I go to the closet and open it. My eyes set its sights on a flying suit hanging there for the taking. How am I going to do this; I want this suit. I take the suit from the hanger. To my surprise, there are two. I look back at the door and listen. All I can hear is silence. I close the closet door and retreat into the washroom, closing the door for a moment. I must do this fast; I take my top off and instead of putting the suits under my clothing I just wrap the garments around my stomach, tying the legs to the arms so that the fabric is snug against my skin. I take the linen top that Newlyn set out for me, put it over top and check myself in the vanity mirror to make sure that there is no evidence of the loot beneath my clothing, or any odd bumps; so far so good. I flush the toilet and wash my hands to make it seem like I was using the washroom and go back into the room just as Newlyn is coming through the door to the bedroom.

"I made you and Shaylo a sandwich let's get you back to the stable." We leave the house. She walks me back to my stall. Newlyn does not stay to chat and just locks the stall door behind me and leaves. I have the sandwiches. I quietly walk to Shaylo's stall and peek over.

I don't see her. Where is she? "Shaylo" I whisper.

Chapter 28
How to Vanish

I grow frantic inside, but succeed in calming myself and whisper, "Shaylo?" I hear rustling, I know it is Shaylo, but I don't see her right away. The board moves, Shaylo slips through, I step back. "What are you doing, are you okay?" I give her my hand to help her up and give her a warm embrace.

She answers, "Yah, I am fine, they're only bruises and will clear in a couple days." She sighs and asks, "How about you, did Newlyn hurt you?"

"No, she just gave me a stern warning and reminder of my place here." I am not really telling a lie; it is a half-truth and Shaylo doesn't dwell on it. "Why are you in my stall?" I ask.

"We are leaving tonight." Shaylo answers in a hushed whisper.

"What, how?" Not tonight and after she had been ruffed up, this was the last thing that I was expecting.

"I will explain once we are safe. Right now, I need you to do as I say."

"Okay Shaylo." What am I going to do? I knew that this was coming, but not now. I guess her encounter with Newlyn was the final straw. She takes a key from her pocket and quickly, but quietly unlocks the door to my stall.

She bids, "Go get two bridles and leave the saddles." I run to the tack room and retrieve the equipment.

Shaylo has two athletic horses picked out. They are large and look like they are born to run. I hand her a bridle. She quickly, but quietly adjusts the size and fits it onto the horse's head. I do the same to the second horse. She approaches the barn door, which locks, from the outside and she simply clicks the door open by sliding her twig in the space between the two doors. Somehow, it works because we are now outside in the open but sheltered by the darkness. The horses follow behind while we walk down the path and through Newlyn's front gates.

Shaylo gives me a leg up onto the large horse and explains, "You need to keep pace." She hops onto her horse, starting at a walk. My guess is to make the tracks less obvious and to reduce the noise, avoiding the sound of galloping hooves near Newlyn's home where ears could hear and cause for alarm. We walk in silence. I don't bother to say anything, Shaylo is thinking through our next obstacles. I believe that this could work, neither Shaylo nor Newlyn know that I managed to snatch a couple of flying suits the only downside to them is we can't use them now in the night. I don't believe they have seen the sunlight in a long time. I also have our sandwiches in my pant pocket. We walk for what seems like forever it feels like we are moving at a snail's pace. I can still make out the outline of Newlyn's home in the distance. We enter the tree line, and Shaylo takes off at a gallop, I follow not far behind. In the dark of night, it is hard to tell the direction we are moving in, but the faster pace calms my nerves since we are putting distance between Newlyn and us. These strong horses enjoy running and are snorting up a storm; it was a good thing we walked away in the beginning of our escape. After a while, the horses slow to a canter then, to a trot and finally to a walk. It is still the middle of the night, but we made a clean getaway. We have cleared the trees and are moving at a brisk walk across open fields, we pass herds of giant animals grazing and paying little to no attention as we pass. It is hard to tell because it is still in the night, but I catch a glimpse in the horizon just off to the left, the town where Rosaleen and I spent the afternoon and rented that solar bike. We are traveling in another direction, not towards town. We continue to ride in silence, trusting the eyes of our horses. We cross the vast field on to the next tree line, which leads to the mountains. The horses will need to be let go from here, they won't make it over the mountain. It is as though Shaylo just read my mind because she has just brought her horse to a stop and has hoped off, I do the same.

Shaylo says, "Remove his bridle." I tend to my horse; she does that same and gives her horse one firm slap on the hindquarters and he whinnies and gallops off. A gentle pat suffices for my horse is eager to catch up with Shaylo's and he gallops off to catch up.

Shaylo speaks up, "They will find their way home."

"Yah it's neat how they remember." The sky is starting to change colors to an orange pink. The sun has not yet come over the horizon but will soon.

"We need to get over these mountains and then we will cross the shallows to the next island." Shaylo explains.

I remember the flying suits tied around my torso, "Shaylo you may want to see this?"

"What?" She asks.

"Look." I lift my shirt to reveal the suits.

Shaylo is confused for a second and recognition sets in, "When did you get those?"

I smile and reveal, "Newlyn locked me in a room for a few minutes while she prepared some food. I searched the room and found these hanging in a closet."

"Taylan you amaze me!" She laughs and gives me a joyful pat on the back.

"I don't think these have been charged. We will have to drape them to catch the sun's rays. The only drawback is they are reflective so it could make us easy to spot."

Shaylo regards them, "Good point well, let's rest now and let them charge, we should climb up a tree and use the horses' bridles to secure ourselves."

I add, "I think we can get away with wearing the suits and putting the linen jumper over top. The linen is thin the sunlight should get through."

"Let's do that." Shaylo confirms. I hand Shaylo a suit and we each striped down to put them on. Just as I thought, they are not charged; I slip the linen jumper over top, and then climb the rocky incline into the forest. We pick a large tree; its trunk is straight and thick at the base; it is too large to wrap your arms around to be able to touch your fingers on the opposite hand. There is a steady path of branches, which are ideal grasps for climbing. Shaylo gives me a leg up into the tree and follows. We climb to the canopy and each settle on a branch on opposite sides of the trunk. Shaylo adjusts herself so that she is in a sitting position, legs extended along the branch and back against the trunk. She takes the horse's bridle, wraps it around her waist, and then loops the reins around her branch. I watch and copy her, securing myself to my branch. Fatigue is starting to take over as I gaze out from my perch over the open field below. The sun is now peeking over the misty horizon. A sweet warm breeze trickles through the branches and relaxes my senses.

"Shaylo, do you think we will see our families?"
"I'm not answering that, get over it and get some rest."

Chapter 29
A Fool's Chase

I wake to a familiar touch on my shoulder, and open my eyes, my own blood, Ashlea. With her finger held to her lip she signals, to keep quiet. She unties the bridle and takes flight, waving me to follow, leaving the sleeping Shaylo behind. We fly high up into the sky, soaring above the clouds and then back down to a remote small island, traveling at a speed that is causing my eyes to tear. We descend and choose a soft, sandy warm beach. Saying nothing at first, just hugging and holding each other, neither of us holding back our tears of joy.

I break the silence, "Ashlea you have no idea how much I have missed you." I gasp and hug her again.

"Ah Taylan I can't put it to words how much I have missed you little sister." She gently rubs my back in a returned embrace.

"How did you get away? How did you find me?" I ask.

"Newlyn only has a small crew at her home caring for her property. She had started a search team, but called it off soon after and then contacted Rosaleen for help so now, here I am."

"Are they mad at me?" I ask.

She says, "Yes, they think this is your fault, for not telling them." Her eyes accuse and she frowns. It is my fault. "You should have told them. Why didn't you say anything?" Ashlea asks.

"I didn't know Ash." I look at her to see if she believes me, she just returns a blank stare, emotionless. I feel suddenly dizzy and sick. "Ashlea, I swear to you, I didn't know that his would happen. Shaylo talked about wanting to escape, but she never said when, or how." I look to her, pleading inside for her acceptance, love and understanding, but she shakes her head at me in disappointment.

"This is your own web; you will need to kill to get out. They are chasing you." I feel my body grow warm and sweat droplets forming on my forehead and neck, trickling down my back.

"Who is chasing me? Ash, can't you make them stop?" Ashlea shakes her head no; she repeats that they are chasing me. I stand, my body is trembling, but lose balance, all is black.

I wake to the afternoon sun beaming through the canopy of the trees. I can't ignore the unpleasant damp feeling all over my skin, a cold clammy sweat. I know that I have rested, but I don't feel rested. Where am I? Where is Ash? I absorb my surroundings. I am high up in a tree. The only thing is that I am hanging sideways from the branch. If it were not for the bridle straps, I would be on the ground, or worse floating away. I look around and over my shoulder for signs of life. Shaylo is not strapped behind me to the parallel branch. My eyes dart around the canopy for signs to where she could be. Would it be a good thing if we parted ways? Does she need me, and do I need her?

I know that I certainly need her in this moment. I know that Ashlea's destination is the Palace, and I have never been there. I need her as a guide. The other option would be that I could return to Newlyn's home, but something tells me that if I were to do that my life would become much more complicated. It is best to stay with Shaylo for those two reasons. She is smart enough to know better than to just leave me. For one thing, Shaylo knows a thing, or two

about traders with having played the mind games that comes with palace life. The risk of me returning or being found by Newlyn is too big of a risk for her. She has been around long enough to realize either way that if I end up in Newlyn's hands, whether it was against my will, or not, I would be used to help track Shaylo down, and they would get the information from me even if I was on her side. The other thing, although it is much less significant is, I am her witness to the imprisonment. Should there be any trials conducted by the imposter King Wolfrim, I could vouch for Shaylo.

It is time to get to work; I untie the bridle that was used to secure myself and climb down the tree instead of flying down by using the suit. I can't risk snagging the material in the branches, and besides, I am not even sure it is charged although it should be charged with having slept in the sun.

The sun paints an interesting image on the forest floor with the odd shrub and plant appearing to glow while others are shrouded in shadow from the canopy. I am still at the base of the mountain and figure that the ocean should just be on the other side. I can hear running water and follow the sound. I need to quench my thirst. The earth dips down a bit as I make my way towards the sound, the trees open a bit to a small brook trickling over rocks. I kneel and scoop some cool water into my mouth. As I drink, I feel eyes watching. I glance up to see my escape partner.

"Where have you been?" I ask Shaylo. I am surprised, but relieved that she didn't abandon me.

"I was just gathering some nuts and berries. I figured you would be hungry because I am. You should eat something before we are back on the move." Shaylo hops over a couple of steppingstones that emerged from the water and finds a nice dry rock near me and sits down to snack on her gatherings. She hands me some food from her pockets and even though my stomach wasn't bothering me, I instantly feel refreshed and energized from the nourishment.

"I tried the suit out, it works perfectly." Shaylo manages to blurt out in between chews. "We are so lucky that you managed to find them."

"I figured the suits would help. It beats having to deal with horses and walking." My nerves are more at ease even after talking and eating with Shaylo. I think Shaylo feels the same. "How far do you think we can get today? How long do you think it will take for us to get to the Palace?"

Shaylo swallows a berry, "With the flying suits, we will cover a lot of ground today; I would say a couple of days at most." A couple of days in the possibility of seeing Ashlea. A couple of days until confrontations happen and a couple of days until the possibility of ending this mess. I know that I am being hopeful, but time will tell, it is going to happen soon and fast. We finish eating and clean ourselves in the brook.

"Shall we?" Shaylo asks, while directing her gaze up. The pressure is real with everything that we need to do and people we need to avoid, but I can feel the energy in the air between the two of us. Shaylo has never said it, but I can tell that she loves to fly like me. My heartbeat is quickening with excitement and anticipation of going up into the sky.

"Yes of course!" I answer. "Hold on a second. What should we do with our linens and the bridles?"

"I think we should ditch them." She shrugs.

"What about keeping them for warmth in the night, maybe we will need the bridles just like we did last night."

She laughs, "Taylan what are you, a hoarder?"

"Well, I am just thinking ahead that's all." I feel a little bit offended that she thinks my idea is ridiculous. If I didn't have the bridle last night, I would have been eating dirt on the forest floor.

"There is no sense carrying the extra weight and stuffing our suits, especially with having to maneuver in the air."

"Good point." I admit.

"Don't worry Taylan we will figure stuff out as we go; sleeping; food and shelter. Besides, if we are displaced for whatever reason, at most it will just be for a day, or two."

"It is decided." I shrug.

We hide the bridles and linen jumpers under some rocks along the brook and back track a bit by descending back into the open field. There is an inviting breeze coming off the rippling meadow grass, just kissing our skin. Ignoring everything around me, I break off into a run and extend by arms like a bird spreading her wings, leaping into the air. The takeoff always feels strange. I can't drown out that bodily expectation that I am going to jump into the air and fall on my face. Up I go with the sensation of being free once more. The feeling is strangely known by heart even though I have only done this a couple of times. I just can't forget that feeling, the excitement, and anticipation; the feeling is sort of like, just knowing that I have always known how to fly, though my heart is in my throat in this moment.

Over the lush green, tree covered mountain and into the sky with Shaylo on my tail; my hair must be changing from a green to a blue color because the sky is all that is in my vision. I don't look back at Newlyn's island, where that cute small town and her home was. Instead, I focus on what is ahead, ocean and a trickle of tiny islands that look like steppingstones in the vast tropical waters. The air is warm and not too humid, we soar, all that I can hear is the whistle of the breeze and the world below is silent.

We exchange few words, it is mostly just smiles, laughs and the "watch what I can do's", as we try to outshine each other by doing flips and tricks in the air and getting the other to watch and then out do the trick with their own new and more difficult one.

We keep on course and are moving at a good pace. After a couple of hours, we need a rest. My arms are tired as though I have been doing push-ups, but it didn't feel like demanding work for the two-hour trip. Now, it feels more like a tired feeling after having done a hundred of them. We glide down to this tiny little island; it is more of a half crescent of sand dune that is just high enough for some grass to take root. I decide to land in the turquoise shallows, in the inner circle of water and walk up to the sand. I plop myself down for a rest.

Shaylo chuckles, "That's exactly how I feel."

"I can use another nap." I lay there, concentrating on the sky for a few minutes. When I was at home with my mom and sisters, I was used to having days full of activity, but now it seems like all the activity is tiring me. It is just the added pressure with being on the run that is making me groggy. Shaylo fusses near to me, she completely strips out of the suit.

She hollers from the water, "We should sit in the shallows to sooth our muscles." I quickly strip down, and we both relocate in the water within the circle of the half-crescent shaped island. The water is a vibrant greenish blue color. We lay on our stomachs in the soft sandy shallows.

"Do you think we are still being followed?" I ask Shaylo to break the silence.

She shrugs, "Probably, but I don't think they are on our trail just because we have the advantage of the suits. They probably think we are traveling by foot or hiding out in the town near Newlyn's." I sense that too. I have a gut feeling that we are in the clear and this is no longer a chase. I hope that we can travel with more ease. The water where we are lying is no more than inches deep. I crawl and roll around in the water and make my way to where the two points of the island crescent seems to line up and from there, there is a drastic drop off. I lie along the edge and gaze down into the deep blue. I see fish, a reef nothing out of the ordinary. Contemplating on going down, I am hungry, there is some sugar kelp down there, or even clams? I close my eyes and soak in the salty bath like water. A splash hits me full on. It is not a little playful splash. It is like a wall of water raining down on me. Suddenly, I am rudely interrupted from resting my eyes. I am not sure what direction it's coming from. My instinct is to blame Shaylo; I give her a dirty look. Shaylo is shaking her head, saying she didn't do it. I maintain my gaze; who else could it be? Shaylo asks me, "Did you see what that was?" She asks, exasperated.

"What?" I can't believe she is playing this stupid game, and then I realize the droplets coming down her face and her soaking wet hair. It couldn't be her, who, or what? Fear hits me, "Shaylo what is going on?" The water is rippling; the sound of a low grumbling surrounds us, like an earthquake.

Chapter 30
Kyle is back in the Swing

The engine turns off; Kyle slides the key out of the ignition, looking out his window at the big grey stone building that was his home away from home a while ago. I say was, because before everything changed, the last days that I was with Kyle he had been out of work with his contract being up. His employers have been in contact with him throughout this entire time, and if the accident had not happened, Kyle would have returned to work weeks before now.

"Kyle!" He jumps at the sound of the voice calling his name, startled by his friend Kevin. Kyle opens his car door and steps out "Hey man how have you been? We have all been thinking about you."

"I'm okay." Kyle manages to say. He has been used to being on his own for the past little while with his parents having returned to their home.

Kevin smiles encouragingly, "Well that's good man. You know if you want to hang out you are always welcome to give me a call."

"Thanks" Kyle appreciates the company, but having been alone, the company of another feels a little foreign now.

They walk into the office together. Kyle goes through the motions of getting a new office pass and meeting his boss after. He returns to a new desk at a window cubicle, which is a thankful bonus from the windowless cubicle he used to have. His morning goes by fast, in a good way. So many of his friends and colleagues stop in and welcome him back.

Noon arrives and he finds his way down to the cafeteria, seeing Kevin and a group of others at the table. "Hey man, I have a spot here for you." Kevin says in a loud booming voice. He waves Kyle over after grabbing his attention, as well as the attention of the entire cafeteria. "So, how's it going? Did you see those retarded test cases that they have us working on?"

Kyle chuckles, "Yah, I asked Steve about them, but couldn't get a straightforward answer. I may just go to Diane after lunch to find out what they want me to do."

Kevin agrees, "Yah Diane knows what she is talking about. Say, I haven't seen you online for a while; how about we make plans to do some online gaming together, you know, stalk up on energy drinks, junk food, and do some quests and dungeon's together, how about it?"

Kyle pauses, not sure how he feels about it, Robin used to be his main partner when it came to playing video games. "Um well, ah yah we can play sometime."

Kevin smiles, "That's great man, how about this Friday night and I can maybe crash at your place?"

Kyle knows that he is not there yet, he needs to get used to the idea. "Not this weekend. I have other plans." Kevin senses that Kyle is feeding him a lie, but does not push it, instead gives an uncertain smile and nod. Kyle sees the effect that his let down has on his friend and uncomfortably he continues, "Give me this weekend to get some work done and by next weekend I will have enough time to pick up a game card and reactivate my online account."

Kevin's ears perk up to the confirmation, "It will be fun, and I heard they have this crazy new expansion." The conversation carries on and before long lunch is over and eventually, the workday is done, and Kyle finds himself back home in an empty house with only Smarty to keep him company.

For the first time in a while, he is happy to be at home from having worked a full day and spending time with his colleagues. He is starting to feel like himself and not some empty shell. He settles down with our loyal little dog Smarty on the couch. The phone rings.

"Hello?"

"Hey Kyle, how was your first day back? The caller asks.

"Oh, hey Dad, it was good."

Chapter 31
A Wall of Water

Shaylo roars, "Out of the water!" We make it to the sand and turn to face the water, just beyond the drop a giant creature breaks the surface, black in color, then several others follow as the first, and come crashing down.

In complete wonder I ask, "What are they?" They are not large fish, sharks, or whales.

Shaylo breathlessly answers, "Manta Rays, they are harmless. Do you want to see?"

Feeling a little weary, my curiosity outweighs my nerves, which are screaming at me not to go. Putting my fears to rest, we carefully and slowly go back into the shallows, to the edge of the drop off. I dunk my head to get a better look down into the deep water and see them, these giant dark creatures, they look like giant birds that are flying through the water seamlessly and with such a graceful speed. They must be at least twenty feet wide from wing tip to wing tip and thirty feet long from the head to the tip of their long needlepoint tails.

Without warning Shaylo descends into the deep. I feel compelled to follow although I am a little reluctant. The temperature of the water in the drop off is not cold, but it is noticeably cooler after being used to the bath like warmth of the shallows. I descend cautiously, but quickly to the ocean floor and the creatures are in the distance, doing the same thing they did before. They all seem to come together at the bottom and then ascend in a circular motion to the surface. It is like seeing an underwater tornado on the ocean floor. I see them break the water's surface up above and then they come crashing down again. I go back to the surface for air and swim back down into the deep. On my way down the manta rays seem to have left their tornado formation and have dispersed. One of the giant creatures spots me making my way through the water and he comes over to investigate. He moves seamlessly, not daring to touch me, his curiosity outweighs any fear he may have. I can move at a nice speed underwater; my fingers and toes are webbed to my first knuckle, but nowhere near as quickly and as effortlessly as these creatures. His movements are effortless. In a single movement, he glides around me like a giant dark cape in the wind. He does a perfect circle, and I am at the center of it. I pause and watch this massive creature. He slows approaching close enough for me to reach out to touch him. Without thinking, I reach out and touch him as he glides by. My hand skims his underbelly. At my touch, he flaps his wings and quickens his speed away from me. I go back to the surface for another breath of air. Shaylo meets me at the surface.

I can hardly contain my excitement, "Shaylo did you see that?"

She laughs, "Do you mean when he circled you and you touched him?"

"I didn't even know creatures like that existed?" I say breathlessly.

Shaylo says, "I have only seen them a couple of times, but never that close, only ever on board a ship looking down at them from a distance."

"I got completely sidetracked watching them. I forgot to grab some oysters at the bottom." I dip my face into the water peering down to see if I am in the clear to swim down without getting sidetracked again by the gentle giants.

"No worries, I picked up enough for the both of us, and even a couple of morsels of sugar kelp." Shaylo reveals two good sized oysters, one in each hand and two long morsels of sugar kelp that look like long strands of green ribbon laced though her fingers. We go to the shore to eat and then we are back in our suits on course, back in flight. It is late in the afternoon or early evening; it is hard for me to tell. We make the decision to come back down on a larger island, similar in size to the island where Newlyn's home is. We land on the sandy shore. It is good that we decided to stop because it gives us some time to settle down for the night before it gets dark. Besides, when it is dark it would be impossible to navigate and who knows if these suits even hold a charge, or where we would end up stopping for that matter?

"I know this place." Shaylo admits. "There is a small town not too far from here; you may have caught a glimpse of it before landing?"

"Yes, I saw something in the distance."

"So, we are going to have to find some clothing, or even better, shelter for the night." Shaylo says as though she is talking aloud to herself.

"I am all ears Shaylo, how are we going to blend in with these suits and get shelter with nothing to barter with?"

"Who says we are going to barter?" Shaylo says.

I am a little surprised that Shaylo would even suggest it and risk us being caught for something else.

Shaylo says, "Follow me." Back up into the air we go, we circle the buildings from afar and once satisfied that she has a good visual of the area, I follow her to a secluded area close to the town in a forested spot.

Shaylo works through a strategy, "This is going to be too easy that it's disgusting, the catch is, we need to do this now before it gets dark and before the shops close for the night. I spotted a clothing shop with some garments we could take what is hanging on a rack out front. I plan to just swoop in when no one is looking grab what I need for the two of us and go."

"Shaylo, we don't need to do it like this. We can camp out for the night. What ever happened to toughing it out? Besides, if we are so desperate for food and clothing, why don't we just go in there like normal people? I can use my pearl necklace to barter with." I look for the tiniest glint of reasoning in her.

"Taylan, I know that your necklace is important to you. We will be quick. We have every right to take what we need after all that we have been through."

"Shaylo this is morally wrong these store owners have nothing to do with your imprisonment and besides, even if I were to turn a blind eye on the matter of morals the one major issue that is staring me in the face is, what if something goes wrong? What if you are recognized? What if we are caught? We are back to square one and even worse what if we are handed back over to Newlyn, then what?" Shaylo laughs at me.

"You worry too much." Before I can argue, she is gone.

I just stand there; I have no urge to follow and be her accomplice. These shops are no different from the one my mom keeps. Why would I take part in this when it isn't even a matter of desperation? I decide to crouch down on the roots at the base of a large tree and wait. She is right. I worry too much and really; we did manage a major escape so in retrospect a little thievery is not a challenging task when you look at what has been managed this far.

I look around. A breeze of wind comes down on me, and then Shaylo is before me with some clothing and shoes.

"I got these from the sale rack." She brags.

"It still doesn't make it right." I say with my arms crossed.

"Your eyes like what they see, I can tell. Look at you; I see that you are eyeing my loot." It is true I am the people that I have come to know all seem to have a natural sense of style and can put together things that you would never imagine would look good. Even in thievery, Shaylo manages to put together a nice outfit. I guess that comes with once having the luxury of money and time to put in a good effort. It has paid off into how she presents herself. Shaylo managed to grab a couple of non-patterned dresses for us with these nifty horizontally stripped jackets to compliment them and a pair of shimmering flats.

"Did anyone notice you?" I ask.

"Yes, the store owner asked if I would like to use her change room inside. I said yes and when she turned to lead me into her store I simply leapt into the air and now I am here." She smirks.

"I can't believe you. Oh, wait I can, all you palace folk seem to feel that the world revolves around you. You have no boundaries, always taking what you want."

"Doesn't it?" She teases.

"Shaylo of all people you? You became a prisoner, have you already forgot that you need to be cautious?"

"It is only a matter of time before Shrago will rescue me, or I rescue him, or King Wolfrim takes notice once the ship has landed to realize that I am not there; a little stealing doesn't hurt."

"It's just not right, that's all I have to say." I roll my eyes. This conversation is going nowhere and how are dresses going to keep us warm in the night? In the morning, we will just leave them behind. Shaylo hands me the clothing, we change out of our flying suits and hide them in the hollow of a nearby tree, walk through the woods towards the town.

"Why do I feel like you are letting your guard down, why now? Can't you just wait a day until we are where we need to be?" I half ask and suggest.

"Please can you just get off it? I got the dresses to blend in; that is not letting my guard down; that is being intelligent. I have been imprisoned for the longest time and this is the only time I will get a chance to enjoy myself because once we get there, I will be right back into the work of sorting all of this out with King Wolfrim, Princess Rosaleen, and Newlyn.

"Fair enough, do you think that we might be spotted?"

"Enough about it, you're like a dog at its bone. This is the last that I talk about this; to answer your last question, I doubt it. King Wolfrim is the front and center of all the attention, my husband and I, who are his servants, are always in the background. The only people that would recognize me are those who are actively looking for me. I'm confident that we are far ahead of them."

"So, what were you thinking, some eats and drinks?" I ask.

"Absolutely" Shaylo answers.

"How, we have nothing." Is she going to have us steal again?

"You will see." She smirks and leads the way as we walk down the path.

The forest that opens to a park with plenty of space for people to lounge, play and relax. There are nicely kept pathways. The area is beautifully landscaped with plenty of flowers, shrubs, and trees. A boardwalk starts, leading its way alongside a beach. We take the boardwalk; its dusk and the sky is a canvas of shades of pink and orange. There are plenty of people around. Some walking barefoot in the sand, others walking along the boardwalk a few swimmers are in the water. Our hair adjusts to the colors of the sky, a pinkish orange color. We settle on a park bench.

"What now?" I am anxious; I don't want to sit around especially in knowing that Shaylo has something up her sleeve.

"We watch and wait." She answers, ignoring my growing impatience to this entire evening.

I just don't get it. I could care less with what happens now. I have played both sides. I am constantly mulling this over in my head. Whether I get to the Palace with, or without Shaylo is not important anymore. It was when we were still far away, in the middle of nowhere, but today when I go over this in my head, if we were to go our separate ways my goal is to get to the Palace and reunite with Ashlea. I know that Rosaleen's ship is destined there and even though I have never been to the city or have set foot in the Palace I am close enough that I no longer would need a guide and that I could find my way without Shaylo. What was I thinking our most valuable belongings the suits were left in a tree?

"What are we watching and waiting for?" I ask, giving into her games.

"I know some people who live in this town, and if I know them well enough, they will likely come strolling down this path."

"Why don't we just go to their home and knock on the door?"

"We could if we need to, but this is more convenient and besides it's more fun when it seems like a coincidence."

"So, who, or what should I be looking for?"

"You don't need to keep an eye out for them; I'll do the looking just talk with me, act interested and not annoyed."

"I can't believe you." I say, rolling my eyes.

"What can't you believe? This is me. What you saw back at Newlyn's; I wasn't myself. I was guarded, and I know that the way you are acting isn't the real you because I get it and know that you are still in the middle of your own nightmare. Trust me I get it; you want to see your sister and believe me you will soon but give me this. We need to rest regardless so why not make the best of the evening?"

"I'll drop it, I promise. On a different note, you never did explain how you were able to get a key to break us out."

"Oh yes, I meant to tell you." Shaylo chuckles, "It really was by pure luck and nothing tactical. Newlyn visited me and opened my stall herself."

"Okay and what is the big deal with that?" I ask.

"Well, you know how Sitrus is obsessed with checking and re-checking the locks and locking them even when we are out of our stalls?"

"Yes," I answer.

"Well Newlyn is not so much. She left the lock undone and led me out to give me grief for not doing the choirs. By luck when she had me on the ground, I caught a glimpse of the key in her pocket and with a quick slight of my hand; I managed to get it without her noticing in my struggle with her.

"What do you mean by struggle, did you fight back?"

She laughs, "No I wouldn't dare, I just shielded her blows and when she forced me down, I was able to slip in and out of her pocket undetected."

"Wow, that is luck, I can't believe that she didn't even notice that she was missing the key." I laugh in disbelief.

"Tell me about it, what's even crazier is she didn't even reach in her pocket to lock the lock, I guess it makes sense seeing that it was not fastened, but still, she simply just clicked it shut once I was back inside my stall and left. I took a chance waiting for you to return because the likelihood of Newlyn realizing that she was missing a key was a huge risk, increasing by the minute. Sure enough, she did not return seeking her key and it gave us the opportunity we needed to get out of there. That is why we left suddenly." Without warning Shaylo stands, looks over my shoulder and starts waving. She hollers, "Hey Oden, long time no see!" The person she is waving to recognizes her and runs over, scooping Shaylo up in a warm long hug.

"Shaylo it's good to see you!" He holds her at arm's length. He is trying to choose his next words carefully, "I see that palace life has been treating you, um what's going on with you?"

Shaylo knows that he is trying to be polite and explains so that the awkward atmosphere that this conversation is causing is put to rest. "I look a little disheveled; I know you don't have to beat around the bush." She winks at him.

"Has something happened?" He asks concerned and completely ignoring the fact that I am there. Shaylo explains and plays down the bad that has happened to the both of us.

"It's a long story and I have just about gotten it sorted out, so everything is good. I'm making my return to the

Palace." Her confidence is convincing, and I believe that he accepts it as a truth.

"Join me for dinner and drinks?" He offers.

"I would love to, but Taylan and I are..." Oden interrupts her in mid-sentence.

"Don't be silly it's been too long since we have seen each other, please you and your friend join me, my treat." He smiles at Shaylo; it is half-playful and half-pleading. Shaylo looks at me as if I am the one who is running the show. I take the visual queue and play her mind game.

I speak up, "I don't see why we couldn't put our plans aside for the evening. Thank you for the invitation."

Shaylo smiles at me and then looks back to Oden with a smile and a nod.

"Wonderful! Well, I am going to head home and get ready. We can meet at Dregit's restaurant in let's say an hour. After that, it is your choice. You remember where Dregit's is right?" Oden asks Shaylo.

"Of course, I remember, don't be ridiculous." Shaylo replies.

"Great, I will see you later!" He gives Shaylo a parting hug, nods to me and continues his walk. We are still at the park bench. I am in total wonder that happened as though it was somehow already rehearsed.

I ask, "How did you know?"

Shaylo smiles, "When you come to be my age you begin to realize that a lot of people stick to their routines."

"That was really lucky of you."

"Not really, I just remembered his routine that's all." Shaylo answers.

"Since we have time before we meet your friend for dinner let's talk about the Palace. So, your plan is to tell

King Wolfrim what; that Rosaleen knows the family secret and that she imprisoned you?"

She replies, "Exactly," appearing satisfied with the thought.

"So, what do you expect King Wolfrim to do, detain her or some other form of punishment?"

"One or the other or both" Shaylo grins.

"I understand that is why you want me there with you to confirm the truth to him, but how do I know that Ashlea won't get caught in the crossfire?"

"Just tell Wolfrim the truth. He will see that the two of you were caught up in the middle of this dispute with the fact that you were taken under Rosaleen's command after it all happened."

"Then what happens to my sister and me?"

"Well, lots of things could happen like, you two could serve me, or you can serve King Wolfrim, or any other of the dignitaries within the Palace." Shaylo looks at me knowing that something is amiss. "You are required to serve out your duties no matter what, and besides serving within the Palace is one of the most prestigious roles you can have."

"Why shouldn't I be able to negotiate my duties? I am doing you a major service with being your witness. If you reveal the warnings to King Wolfrim and mention that I helped you, why can't you lay mention and suggest that I and my sister be discharged?"

She is surprised that I had the nerve even to ask. "That's a big ask Taylan. Whether you serve in the trenches and win the war or assist the elite within the Palace, keep the peace, whatever you do, your superiors expect commitment. They don't give freebies. You serve the length of your term and then you can choose to retire, or continue working, after your time is done, it is your choice if you want to continue. I can't really help you out."

"Could you ask him to shorten my required length that I need to serve?"

"Yes, I can ask, but I doubt it will go in the way that you hope for."

"Just ask for me?" I plead.

"Sure Taylan."

"It would be also for Ashlea." I clarify.

"I understood what you meant; I will ask." Shaylo gives me her word, but as to exactly how much that means, only time will tell.

We spend the hour walking along the boardwalk, strolling down the streets in town, taking in the sites as though we are tourists, or shoppers and not people who are on the run. We make our way to the restaurant to meet her old acquaintance. Oden is standing out in front of the entrance. We meet and all walk in together. To our delight, there has been a reservation made and no wait. We all sit down; the conversation mostly involves Shaylo and Oden catching up with the happenings of their lives. From what I gather, they have not seen each other in years. I find it hard to stay tuned in to the conversation. Shaylo and Oden are failing to include me; however, even though I am bored, I force myself to pay attention in case there is information that could be of use.

We eat, drink and within an hour, finish this part of the evening. I am tired and bored out of my mind and Shaylo seems to be having the time of her life.

Oden says to Shaylo, "How about some drinks at the lounge?" Shaylo looks at me, which catches Oden's eye, "It will be my treat." He finally acknowledges my presence.

"Sure, thank you." The three of us leave the restaurant and cross the street to the lounge. It is a one-story building. The front is made of a smooth plaster and is painted a soft orange. There are skillfully placed shrubs in front; each is covered in little twinkling white lights. There are no lineups. The sound of upbeat music is in the air as well as the humming of many voices within the building. We enter; the place is full of people having an enjoyable time, some talking amongst friends, lovers putting the moves on one another and others dancing. Some are even singing to the song. The place is full, but a good full, the right number of people. There are no lineups for drinks, tables, or the most important thing, the facilities.

Shaylo's old friend leads us through the lounge to the bar and orders drinks for us. I have no idea what kind. I could not hear his order because of the volume of the music. Oden pays the bartender then leads Shaylo and me onward through the lounge. The theme of the white light shrubs outside carries its way into the decor of the inside. Along with a red and white color theme against honey color wood. We arrive at this cozy circular white leather covered booth with a knee-high circular wood table. The servers have reached our booth first. They are setting down our drinks as we walk up. We sit, Shaylo and Oden are already in conversation, but whatever they are talking about, I have no idea. I politely sip my drink, look in their general direction and pretend that I am engaged in the conversation. What I really want right now is to rest, but Shaylo has a second wind. I make a personal note to myself, that Oden has good taste, the restaurant, this lounge, and the drink that he ordered for me. I can taste the faint taste of sugar kelp in this sweet frosty drink, but because I am already tired, this drink makes me even more so. I finish it despite the fatigue.

Shaylo and Oden show no signs of turning in for the night and I need to get up, or else I am going to fall asleep.

"Shaylo, Oden excuse me I am going to go find the washroom." They nod, quickly returning to their discussion as I get up and walk about the lounge. I wander back in the direction of the bar, spot the washroom signs on the opposite wall, and follow them down a hallway into the bathroom. This washroom is elaborately decorated just as the rest of the lounge. Honey colored wood floor and vanity with white square sinks; the stalls are a deep red. The lamps are clever looking things that are made of what looks to be shrubs but hanging from the ceiling with those sparkly little white lights. The only other lighting is these tiny rows of bulbs over the square mirrors on the vanity. I am the only one in here, given the number of people in the lounge and decide on the second stall to the left. I finish, wash my hands, and check my appearance. My hair is a honey brown; my eyes are catching the color of the floor. I pull my hair back to look at my pearl and lightly run my fingers over what is left of the scar on my throat. Soon enough the scar will be completely gone. I am caught up in staring at my own face. Jeez, I look tired. I can't possibly be fooling them. Regardless, there seems to be no end to this night. I finish fussing over my appearance, satisfied that this is the best I can look and exit the washroom. Slowly walk down the hall, only this time there is a man at about the halfway point leaning against the wall. I murmur. "Excuse me?" to pass, he barely takes notice, but lets me by. The attack comes from behind. I need to pay attention to my surroundings more, it is a constant reminder, and this proves to be another.

Chapter 32
A Hallway Headlock

I try to break out of a headlock, but it is of no use; I am being picked up and dragged into the washroom. The hallway is a good cover and no one from the lounge has noticed. No one has come to my rescue. The music is so loud that my struggle can't be heard unless someone happened to be at an arm's length. Fatigue evaporates; I am wide-awake, fighting to break free. Everything is happening in slow motion. It is just a couple of seconds. What did I do wrong and why am I being attacked?

The attacker drags me into a stall. I can hear the latch of the stall door click shut behind me.

"Stop freaking out it's just me." The voice says in a rushed hiss. I stop struggling and he lets me go. I turn to face him.

"Sit? Why did you grab me like that?" I am so irritated.

"I wasn't certain that you would stay and chat with me." Sit answers exasperated.

"You think that I am on her side?" I say with arms crossed and looking up at him.

"Well, you have a motive."

"And what is that? That I risk bringing my mother and other sister, Saydira, into the mix because I left Rosaleen who will go after them. On the other hand, is it that I enjoy the company of my attacker's wife? When Shaylo figures out that, I was the one who sentenced her husband to death and then finished him off myself. Should I just stay in her company and let her kill me?"

He rolls his eyes and replies, "Okay sorry, it's just that I didn't see it like that."

"How did you see it?" I cross my arms and lean against the wall of the stall.

"I thought that you had become her ally, I thought that your motive was freedom and that the entire prison thing had become too much for you to manage."

I sigh and let my breath escape my lips, "It was, but look at the situation you and Newlyn put me in. With being your captive, I needed to act the part. When Shaylo made a break for it, what did you expect me to do; tell her; oh, I will hang back in this horse stall?"

"Sorry," he shrugs, "Well, I'm happy that I found you safe." Sit rubs my arms in a half-hearted embrace and smiles shyly.

I whisper, "Thanks, I missed you and wondered if you would find us. I thought that you and Newlyn would not have thought to look this far?"

"We figured after a rigorous search of the island that you had managed to leave. We are on good terms with the other islanders and no offense, but you two would not have been able to stay hidden with them so I trusted my gut that no one was harboring escaped prisoners in their home."

"Makes sense" I smirk.

"Enough of this let me take you back. You are no longer obligated to continue in this act. We can leave now, and Shaylo will never know what happened."

"Sit, I can't, please don't make me leave?"

"But why Taylan, you can leave this all behind and forget it ever happened."

"I have invested so much into this, and I feel like I am so close to having this play out and finish. There is no point of taking me now?"

"What do you mean?"

"I don't need rescuing; I am safe for now and the whole point of tracking us down was to stop Shaylo from getting to the Palace. We are only about a day away and your saving me isn't stopping her. You can't stop her unless you confront her when she is without her friend, or the other way would be, if you ousted me for being her husband's killer. Her motive is her husband's safety. Trust me. I am fine. This won't play out the way Rosaleen and Newlyn had hoped for, but regardless, it will play out." I see a change in Sit, an understanding, or tolerance.

"I won't return to Newlyn and tell her that any of this happened." He says.

"I should hope not, I don't think that they would take your failure lightly, or my stance on this."

"I'll follow you and stay hidden so that Shaylo doesn't suspect. I need you to do something for me?"

"What?" I ask and wait for his proposal.

"We need to try to slow her down so that we give Rosaleen the chance to conduct her own plan at the Palace. We need to get Shaylo away from these people and her friend. I can try to stop her, but I can't do it here with so many people around."

"I can try my best and see what I can do." I say to him.

"I can live with that." He answers. We embrace while still locked in the washroom stall and seem to come to sense of our own surroundings. I laugh at the thought that we just had a deep conversation next to a toilet. The laugh is contagious.

"We got to get you out of here." I say as I managed to hold in a giggle while trying to stay focused.

"There is no need, you leave first, return to Shaylo and her friend. Pretend that this never happened." He says with a brave smile and longing eyes. I can feel it, he does not want me to leave, and I can feel he does not want to let me go.

"Sit I will miss you. Geez I hope this all pans out so that we can see each other sooner than later." I hold onto him and lose myself in time. I am not sure how long we are together although it is only a moment or two. In unison, our eyes meet. I look up into those clear blue eyes of his; he leans down and gives me an intense kiss. I just want to stay with him. He is warm, tender and I want more. He does too, but we force ourselves to end the bliss, he nudges me.

"Go, you have to." He asserts. I give him one last hug, a kiss on his cheek, and then leave the washroom. Oddly, there is still absolutely no one else in the washroom, but Sitrus in the stall and me just giving myself a final check in the vanity mirror.

I leave and my heart aches. All kidding aside, I knew that I have developed feelings for him even under the strange circumstance, but never thought that I would ever long for him this much. Leaving him brings me to the realization that Sitrus means much more to me than I had ever thought.

Down the hall I walk, a man brushes passed me entering the men's washroom. I hear him say a gentle excuse me as he passes. I enter the lounge. Nothing seems to have changed. The atmosphere is that of fun and laughter, people dancing and friends enjoying each other's company. The only thing that seems to be different is that Shaylo and Oden are not where I left them. I see this before approaching the round white leather couch; however, I don't veer off my intended destination. I stand there for a moment looking around for a sign of them, but only catch a few glimpses from strangers' curious glances. They have not been gone for long because their empty drinks have not been picked up, and no one has taken over our spot. I decide to sit and wait for them. A server walks over; picking up the empty glasses and says to me, "I was asked to tell you that your friends are just outside." They are not my friends.

"Are we all paid up?" I ask to be polite; regardless, I have no kiros anyway.

"Yes, your friend covered the tab." The server answers.

"Okay great."

"Have a good night." She smiles, leaving with a full tray.

Well, that is weird. Why would they be outside? They had not really shown much of a desire to leave anytime soon. I have a strange feeling that something isn't right. I casually get up and approach the exit, sure enough the two of them have continued their catching up outside. I come out into the warm night, and they spot me, waving me over.

"What are you two doing out here?" I ask.

Shaylo answers, "I know you're tired and I am to, I figured that we would call it a night."

Oden pipes up, "You are both welcome to stay at my home for the evening. It's not an inconvenience."

Shaylo answers before I open my mouth to speak. "Thanks, so much Oden, but I am afraid that we have an early start to our day tomorrow, we wouldn't want to disturb you. We are going to find a quiet place to rest for the night and tomorrow we will make our way to the Palace." Before Oden can make a second attempt at convincing her otherwise, Shaylo cuts right to it, "Thank you so much for the diner and drinks. I can't remember the last time that I enjoyed myself as much as I did this evening." She gives him a hug and a kiss on the cheek.

"When I see my better half, I will tell him how well you treated my friend and me."

I must take note of how Shaylo does that. She has Izavelle's skill with having a good relationship with others, but also, she is good with transitioning and does it in a way that doesn't make it sound short or cut off. She also pays attention to the feelings of others.

Oden smiles and pulls her in for one last hug, "It was so good to see you again have a safe trip and say hello to Shrago for me."

"I will and thank you." Shaylo puts her arm into mine like a chain link and we walk in the opposite direction that Oden is headed. We head back to the shore and through the park, down the boardwalk. I am beyond tired, but after seeing Sit I have butterflies in my stomach and have a much-needed boost to get me through this last leg. We walk in silence. Normally I would question her on where we are going next, or what are we going to eat, or where we should rest; come to think about it, where are we going to rest? At the beginning of the night, I would have guessed that Shaylo would have taken Oden up on his offer to rest at his home, but I guess with no money to pay to stay at an inn I guess we are camping outside like we have been doing. I doubt that she is going to have us travel by night and I know she has been up as long as I have so travel at this hour is completely out of the question. I decide to keep quiet and just wait out until she decides for us. I think I have done well for myself playing the part of Shaylo's partner and the chemistry between us is amicable. This could have gone bad, but it hasn't, and I can honestly say that I am proud of myself for being so strong and give myself an invisible pat on the back.

We walk back to the spot in the forest where we left our solar suits. I pay little attention to Shaylo and instead get to work with finding a comfortable spot to rest my eyes for the night. There is not much of a breeze, which is good because the temperature is comfortable without the wind. The trees are a good barrier from the ocean. I crouch down but hesitate because the sound of Shaylo's footsteps approach me from behind.

"Shaylo, I didn't think I would ever get to rest with the way you and your friend were catching up." I decide on resting up against a tree trunk, back against the trunk and my legs extended. I look up at her; she is only a shadow in the moonlight. "I was so sure you were going to take your friend's offer at a nice comfy bed." I cross my arms to a comfortable position. "Your decisions always surprise me." There is a moment of silence, and I blink to try to get a better look at Shaylo, but it is of no use she is still just a shadowy silhouette in my vision.

"You sure had me fooled." A stern voice projects into the night.

"Shaylo, what are you talking about, can't we just put whatever it is aside and get some rest? We can talk about it in the morning." My heart is starting to race. Does she know about Sitrus's visit?

"You can stop pretending. I heard everything."

Chapter 33
Shaylo's Game Change

My heart is racing, what did she hear? Having no chance to move, she straddles me, pinning me down. Shaylo takes my wrists holding them above my head. While glaring at me, she roars, "You killed him?" I am shaking, trying to force myself from her grasp.

"Shaylo I," I am still fighting to break free. The sudden burst of rage from her slams my wrists back into the dirt. The back of my hands sting from the pebbles scraping my skin.

"You are nothing to me." She hisses, red in her eyes. I am trying to roll over and wiggle free. Her weight is too much for me.

"I could take you right now; maybe step on your throat?" She holds me firmly as I struggle; Shaylo is stronger than I am, I am panicking, struggling to take a gulp of air. "I don't want to die." I manage to choke out.

"Why?" She screams in a raspy voice, but tears are streaming down her face. A couple of them drop onto mine and trickle into my mouth. The salty taste of a tear, there is no mistaking what it is. She shakes me hard and screams, "Why?" Angry sobs, with her hands on my wrists she punches my own hands into the dirt, and I start to feel the warmth of blood.

I whisper, "Please."

She looks at me "What?"

I gently say, "Please, he attacked me."

I set her off the deep end and she yells at me, "Liar!"

My heart is still pounding in my chest more so than the night her husband Shrago attacked me.

"Please" I say in a raspy voice, "Look at me," I cough on the saliva mixed with dust from the struggle going down the back of my throat, "Yes, I kept things from you." Shaylo is shaking; I can feel with the weight of her body that her muscles are tensing up more than they already are; she is getting ready to let me have it.

"Understand; he attacked me while I slept. Remember the wound on my throat when I first stayed in the stall next to you?" I am panting, but she is starting to listen. "Do you remember?" I need her to acknowledge.

"Yes" She answers.

"It was Shrago that did that to me."

"No!" She screams, but the red is fading in her eyes.

"Yes" I whisper.

"No" She repeats, only this time the rage is being replaced with sadness. The muscles in her body start to relax.

"Please let me explain." I test her by trying to lift myself and manage to sit up from the ground. It is as though she forgot that she was pinning me down. "It wasn't my will; I didn't wish to hurt anyone." I pick up her hand and cup both my scraped hands around hers. "Please look at me, I didn't wish his death." Shaylo looks up at me, tears flowing down her face. She is ashamed of them. Shaylo tries to stop them, but it is not working. "Please let me explain, will you listen?"

She breathes in and forces the words out in a sob, "Yes, I need to know what happened to my beloved."

My own heart starts to slow to a steady beat, we sit cross-legged at the base of the tree, face to face, and I have not let go of her hand. All I see is the faint sparkle of her glassy eyes in the darkness. She is still a shadowy figure, and I tell her everything. I don't know what has come over me because she could try to kill me after I finish. I have the feeling that more than just Shaylo's eyes are on me. I gamble and sneak a glance in the direction where I sense it and sure enough, there is a shadow in the darkness not far off, watching. It comes as a relief to me in case something goes wrong. I know that it is Sitrus.

Chapter 34
Shaylo Knows

I am not sure when but eventually, we get some rest. I'm relieved that Shaylo at least understands why I did what I had, and I can understand why she doesn't agree with it, but at least she knows. It wasn't cold in the night, but I wake before dawn to find that we are both still in our dresses and are snuggled up to one another. The extra warmth is not required, but it is welcomed. I hardly move and just look around but see no signs of Sitrus. Last night after Shaylo was caught up to speed on her late husband she asked about Sitrus. Straight up she had asked if he was following us and without being certain as to how much she overheard in the lounge washroom I sort of beat around the bush and said without sounding over condescending, "What do you think?"

She had given me an uncertain look and as loud as she could yell, she calls out, "Sitrus" and listens and again, "Sitrus, I know that you're there." She listens. I never said that he was following us; I never said anything about his whereabouts. I won't say anything to her about it. She eventually gives up on calling Sitrus out of hiding, and I am a little surprised that he has not revealed himself. He hears her. He is using his cover to his own advantage. He could be out of earshot and instead will track us from a distance. Who knows with Sitrus?

Shaylo eventually settled and cuddled up next to me last night and this morning I wake to her head resting in my lap. I guess at some point I had been rubbing her head because my hand lightly place almost cradling the crown of her head. Looking down at her, I have a moment to look at her more intimately. I can imagine that her beauty was key to getting her to the prestigious role of a wife to an important man. I wonder if she had any knowledge that her husband could be as brutal as he was or if she even saw that side of him. I knew who he was, as a servant to Rosaleen, but I had no idea Rosaleen had robbed him of a powerful position. He was the right-hand man to the imposter King Wolfrim and Rosaleen thought that her stepfather had chosen Shrago to be her undercover bodyguard while traveling on her ship and acting out the position as a server to onlookers. His charade sure had me fooled. After being attacked by him I know that he was not a gentle creature and that he took what was his and let those around him know when he was not happy. Shaylo is a strong woman and last night was the first time that I saw her lose her edge. As brutal, as Shrago was to me, he was still loved by Shaylo. I wonder how they were together. I have a tough time visualizing it, two strong people mentally, physically, and seemingly fearless; their bond must have been intense. I sit there and feel bad, but not sorry for ending Shrago's life. I don't feel sorry because it was his decision to be brutal, not mine. I feel bad because I have developed some sort of backwards friendship with Shaylo and wonder if I had known her outside this setting if I would have had a good relationship with Shrago?

Shaylo stretches and opens her eyes, looks at me while calm in her element, but I can't tell if she has moved passed the fact that it all stems down to me. Her eyes have an element of strength in them, but there is also sorrow. I have said everything that I needed to. It is up to Shaylo to choose if she wants to forgive me.

"Did you rest?" She looks up and asks while stretching.

"Yes" I answer in a whisper.

She lifts her head from my lap and gets up carefully. She starts pacing slowly back and forth, arms crossed and head down to the ground. She is thinking through something, what I told her last night, or she is going through our plan for today with travel. Back and forth she slowly walks, stretching her limbs out of rest. I leave her alone for a few minutes and sit back letting her work in silence.

After some time has passed, in a faint voice I say, "Shaylo?"

"Can you just shut up for a second and let me be." She answers curtly.

I get up from my spot at the base of the tree, cross my arms and walk off in the opposite direction to the park. I duck and creep around branches and manage to get around the obstacles. I walk to a clearing that provides a clear view of the ocean. There is a bit of a cliff here. I am about ten feet above water level. It is a grey day; the waves are crashing against the cliff and the wind is strong which is good in a way because it is in our favor if we are continuing in the same direction. My arms are crossed as I stare out into the open. I am longing for my mother, sisters and Sitrus. I hold my pearl on its chain. It rests around my neck. I am brought back to the North Shore. The day my sisters and I uncovered the pearls and feel comfort with that memory. Shaylo has not tried to kill me. Her reaction: although intense, it went well. I had anticipated a fight. I turn to walk back but when I turn, Shaylo is standing in my path.

She snaps, "Do you think you can just walk off like that?" Her eyes are burning into mine.

Surprised, I tread carefully, "Shaylo I... I thought you wanted a few minutes to yourself?"

She spits back at me, "I asked for you to be quiet, not to leave."

"Sorry!"

"We are leaving now suit up." She barks; I comply to avoid confrontation.

We both strip down leaving the dresses behind by tucking them into the crevice of the base of the tree. She takes off. Leaping into the air in one bound. I follow. We travel all day, soaring at cloud level. She pays little attention to me as we fly, and well, she is paying little attention to anything for that matter except for the direction that we are traveling. I don't bother trying to make an attempt at conversation. It is best to leave her alone and let her grieve. My mind wonders off to Sitrus as we glide, pondering where he is? I have not caught a glimpse of him. He is good at what he does. We touch down momentarily for a break to relieve ourselves, drink and eat. The stop is of no interest, just another small, unoccupied island. Then we are off again and still, Shaylo has said nothing, I am not sure if it's Shaylo's silence that bothers me, or that I am just missing the companionship of others, maybe a bit of both. I am feeling anxious with the thought of getting there, not only for the main reasons, but for knowing that there will be others there to talk to also. Let me be clear that I am not mad at Shaylo for the way she has come at me, or for her silence. I know that being upset effects people differently. I am just anxious for new company and hoping to see Ashlea.

It is rolling into the evening, and we are still on the move and can see the city in the horizon. The city grows larger as we approach. The buildings appear large, and most seem to be comprised of glass because the buildings reflect the sky and right now, it is a grey color with a faint orange as the sun is starting to set. The city, despite its size, is like all the others that I have visited, in that it is next to the ocean. The only differences are instead of the more natural settings of the small island towns, it has city walls and is a glass jungle. It looks foreign to me, but pretty. The shore is surrounded by many ship docks and the ones that catch your eye are the docks for the larger ships. In the distance, you can see the Palace erected on a hill, which makes it look that much grander. Its white stone walls make it look like a sandcastle in a sea of sparkling water.

Shaylo dives down as we approach. I follow. More things come into focus, small boats in the water, building details and people. Just off to my right something catches my eye, Rosaleen's ship! My heart flutters, knowing that my sister is nearby. I don't need Shaylo anymore to guide me and I am not playing any more games with her. She knows the truth about Shrago and what is even better in a twisted way is Rosaleen has not docked ship yet meaning her confronting King Wolfrim has not commenced, which means that neither Shaylo nor anyone for that matter has confronted this imposter, King Wolfrim. Shaylo is a lost cause; let her warn the imposter. I know I don't have the physical strength to stop her on my own unless I can lead her back to her enemies. Shaylo is still ahead of me; this is my chance, if Shaylo chases me it might work out that Rosaleen's people can catch her if they see me coming? It is a chance, and it needs to happen now. I make a break for it.

Chapter 35
Taylan's Dive

I dive down towards the ship, gaining speed in the descent. The wind is rushing past, and my eyes are tearing up. The ship is getting closer, I ease up to slow my speed as I approach. Feeling confident, I look back and don't see her. I look forward, still moving swiftly, but something doesn't feel right. It's the ship; it's not Rosaleen's? The sinking feeling of being so very wrong sets in and my stomach turns. I won't see Ashlea. Forgetting for a moment just why I was going so fast, I slow my speed in bewilderment. I was so sure that, that was "the ship," Rosaleen's ship. My heart aches, how could I be so wrong?

The wind is knocked from my lungs. I can't breathe in and find myself falling, like a kite falling from the sky, dropping towards the water. I am more alert and awake than ever, and my heart is racing as I fall. Time has slowed down as I try to correct myself, extending my arms and flapping, trying to catch myself, but it is not working. I hit the water hard with the back of my shoulder and sink fast. The suit is awkward in the water; I can't get out of it. Normally, I can stay under the water for a few minutes at a time, but without air in my lungs, I am struggling to breathe and need to get to the surface. Down into the deep I drop, somehow, I struggle to get out of the suit. The water is dark with the sun low in the sky. There is no reef here. It is a shallow looking sandy bottom, but the water is deceiving. It is another twenty feet before I touch bottom. I don't want to touch bottom. I need air. The suit that I have scrambled out of sinks, I am naked and racing to the surface with all my energy. My arms are tired from flying all day and I am sore from the hit and impact of the water; I need to reach the surface now. My eyes are open looking up, I am getting closer to a breath of air, but it is not soon enough. I kick my legs and extend my arms to swim as hard as I can, but my vision goes dark, I am still alert and kicking. I know my eyes are open, but I can't see anything. I feel tired, but I am not giving up, I can't, not like this. My chest hurts and body just wants to inhale, but I force myself not to. This isn't supposed to happen; I want to see Ashlea, just a little further. Where is Sitrus when you need him? I thought he was following Shaylo and me, I am a fool to think that he would come to my rescue. Everything goes silent except for a wringing in my ears. That is the last thing that I remember.

Chapter 36
Taylan's Darkness

Am I home? Is this a dream, or am I dead? It is eerily silent. It is dark. Somewhere in here there is a dim light casting shadow. I blink, opening my eyes wide to see clearer. This is a bedroom, but I'm not sure if this is my bedroom back home? I'm on my back and comfortable, warm, and dry. I touch myself to make sure that this isn't a dream. I am here, wherever here is? I run my fingers through my hair and check the color; black which means that I have been resting for a while. Slowly and ever so quietly, I sit up. No one is here. I lift the sheets and examine my body, running my hands over to feel for pain and areas that I can't see just to make sure that I am okay. I seem fine. This is so weird. The last thing that I remember is the thought that this was it; I was dying alone because I couldn't bring myself to the surface. It was the hardest thing that I ever fought for; a breath and knowing that the battle was lost; that was my last memory. I think hard, was there something that I missed when I was in the water? No, I was for sure alone before it all went dark; there was no site of Shaylo coming to my rescue, or even Sitrus for that matter.

The bed is just like my bed at home, silky sheets and netting surrounding the bed. The air is warm, and it is the middle of the night. Restless and uncertain on where I am, I get off the bed and walk around the room. The walls are a sphere and are all finished warm wood textures. I touch them recognizing the pattern of grooves from the grain. A single arched at the top closed door is on the opposite side from the bed. There is a window on the left off to the side and it is open with a breeze coming though the sheers. My limbs are working, muscles are a little sore, but nothing is broken. My lungs are tired and sore, as if I have been running full force for hours, but none the less, I am okay. I approach the window and look out trying to figure out where this is exactly. I look out and learn that I am up at least four levels. The window is big enough that I can sit on its wide ledge and lean out to get a better view. I am in some kind of tower; it looks to be a corner tower. I do not see any other window ledges nearby, but it is hard to tell with the spherical shape of the structure and with the fact that it is dark. There could be another window a level above, or below that is simply just out of sight. The adjacent flat walls that extend from the tower do have windows and the one closest to me is a fair distance. If I shouted, I am sure that if someone were in that room, they would hear me. The window over there is open. There is no sheen from glass, and I see the faint movements of its sheers. It looks like there is a dim light projecting through. Below my window is a yard that looks to be set up for leisure. There is grassy open flat space that starts on the far end and near me; there is a pool with a large fake waterfall surrounded by lush vegetation, trees, and the glimpse of flowers and plenty of shrubs. A patio surrounds the pool with chairs and lounge beds. I know where I am; I leave the window, setting my sights on the door, tip toeing towards it and try turning the knob. It is not locked! Hmm I have no idea how long I have been here, or what has happened. Could this entire dilemma with Princess Rosaleen and King Wolfrim be settled? My heart starts racing and the sudden surge of adrenaline hits; I want to know what has happened and who else is here.

Staring at the door, do I dare? Yes, do it. I slowly open it without a sound and peek through to a dark hallway with red carpet laid out on a grey stone floor. It is quiet, too quiet, but despite the eerie feeling that I shouldn't be doing this, my curiosity takes over. It is making me brave or stupid. I am not sure which? I creep down the hall and around a corner. There are more hallways only this time I see the glimmer of a faint light under a closed door. This must be the room with the open window. It's quite a way down, I cautiously tip toe forward and listen, nothing. I become aware of what I am wearing, a sheer nightdress and I am barefoot. My toes are cold from the stone floor. I won't go back. I am already halfway there. Still no noise, as I approach this closed door. I make the effort to stand up straight and knock gently.

Tap, tap.

I wait and listen. I hear rustling and wait. I am about to knock again when the door creaks open. Shaylo.

In a hushed voice she asks, "What are you doing up?"

I wanted to ask the first question, and I lose for a second my train of thought and ask, "What do you mean, what time is it? How long have I been asleep?"

She yawns as she answers, "A couple of days. Come in, there is no sense waking everyone up, it is the middle of the night." I follow her into the bedroom.

"You rescued me?" I question.

"Yes, I pulled you from the water just in time and brought you to the shore. Once I knew you were breathing, I went for help, and we eventually made it back to the Palace." She takes a seat on a red velvet couch, and I take a seat on a cushion chair.

"I thought you were going to let me die."

"I thought about it, but where would that get me? It won't bring Shrago back and besides none of that would have happened without Rosaleen, or Newlyn setting things in motion. It's more their fault than yours." My palms start to sweat at her candidness.

"Are you mad at me for what happened to Shrago?" I ask.

She reaches for me and pulls me close so that we are face to face, in a strained whisper she answers, "Not a day goes by that I don't think of him, wishing I could see his face, touch him and hear his voice." I gulp; I feel her grief, she is angry, "You killed him, you stupid girl." Her fists are clasped so tight holding the collar of my nightshirt that I feel her trembles.

"Shaylo, I didn't have a choice."

In a slightly raised, but strained voice she answers, "You're not kidding anyone, you had a choice." She lets go of my collar and I call back in the chair.

I can't let Shaylo win this argument or have her convince herself that this was how it was, because how she understands it is not right. "Shaylo, you listen to me, Shrago was already as good as dead when I brought on his death; his head was smashed in. If I had done nothing, he would have died a more painful death. This is why I had done what I did." She's gazing hard into my eyes and grasps me firmly again holding me there; I continue, "Yes, he attacked me and had he not been on the brink of death I would have given Rosaleen a non-death type of sentence for his assault on me, I swear this to you." Her stare cuts through the dimness into me. Shaylo is debating on taking her frustration out on me again. She just pushes me away in one strong shove. I don't say anything about it, there is no point.

She paces the room for a few minutes to calm herself. "Shaylo?" I whisper.

She sighs, "What?"

"Where could I make myself a snack?"

I catch her surprised, sideways glance, but quickly, she changes her expression as she realizes that my hunger is weighing more heavily on my mind than her grief; it has been a while since I last ate.

"Come with me." She grumbles and we leave her room, exiting right and walk down the hall. Then down the stairs that seem to go around and round as we descend. My eyes are fixed on the red carpet as we walk, then through a short hallway that opens into a large space. It is unlit and we tiptoe across to the opposite side. There are giant windows down the right, overlooking the same view that I had from my bedroom. We enter a second hall and at the end go through swinging doors that make a creaking sound. We are in some kind of grand kitchen. Not one where you would sit to eat a meal, but one designed for food preparation. Shaylo turns on the lights as she crosses the room, gathers two stools and brings them over to a counter, motioning me to sit down.

She prepares some toast with some sort of dark sweet spread, brings our snacks over to the counter, and hops up on the second stool next to me and we eat.

I ask her in a hushed voice, conscious that the building is quiet, and the Palace is asleep, "Why did you bring us back here?"

"Taylan, just let it go, you know why."

"What good does this do? It won't bring him back."

She swallows a bite, "I know that, but you need to understand that I need to get even. Locking me up in a horse stall and then killing my spouse, and never telling me what had happened. They need to pay for this, and I will make it happen and you my dear are going to validate everything." She sips some water to wash down her toast. I have already finished mine. She takes our plates to the sink, cleans, and puts them away in an overhead cupboard.

I ask, "How does any of this help me get my sister back? Did you even take a moment to think how all of this would affect me? You are putting me right in the middle and I don't want to be a part of the feud. If I do what you ask, then what happens to my sister? Did you even take a moment to think about me?"

"Don't be all self-righteous, your sister won't come into harm's way, your right, you, and Ashlea aren't a part of this. I promise that she will be kept safe."

I don't know what to do here. Everything is in the balance. Ashlea, being able to see my mom and Saydira again, and I think the start of a forming relationship with Sitrus, although he has lied about keeping watch over me while on this journey with Shaylo. If I side with Shaylo, Sitrus will view me as a traitor and so will the Princess, her servants, and her mother. If Rosaleen somehow overcomes this dilemma, I can guarantee some form of retribution will come to me either directly, or indirectly. The truth of this matter is there is no good side. This imposter King Wolfrim took control because he was once being controlled and Princess Rosaleen is no angel either. She has blood on her hands. The truth is, I must decide and right now, it is to side with Princess Rosaleen because my family and loved ones are within her grasp, however way you look at it, but Shaylo doesn't need to know this.

Shaylo whispers, "Let's head up to bed."

I am anything but tired. I can investigate my room in hopes that it will speed up the day to come. There is one last thing that isn't answered that I need to know, I murmur as we are walking back through the Palace, "Shaylo do you know where Rosaleen is?"

"Not for sure, some have spotted her ship not far from here, but those reports haven't been confirmed."

"Do you think she will return?"

Shaylo shrugs and with a smug expression she says, "It all depends on if she has good insiders, or any for that matter. If she knows that I have returned to the castle, the best thing for her would be to turn that ship around, go as far as she can and never return. I know her type, Rosaleen is too proud, she may return, or she may not, but I am sure that we will know soon enough."

We have made it to Shaylo's bedroom door, "Good night, Taylan."

"Good night" Shaylo closes the door behind her, and I walk down the hallway and around the corner to my own room. It is odd how she considers me a key piece to her game and yet she doesn't worry herself with watching over me, but then again, we have stayed together during the entire time of traveling. She knows that I have nowhere to go. I have no idea how to get home, no understanding of where Ashlea is right now, and I haven't a clue how I would leave without being noticed, or if anyone is watching for that matter? Shaylo knows me too well. This is no good, will Rosaleen return with Ashlea?

Chapter 37
Shaylo's Demand

Shaylo comes barging into my room. "Taylan, get up." She sounds annoyed and I have done absolutely nothing.

I roll over, "What time is it?"

"Mid-morning, you need to dress and eat; you're meeting King Wolfrim with me at noon."

I sit up and rub my eyes open. Shaylo has drawn open the sheers, letting in as much light as possible, which does not really change the lighting because they are sheers, but it lets the breeze in a bit more. She plops a dress on my bed and other clothing for me to wear. I get dressed. She lays a pair of shoes down for me to step into and wear. It is a simple blue outfit nothing over the top fancy, but a dress with straight cut lines and the shoes have a heel to them.

"Shaylo I can't walk in these."

"Practice," she barks. I start to walk around, managing awkwardly.

"Not like that." She sighs. "Like this," Shaylo is bare foot, standing next to me, "Balance, like you are balancing on your tiptoes. When you step, your shoe will hit heel first then toe. When your shoe is completely touching the ground, you must remember in the back of your mind that you are on your tip toes, but you can use the heel to rest some of the weight so that your feet don't get sore." I hesitate and she urges, "Practice" and leaves the room in a rush, her blue hair trails behind her.

I walk around in these heels stopping at my window to see if I can see anything new since it is now light out. Just beyond the wall in the horizon is the ocean and sky. The water is full of different sized boats and ships. I wonder where Ashlea is. I turn just as Shaylo returns to the room with a bag full of different grooming products and makeup.

"Come here." She demands and I sit where she gestures.

"Close your eyes." Shaylo commands.

"Why?" I ask.

She sighs, "Taylan your meeting King Wolfrim today. I need you to look good, groomed, and polished, and most importantly credible so that you can be taken more seriously. I'm going to put some makeup on your eyelids and maybe a bit of powder and blush, but not too much, just enough to make you look more polished." I close my eyes and allow her to do whatever it is that she needs to do.

"Shaylo tell me again, why can't he just take your word alone for everything that has happened? You and your husband have been loyal to him for many years. I don't see why that wouldn't count for anything?"

"He respects me. It is not about the need for him to believe me; it is about my word versus Rosaleen's. Over the years, as twisted as this sounds, he has come to love her like she was his own daughter and even up until her departure Rosaleen and Wolfrim have a strong bond. He trusts her just as he trusts me. My fear is he views our loyalties on an even playing field and that is where you come in, to solidify my truth." The makeup brush leaves my face, and she is back in her bag digging for something else. She pulls out a bottle of perfume some tinted lip balm and some blush, then turns to me, and continues with my grooming. She brushes my silky hair into some sort of up-do and pins it in place.

"There, much better." I am not sure why, but I am reminded of the day that I put her husband to death. I remember now, it is because Princess Rosaleen said the exact words and made the same gesture when she fixed that red scarf around my neck to cover my wound. I sit there and instinctively touch my neck. It has completely healed now.

"We have some time to kill would you like me to show you around?" I startle at Shaylo's choice of words, kill, but realize that there is no hidden meaning behind them.

"I would like that. I have gazed down at the courtyard that my window overlooks. Can we see it?" She nods, leading the way through the airy hallways down the winding stairs and into the great room. Instead of crossing the room to the kitchen, like we did in the night, we make a turn to the right and open a glass door to the yard.

In the courtyard, everything is symmetrical. The gardens and pathways are all straight lines, the ground is level, and the grass is cut perfectly. We casually walk down the pathway towards the pool with the waterfall.

On the way, Shaylo says, "For a while, when I was held at Newlyn's I didn't think I would ever set foot in this place again." She smiles as we stroll down the path, and that is the first one I have seen since waking up in this place.

I ask, "After we all talk with King Wolfrim today what happens to me? Do I stay here with you, or do I return to my mother?"

"That will be the King's decisions not mine."

We approach the pool; there is a group of ten, or so attractive women. Some are swimming in the pool; some are under the waterfall soaking their heads in the steady stream and some are resting on the outdoor lounge beds. Apart from all being stunning, they are all nude. As we walk up, I ask, "Who are they?"

She smiles at me, "Some of King Wolfrim's servants." As we approach, the women recognize Shaylo, and she is greeted with warm welcomes. I hear them say things like, "We thought you were never coming back!" "How is Shrago?" and "Has Princess Rosaleen returned with a decision on who she will wed?" Shaylo fabricates lies for answers. These women are clueless to everything that has happened, and it is something that Shaylo feels that the king should know first. She sits on one of the lounge beds and a group of them get comfortable by her side as she brings them up to speed on her trip. I can't listen to her lie or be there to affirm them. I can't play that part of the game well. I decide to leave the social circle and investigate the pool area. The pool catches a lot of the sun, but it is also surrounded by a lush and tropical garden full of flowering plants that vary in different shapes and sizes. The waterfall is artificial, it's water that is pumped out of an artificial rock mound. It looks like a miniature mountain. I had not noticed this from my window, but the pool is not just a square shape with a waterfall. On the other side of the waterfall is a fabricated lazy river. It weaves its way through the garden, and it rejoins on the opposite side of the pool? I decide to explore, but first take off these stupid high heels and tuck them under a lounge chair. I walk bare foot along the water's edge. I duck under branches and carefully step over and around flowerbeds, making my way to a spot that is still surrounded by lush vegetation only there is a bit of space that I can sit and dip my feet into the refreshing water. It is nice here, quiet and I am just out of earshot of the discussion Shaylo is having with those women. The trickle of water is always so relaxing to me, and I sit and close my eyes, letting my feet dangle in the mild currant. This must be the calm before the storm.

Maybe the talk with King Wolfrim will go well, I don't know, it's just I have been envisioning it to go bad for so long because I know how Shaylo reacts. Anyone who is not with her is against her and she has a temper. I think of home, my family and Sitrus. Relaxing and reflecting, that is all that is on my mind, all that I can think of, and it is weighing hard on me.

"You are sad." A high pitch, mousy like, but sweet-sounding voice startles me out of my daydream. I look towards the sound of the voice and there is a woman in the lazy river. She wades up and grabs on to the ledge just in front of me so that she doesn't float away. She is naked and her hair is undone, but the water has skillfully placed it so that all the strands have been pulled back, as though she is wearing an invisible headband.

"You are sad, and you shouldn't be." She says again.

"I'm not sad." I whisper.

She ignores my reply "I have learned that there is no point in being sad or dwelling on things of the past." I stare blankly at her. What does she know? Who is she? "I used to be like you, and I know what you are going through. You need to let go of the past, embrace the present and look toward to the future." I say nothing and just stare at her confused. "You don't understand, but you will. I love my life, and you will love yours. You will see."

I get up the courage to say, "you are mistaking me for someone else. What is your name?"

She lets go of the ledge so that the light currant can move her along, she replies, "My name isn't important, your happiness is." She disappears out of sight beyond the bend of the river. I sit there for a moment dumbfounded and then I am pulled back into reality. I can hear Shaylo's laughter. I need to do what is best for me and go back to where Shaylo is socializing with the other women.

Shaylo looks at home here, and the woman that had just spoken to me a few minutes ago is nowhere to be found. She has not joined Shaylo by the poolside as I had thought. How strange, but then again, I did take my time with returning and she could have very well gotten back to the main pool, got out and returned to the Palace.

The women who are socializing with Shaylo glance at me and smile politely, but don't say anything and some of the others have retired to resting in the lounge beds taking no notice of me, or anyone else for that matter. This is socially awkward, and I feel so out of place. Shaylo gestures me over. In a whisper for only me to hear she asks, "Shall we?"

"Yes, sure" I answer. We walk back together through the courtyard and into the great room. Directly across the entrance is a fireplace with some sofas that are arranged around it. From a distance, the set up looks so tiny and to be honest I never noticed the arrangement. I know that I have walked past it a couple of times since I woke. I sit on a sofa and Shaylo on a single seat sofa. I am unsure of the time, but we wait and wait some more. The guards have time to exchange thoughts amongst themselves while Shaylo and I sit in silence not because we must, but simply because we have nothing to share. We both know what we need to do. A guard comes through the closed doors next to the lounging arrangement, but it is a false alarm. He was not calling us in; he was just looking for a fellow guard. We continue to wait, and I fidget with my pearl pendent. Touching it triggers the not so long-ago fond memories. I close my eyes, and I am brought back to the North Shore the day my sisters and I found the pearls.

Startled by the creak of a door, I am not sure why, but I always imagined that when first meeting King Wolfrim, he would have been announced upon arrival instead, the palace guards are distributed around the room like silent statues keeping guard. He enters the room, and I set my eyes on this short fat; let me re-word it; he isn't overly short for he is a wee bit taller than I am, but for a man he is short. His hair is curled which is odd. It looks unnatural. Maybe someone curls his hair? His locks are a golden brown, which is strikingly close to the elaborately embroidered gold colored robe that he is wearing. His skin has a pink tint to it and his eyes are black. He waits for no one and marches up with every footstep making an echoed tap as he moves to the loungers. Shaylo immediately stands to greet him; I copy her and shake his hand.

He gestures to Shaylo, "We have lots to talk about, come with me." He explains, leading her back through the doors that shut in one loud sharp sound like the cover falling hard over the keys to a piano. Standing there dumbfounded, was I supposed to follow them?

I look around at the guards and decide to approach the closest one, I ask, "Should I go in?"

He answers curtly, "No you wait until he calls you."

"Okay thank you." I murmur and return to the sofa to sit and wait. I really hate waiting and it doesn't matter if it is for a King, it is still awful. I'm not sure how much time has passed, but I am fidgety and decide to stand and walk around the room, counting all the guards that I see inside and outside and glancing at all the artwork and sculptures' that boarder the room. I wonder if these guards were all called to serve, or if they applied for the job. I want to ask, but I find my shyness taking over, I will have a chance to ask later.

I am startled by the creaky sound of the large door and pivot on my heel to face the sound. Shaylo is in the doorway. She says nothing and I know that King Wolfrim is ready to hear me speak. I follow her and a small gust of wind is felt along my back as I step through the entrance and the door shuts behind.

Chapter 38
Wolfrim's drafty Hall

We walk down a dark drafty hallway, up a serpentine staircase; outlined by light on the other side coming through space between the door and frame. We approach closed double doors. Shaylo takes care to open them quietly and we both enter. Unlike the hallway and staircase leading to King Wolfrim's chambers the room is well lit. The thick red velvet window coverings are drawn shut despite that it is the middle of the afternoon. Only the lamps are lighting the room.

"Sit," he orders, "both of you." I take a seat across from Shaylo on a sofa; Wolfrim sits across from us so that Shaylo and I are on his left and right, like a triangle. This chamber is massive, there is a lounging area where we are sitting, and at the other end there is a giant lavish four poster bed with a red velvet canopy draped around so you don't see the pillows, or the bed unless the canopy is opened. There is a fireplace beside us and next to the bedside; there is some sort of cabinet and elaborate table. I spot a few fancy stemmed drinking glasses and an assortment of liquor. I look at him, then at Shaylo and then back to him. In what I guess is the calmest tone he can speak, given the situation he says, "So I understand that you are one of my daughter's newest hires?"

I try to swallow, but my throat is dry, Shaylo encourages, "Go on Taylan, you can tell him the truth." I look at her and then back at him, unsure.

I blurt out, "I don't know what you're talking about." My heart vibrates. Shaylo's eyes meet mine. She glances down for a second then back up without saying anything except I know she is urging me while dumb founded. I am too afraid and look down to avoid either of their eyes.

"Taylan go on you have to tell him." I don't think she realizes; it is not nerves holding me back. It is the decision that I have made. I want no part in this game. I am not taking sides.

I investigate King Wolfrim's black eyes, secretly coaching myself to keep eye contact, appear confidant and certain, though I am a pile of nerves on the inside, "I have no idea who you are talking about, or what this is all about."

There is a moment of utter confusion from Wolfrim and Shaylo. They stare at one another. No one knows how to react. Wolfrim stares back at me realizing that what just came out of my mouth is untrue but knowing that I have made a choice. Shaylo is fuming on the other hand. As I glance at her, she explodes.

"You brainless twit," she shouts, "after all we have been through!" She takes a step closer. "I even forgave you for killing my husband. All that I ask for you to do is tell the truth." She takes another step closer. "I have even taken the courtesy of bringing you to the Palace for an opportunity into a life only a few will ever see." I hold my ground saying nothing. Shaylo continues, "You choose to not even give me the gratitude of avenging my captors, or Shrago's real killer." She lunges at me, clutching her hands around my throat. I stumble, my legs fighting to stay up, I kick off those stupid heels, struggling to break free, clawing at her hands while trying to kick her, but it only makes her angrier. She tightens her grip, I am not making progress, I can't breathe, and I am starting to feel dizzy as I struggle to get out of her grasp. I catch a glimpse of Wolfrim, who is amused, and everything goes silent, it is out of my control. I drop to the floor.

I must have only been out for a moment because when I open my eyes, it is to Shaylo straddling me on the floor; she must have loosened her grip enough for me to come around. I stay still and squint my eyes, into tiny slits so that neither Wolfrim nor Shaylo know. She has one hand on my throat and her main hand is reaching into her breast for something. To my horror, it is a dagger. Without hesitation, she maneuvers it to drive it into my throat with all the speed and force she can muster. I react, rocking my weight to roll over and get her off me. The force is enough; she misses my throat and drives the blade through the rug and into the floor. Shaylo struggles to free the blade, and I have opportunity to get her off me. With the force that I can muster, I get on my hands and knees, scrambling to rise after forcing Shaylo off me. Shaylo also gets up with a stumble and she reaches to free the blade. Panicked, I lunge for the blade, managing to pry it free and face her; we are moving together like a dance, slowly step by step, I with both hands firmly gripped on the dagger and facing her. Fearless, Shaylo thrusts at me roaring of rage and without anything to defend herself she goes for both my wrists and latches on to one. I flick my wrist, and she lets go. Just as she is about to strike again, I give her the generous contact of the blade, edging it along her throat, just as though Shrago did to me. Her rage evolves into panic. She backs away. I watch her, while still grasping the blade. Shaylo touches her hands to her throat, feeling the oozing wound and lets out an angry sob. Still looking at me, but addressing King Wolfrim, "Do something!" Wolfrim says nothing and watches with those emotionless black eyes. Frantic she cries, "Do something!" Her gait is wavering; she stumbles and then falls. It is hard to watch, and it is taking me back to the day that it happened to Shrago only this time Shaylo is alert and knows what is happening to her. She is whimpering now, incoherent words, sounding like she is asking Wolfrim to help her. I back away, frozen, but at the same time, I can't take my eyes off her. She whimpers to no one, "Come here." I approach reluctantly, but I do so and stand above her so she can see me. She peers into the centers of my eyes; she knows it is me, "Why couldn't you give me this?" Shaylo says in a quivering whisper.

"You know why." I answer in the faintest whisper, practically mouthing the words and back away. She is dying; it is slow, messy, and hard to watch. She does not say anything else and slips into unconsciousness, she will be dead soon. I am reminded that I am not alone by the feeling of eyes watching me. I glance at him. He looks amused and applauds me, slow loud claps. It is an uncomfortable applause.

"Well done, you know, I wasn't really a fan of her husband, or her for that matter." I say nothing, Wolfrim continues, "Sure they helped me get to this status, but between you and I; I know that Shrago was looking for a bigger piece of the pie." He winks at me. "Truth is a funny thing don't you think?" I swallow saying nothing, he continues, "I know that Shaylo wasn't lying to me." I breathe and wait for him to continue, "That leaves you and me dear. Your silence speaks more than any words, but do you know what, I admire you. You just took down one of the most intimidating women I have ever known, and you took out her husband too? Amazing, is all I can say. You know dear I will give you two options, are you ready?" I stare at him, "Option one, you stay here in the Palace and work for me." He seems amused with himself, closing a hand and glancing at his own neatly groomed fingernails for a second. He continues, looking back up at me, "Option two if you don't choose to work for me you can still stay here, but you will be living out your days in confinement and who knows, maybe your life will be short lived?" He has the look of a cat when it has caught a mouse by the tail. I am not going to have any of this. I back away from him and Shaylo who is lying in a spreading pool of blood. My back is now touching the door, he is waiting for my answer, but I say nothing. "So, I guess you have made your decision? Well, in my opinion it's a poor choice." He smiles a confident, condescending grin, which causes me to shiver.

Still with my back to the door, my hands find the knob. I twist it open and make a break for it. I fly down the hallway at a sprint, down the serpentine stairs, but stop dead at the closed door to the great room. If I open the door, I will need to face two guards. I can't do this; do I go back up the stairs, apologize and plead with Wolfrim to take the kinder option he proposed? My heart hurts and I back away from the door and up against the wall of the serpentine trying to urge myself to choose. When I touch my back to the stone wall it feels as though it moved as though my shoulder sunk into the wall. I turn and push against the wall, a secret passage opens. I shimmy through. The stone wall closes behind me and I find myself in complete darkness and silence. I have no idea if Wolfrim has approached the stairway, or what, but there is no time to ponder. I feel my way along the edge of the wall by crawling and making haste through the darkness. There are no corners; however, it feels as though this passage gradually turns, I never feel a corner. My eyes adjust, there is light at the end, coming from a space under a door. I crawl up to it and try to push, but it won't budge. I get off my hands and knees to feel along the wall for a latch, or something. I am in luck; a lever, I pull it and the door creaks open. The room I come into is almost blinding, there are windows, and I run to them for my exit, but in the same moment I stop dead in my tracks.

"Where are you going?" She asks. It is the mysterious woman that spoke to me from the lazy river.

"Please I need to get out of here." I beg.

"What about Princess Rosaleen? She should be here soon, and you serve her." She says confused.

"Please, I'll explain later just help me get out of here unnoticed."

She looks at me, as though deciding, as though she is contemplating if I am being truthful, she says, "Okay."

She walks briskly to her closet, gets a change of clothes for me, "Here put these on." I strip down, tossing away the bloody blue dress Shaylo gave to me, not wasting any time and we switch. She tosses my dress in the back of her closet, and I put on this emerald, green satin robe, she is already in a blue one and puts her hood up; I do the same. She instructs, "Follow me." She steps out of the window; I follow. Her room is on ground level, so we just step down into and around some shrubs that are below her window. She leads me at a steady walk to the pool area.

I murmur, "We need to move faster."

"Not unless you want to draw attention to yourself." She answers through her teeth while faking a smile.

There are only two other women at the pool. They are sleeping on the beds. Quietly we approach and walk by completely unnoticed. She leads me through the same path that I had strolled through only hours before. We approach the spot where we had talked, deep in the garden, along the water's edge of the lazy river. She disrobes and jumps in; I do the same. "Grab your robe in a bunch you will need to dress once we get you to somewhere private." The currant guides us through the lazy river; my mind is playing games with me because I could swear that I hear the shouts of guards and fear that the shouts are related to finding me.

She starts swimming towards the side; I copy, grabbing the edge and she reaches down and pops a grid off. She instructs, "Go through." I duck under water, and she pushes me through a dark tunnel and then follows behind. There is enough air at the surface to bring our heads above water. She fidgets with the cover and manages to snap it back in place then urges "Keep swimming forward so that we can get out of earshot." We move through this water tunnel and are soon engulfed in darkness.

"Okay tell me what this is about?" She demands.

I let out a breath and explain, "The short story is, King Wolfrim is an imposture and has been living this lie for a long time. Princess Rosaleen knows this now and the imposter knows that Rosaleen knows. I need to return to Rosaleen and my sister. I am leaving because I didn't want to be on the opposing side. Rosaleen will return, but not under amicable circumstances and my plan is to return to her before she returns to the Palace. Please you can't share this with anyone." I beg her.

"Okay" She assures. I have no choice but to trust her.

"Please can I ask a favor?"

"Yes sure." She says.

"Rosaleen wants to return, but she probably wants to return unnoticed. Could we use this way back? Or um let me re-think this, could you leave your window open so that we can make our way back in?" I have nothing more to offer Rosaleen other than showing her this secret passage as a show of my dedication and gratitude to her and she will believe me when questioned about the escape with Shaylo.

"Yes, anything for the Princess and for a friend." She answers. I can only trust her in that; this will not be a trap.

"Now that I am up to speed on things, let's move." She suggests. We continue blindly down the tunnel, making our way to a cavern and the mouth opens to a beach. To the passerby, this would be a hard opening to spot because it is surrounded by many rock clusters, and the opening is only big enough for a couple of people to wade through at a time. We approach the shore, and both put our wet silks on, once again, another sunset to mark another pivotal day.

"Thank you." I say to her.

"You're welcome and let's hope that this works." She says encouragingly.

"Can I ask you something?"

"Anything" She answers.

"I have no idea where to find Princess Rosaleen. If she wanted to dock her ship in an alternative harbor from where she usually docks, or anchors in shallow waters, whatever, do you have any guesses where I should look?"

"Yes, actually there is a second harbor about an hour journey by solar bike west of here and about another half hour west from there is a good spot where a lot of larger boats anchor."

"Great thank you." I don't know if I should give her a hug, shake her hand, but I settle with a polite smile.

"Oh, I forgot; that robe has an inner pocket, inside the pocket there's a pouch with some kiros just to get you by until you return." She says.

"You don't know how much this means to me; I can't thank you enough. You know, I never got your name?" She smirks at me.

"I'm Jodis."

"Nice to meet you officially and if everything works out, I will see you in a day, or two. Before I forget my name is Taylan." I smirk back.

"Nice to meet you officially, I wish you a safe return, see you soon." Jodis waves me off. I catch a final glimpse of her hopping along the stones as I pause to look back after walking for a moment, and then she is out of sight.

I have a long walk ahead of me and make my way around the rock crevices. I pick up three rocks and place them on a nearby bolder as a marker to tell that the entrance is near.

The Palace from eyesight looks to be elevated like it is sitting on a stage overlooking its city; however, the courtyard must be at level with the ocean because from the tunnel I escaped through the pool is fed fresh ocean water. I take a moment to look at the Palace and then back in the direction of the city. My eyes are just playing tricks on me, and it must be the grand size of the Palace in comparison to the buildings of the city. It takes a long time to maneuver the rocky shore and soon find myself walking in the dark, which doesn't help, but eventually I reach a street.

I look around seeing some restaurants and shops, but nowhere do I see where I can rent a bike. I do spot a couple of parked water powered taxis and jog over and tap on a window, "Yes, where would you like to go?" The driver asks in a deep, slow, but steady voice.

"Do you know of any solar bike rentals nearby that are open?" I ask because I don't think that I have enough to cover a taxi for such a long trip, and if it turns out to be a dead end then I won't have enough to make it back.

"Yes, get in." The driver assures in his deep voice. The driver takes me to where I need to go, and within no time, I have a bike rented and find myself on my way west.

The first stop is well populated there are many streets and buildings, and the harbor is full of all sorts of docked boats and ships. In the bay, it is easy to see everything in the moonlight; the water is trickled with sparkling lights from anchored boats and ships. I walk to the end of the pier and look. If Rosaleen is here, her ship is anchored out there. I scan the bay and do not see anything that I recognize as Rosaleen's ship, but there are quite out there. A few that could be hers. It is hard to tell, and I hate this second-guessing myself. It is nice that I can see them in the moonlight, but I can't be sure and decide to stop and think. I take a seat on the edge of the pier.

I hear the holler of a man not too far; he must be on the next pier. "The boat's lowered and ready to go ladies!" I know that voice! I race over to the next pier where it is coming from, stopping at the edge, spotting the man that called out. He is the one that lowered the boat for Rosaleen and me to go to Newlyn's Island, the day I killed Shrago. Ashlea and Izavelle are approaching from behind, walking down the pier towards me. My heart stops for a second and the next, I am running as fast as my legs can carry me, so fast that I think Ashlea doesn't recognize me. I wrap my arms around her, sobbing happy tears. "I didn't think I would ever see you again." I blurt out in between sobs. Without saying anything, she knows it is me and returns my embrace. I know she is feeling the same.

Izavelle wraps her arms around the both of us and whispers in my ear, "We thought we had lost you." I managed to peel my arms off Ashlea; everything is a blur from the pier to the ship because I am just smiting about my reunion with Ashlea, and I am exhausted.

In no time, I am reunited with Soolena and Princess Rosaleen. Rosaleen seems happy to see that I have returned, however, I can tell that she is, wondering why I have come back.

"Shaylo is dead, and King Wolfrim knows that you found your mother and know his secret." I tell Rosaleen with everyone listening.

Rosaleen answers, "You have to explain, so Wolfrim knows that Shaylo is dead?"

"Yes" I answer, but then shake my head, "Yes that's right, but that's not what I meant to say. King Wolfrim knows that you know that he is not your real father, and he knows that you know that he was the one who broke up your family and exiled your mother." It is obvious that Rosaleen had already assumed that.

Rosaleen asks, "How is Shaylo dead?"

"I killed her, in self-defense; she found out that it was me that killed Shrago and as much as I had explained why I had, she couldn't forgive me."

"Where is Sitrus?" She asks. I need to tell a small lie because I am not sure how they would react if they found out that he didn't exactly follow orders in finding me and failing to return me to Newlyn.

"I don't know?" It is the only thing that comes to mind.

"I see; how did you find your way back to us?"

"A woman, her name is Jodis; she helped me escape and suggested different areas for me to try to find you. She's waiting for our return, she's on our side." I come to the realization, "Rosaleen, you need to move your ship. If she knew where you would be, I am sure Wolfrim, and his servants would guess the same. I am not sure how much of a head start we have if he has placed orders to find you?" Why didn't I think about that sooner?

"Thank you, Taylan. Izavelle, Soolena and I will decide. Ashlea, take your sister to your room. You both need to rest, and we will call on you once we have decided." I want to tell them more, but decide they have enough information, I don't object.

Later, after resting with Ashlea in her room, we wake suddenly. It feels as though it is the middle of the night, "Get up we are leaving."

Chapter 39
Ashlea and Me

Ashlea and I don't question the interruption. We know what it means. I had a dreamless sleep. I am not sure if that means anything, but I am happy in knowing that I was able to get some rest. Ashlea and I follow Soolena from our bedroom up to the room that has all the different suits. We enter the room, and the twilight sky is seen through the windows on the ceiling. We follow Soolena's lead and suit up. Rosaleen barges in, "Good, you guys are dressed. We are leaving soon." She is gone in a rush and from what I see Rosaleen is also suited up for flight. We exit the room and meet Princess Rosaleen and Izavelle for breakfast. I just noticed this now; the ship is on the move from the mild vibration felt on the bottom of my feet. I can only imagine the reasons why, but I am not certain on where we are headed, and I won't ask. I am where I need to be, which is by Ashlea's side. We sit down to a hearty breakfast. The air has the aroma of fried meats, warm breads, and the sweet smell of fruit. I fill my plate because I know what being hungry is and have a feeling that the next time that I have a chance to eat will not be for a while.

Rosaleen brings us out of the dark by explaining the plans, "We are going to move fast, travel quickly and lightly, and we are going to settle all of this today. The sun should peek over the horizon soon and we are going to take flight to the castle. The key is, we need to act quickly, and the unfortunate thing is that the king knows, and we must assume he is now taking precautions to protect himself and seek me out before I seek him out." Rosaleen takes a large bite of meat, swallows and continues, "I really can't say what we are going to do once we make it to the castle. We are going to have to look at our options once we are there and decide what is best. The precautions I have taken to avoid capture of this ship is it will remain on the move until I return to it. Taylan was able to find us on someone's assumptions, and its sheer luck that she found us before Wolfrim's guard did. I know that Wolfrim would have sent them." Rosaleen's manners have fallen to the wayside. She takes her fork, shovels in another large bite, and looks at all of us, expecting us to chime in.

I nod, "These plans work for me."

"Yes, me too." Ashlea adds and Soolena with her mouth full nods in agreement. Izavelle does the same.

Rosaleen adds, "Izavelle is going to stay aboard the ship and make sure that my directions are followed." No one objects to this; we finish our food, and then other servants clear the table. Most of the faces are new to me, however, I do recognize one of them being Zethel and she quickly gives me a smile and a wink when I catch her eye just as I am leaving. We all head out to the deck and all of us except for Izavelle are suited. Izavelle is there only, to help see us off.

Izavelle pulls Ashlea and me aside, "With flying you really have no choice, but to travel lightly so when you get to your destination make sure to pay attention to your surroundings. If you see something that you think you can use, take it. Your suit has little to provide for self-defense and protection, but I wasn't going to let you two starts with nothing. In both cuffs, you will find a small blade. It's not the greatest of weapons, but I think it's safe to say that with your training and experiences I don't need to teach you how to use them." Ashlea and I feel our cuffs and sure enough, a small sheath can be felt.

"Okay ladies let's do this!" Rosaleen's voice booms. She is the first followed by Soolena, Ashlea and I, we run and leap into the warm dawn sky. I guess it doesn't take much sunlight for these suits to work. It is not long before the skyline reveals a land mass and Rosaleen guides us straight to its shore. We eventually find ourselves close to the exit to the cave where Jodis and I parted the day before.

I ask, "Rosaleen have you been through the passage that leads to the castle's yard?"

She turns to me, "No, what are you talking about?"

I realize that I left those details out, "Jodis got me out by using a passage near to here. I marked it by placing three rocks not much larger than my hand in a pile on a bolder near the entrance. We could try to use it to get back in?"

Rosaleen answers, "That's a promising idea. I am reluctant for us to fly all the way to the Palace walls. We would be easy to spot and knowing Wolfrim, his guards would be on the lookout." Rosaleen addresses everyone, "Let's spread out and find the marker." We search along the shore and maneuver around the large boulders. I am glad that I decided to lay down a marker because there would be no way anyone would be able to find the mouth of the cave without it. Ashlea has the legs of her solar suit rolled up and is walking through the water about ankle deep. I guess that maneuvering around boulders isn't really her thing.

Soolena hollers and waves us over, "Over here I've found it. We all close in around the rock pile.

I explain, "It's within a few steps of this pile." We all glance around the area; I spot the mouth of the cave first and am happy with myself, "Look there!"

Rosaleen answers, "We should all go in together. There is no point in splitting up yet. We have no other cover and no alternative plan."

"Agreed" Soolena adds.

I am still listening, but at the same time, my eyes are distracted, spotting something on Ashlea's calf. "Ashlea turns around."

Confused she answers, "What?"

"I thought I saw something on your leg?" She swivels on the spot and sure enough, there is an insect the size of a hand gorging itself on her blood. Ashlea panics, trying to swipe the thing off.

Soolena yells, "Stop!" She darts over with a rock in hand; I didn't even see her pick it up. Instead of squishing the bug, she puts the rock to Ashlea's skin above the insect's head and rubs the rock toward it and in one swift movement, the parasite drops to the ground, still alive. Soolena tosses the rock on top of the bug and steps on it, squishing the thing like a rock jelly sandwich. The crunching death of it and its blood curdling shrieks sounds like a baby screaming at the top of its lungs.

For the amount of blood that is trickling down Ashlea's leg, her injury is not as bad as it appears, given the size of the parasite, it only made a poke mark to siphon her blood.

"Ash how could you not feel that?" I asked astonished.

"I don't know, but I feel it now, it is kind of a burning itch." Ashlea describes.

Soolena, who is just behind me says, "They inject venom so that you don't feel them when they latch on. It was a rock piercer, and they are found by rocky shores like this. Fortunately, they only feed in the early hours of the morning; after the sun rises in the sky, they seek cover and shade under the rocks to protect them against the sun and its predators."

Ashlea asks, "What are their predators?"

"Predatory birds, sea turtles nothing that's a threat to us." Soolena assures.

"Let's get moving." Rosaleen says and we enter the dark cave.

"What should I do about this bite?" Ashlea asks because we are about ankle deep in water now.

"Touch you hand to the bite." Soolena says.

"Okay, I'm touching it." she answers.

"Is the blood dry?"

"Yes" Ashlea replies.

"You don't need to do anything except just make sure to not scratch it." Soolena says.

Making our way deeper into the cave we eventually must feel our way along the walls, soon we are submerged in water; the current helps us with figuring out the direction. It feels like this trip back is a lot shorter than it was on the way out and in no time, we find ourselves at the grid. It is mid-morning, by now I would assume that most have finished their breakfasts and are starting to go about their day. Rosaleen is at the front of the group. The tunnel is so narrow at this end. Only Rosaleen can look through the grid. She is uncertain on whether to go through, or to wait it out until night.

Rosaleen whispers back to Soolena, who is behind her. "I don't know what to do. What do you think?"

Soolena whispers back, "Describe to me what you see."

Rosaleen scans the area and whispers, "An empty lazy river and plants, I can't see anything else."

Soolena asks, "Do you hear anything, or smell anything?"

"Just the sound of moving water and the aroma of the plants," Rosaleen replies. Soolena is going through scenarios and trying to use every sense to decide.

Finally, Soolena suggests, "Let's split up. We send two of us into the lazy river and then they can navigate the grounds to seek out Jodis. The other two will wait until nightfall and then make their way in. I think that we can slip in unnoticed if it is only two at a time."

Rosaleen replies to Soolena, "Okay, I was also thinking along those lines. So, if we go with this plan then the next decision is who? I am just weighing the options. If I go in the first wave, it will at least give me the chance to get in without giving them the heads up, instead of if I were to wait back and go in the second wave. I should bring Taylan because she knows the most recent happenings within the Palace and should anything happen, you and Ashlea can make it through on the second wave."

Soolena agrees, "I think that is probably the best move. They are on alert now, and if you were to wait until the second wave to send yourself in after the great possibility of our first wave, being discovered it will be a massive failure Rosaleen. You and Taylan must go first, and Ashlea and I will be your strength to follow."

I lean over Ashlea's shoulder, I am the last in line and in a muffled voice, I direct my question over to Soolena, "Do you know where Jodis' window is?"

"It's on the opposite side. The first window from the corner, do I have that right?" Soolena confirms.

"That's right." I answer.

Rosaleen confirms, "Okay after sunset we will meet again, head for Jodis' room."

Ashlea and Soolena respond in unison, "Okay" I can feel the nervous tension starting up in all of us. I can taste it and Rosaleen knowing her Palace instructs, "Taylan you need to undress, pull your two sheaths out of the suit cuffs, there are straps" Rosaleen reveals and continues, "Ashlea help her tie them to her forearm, blade and sheath on to the inside of her forearms." Ashlea turns to face me in the shadows, and I am out of the suit with the blades secured to my arms. Ashlea wraps my suit around her torso and ties it in place, like a belt so it does not float away. I think that Soolena does the same with Princess Rosaleen's suit. Ashlea and I do a shuffle so that she is now in the back and then I do a shuffle with Soolena so that I am right behind Rosaleen. Rosaleen looks me up and down and satisfied with what she sees she snaps the grid out of place, hands it back to me and I hand it back to Soolena. We both swim through into the blinding light.

Chapter 40
Rosaleen and Taylan in the River

My heart is on vibrate as we float down the lazy river. We say nothing and I follow her lead with trying to appear as casual as possible. The river loops around and we are now coming into the main pool. We both walk up to the steps where the lounge beds are and to our luck no one is there this morning, and fortunately some towels drape over the chairs to dry. Rosaleen walks up and casually grabs a towel and hands it to me to dry off. She takes a second one for herself, taking her time with patting herself dry.

She asks me, "So how was your breakfast?" While leaning over and towel drying her hair. She is trying to settle my nerves and make us blend in. No one is here, but it does not mean that there are not ears that could hear us in the vicinity. There are open windows to the nearby rooms, guards are patrolling the wall from above and there could be people out enjoying the nearby gardens on their morning stroll. We dry off and casually walk down the garden pathways and around the castle wall to the side where Jodis' window is. Luckily, the only people who are outside are the guards and they take little to no interest at all because we look like any of the other women who use the pool. Jodis' window is open, and we each take a quick glance of our surroundings, no one is watching, and we enter through the window.

The room is empty, and Jodis' door is closed, but not locked. Rosaleen whispers to me, "You know we could wash up."

I feel comfortable, my heart is back to a normal rhythm and clearly, we are not on the radar, "I am okay with that." Jodis' room, like many of the rooms within this castle has its own suite and we each take turns showering and then dressing in her clothes, each of us picking a comfortable dark colored simple shirt and pant. The knives that are around our wrists are concealed.

After a while, Rosaleen paces the room, "What do you want to do to pass the time?"

"I should show you the passage I found by accident." I suggest.

"Good idea." I show her the secret entrance. We slip through and walk along the corridor, blindly and in a whisper, I tell her, "The other end opens to the wall of the serpentine stairway that leads to the King's chambers."

She stops me with placing her hand gently on my forearms. "You know what this means right?"

"That we have direct access to Wolfrim?" I answer unsure on where she is going with this.

"That's given. This is a passageway for lovers. Their bedrooms connect. You know what this means right?" Rosaleen explains but looks as though she has already been defeated.

"Rosaleen it's not like that, Jodis isn't on his side. She's on yours." I try to assure her, but in the back of my mind, I am starting to question my own instincts.

Rosaleen says, "I knew Wolfrim had women, and I figured these passageways existed. I have discovered my fair share while living here all these years, but the two passages, this one and the one in the pool that you have shown me I had no idea they existed. I do consider Jodis a friend, but I had no idea she engaged in King Wolfrim's romps and that makes me worry." She admits.

"Jodis can't be on his side. Everything happened so fast. There would have been no time for plans to be devised. She chose to help me to bring justice for you. There was no way that she was letting me go to reel you in."

"You believe that, and I want to believe that you're right. Let's just play it safe and we will remain here in hiding until either one of them makes an appearance." Rosaleen says.

"Okay" I whisper.

We wait in the darkness and take turns on listening at either end of the tunnel, then checking back with each other; it becomes a bit of a routine.

"Rosaleen, can I ask you something?"

"Sure, go on."

"Where is your bedroom?" I ask in a whisper.

"It's at the opposite end of the castle in one of the towers." She answers.

"Are there any secret passageways to and from your room?"

"No there isn't any however, my room does have lofty ceilings, so I do have a staircase that leads up to an indoor balcony, and I also have a bathroom, walk in closet and a den. The only thing that comes remotely close to a passageway is one of the tower windows, if you lean out and over you can see that in the brickwork, the masons created footholds that lead to the ground for a quick escape. I have never had to use them." As she is speaking, I can hear the faint sounds of a door thumping shut and our conversation takes a halt. Rosaleen hears it too.

In a whisper, Rosaleen says, "I think that was from Jodis' room. Let's go check." I tiptoe and follow her to the end of the passage. Rosaleen opens the secret door for a glimpse into the room; with a startle, she jumps back onto me. The passage opens.

"You two weren't discreet when taking up residence in my room; as soon as I entered, I knew you had returned." Jodis gives Rosaleen and then me a hug.

Rosaleen admits, "It's been way to long Jodis, I should have brought you on my tour."

"No, you were right to leave me here, and everything for the most part has gone well." She assures Rosaleen.

"Jodis, I had no idea you were one of King Wolfrim's personal assistants? You should have told me."

Jodis smiles shyly, "Some things are better left not said; anyway, we have to focus on what lies ahead." Jodis continues, "Wolfrim uses that passageway so hiding there isn't a promising idea if your plan is an ambush. He always has two guards that will be with him. They don't go through the passage, but instead, they will go from guarding his chamber doors and walk down the hallways to guard mine. They never come in unless they are called in. So right now, you have three people to deal with, King Wolfrim and his two guards. The options as I see it are, we can ambush him here in my room, or we can try to get into his room un-detected and surprise him there."

Rosaleen interrupts, "We will do it here."

Jodis says with a smile, "Well in that case we will need to hide you here and not in the passageway and then when he cries out for his guards, we need to deal with them quickly."

Rosaleen says, "Where can we hide?"

"Taylan can hide underneath the bed, and you can hide in the closet, or vice versa."

Rosaleen says, "I want Taylan to be the ambusher, should anything go wrong she will be the one who will pay the crime." She is ready to do away with me so easily. Rosaleen elaborates as though she is reading my mind, "This is what I was talking to you about on those first nights on the ship; you have to trust me on this."

"Okay" I have no choice.

Jodis asks, "Do you have weapons?"

"Yes, we each have concealed daggers." Rosaleen confirms.

Jodis adds, "Now that I think about it, Wolfrim also has a concealed blade, but that shouldn't be an issue because we can have you two waits until he makes himself more comfortable. His clothes will be on the floor so; we will need to pay attention, we can't let him get in reach of his blade."

"Good point." Rosaleen agrees.

Jodis hurries us "Let's get you out of sight before he comes." With her warning, Rosaleen and I move to our spots and wait while Jodis gets ready for her evening with the King. This day has been full of waiting, but I welcome it because it buys me time to prepare mentally. I am on my stomach under the bed resting my eyes while fully conscious of my surroundings. Rosaleen is in her spot and Jodis is brushing her now dark blue hair while sitting on the bed and looking out at the evening sky waiting. I open my eyes to the sound of the passageway door opening. He walks in saying nothing. I can't see him fully because I am peering through a bed skirt that I dare not lift. All I can see is the outline of his figure. I know that it is Wolfrim. I wonder how such a chubby man can fit through the passage.

In a flirtatious voice Jodis says, "Oh, my king I am so happy that you have come to visit me tonight."

In a friendly tone that I have not heard from him, which I would have never expected he answers, "Are you now? Tell me why?" He asks. Surprisingly, he seems good, relaxed maybe even happy?

"Because, I have been thinking about you all day," Jodis confides. I see his clothes start to drop piece by piece to the floor; one foot followed by the other leaves the floor to the bed.

"What have you been thinking about, tell me?" I hear him say.

"I was thinking about just how good you are to me." She answers in an intoxicatingly sweet voice.

He has a booming laugh that is startling, "It is you that is good to me." They are both on the bed and this is my queue. I first drag his clothes under the bed so that there isn't a chance he can conveniently pick up his weapon. I creep out from the foot of the bed; his back is towards me. I come from behind and scoop my blade around his neck, holding it so that it is touching his throat.

Unwavering I say, "Stop" he is more surprised than anything. He gets off Jodis who gets up and backs away to the closet where Rosaleen is concealed.

"I should have known that you were still here and to think that my little pet was involved. I should have known; you got away with hiding too easily." Wolfrim says with laugh while glaring at Jodis.

"So, what are you going to do girl? Are you going to kill me?" He dares.

Rosaleen emerges from hiding and in her booming voice says, "I think we should. You killed my father; a life for a life, I think is fair?"

He turns his head slightly towards Rosaleen's voice, his words directed at me, "Ah I see, so that's where you ran off to, if I were to guess, I would have assumed Taylan, that you had ran off to find your friend Sitrus." Wolfrim smiles, knowing that he has my attention and continues, "Oh my, you thought that I didn't know about your little friend?" Stay focused, I repeat silently to myself, I stay quiet, but my anger is building up.

Rosaleen holds her ground addressing him, "Be reminded that I can do anything I want now and there is nothing you can do."

He answers unbothered, "You could, but you won't, you say a life for a life how about an exchange?"

Rosaleen answers, "You have lied for my entire life, and I know you are going to say anything to get out of this, your words mean nothing." Rosaleen approaches us and she holds her blade to his throat so now hers and mine are touching his soft skin. "How dare you, kill my father and drive away my mother. What was this for?" Spitting out her words like an awful taste in her mouth.

His voice is still calm and his heartbeat steady, he says, "Yes, my dear, it was part greed, but do keep in mind your father was no angel. If he wanted me that bad to act the part and play his role, that it was mine for the taking." Wolfrim laughs, "You know what Princess, his death was by his own sentence not mine and all I did was switch places with him." Rosaleen stares at him long and hard, with significant effort removes her blade from his throat.

Rosaleen commands, "Jodis find something to bind his arms." Jodis starts looking through a drawer, finds a belt from a robe and hands it to Rosaleen. She binds his arms behind him and gives me the nod; I remove my knife and hold. Rosaleen grabs a robe from Jodis and tosses it at him to cover him. Wolfrim can't really do anything, but let it drape over if he wants to stay covered.

Mockingly he says to Rosaleen, "What are you going to do Princess, you do realize if I call out there are two men standing guard outside these doors." Rosaleen walks over to him then gags him and bends down so that they are eye to eye she says in a faint voice, "I nearly forgot, thanks for reminding me." She returns an over-confidant smile back at him.

Rosaleen asks Jodis, "Sitrus, do you know of him?"

"No, this is the first that I have heard the name." She admits.

"You are going to tell the guards that King Wolfrim wishes to see Sitrus here and now."

"Get off the bed." Rosaleen says to Wolfrim, the robe falls to the floor. She looks to me, "Taylan help me take him into the washroom." We close the door and wait, in no time Jodis quietly opens the door to the washroom and in a whisper, she informs us, "One of the guards is still standing outside the door and the other has gone to get Sitrus."

"Okay thank you." Rosaleen says to Jodis, "Wait out there for us?"

"Yes Princess." She shuts the door.

The three of us wait listening. A few minutes later, there is a faint tap at Jodis' bedroom door and a deep voice says, "The prisoner, as King Wolfrim requested."

"Thank you, could you leave him here and stand guard outside?" Jodis asks the guard.

"I am afraid I need to remain with the prisoner. It's not safe." We can hear the guard say to Jodis. They are just outside the washroom.

"Okay, the king is just washing up; I will let him know that you have arrived." We all back away from the door and Jodis carefully slips in, closing the door behind.

Her voice is a frantic whisper, "Rosaleen the guard won't leave what should I do?"

"Is it just one guard and Sitrus?" Rosaleen asks.

"Yes" Jodis says, "The bedroom door is closed and there is still one guard outside."

"Taylan stay here with Wolfrim, I will talk to the guard." Rosaleen leaves me alone with him. His overconfidence is evaporating quickly and being replaced with anger which is starting to fester. I turn my ear to the closed door and listen.

I can hear the guard's confused voice, "My Princess, what are you doing here?"

"I returned today and wished not a grand entrance. That man that you are keeping captive I command you to release him."

"My princess, I am afraid that I can't, I am under strict command from the king and have been instructed to take orders from him only."

In a calm voice Rosaleen answers "I understand," than calls to me, "Taylan come out with Wolfrim."

I turn to Wolfrim who is staring at me with his hands still behind him. I command, "Let's go." He doesn't move and feeling rather annoyed, I don't want to have to waste my strength on him to drag him out before everyone. To be honest, I am starting to feel the drain on my body especially having only eaten this morning. He is defiantly standing his ground, "What is your problem? Let's go!" I step closer to him, reaching for his arm. He dodges my grasp, pushing me hard and I fall to the ground. Before I can get to my feet, he has the rope that bound his hands around my throat and pulls me up to my feet. My hands are working to pull it off.

He whispers through his teeth into my ear, "No one rules me, do you understand?"

I choke the words out, "Yes" and a couple of tears escape, trickling down my face.

He opens the door for us to meet everyone. Instinctively Rosaleen starts to come to my aid. Sitrus tries to break out of the guard's grasp and Jodis backs herself to the doors of her room. Her instincts are telling her to run, but Jodis is frozen.

Wolfrim's booming voice startles Rosaleen into an unwanted halt, "Don't take another step, or it will be the last of this little pet of yours." Sitrus also stops struggling with the guard even though the order wasn't for him. "You listen to me; I have worked too hard to lose everything to a spoiled little brat, guards, GUARDS!" He yells for the one standing out in the hall, the knob twists; the only thing about Jodis being frozen with fear is that she at least has control of herself to remain as a barrier. She uses all her weight to keep the other guard from entering her room. Rosaleen starts toward the door and Wolfrim starts up again with his commanding voice, "Rosaleen don't move. Jodis let him in." Jodis stops struggling with the door not wanting to be the cause for me getting hurt. The guard pries the door open and hesitates when he sees that the princess is causing trouble. "Seize her!" Wolfrim commands to the reluctant guard. Rosaleen holds both her blades firmly and ready to put up a fight. He has a sword to combat her.

Wolfrim shouts, "Rosaleen don't be stupid, this is over." Rosaleen takes a couple of steps back; the guard slowly advances. I get the feeling that the guard does not want to hurt Rosaleen however, he is stuck having to obey his King. Everything that we have been working towards is lost and I don't see a way out, but Rosaleen is going out with a fight and Sitrus and I can't do anything, it is over for us, and I know that Wolfrim is going to do away with me if Rosaleen doesn't comply.

A flash crosses my vision; the guard that was taking on Rosaleen lowers his sword; Rosaleen stops and looks at the guard. He looks down at his chest, a blooming blood flower, with a dagger handle for the center, emerging from his chest; he looks at Rosaleen with red in his eyes, raises his sword and takes a final lunge at her screaming, "Why?" Sitrus breaks away from the other guard's grasp and dives, pushing Rosaleen out of the way, but is struck down from the attacking guard's final effort. Sitrus hits the ground hard, and I feel the vibrations in my chest from my own screaming, but I hear nothing, only ringing in my ears. I am not sure how, but I fall to my knees and crawl over to where Sitrus lies, not knowing, or caring at his point where the king is, or anyone else for that matter. Sitrus is in pain. There is so much blood. A fight is going on around me, but I don't care. I take off my pants to use as a bandage and try to remove the sword from him. It is only making it worse, and I can't stop the tears.

"Hang on." I tell him, as I struggle to help, but he doesn't listen, I can see him starting to slip away. At this point, I shred the pants with one of my blades. He is on his side, and he reaches out and touches my forearm. I stop, catching him looking at me with those eyes that can see into my soul.

He whispers, "It is okay," I gaze into his beautiful eyes not wanting to give up on him, but again he says in the faintest voice, "Just hold me." I lie on my side facing him and holding him close, feeling his heartbeat and smelling the faint scent of his breath. He is going to sleep. I can't do anything. He shivers and I hold him ever so close to keep him as warm as I can. He asks, "Taylan?"

"Yes" I whisper.

"I will be with you always." He closes his eyes, and I feel him fade away, but I don't let go. I close my eyes to the chaos around me and imagine him alive and well. The day we first met, sleeping by his side, our time at Newlyn's beach and when I had tried to escape, and he found me. All of this happened in a fleeting time, but I felt that I had known him forever, perhaps in a past life. I love him.

Time stands still. Eventually a gentle hand rests on my shoulder, "Taylan, he is free." Ashlea says. My eyes are sore, and I look around the room, Ashlea and Soolena are here. One of their blades must have hit the guard. Sitrus had gotten in the middle when the guard was after Rosaleen. King Wolfrim is also laying on the ground dead, another blade no doubt from either Ashlea, or Soolena. It explains how I was able to crawl over to Sitrus in the middle of all of it. The guard who was holding Sitrus captive begged for mercy and Rosaleen has granted it. Rosaleen knows the guard and Soolena keeps watch over him to prevent anything further.

Rosaleen approaches and says, "We will all miss him; there is nothing I can say to you to make this easier, just know that I am forever grateful. Sitrus saved me." She crouches down and touches his shoulder.

There are a few minutes of quiet between us as we sit there gazing at his empty shell. "I know that you won't like this, but it's the easiest way to explain to the Palace what has happened." I look at Rosaleen as she explains. My tears are dried up. "The guard and Jodis have confirmed with me that the rest of the Palace has no idea for the reason why King Wolfrim alerted the guards to keep watch of my return. The assumption was that he was just anxious to see me home and wanted to be notified immediately.

Fortunately, he kept his real intentions secret, hoping that there wouldn't be a fight. That is the good news. We can continue in keeping the truths surrounding my family secret."

I ponder and then ask, "I didn't think you would have wanted to keep the truths secret?"

She forces a smile, "I don't, but it's easier this way, either way I am the queen now. Explaining death is one thing but having to explain a death and many years of lies and deception is an entirely different matter. It's a mountain that I don't wish to move."

"I understand." I think if I were in her shoes, I would feel the same. While looking upon Sitrus' face I ask her, "Do you have any idea how Sitrus ended up in bad company?"

The guard who begged for mercy explained, "He was reported by a man named Oden who accused him of trespassing on private property. What was peculiar with the entire thing, rather than handing out a fine, King Wolfrim moved the issue between Oden and Sitrus behind closed doors to deal with. Soon after, for reasons kept secret Sitrus was imprisoned. I had assumed that he refused to pay. None of the guards questioned the king about it." I understand now. Oden must have seen him the night Shaylo, and I had been treated to dinner because I never caught a glimpse of Sitrus following us after that night. I sigh crossing my arms over my stomach and look down at him. My heart hurts.

Rosaleen continues what to do next about Wolfrim, the guard and Shaylo, "We have three that are dead. We need to explain why. This is the part that I know you won't like Taylan. It is better this way. We have decided to have Sitrus take blame for the deaths and sum it up to that his constraints weren't properly secured, He broke free and got a hold of other weapons, he attacked and killed before he was ultimately stopped. Soolena was able to put a stop to the attack by ending his life." Rosaleen is right. I am not happy about it, but I suppose this makes sense if they want to avoid questions. Rosaleen continues, "You and Ashlea can leave. Soolena can take you back. She knows the course that the ship is on." Rosaleen calls, "Soolena would you be so kind and take them back?"

"Yes, my Queen. You don't need my security?"

"No this is my Kingdom and Jodis speaks the truth, I am home now."

Soolena, Ashlea and I exit through the window of Jodis' room. The flying suits were hidden within the passageway of the pool that leads to the ocean. It is dark and they have little to no charge left in them. We suit up in them anyway. They are drier than the clothes we are wearing. Soolena leads us along the rocky shore that leads to a foot path, and from there we walk to the pier that is near the castle. The ship is not docked there as it normally would, however, there is a small boat waiting for us. We jump in and Soolena drives us back.

Once Ashlea and I are settled on board Rosaleen's ship, Soolena leaves, returning to the Palace. Izavelle comes to see how we are.

Izavelle gently taps on our door and peeks in, "I was thinking of you both the entire time." She approaches us quietly, like cat. "I understand that you both performed well. Taylan, showing the secret entrance was key. Ashlea, I heard from Soolena that you have a straight throw." It is obvious that Izavelle has already talked with Soolena.

Ashlea treads carefully, hoping that Izavelle's appreciation in our help for Rosaleen and her people is enough, "Thank you for your flattery." Ashlea looks down to her hands, takes a breath and slowly looks back up at Izavelle, "Does this mean that we fulfilled our work for Queen Rosaleen? Can we return to our home?"

I sense Izavelle is slightly disappointed and simply answers, "No, I'm sorry, but Rosaleen wishes are for the two of you to continue to serve her." I feel like I have been punched in the gut. I close my eyes to stop the tears. Izavelle does not want us to dwell on it and says, "Ladies please get some rest, we have more to talk about and we will talk tomorrow." Izavelle quietly lets herself out.

Ashlea and I are beyond tired; my emotions are all over the place. I am happy to be with Ashlea again, but grieving the loss of Sitrus and feeling defeated, with all the work that I have done and risking my life for Rosaleen's cause. We have been apart for so long, yet it feels like nothing has changed. We are still in this same predicament of not being in control of our destiny. We exchange few words, not because we are upset with one another. It is because there is nothing to say that can make this situation better, we both know how the other is feeling it's bittersweet, happy that we are reunited, but reminded that we are still missing loved ones and not free. I crawl into bed after Ashlea, nuzzle up close to her, and close my eyes. The last thoughts to run through my head are of Sitrus, his lips moving and saying those words, I will be with you always.

Chapter 41
Taylan and Ashlea

That next morning Izavelle explained everything that was planned for Ashlea's future and mine. Queen Rosaleen momentarily returned to the ship and passed command of the vessel over to Izavelle. The Kingdom was now Rosaleen's; she glided into the roll smoothly with little questions asked surrounding the death of King Wolfrim, Shaylo, the guard and Sitrus. Sitrus was given total blame for the blood that had been spilled. Ashlea and I returned to Newlyn's home to carry out our work of serving the queen. Eventually, Newlyn returned to the Palace to be closer to her daughter and help her out in the new role.

As I mentioned, Izavelle had spoken to Ashlea and me like she promised that following morning, which was now a few months ago. Izavelle explained that we would forever serve the Queen. It was upsetting news at the time however looking back, it was the best news we had ever received. What it really meant was yes, we are forever to serve our Queen, but the job is that we are caretakers and guardians of Newlyn's home, property, and its wealth. It would have been Sitrus' job, but he is gone, and Newlyn is now residing at the Palace and little Sid is too young to care for everything on his own. Ashlea and I see Queen Rosaleen and the Queen Mother Newlyn from time to time when they visit the property. We work as hosts to them, but most of the time we are just caretakers and guardians, and it all means the same thing. This is a happy compromise for us, it is a job like any other and we do it well.

Saydira and our mother, Nafeeza have re-united with Ashlea and me. We all live here at Newlyn's home on the island. Time seems to heal and within the few months, life has returned to normal. I have my family, and this place is starting to feel like home, but on a much larger scale.

Ashlea and I have taught my mother and Saydira my favorite activity, how to fly. They have also learned how to ride horses and when we have finished our chores, all of us, including little Sid usually relax at the beach just outside of the property's walls, or in the small town enjoying a meal at one of the quaint little restaurants.

This is my life and who I am that was forever, long ago.

Chapter 42
A Walk with Kyle and Smarty

I am sharing this information with you while I still know and understand, and before I choose my next life. In this state, these lives, memories, souls, your soul and mine, your likes and dislikes, your desires, everything stays with you forever. They move with you into the next life, though not always as expected, or known for that matter. Kyle was my Sitrus, in that world. There are others that I have mentioned from my tale from long ago of my life as Taylan whom I have also mentioned in my life as Robin, but I will let you make those connections. It is comforting in knowing that the souls that connect to you never really leave you. They will follow you in their own strange way and being in this state of flux, I can appreciate understanding the feeling that you sometimes get when you have just met someone, and you connect with them and feel that you have known them forever. Chances are that you have.

Kyle has been busy healing since I left, both physically and emotionally. A few months have passed since the car accident and life for Kyle, his family and Robin's family is getting back to normal. They are still grieving; however, time has made the loss a reality and everyone is coming to terms with it at their own pace. Kyle is out of the hospital and his bruises have faded away. He returned to work three weeks ago and fortunately with all the finances, being the mortgage and car, he won't need to sell because Robin's life insurance will cover a sizable chunk, allowing Kyle to manage the difference with his own income.

It is the end of summer on the cusp of fall and Kyle has decided to take our little dog Smarty out for a walk. He looks good, this is one of his better days and Smarty for the little dog that he is, has done a huge favor to Kyle with helping him get his mind off things by making him play and smile. They walk down the sidewalk. Smarty stops to look at something. Kyle tries to pull him with the leash to continue the walk, "Smarty come here" the ten or so pounds of Smarty holds strong and is clearly focused on something. Kyle stops tugging on the leash and instead goes to see what has Smarty's attention.

"What Smarty?" Smarty stares a few paces in front of him in the grass and Kyle follows his gaze. It is a young robin in the grass, fallen from a nearby tree, not injured, or anything, just a little clumsy as she is learning how to fly. The little robin looks up into Kyle's eyes. He crouches down, holding Smarty and looking back into its clear dark eyes and a strange feeling comes over Kyle as though he recognizes something in himself, or that little bird and he can't put a finger on it. He can only watch the little creature as something inside of him burns with the familiarity of knowing, he can't make the connection in his mind, but that feeling is, that his heart knows and the same holds true for the robin, she feels it too, but she also knows that she needs to take flight. She takes one last look into Kyle's eyes and musters up all her energy, taking flight.

Chapter 43
Final Notes from Taylan

I thought that the dark events were far behind, and that my family and I had overcome the hardest challenge that would ever face us, but that was not true...

Months later my family had the honor of a visit from Jodis, she had travelled by ship and had made it to shore, to our quiet little island town, and not long after making her way to Newlyn's home, the same way that Rosaleen and I had travelled long before. The visit was unsuspected, and we reunite at the beach, just beyond Newlyn's walls.

"Taylan, hello" I hear a familiar voice and lift my head from lying in the sand to see that it is Jodis.

"What are you doing here?" I ask.

"That isn't the kind of welcome I was expecting, how about a hug?" Jodis says.

"I didn't mean for it to sound like that, come here, how are you?" I say, happy to see her.

"I am well. The journey was good, but I fear that I come here with ill news." Jodis answers.

"Tell me, is everyone well?"

"Yes, everyone is well, but I fear I have been keeping something and worry that the wrong people have control." Jodis explains.

I shrug, "Jodis, we just choose what is best for us. I have learned to sleep at night knowing that Queen Rosaleen and her family have blood on their hands. I know that they have done terrible things, but I do believe that they try to go through life with their best interests in mind. They have treated my family well."

"That is the difference between you and me." Jodis looks down, disappointed that I have already formed an opinion.

"Jodis, don't let my opinion silence you; you saved me. Please tell me what drove you to make the journey here?"

She says, "You know who I was to the King?"

"Yes" I murmur.

"He used to tell me things when we were alone." Jodis explains.

"Please go on, it's okay, I will keep it secret if you want me to, just like you kept my secret."

"Your Imposter King Wolfrim was Rosaleen's real father." Jodis explains in a breath.

I take a moment to process, "Jodis, you have had a long journey, please let's go inside and get you settled."

Acknowledgements

I would like to thank everyone that supported me when this novel was only an idea. My friend, Mylene, who read the first drafts and recruited others to do the same. She provided me with the feedback that developed this book into the story that it is today. My mom, Christine, who helped in deciding on the names of the characters and my dad Michel who encouraged me to publish. I thank the rest of the family that read the different drafts until the final draft was ready for the public.

Special thanks to my husband, Curtis for being supportive of my writing, so much so that he purchased a laptop for me to write wherever I wanted as well as many other electronics and gadgets to help in the creation and design of this novel.

About the Author

Carolynne Raymond is an Ottawa-area based author who writes science fiction, fantasy, and children's fiction. When she's not crafting tales, she enjoys reading, painting, and spending quality time with her husband and son.

Connect with Carolynne on:

Twitter: @cshaylo
Facebook: http://www.facebook.com/cshaylo
Instagram: carolynne.raymond
TikTok: @carolynneraymond

What is Next

More novels. I am writing the third and final novel to The Earth & Airus Series, my science-fiction series, wrapping up Taylan (Robin) and Kyle (Sitrus) stories.